AF417992

A Taste of Revenge

A Twisted Princess Collection

AMBER BUNCH

For all of those who have wondered what it's like to be fucked
in an interrogation room.
You're welcome.

-Death
-Gore
-Sexual Assault Reference
-Child Loss Reference
-Police Brutality
-Corruption in the Judicial System
-Murder
-Wax Play
-Explicit Sexual Content
-Infertility
-Loss of Loved Ones
-Explicit Language
-Mention of Racism

Please note: If I have missed any warnings, please reach out to let me know.

Contents

XI
JUSTICE

Prologue

"Is it going to work?"

"Only one way to find out."

The professor hands me the vial of the crystal clear liquid—a poison we have worked years to perfect—untraceable by even the most advanced technology and toxicology tests the government has hidden away from the world's eyes.

It kills the person who ingests it by either mimicking cardiac arrest or asphyxiation, whichever they succumb to first.

Well, at least it's supposed to.

The lucky recipient strapped to the chair in the underground cellar of my home will let us know soon enough.

I know what you're thinking—*"How can you just kill an innocent person?"*

For starters, this bastard is far from innocent. He's just another corrupted part of this demented judicial system.

And why is that?

Because he's a dirty fucking cop. That's why.

He's gotten away with countless murders—six to be exact, but who's counting?

Certainly not the police department or the judge that deems him not guilty—Every. Single. Fucking. Time.

I knew this was a thing in America but it's just as disreputable here in London, which I hate to admit, caught me off guard.

I don't know why I expected it to be different. I was only kidding myself, to be honest, but I was still an angry, naive child when my mother and I first moved here from the States.

It feels like a lifetime ago now.

"Alright...Noah, is it?" I glance over at the barely conscious man. "I sure hope you're hungry, sugar. Because I have a meal for you that's just going to make your tastebuds explode."

He struggles against his restraints, his forehead creased with sweat as he stares at us, his eyes wild.

"Professor," I take a step towards the door, looking over my shoulder as my hand wraps around the cold metal of the doorknob. "Keep Noah here company for me while I prepare his supper. He is a guest here after all."

I wave to the two gentlemen before exiting the room, my mind still trying to wrap around the fact that I may finally be able to go back home to New Orleans—back to Papa.

My flesh tightens from the slight chill in the air, the small hairs on the back of my neck standing to attention as I make my way through the dark tunnel-like hall to where the elevator is located on the other side of the vast cellar.

London autumns are colder than they are in NOLA, and I never did get used to them. The warm southern air will be a lovely acquit from the London fog.

I bought a large building in the center of the French Quarter that has been going through minor renovations for the past few years now. Mainly structural—the interior will be completed once I get there and let my ideas run wild. But it's been ready for about eight months, patiently waiting for the grand opening of Le Rêve Brisé.

She's been my dream for as long as I can remember and soon, I will make that dream a reality.

"I just have to make sure this works," I think to myself, my hand clutching the vial for dear life.

The elevator dings and the doors split apart revealing the prestigious cigar room/library.

My heels click, echoing loudly off the taupe porcelain patterned floor, my dress flowing playfully around my ankles as I cross the large open space.

The dining room opens up into a large kitchen with an open floor plan. A large gold-trimmed vent hangs above the seven-burner stove that centers a rustic stone backsplash.

The small glass in my hand clinks when I place it on the countertop and grab a large pan from the cabinet below the double oven nestled in the stone wall.

I let out a low sigh as I rest my back against the counter and begin flipping through the worn pages of my cookbook.

It's had so many new additions over the years since Papa started it for me on my sixth birthday, though his recipes will forever be the ones I favor.

My fingers skim through the pages, the memories seemingly dance on the pages in vivid colors before my eyes, nostalgia hitting me like a gust of wind.

A few minutes pass by before the recipe for Crawfish Etouffee snatches my attention and a smile spreads slowly across my face.

If this isn't a perfect last meal—I don't know what is.

What did Noah do to deserve such a terrible fate?

He murdered his girlfriend's eight-year-old daughter—beaten to death because she was crying after fighting with her best friend at school that day.

He had been off duty, drinking all day. His blood alcohol level was almost triple the legal limit. He pled not guilty after his lawyer used some bullshit sob story about how he was a hero to society, and he wasn't in his right mind.

And naturally, because of his badge and uniform, he was absolved of any wrongdoing.

The mother of that innocent child never received the rightful justice she deserved.

But she will now.

I take a deep breath, trying to shake off the heaviness that has settled in my chest.

The Crawfish Etouffee simmers on the stove, the aroma filling the room with a familiar warmth of home. I stir the pot, the wooden spoon clacking against the sides as it creates a rhythm of its own.

This dish is a culinary journey, a dance of flavors that has been passed down through generations.

It's more than just a meal—it's an art.

I pour a generous amount of the simmering etouffee into a large serving dish, the steam escaping and curling into the air like tendrils of smoke.

The sight and smell of the dish bring me back to my childhood, spending time with Papa and learning the secrets of Cajun cooking.

And now it carries a darkness with it, a shadowy presence that will never leave.

The desire for vengeance floats through my mind like a ghost, a lingering specter that haunts me, a constant reminder of why I am doing this, and I'm going to make sure they all pay for what they have done.

You know what they say...revenge is a dish best served with a side of bread and a dash of poison.

CHAPTER ONE

Tia

The restaurant has always been one of my favorite places to be.

Momma said even as a baby the only way to get me to stop fussing was Papa holding me in front of the stove as he cooked.

Papa says it's not much and it pays the bills, but for me, it's the most magical place on earth.

The people, the smells, the food—it's all so incredibly wonderful.

My dream is to one day open up my own place.

I want to travel the world and infuse my cooking with other culinary wonders of the globe to create something fresh and new, something that will make your palette dance with delight.

"Hey, princess. You wanna help me serve these over there to that table?" My father nods over to a table of three rowdy white men.

"Of course, Papa!" I smile, grabbing two of the plates, one with a steak dinner and one with his famous fried chicken, and follow closely behind him. Papa carries a tray of piping hot Gumbo, a family recipe carried down for generations, and also one of my favorites.

My little legs struggle to keep up with his long ones as we weave and bob in and out of tables and the crowd of people.

Papa is a big man, but a gentle one.

He would give you the shirt right off his back. He's always helping out in our community in any way he can, and the restaurant's regulars absolutely adore him.

"How you fella's doing tonight?" Papa asks as we walk up to their table and they all stop talking and stare at us like we're interrupting an important conversation.

"You know, I'm glad ya asked because my soda tasted pretty flat and I expected better after so many fine folks in this town spoke so highly about this place." The man with greasy hair, a crooked nose, and a lip full of chewing tobacco says.

"My apologies, sir. The machines in the back must be out. I'll go fix that right away and get you some fresh. What were you drinking?"

"Yea, I'd appreciate that." He says. "And I want a Diet Coke."

"Absolutely," My father replies.

We hand out their food, and the entire time that we're placing the dishes on the table the guy on the left of me is burning a hole straight through me with the intensity of his stare, his eyes gliding up and down my body.

I recognize him as one of the policemen from the New Year's party Papa catered for earlier this year, but I must admit, he's giving me the creeps.

I do my best to block him out and concentrate on my work, but he continues to stare at me with the intensity of a thousand suns.

My heart pounds heavily in my chest as I begin to grow more and more uneasy under his burning stare.

I glance over at Papa hoping he's noticed the man's behavior, but he's completely engrossed in serving the other two customers.

"Please, excuse me. I should go check on everything in the kitchen." I say, getting Papa's attention.

He notices the dejection in my voice, and quickly turns around to check on me.

I shift my eyes to the man making me uncomfortable and Papa gets the hint.

"Please do, Tiana. The beignet dough needs to be rolled out and cut if you could."

I nod and make my way back to the kitchen.

A few moments later my father comes in, his voice shaky, "Are you ok, princess?" He's trying so hard to not lose his patience and go off on those men.

"I'm alright." I smile, pulling the cloth off the big round wooden bowl that has soft beignet dough comfortably rising inside it.

I'm used to it.

I have more curves than most girls my age do, and men really seem to take notice.

Momma says as a woman it's a common occurrence and it will only get worse as I age, but she says she eventually learned to brush it off.

Besides, we have Papa to protect us.

"I'm gonna go trade out the soda for the soda machine. I'll be right back to help"

"Okay, Papa."

The flour resembles a snowy winter morning showering down as I dust the surface of the countertop, preparing to roll out the dough.

It's soft in my hands, like a slightly moist and sticky, pillowy cloud.

I roll it out until it's about two inches thick, grab the knife next to me on the counter, and begin slicing small triangular pieces of dough, arranging them on the large baking sheet to the right of me on top of the stove.

By the time I get the last few of them arranged on the pan, Papa walks in.

"Are you sure you're okay?" He asks, his brows pulling tightly together as he places a hand on my shoulder.

I nod, smiling up at him, "Yes, Papa. I'm alright but I don't think that man should even be allowed to be an officer. Did you see the way he was looking at me? It's disgusting."

"Oh, I saw, and if it weren't for the strength God is giving me in this moment, I would probably be putting his head through the wall, but violence won't pay the bills." He sighs, slamming his hand down on the counter.

As the anger ripples through the room, I watch my father, his broad shoulders tense with suppressed fury. His calloused hands tremble slightly on the countertop, veins pulsing with the weight of his restraint.

I'm not used to seeing him look so...powerless.

"Papa?" I place my hand on his shoulder, and he offers me a tight, yet gentle smile and places his hand over mine, giving it a light squeeze.

"I'm okay, Tia. I'm just—I'm so sorry you had to experience that."

"Oh, I'll be fine," I reassure him.

He purses his lips and wipes his hands on the front of his apron, "Help me fry these up?" He nods to the beignets.

I grin, "Absolutely! Can I make some with hazelnut spread and a triple berry jam inside?"

His eyebrows almost reach his hairline, "Triple berry jam, huh? Well, that's different but I'd sure love to try it, so why not!"

As I carefully pipe the filling into a triangular shape of fried dough, a sense of comfort washes over me like a cool breeze in the sweltering heat of a hot Louisiana summer day.

As Papa tosses another batch of beignets into the hot oil, the rhythmic sizzle provides a comforting backdrop, drowning out the troubles of the world just beyond these walls.

Standing here with him, creating a hurricane of flavors, I'm transported to a place of peace and joy. It's the times like this that bring me solace and true happiness.

I can almost forget the ugliness that lurks outside our humble kitchen, the darkness that threatens to consume our dreams and aspirations.

During these fleeting moments, the shared love of cooking between my father and me acts as a shield, shielding us from the unkind truths of our daily lives.

"These look decadent," Papa beams proudly over my shoulder at the tray of beignets.

The powdered sugar dusting the golden pastries almost glistens under the glow of the warm kitchen lights, enticing my tongue with the promise of its soft pillowy inside bursting with sweet, delicious filling.

He reaches for a beignet and delicately nibbles on it, letting out a contented sigh as he relishes in the burst of flavors.

A smile twitches at the edge of his lips, "You have a knack for creating unique flavors. I have absolutely no doubt that these are going to be a hit during tonight's dinner rush." He compliments me, finishing off the final piece of fried dough in his hand.

"Thanks, Papa!"

"Let's go get these stored away in the case now, okay?" He nudges me with his elbow before he makes his way over to the sink and washes his hands. "You grab that smaller tray there." He gestures, drying his hands on a paper towel.

"Yes, sir." I assent, carefully balancing the tray as I navigate through the sea of people and tables filled with lively chatter and laughter.

As I approach the display case filled with an array of delectable treats, I can't help but feel a swell of pride in my chest.

The aroma of freshly baked pastries dances through the air, captivating the senses of our customers and beckoning them to indulge in our culinary creations.

"Well, don't those look stunning!" Mrs. Charice quips as I begin filling the empty spot in the glass case with the stuffed beignets.

Papa and I took the time to garnish the golden pastries with thin slices of juicy red strawberries and fragrant sprigs of fresh mint, adding a pop of color to the top of them.

They look almost too beautiful to eat.

"Thank you!" I grin, pride blooming in my chest.

Papa walks up behind us, "Looks like it's going to be a busy night tonight, ladies." He says just as a large party of folks walks in.

"How many tonight?" Mrs. Charice greets them with a big welcoming smile.

"We have a few more that will be arriving soon, so a total of eighteen." The tall balding gentleman in the front confirms. "I hope that's okay?"

"Of course!" She grabs a handful of menus. "Right this way, please."

"Can you finish up here while I go get some tables pushed together and inform the kitchen of their arrival?"

I reply quickly without lifting my eyes away from the case, too focused on arranging it neatly for a cleaner presentation.

The rest of the evening seems to fly by and before I know it, it's time for us to close up for the night.

I'm tired but I feel accomplished as I wipe down the counters and tidy up the remaining two tables that still have yet to be cleared.

As Papa predicted, our beignets were a hit and sold out within the initial forty minutes of the dinner rush.

"Anything else you need from me, Mr. Williams?" Charice asks as she gathers her coat and keys.

"No, Charice. You've done enough. Thank you so much for staying late to help us close up tonight."

"Anytime." She waves, heading out the back exit door.

I turn off the lights and lock the front door, Papa comes up behind me, placing a gentle hand on my shoulder. "You ready, cupcake? Momma has a pie cooling off that's calling my name and I'm ready to rest these old bones."

I nod with a tired smile, "I'm ready Papa."

We walk out into the cool night air and the sounds of the bustling city ring down the long strip of the French Quarter.

The streets are alive with the intoxicating energy of New Orleans. Jazz floats through the air, mingling with the laughter and buzzing voices of the people strolling by.

"Oh, no! I forgot to lock the safe." My father's deep voice resides in my ear as he places a hand on my shoulder halting me. "Stay right here for just a moment, I'll be right back, okay princess?"

I nod my head acknowledging his command and sit down on the top step of the concrete stairwell to wait for his return before he disappears back inside the restaurant.

The shadows creeping down the alleyway make my skin crawl like little beetles scratching just under the surface biting and clawing until they consume me whole.

I shiver, pulling my arms tight around me, and glance nervously at the dimly lit street. The flickering streetlamp casts eerie shadows on the cobblestones, distorting the familiar shapes of the buildings that line the road.

Minutes pass, but it feels like an eternity. Impatience grows within me as I tap my foot on the ground, my heart beginning to pound in my chest.

What is taking him so long?

My body stills, frozen in fear when a familiar voice rakes against the soft flesh of my brain.

It's the man from earlier tonight who kept undressing me with his eyes.

"PAPA!" A shrill cry escapes my mouth, piercing the air and echoing off the walls.

It's a deafening sound, one that could potentially startle the corpses in the nearby cemetery if they were alive.

"PAPA!" I scream again just as I feel the man's strong arms snake around my waist.

A sharp pain lances through the back of my head when he slams me against the brick wall, my struggles mute to his iron grip.

"Shh," he hisses, "Don't be afraid, I just wanna have a little fun, darlin'."

I can feel his hot breath in my ear as he presses himself close to me, his body odor and the stench of alcohol making me want to gag.

"Please! Just leave me alone!"

His erection presses into my stomach, and a low cry leaves my lips and my stomach sinks to my feet, leaving a wave of nausea in its wake when the realization of what he's going to do to me sinks in.

I writhe and try to break free, but he only tightens his grip, his eyes gleaming with sinister intent.

I hear the shuffling of feet and more voices join in, "Come on Ralph. You're drunk. Just leave the girl alone and let's go to the speakeasy down the street. Starla is there tonight." His friend tugs on his shoulder but Ralph shrugs him off in an angry haste.

Ralph narrows his eyes and glares at his friend before spinning me around and pressing me against the bricks, his grip on my arms now tightening to the point of pain.

"Fuck off, Carl," Ralph growls, his voice slurred. "We're just having fun. Ain't we girl?"

"What do we do, Allen?" He asks a third man from somewhere behind me.

"What the fuck can we do, Carl? He's our fucking boss. We say a word about this, you know he'll have our badges, and Jenna will kill me if I lose my job, especially with us having another little one on the way." The man replies.

A whimper escapes my throat, feeling defeated by their words. There is no escape, no hope left for me tonight. The rage and desperation coursing through my body is a lost cause because I know there is nothing I can do to escape this nightmare.

I want to scream, to fight back but I'm frozen in terror, my mouth is dry and there's a lump forming in the back of my throat, choking the air out of me as hot tears swell in my eyes, falling silently down my cheeks.

I can hear him unbuckle his pants, though he's still pressing me hard into the wall. His hand slides up the back of my pale yellow work dress and I try my best to steel my nerves.

"You will survive this," I whisper to myself and grip the brick wall, preparing for whatever hell is about to descend upon me. *"You have to."*

My heart races in my chest, pounding against my ribcage as if it's about to burst from my chest.

Suddenly, Papa busts through the back door, baseball bat in hand, "Get your filthy God damn hands off my daughter!" He roars, and I let go of the breath I had been holding.

I sob in relief as Papa spins the man around and drives the tip of his bat into his stomach. His expression twists with rage as he swings the bat forcefully, each strike landing on its intended mark with accuracy.

The man grunts in pain, his head whipping back with each strike, dark bruises begin to form on his body, and blood starts to seep from some of the wounds.

The bat strikes the man's body with a sickening thud once again and I can see the determination and fury in my father's eyes as he rains down blows on the man who was trying to rape me.

"You're gonna fucking kill him, man!" Allen screams, diving for Papa and tackling him to the ground.

The impact of their bodies slamming against the ground jolts me out of my terror-induced trance. The scene around me is chaotic and gruesome as both men roll on the ground.

People just continue to stroll right past the alleyway, turning their heads as if there isn't a life-or-death struggle happening mere yards from them, right in front of their eyes, yet, they turn their heads.

A surge of frustration and powerlessness consumes me as I come to the realization of how easily society disregards us, and our empty pleas for help.

Allen tries to wrestle the bat out of my father's hand and the handle connects with Papa's face, blood instantly begins pouring from the large open gash right above his left eye.

"Get off of him!" I scream, jumping on Allen's back, punching and ripping at the hair on his head in a desperate attempt to get him off my father.

Strong hands grip me, pulling me away from Allen. It's Carl.

"Let me go!" I kick, flailing my legs as he lifts me up and away from the men fighting on the ground.

"Please, I'm trying to keep you from getting hurt." He says.

"You didn't care when your friend was raping me!" I spit, slapping him in the face. "NOW, LET ME GO!" I strain against his hold, but he's too strong for me to break free.

I watch in horror as Ralph begins to stir on the ground next to where Papa and the other man are fighting and he stands up, pulling a gun from his pants.

"Whoa! What the fuck Ral—"

The air fills with a loud crack, and the flash of the muzzle and the thunderous reports fill my senses.

The world comes to a sudden halt and I am left disoriented, struggling to make sense of what is happening.

The moments seem to last forever as I witness a hand move and then release, signifying the end of the struggle between my father and Allen.

"Da—Daddy?" I whisper, though, there is no response, only a deafening silence that seems to swallow me whole.

"We gotta get the fuck out of here." Carl releases me and I fall to my knees on the ground.

"What about the girl? She saw everything."

"Leave her."

"What if she tells someone?"

Blood smears Ralph's face, the rain starting to fall creating shallow pink rivers in it as the small wet drops trickle down his chin and fall to the dirt, mingling with the crimson of my father's wound that taints the ground around us.

His gaze pierces into the depths of my soul, his eyes reflecting the emptiness that has already begun to fill my heart.

He casually tucks his gun back into its holster, "I'm the goddamn Sheriff, Carl. Ain't no one gonna believe the likes of her over me. Besides," He laughs. "Even if someone did manage to believe her, it was self-defense. The charges would never stick. Oh, and call this in will ya? Annie is expecting me to be home any minute for supper and I'd sure hate to make that woman mad."

I'm left alone in my anguish as I watch the men walk away, leaving my father's lifeless body behind, I feel a chilling numbness cloak my entire being. Despite the pounding rain, I feel the icy tendrils of fear and despair begin to seep into every part of me.

Forcing myself to my feet, I stumble over to my father's side. My thoughts are clouded, my heart shattering as I take in his condition. His clothes are drenched in blood, and his face is contorted with agony as the light fades from his deep brown eyes.

Tears stream down my cheeks and I reach out to touch him, but even the small distance seems insurmountable.

Rain pelts my head, dampening my clothes and hair with its icy embrace. With desperation in my grip, I cling to Papa's hand, "Wake up!" I plead, the gasps of my sobs echoing in the dimness of the dark alley.

My free hand searches frantically for the keys to the restaurant so I can call for help but they must have fallen out of Papa's jacket in the chaos and commotion.

"PLEASE, SOMEBODY HELP ME!" My throat burns from the sharpness of my scream.

As if only a whisper, Papa's hand weakly squeezes mine, "Papa!" I cry out.

He gives me his biggest smile, "Hey cupcake, don't you fret about me, okay?" His voice is strained. "I need you to be strong now. Can yo—Can you do that for me, princess?"

No longer able to process my thoughts or emotions, I nod uncontrollably through my tears, kissing his cold, clammy hand.

"I want you to leave. Run as fast as you can home to your momma, you hear?"

"No. Please, no. I—I can't leave you."

His gaze softens, "Tia, listen to me. You have to. Your momma will get help and I'll be right here, okay? I'll be right here, baby. Now, I need you to put on your bravest face and go."

With a heavy heart, I reluctantly nod my assent, swallowing the lump in my throat.

I have to be strong...for Papa.

Enveloping him in my embrace, I offer a tender squeeze before reluctantly pulling away. As I rise to my feet, I delicately brush away the tears that have gathered on my cheeks, watching as the rain gracefully falls and dances around us like a symphony of nature.

I can do this. I can save him.

I take a deep breath, pivot on my heels, and get ready to run as fast as I can.

But before I do, I steal one final glance at the man who has been my anchor, my source of resilience, and my closest companion. A wave of sorrow washes over me, threatening to pull me under as I come to terms with the possibility that this may be the last time, I see him alive.

"Papa?" I choke out, my voice trembling with emotion. "I—I love you."

A faint attempt at a smile graces his features, though it fails to reach the depths of his vacant eyes. But even so, I can't help but sense the lingering warmth in its presence when he whispers, "I love you mostest, princess."

CHAPTER TWO

Tia

"**M**s. Williams, your car is ready." My driver Angelo informs me, pulling me out of the fog my mind drifted into.

"Thank you, Angelo."

I step outside the grand mansion, my heels clicking against the cobblestone path that leads to the waiting car. The night air is heavy with a mixture of anticipation and trepidation as I approach the sleek black vehicle.

By morning I'll be back in New Orleans.

My stomach churns at the thought. It's been almost twenty years since I've stepped foot in the Big Easy. Not since—.

Angelo tips his hat, opening up the back driver-side door, a polite smile stretched across his softly wrinkled face, though his eyes betray him as I can see the hint of concern in his friendly features.

I push the thought aside, steadfast in my determination to avoid being engulfed by the tempestuous waves of emotion that would inevitably accompany any conversation between us.

Memories, both pleasant and painful, flood my mind as I settle into the backseat of the car. The leather seats are cool against my skin, offering a small sense of comfort amidst the rising unease.

Angelo starts the engine, and we pull off into the night, the city lights of London fading into the distance behind us. As we make our way toward the airport, where Momma waits, I find myself entranced by the passing scenery outside my window, lost in a medley of introspection.

I wanted so badly to get the chance to see Alice before I left, but I haven't seen her, or heard from her as a matter of fact, since the night of my masquerade party.

She was so upset when I told her I was leaving but not to the point where I thought she would just ghost me like that.

I hope she's okay.

I sigh deeply, grabbing a bottle of champagne and a glass flute from the mini-bar across from me, then carefully pop the cork from the bottle and pour myself a glass before settling back into my seat.

I've come such a long way from my days when I was thought of as nothing more than the little colored server girl from Soul of the Bayou.

As I take a sip of the champagne, the bubbles tickling my tongue, I can't help but reminisce about my journey from humble beginnings to where I am now. But despite the success and acclaim that I have achieved, a part of me still longs for the simplicity and warmth of those days.

The voyage from the vibrant streets of New Orleans to the bustling metropolis of London had been my salvation, my opportunity to forge a fresh existence, far from the dark phantoms that plagued my past.

Yet, despite the searing pain in my chest and the haunting memories that flood my mind, I find myself running back to the same town that destroyed me, knowing that in every corner, every hidden shadow, I'll be reminded of the shattered pieces of my heart, scattered like broken glass through the bright unforgiving city.

A masochistic part of me wonders if I deserve this punishment, if I'm somehow drawn to the chaos and torment that await me. But another part of me, a small voice buried deep within, insists that I must face my demons head-on, confront the past that haunts my dreams, and find the closure and revenge I so desperately need.

Maybe if I had been a little bit faster—ran a little bit harder.

The familiar sound of my phone chiming interrupts my thoughts. Most likely Momma, her tendency to be fashionably late ingrained in her DNA. Papa always teased that she would even be late to her own funeral.

As expected, the message that pops up on my phone screen is to inform me of her delay. The words are short and to the point, but I can sense the slightest hint of an apology hidden behind them.

I suppose some things never change.

A chuckle forms in my chest as I set my glass of champagne down, the bubbling liquid temporarily forgotten.

Glancing back down at the text from my mom, I can't help but feel a mix of relief and frustration. Relief because her delay buys me more time to gather my thoughts and prepare myself for what lies ahead. Frustration because her tardiness means that we might very well miss our flight.

Oh, well. Should that happen, I'll just find us a hotel nearby where we can pass the time until the next available flight.

As the limo speeds over a seemingly large pothole. my phone flies off my lap and hits the smooth leather with a loud slap. We make a sharp turn immediately afterward and I catch myself cursing under my breath, and leaping for the small device before it has a chance to slip onto the floorboard, and under the massive seat, lost forever among the labyrinthine wiring, mechanisms, and forgotten stale Cheetos from drunken Friday nights.

A resounding sigh escapes my parted lips as I recover my glass of *Dom Perignon* and sink back, relaxing my shoulders and allowing myself a small moment of reprieve.

After polishing off three drinks and a candy bar, we arrive at the airport. Throngs of people race around us, some hugging and kissing their loved ones goodbye, while others frantically check their watches and drag heavy luggage towards the departure gates.

It's pure chaos.

Although my private jet was an option, I opted for a more subdued arrival into town, wanting to remain low-key for a bit while I take the time to get the restaurant up and going.

Precision and caution are essential for my plan to succeed. A single misstep could jeopardize everything. . .And failure is not an outcome that I'm willing to accept.

Reluctantly, I slip my feet back into the heels that I kicked off during the ride, pick up my phone, and dial Momma's number, listening for the ring before I place it on speaker.

"Hello, sweetie," my mom's voice greets me through the phone.

"Hey, Momma," I say, fully aware that she's about to tell me about another pit stop she just *had* to make so she could say goodbye to another one of the many friends she had accumulated over the years.

A wave of dread washes over me, and my stomach lurches as if it's trying to escape through my throat.

My senses are on high alert, every nerve tingling under my skin, tingling with apprehension. I know this move is hard on her too, maybe even more so than me.

She had a really good life here but once I told her that I was moving back to New Orleans after purchasing the old brewery warehouse on Bourbon to open up that brasserie me and Papa always talked about.

"I'm almost there, I swear!" Tears choke her voice, and I feel my heart shatter even more.

"It's okay, Momma. There's a nice hotel nearb—"

"I'm going to be there!" She says with certainty. *"There's no way in Hell I'd miss my baby girl living out her dream."*

"Alright, alright!" I laugh, feeling a little lighter as her sadness is quickly replaced with excitement.

"Do you know if they allow us to bring snacks? You know how hungry these trips make me."

"I'm not entirely sure, but I believe they have their own selection of items on the plane."

Perhaps we've become too accustomed to the spoil of riches.

It feels like a double-edged sword, this wealth and privilege that's been bestowed upon us. On one hand, it has afforded me the opportunity to pursue my dream of opening a restaurant, but on the other hand, I worry that it may have pulled us too far away from the roots of our humble beginnings.

After a few more minutes of trifling chatter, we hang up and my mother arrives shortly afterward in her old beige and brown rust bucket. Though I've made many offers to buy her a new car or get her a driver, she's refused, saying she has all she needs.

I don't think she'll ever drive another vehicle. This car holds a special place in her heart; it was the first—and only—car that she and Papa picked out together.

I have arranged for it to be sent back to the States for her. It should arrive around the same time we do, or at least within a week of our arrival.

Alfred opens her door, offering her his hand, "Thank you, Alfred. Always the gentleman."

"Ma'am" He tips his hat after he gently lifts her from the driver seat.

Our bags have already been shipped, so other than our purses, we have no other belongings to worry about while going through customs, it makes things easier that way.

Momma takes my hand, her smooth skin feels so frail against the callouses on mine, "You ready, sugar bug?"

Gently clasping her hand, I attempt to calm the butterflies fluttering in my stomach. "I'm as ready as I'll ever be, Momma."

CHAPTER THREE

Agent Holloway

I fucking hate donuts.

A sugary good-for-nothing carb that tastes like the love child of cardboard and disappointment.

But here I am, sitting in this quaint little cafe, sipping on lukewarm coffee and staring at a glazed donut like it's the solution to all my problems.

Perhaps it is.

The bell above the door jingles and I glance up to see him walking in—Franciso, a member of the Rivera Cartel.

He's been a reliable source and a familiar associate of the FBI for many years.

"You're late."

He slides into the booth across from me, his sharp eyes scanning the room, paranoid as usual, before settling on my face. "And you look like you've had a rough night," he remarks casually as if we're discussing the weather.

I fight the urge to roll my eyes, "Well aren't you perceptive." Barely containing the sarcasm dripping from my words as I shove the plated donut in front of him.

He chuckles, a low sound that rumbles in the quiet cafe. His eyes twinkle with amusement as he picks up the donut, taking a bite with relish. "You know," he starts, wiping a stray crumb from the corner of his lips, "You'd think you'd be nicer to the guy that knows where the bodies are buried."

I raise an eyebrow, unimpressed. "Please, you probably helped bury them."

His laughter is forced, his eyes not reflecting the humor. Like me, he has a darkness in him. It's what drives us both to excel at our professions, however different they may be.

"You're not incorrect. However, you know very well that I have no say in the matter," he stuffs the remaining donut into his mouth, causing his words to be muffled by the pastry and sending crummy bits flying from the disgusting hole in his face. "Besides, I wouldn't have been able to give you this."

His elbow bumps his fork sending it tumbling to the ground. As he leans over, his fingers brush against my ankle, and I feel a small object being tucked into the top of my boot.

Considering the way it feels pressing into my skin, I can surmise that it's rectangular in shape, hard—likely plastic—and from the slight pinch I get when I roll my ankle, it has a covering.

It's a flash drive.

When he sits back up, our eyes lock. Sweat beads above his brow and I can see the fear swimming in his baby blues.

This will be the final encounter I have with him before someone discovers his body and calls it in.

It's bittersweet. However, we finally have all the necessary resources to dismantle his boss's entire drug operation once and for all.

"Did you know that wolves are excellent communicators, and they tend to sacrifice themselves for the sake of their pack when the situation is dire enough?"

My deficiencies lie in expressing proper farewells and accurately conveying emotive responses. As a youth, I was diagnosed with high-functioning autism, rendering me unable to process situations in the same manner as neurotypical individuals, but since I know from our many discussions that he likes wolves; it seemed like the most appropriate response.

"Take care of them, will ya?" For a brief moment, his stony expression wavers, and a single tear falls onto the worn tabletop of the old diner.

He's referring to his son and his wife waiting for him back home. For someone as deep in this shit as he is, he knows death is the only way out now.

His loved ones will be placed under the careful watch of the Witness Protection Program, their identities erased and replaced with new ones. They will be relocated to a distant home, far from the crowded streets of New York City, where they can begin anew, free from having to look over their shoulder for the constant threat and danger lurking at their every turn if they were to stay here.

I tilt my chin up slightly, shifting my gaze down to my hands. My thumbs fiddle back and forth in a game of their own, a nervous habit of mine.

"Of course. You know I'm a man of my word. They will be well taken care of."

"It's been—"

"Shit. It's been shit."

His mouth twitches on a lost smile and he hesitates for a moment, his gaze flickering towards the entrance as if he's expecting trouble to walk through the door at any second.

"C'mon Holloway, it hasn't *all* been bad."

Indeed, not all of our encounters have been terrible. His presence in my life has been a mixture of chaos and protection, danger and solace. He's been the ear that I never knew I needed, regardless of whether I was complaining about the weather, stating random and weird facts that no one asked for, or talking about the woes of the job—he always listened.

"I appreciate everything you've done. Despite your—involvements."

He leans back in his chair, the weight of the world evident in the lines etched on his weary face. The diner is quiet, save for the gentle hum of the neon sign outside, casting an otherworldly glow through the grimy windows.

"We've been through hell together, haven't we?" he muses, a hint of nostalgia lacing his words.

I nod my head, recalling all the close calls, the almost disasters, and the nights spent divulging secrets and indulging in greasy food at this rundown restaurant.

It's strange.

This feeling.

An emotion I'm not used to and yet can't quite shake off. It's like a whisper in the wind, faint yet persistent, urging me to acknowledge its presence.

I reach for my coffee—probably cold now, and take a sip, the bitterness of the liquid mirroring the bitter reality of our situation.

"How long?"

"I'd assume once I leave here and I'm no longer in a public area."

The black SUV that's been sitting down on the street corner for the past hour, almost hidden in the shadows, seems to be mocking him, a silent threat that he knows he can't outrun forever. His eyes flicker to the entrance once more, calculating his chances of making it out without being noticed.

"You could take the back entrance—skip town."

"Shit Holloway, you know just as well as I do that's not gonna do me any good. They have the entire fucking place surrounded."

"Do they know about the fl—?"

"No." He snaps, anger flashing in his eyes. "But they know that you're FBI. You're going to have to watch your back."

It's not time for them to attempt murder yet; they want to gather information first. They'll take a few months to study my daily routine and behavior thoroughly.

I know they're waiting for me to feel safe, to let my guard down, and move on with my life as if they don't even exist. And just when I think I'm in the clear, that's when they'll strike.

But I can't just sit around and wait for them to make their move. I need to be steps ahead and anticipate their every move before they even think of it.

It's not just about me anymore; it's about protecting those I care about—protecting *her*.

I've seen the aftermath of this drug empire's *"information gathering"* phase before, along with the twisted wreckage and broken bodies they leave behind as a warning to anyone else who dares to cross them.

I can't let that happen again.

I won't.

Glancing back out of the dirty fingerprint-smudged window, I wave to Cynthia, the bottle-blonde waitress who always works the late-night shift in skimpy little outfits, to bring my check.

"Don't you go worrying your pretty little head about me," I scold. "It would be wiser to concentrate on the pressing matters of those who eagerly anticipate your impending demise."

Cynthia skips over and leans over on the table, pressing her ass in the air, her large breasts spilling out of the low v-cut of her crop top, "Can I get you boys anything else?"

"I'm good, thank you," I reply.

"What about you, Francisco? You look awfully stressed tonight. If there is *anything* I can offer you to help with that, let me know."

"I think I'll be okay, Cynthia. Thank you for the offer." He replies.

She playfully winks at him, popping a bubble with the blue gum in her mouth as she swipes the card from my hand, her bright red nails coming dangerously close to my face before she saunters away with a confident stride and swinging hips.

He chuckles watching in amusement as she walks away, "I may be a dead man, but I'm also a married man."

A hint of sadness tinges his bright blue eyes, "You ever smoke before?" He asks.

The question catches me off guard, "No. I can't say that I ever have."

He pulls a pack of cigarettes from the pocket of his jacket, "Me either."

His attempt at a last hoorah.

"Catch you on the other side, agent?" He holds out his hand for me to shake.

I stand up, swallowing hard as I tightly grasp his hand, "Catch you on the other side, Fransisco.

CHAPTER FOUR

Tia

"Isn't it beautiful, Momma?" I swirl around the vast empty space of the old building.

"Well, it's definitely. . .something," she says with a slight wrinkle in her nose that tells me she's not impressed.

Granted it has been undergoing renovations for quite some time, it's still going to need a little extra love and attention before the Grand Mardi Gras Opening.

I can't blame my mother for her lack of enthusiasm. The old building has seen better days, that's for sure. But there's just something about it that calls to me, something in the way the light streams through the broken stained-glass windows and illuminates the dust motes dancing around in the air. I can feel the history painted into these old walls and see the potential seeping from the wooden bones of the structure, even if my mother can't right now.

Her imagination never was as visual as mine and Poppa's, but she was always there to support us and cheer us on in whatever crazy endeavors we wanted to pursue.

"Oh, come now. Just picture it, Momma," I say, ushering her over to the staircase that leads up to the second level that will eventually overlook a grand ballroom/dining area. "Imagine the ballroom brimming with people, the smooth sound of jazz floating through the air, and the sounds of laughter, and joy bouncing off these walls as friends and family gather over good food and conversation. This place will be a beacon of light in the city once we're done with it."

Though I can see the skepticism in her eyes, there's also a flicker of hope residing in them too.

Her forehead furrows, the creases in her dark complexion a testament to the struggles and sacrifices she has endured over the years. "You certainly are your father's daughter." She laughs as she grabs a broom one of the contractors must have left behind and sweeps it across the floor, upheaving a cloud of dust as she does. "Don't just stand there," She scolds, "This place isn't going to finish itself. Why don't you run to the store and grab more cleaning supplies while I open up some windows and kick a little more of this dust up?"

"Yes ma'am." I nod eagerly, grateful for the opportunity to step out into the warm embrace of the afternoon sun. "I'll be back soon," I promise her, turning the knob of the front door that leads straight out into the city in my hand.

"Tiana?" Her voice cracks, stopping me right in my tracks before I have a chance to step out the door.

"Everything okay, Momma?"

"I just—," She wipes away a stray tear that had fallen to her cheek, "He'd be so proud of you, you know?"

I quickly rush back over to her and throw my arms around her shoulders, pulling her into a tight embrace "Thank you, Momma. For everything." I whisper, my voice choked with emotion.

She squeezes me, the memory of my father lingering between us for a brief moment before she gently pats my back and pulls away, meeting my gaze with a bittersweet smile hugging her face. "Now go on and get, child. Time's a-wasting."

I can't suppress the deep belly laugh that tumbles from my parted lips, "Okay, I can take a hint." I throw my hands up, "I'm going. I'm going."

As I make my way through the French Quarter, the lively energy of New Orleans seeps into my bones, infusing me with renewed determination.

My main priority right now is getting the restaurant up and running successfully. Once that's taken care of, I can shift my focus to my ultimate goals and start putting my plans into action. Being able to accomplish this sooner rather than later would be best because the anticipation is almost crippling, but there's a silver lining: it *will* all be over soon enough.

The mellifluous taste of vengeance lingers on my lips, and I can taste its sweetness on the tip of my tongue. Like a wild animal consumed by blood lust, I crave the satisfaction of extracting every last drop of life from those who have wronged me. The time for retribution is near and they will face the consequences of their actions and finally pay for their transgressions.

I cautiously push the creaky door open, and the small bell attached above it jingles softly to signal my arrival. The interior is dimly lit, giving off an old-fashioned vibe, but this place is a familiar sight to me.

I visited this store almost every day with my father as a child. The owner was a sweet man, always ready with a kind smile and an ice cream from the cooler next to the front counter for me when Poppa and I would visit.

I adored the stories he would share with his customers about the history of the city and the old lore of the ancestorial magic that is said to be ingrained deep inside the heart of New Orleans.

But those days are long gone, and the joyful tune of nostalgia must be silenced. There is still too much work to be done, and I can't afford to get lost in my memories. These intense emotions, this anger, must be controlled until the right moment arises.

"Can I help you find anything, Miss?" As I look up from the dusty shelves of forgotten tourist trinkets, I meet the eyes of the new shopkeeper.

He's young, and handsome, with a sharp jaw and eyes the color of aged whiskey. His presence exudes an enigmatic quality, and I can sense a profoundness to him as if there is more beneath the surface of his amiable smile than meets the eye.

His gaze lingers on me for a moment too long, as if he's trying to place who I am and silently questioning himself on why I seem so familiar to him.

He's the old shopkeeper's grandson, Elliot. A boy that I used to sit next to in class and play with in the creek on long hot summer days. Long before the innocence of childhood had been replaced by the heavy burden of adulthood—before the darkness crept into my heart and turned my world bleak and cold.

I can see glimpses of the carefree boy he used to be beneath the mask of composure he wears now, but rather than acknowledging his questioning gaze and our very short-lived past, I instead compose myself and offer him a polite smile in return.

"Just browsing, thank you," I reply, my voice steady despite the storm of emotions raging within me.

"Take your time. If there's anything I can help you find, please let me know."

I nod a silent Southern thank you and continue my search down the aisle for supplies I'm not even sure exist here.

"Actually," I call after him, "Do you happen to have any cleaning supplies available?"

"Cleaning supplies, huh?" he muses, a playful smile tugging at the corners of his lips. "Hold on a second, ma'am."

He disappears into the back room and the faint sound of shuffling boxes reaches my ears before he emerges once more, now holding a small wooden crate filled with an assortment of different types of cleaners, sponges, and other small supplies.

"Will these do?" He asks, setting it up on the counter in front of me, the basket clanging loudly against its smooth surface.

Elliot's eyes crinkle at the corners as he watches me inspect the products in the crate.

"Thank you, these will be perfect," I say, grateful for his help but also eager to see him disappear back into the shadows of the shop so I can go on about my business and try to forget the past that threatens to resurface with every lingering glance between us.

I'm not ready to be recognized just yet. It's too early, and if I'm being completely honest, I don't want to stir up any unwanted attention at the moment.

Grabbing my wallet out of my purse, I grab the green and black debit card from the second cardholder of my wallet and swipe it through the old machine.

The machine processes the transaction as quickly as something as outdated as it is can and Elliot hands me the supply crate.

I balance it on my hip as I walk to the door, pushing it open with my free hand.

"Would you like me to carry it out to your car?" He calls after me.

"Oh, no thank you. I'll manage." I reply.

"Alright then. Have a nice day, Tiana." As I hear him speak my name, a chill runs down my spine.

Shit.

So much for going unnoticed.

I quickly compose myself, forcing a cheerful grin as I turn back to face him. My heart beats wildly in my chest as I inhale deeply, attempting to conceal my disappointment at his recognition of me. "Thanks, Elliot," I murmur softly, feeling a flush of embarrassment spread across my cheeks. "You have a good day as well."

The sun shines brightly through all the windows Momma opened during my store run, when I arrive back at the restaurant, flooding the place with light and a sense of warmth and the feeling of home.

The floors have been meticulously swept already, and my mother is in the back corner of what will eventually be the hostess area, using the broom she found to battle a stubborn cobweb from the ceiling.

The place is slowly transforming into something spectacular, like a diamond that has been waiting for years to be unearthed from the hard-crusted earth that it lies beneath.

The weight of the crate suddenly becomes apparent, making my arms feel heavy and strained. With a small exhale, I shift the weight and set it down on the floor near the front wall by the door. Stepping back, a huge grin spreads across my face like wildfire as the thrill of accomplishment washes over me.

Everything is slowly coming together and

I feel a surge of pride and satisfaction as I take in the progress made. The restaurant is beginning to look like the dream my father and I had always envisioned.

This dream, our dream, is on the cusp of realization.

Through countless sacrifices and unwavering determination, we are now reaping the rewards of our diligent efforts.

I reach up and touch the locket hanging from my neck, the one with a picture of me sitting on my father's shoulders after winning my first relay race. My hand tightens around the metal, holding onto the memory tightly.

We're almost there, Papa.

CHAPTER FIVE

Agent Holloway

"The suspect is about six-two, he weighs approximately one hundred eighty-five pounds, he's armed, and he's traveling east on foot through the woods located in the back of the property." My adrenaline kicks into overdrive as I pick up my pace and relay the information over to the rest of my team.

Damn it!

I had him. I fucking had him, and I didn't take the shot.

The teenage girl who'd been trapped in his house of horrors was already terrorized and frightened enough as it was when we infiltrated the place, and I didn't want to be the one to add to her growing list of traumas by blowing brain chunks all over her face while she was being used as a meat shield so the asshole could escape.

Now, we might lose him again and have to worry about yet another person falling victim to his depraved crimes.

No.

Fuck that.

We're ending this shit tonight.

"Copy that. I've positioned several cruisers along the tree line leading out to the main road, we're ready to intercept him if he heads toward this area." Sloan's voice greets me back over coms.

I carefully survey the dark trees around me as I trudge silently through the woods, making a conscious effort to avoid making any noise.

However, my footsteps cause a soft crunching noise of their own, but it's the eerie silence surrounding me that is almost deafening.

All of a sudden, Sanders is jabbering his complaints into my ear causing my heart to do a little flip flop from the abruptness, "Just so we're clear, this is not how I wanted to spend my Friday night."

"Yea well, neither did I, but this is the life we chose so suck it up, sweet cheeks," Reyes responds gruffly before appearing out of seemingly nowhere, about forty yards to my left.

He's like a damn ghost.

I've never had to question why the FBI hired Reyes. He's a complete anomaly—a terminator of sorts, a man who can move in absolute silence through the shadows and emerge from the most precarious corners unnoticed. I've seen it countless times, yet it never fails to make my hair stand on end.

And even though some might say he's as strange as they come, he's a fucking good agent. There's no denying that.

He signals to me to let me know he's ready to move forward, I nod in a silent acknowledgment, and we continue to push on, combing through the dense forest around the perp's property with our weapons drawn and senses on high alert.

Every rustle of leaves and snap of twigs sends a jolt of electricity surging through my veins.

My hand clenches around the cold, hard metal of the gun, fingers trembling with anticipation as my grip tightens. The air is tense, with each breath I take feeling heavier and more labored than the last. My heart hammers in my chest, drowning out all other sounds except for the deafening pounding of my pulse. Every nerve in my body is on edge, ready for the chaos that will soon unfold.

"I see movement up ahead," Sanders whispers, his voice hoarse. "He probably thought he was being clever by doubling back. I'll try to flush him out towards you gu—" Suddenly, gunshots ring out, cutting his words short.

My mind whirls with a million questions.

Did Sanders shoot or did the perp?

Did one of them get hit?

Is one of them dead?

Or both?

Cursing myself under my breath for not taking the shot earlier when I could have just ended this, my feet pound against the foliage of the forest, Reyes already a few yards ahead of me, barreling towards the source of the gunfire.

As I push deeper into the forest, the thick vegetation closes in around me, suffocating me with its darkness.

My flashlight casts a weak beam, like a struggling candle in a sea of blackness, but the shadows seem to reach out and consume its light, each step I take plunging me further into the clutches of the night, and every rustle and whisper of the trees making my heart race as I become a helpless victim of the forest's embrace.

I can make out a small opening—it looks to be a hidden trail that someone has walked maybe only a handful of times.

My gut is telling me to leave Reyes and venture down this man-made path, so I do the only logical thing and take off down it, sending up my Hail Mary's just in case I'm wrong and my instincts are leading me astray. Not that I'm a religious man, but after working in this field for a while, I've learned it's wise to keep your options open—just in case.

The silhouette of a person lying on the ground appears a short distance ahead, however, it's too dark and I'm still too far away to be able to make out whether it's Sanders or the suspect.

The barrel of my gun is tipped down, a steady aim settled on my target—I can't afford any hesitations or mistakes this time.

I inhale deeply and edge closer to the figure, squinting to make out the faint outline of his face.

It's Sanders.

Thank fuck.

I can see his chest rising and falling, a sign that he is still alive. His vest has been removed and it looks like most of his equipment is gone as well.

Based on my observations, it seems that he has escaped any long-term or fatal injuries. There is a bullet lodged in his left shoulder, accompanied by contusions on his face and a potentially fractured nose.

I lift his shirt next, examining his abdomen and I identify four more wounds that appear to be inflicted by gunfire. Fortunately for him, it appears like his vest absorbed most of the impact, so he'll be fine for the most part. Though, I'm sure he has a few cracked or broken ribs.

So not only is our suspect posing as one of us, but he also has a bulletproof vest to help protect him now.

Damn.

The bastard is smart, I'll give him that.

Although the majority of his kidnappings and assaults have occurred in New York, he has remained concealed on the fringes of the state, just beyond the Pennsylvania border. He's been able to elude the police thus far, hence why the FBI was brought in to assist with the manhunt.

My flashlight flickers across the surrounding trees, searching for any signs of the perp but I know he wouldn't chance sticking around just in case more than one of us showed up. No. He's going to try to take us out one by one.

"We have an agent down that needs immediate medical attention." I quickly relay over to the rest of my team, giving them the coordinates to our location.

Sanders groans from beside me as he begins to stir, "He has my fucking coms."

Sure enough, as soon as the words leave Sanders's lips, the twisted individual we're pursuing chimes in with a taunting voice, "Try to catch me if you can." I grit my teeth as his cackle echoes through my earpiece.

"You son of a—"

The sound of a young girl's scream reverberates down my spine, cutting Reyes off in mid-sentence, "Ah. Ah. Ah. You shouldn't be so hasty with your words, agent. You hurt my feelings again, and I'm going to hurt her again. Okay?"

Sanders's eyes meet mine, reflecting the confusion I feel at this moment.

How did we miss her?

My heart races as I try to think of the best course of action. We need to move fast, but we also need to be strategic.

"Alright." I agree. "We didn't mean to hurt your feelings, Nathan. My colleague can just be a bit short-tempered and rude sometimes."

"We're going to play a little game of hide and seek."

Reyes breaks through the clearing nearby, lowering his weapon once he realizes it's just me and Sanders.

"Your—" I hold my hand up to Reyes in hopes of silencing him before he antagonizes the perp further and he nods, getting the hint. "You're on." Reyes smirks.

"What did you have in mind, Nathan?" I use his given name in an attempt to establish a personal connection.

Nathan's chuckle is eerie, a mix of manic laughter and violent glee, "Good. I'm glad you decided to do the smart thing and play along. The girl is hidden somewhere. She doesn't have long though, you see. That pesky little explosive I shoved in her mouth right before I taped her pretty little lips shut only has about five more minutes before her head pops like a virgin's cherry. And guess what, kids? That's not all!" Nathan's voice cracks with excitement. "You have a choice to make...find the girl and save her life or come find me and let her die." He pauses, letting the gravity of the situation sink in, "Your countdown begins now."

A chill grips my veins with icy claws as I observe the calculated cruelty of this man.

He embodies all the traits of a true psychopath—callous, lacking in empathy, and deriving pleasure from manipulating others like pawns in a game. His intellect is sharp, his wit cunning, and his charm disarming, making it easy for him to deceive countless innocent girls and women. It's no wonder he continues to evade justice with ease.

A medic arrives for Sanders just as Nathan ends his ominous monologue, handing Reyes and me a new earpiece with a private line to Sloan.

The situation is dire, but I remain composed, understanding that showing any hint of vulnerability will only make the girl's suffering last longer, "Sloan what's your location?"

"On my way to you."

"No." My eyes scan through the trees, my brain working overtime, and my gut telling me something isn't adding up.

The girl—how could we miss that? Who *is* she?

"Sloan, stay where you are and contact Mels. I think Nathan has somewhere to go—a place he would feel safe at. Possibly underground. Ask her to look into the surrounding area and search for any abandoned coal mines or caverns."

"You got it." Though there is disappointment in her voice, she doesn't argue.

"Reyes. I think you should head north, where we first heard the screams."

He gives a quick nod before vanishing into the dense pines. I take one more careful look around, my thoughts racing as I try to connect the final pieces of the puzzle.

"Holloway, Mels said there's an old mining cave roughly about a mile west of here. There was a collapse years ago killing over thirty of the people working the mines that day, and it's been condemned ever since. I'm sending you the coordinates now."

"Copy. Thanks, Sloan."

"You got it."

Okay, I'm quite confident that he will be making his way there, but that still leaves us with the task of finding the girl's whereabouts.

It's highly unlikely that he would keep her at the mines if it were meant as an escape route, and considering his knowledge of the tunnel system, he'll have a significant advantage over us once inside.

I glance at the time on my watch.

Shit.

We only have four minutes left to stop him from getting away and to locate the girl.

"The girl. The girl. The girl." I speak softly, my words carried away by the wind like delicate secrets, only to be whispered back into the rustling leaves of the trees surrounding me.

"Reyes, do you remember that cold file we were looking at a couple of weeks ago? That case we thought might be linked to all of this—the one where the girl's body was never found?"

His response is hesitant as if he's unsure of where I'm heading with my question, "Yeah, but the way it was done doesn't match the other crime scenes, right?"

"Precisely. According to the police report, there was no evidence of forced entry or a struggle, yet the girl's blood was discovered in various parts of the house. The mother of the girl, who was found deceased in her bed, showed no signs of fighting back despite receiving thirty-seven stab wounds. The scene was sloppy, chaotic, and from the fifty-seven stab wounds the mother received my guess would be, it was also personal."

"What does that have to do with anything?" Reyes's confusion is evident. "That was almost twelve years ago."

"Think about it. What if the girl was never a victim? What if she let the perp in that night—helped whoever it was with her mother's murder and now she's helping with more?"

"Jesus fucks, Holloway. You think this girl is the same one?" Reyes responds.

"I do," I confirm. "And I believe she's been involved with helping Nathan kidnap, torture, and murder all of his victims ever since."

I can hear Sloan suck in an exasperated gasp, "That would make sense on why there was never a body recovered."

Reyes and I catch back up with each other, exchanging that—*I hope to hell we're not wrong*—kind of look, and continue our venture through the broken bush and rotting leaves of the forest.

"All units are en route to the mines for backup," Sloan announces.

The area around the old caverns is like a ghost town, the scent of death lingering in the air around us while the distant echoes of our footsteps ring in my ears.

My heart is a war drum sounding off in my chest, a mixture of adrenaline, excitement, and the fear of what will happen if I'm wrong about this as we approach the entrance to the mine.

The dimly lit opening looms before us, a sinister invitation to venture deep into its belly.

The stench is horrendous, almost unbearable, an odor so putrid it makes bile rise in the back of my throat. Good thing I skipped lunch, or I'd probably be wearing it right now.

Reyes and I trudge through the moist, dim, tunnel, our boots crushing the loose rocks beneath us as we delve deeper into the dark, long abandoned passageway.

"Sloan," I speak low into my com, "We need a direct line to Mels. There are too many tunnels. I want her in my ear with directions as quickly as you can get us connected. We don't know this place the way Nathan does." Sloan acknowledges my request and I hear the crackling of static as the connection is made.

"Mels, can you hear me?"

"Loud and clear, Holloway." She responds, the sound of her popping gum loud against my eardrum. "Okay, you're at the West entrance. There are two more exits, one on the south side and another one located on the north side. Hmmm—" She pauses, and I can hear her fingers clicking off her keyboard at excess speed. "However, there's a river on the north side. It's possible he could be heading that way, but I can't find anything connecting him to any kind of ownership or access to a water-craft."

"Units are being dispatched to both locations as we speak," Sloan announces. "I'm on my way to the North entrance now.

Hopefully, if they're heading there, we'll be able to cut them off before they reach the river."

"Cade" Reyes calls out, gesturing to the opening on his left. It appears to be a room of sorts.

I nod, making my way over to him.

As we prepare to breech, the pungent stench of death intensifies, invading my nostrils with an overwhelming force. The room is barely illuminated by the feeble light of our flashlights, casting grotesque shadows that dance on the damp walls.

There's a mattress against the back wall old and tattered, with springs poking out of the ripped fabric. The surface is covered in various colored stains, most likely from the countless nights of horror that the naked decaying girl who is handcuffed to it had to endure.

I turn to Reyes and see the same emotions mirrored in his eyes—revulsion, rage, and determination to bring this son of a bitch down so no other person has to go through what this poor girl did.

The butterfly tattoo on her wrist is a match to one of the missing girls we've been searching for—Sarah Benning, a seventeen-year-old who went missing from the Upper East Side about six weeks ago, and based on the level of decomposition, it appears that she's been deceased for at least three or four of those weeks.

A soft, feminine voice speaks through the intercom, causing a chill to run down my spine. "I see you've met my friend," she says with a tinkling laugh.

Reyes's body freezes, his gaze jumping up from where he's crouched on the floor, "You were fucking right." He mouths to me.

I wish I could say that I never had any doubts about being right, but that would be a lie.

"I'm glad to hear you're alive," I say back to her, not knowing if she can actually hear me or not.

She laughs again, "I wouldn't have been if I was waiting for you to save me."

"If I had followed that pointless and futile pursuit, then I wouldn't have been able to be here with you, meeting your friend and having this conversation."

She laughs again, a haunting sound echoing through the room. "You still don't get it, do you?" she says, her voice now cold and distant. "You're never going to catch him. He's a savior, and what he's doing—rescuing these girls from a life of endless suffering, it *needs* to be done, and they *want* to be saved."

She exhibits signs of being heavily influenced and manipulated by Nathan, as evidenced by her childlike demeanor and unquestioning loyalty. This prolonged grooming has likely deeply ingrained psychological patterns that may be difficult for her to break.

He's brainwashed her into thinking he's a hero—a god, and in some twisted way, it's the only world she knows and believes in.

"And did he save you too?" Reyes asks the girl.

"We saved each other," I don't miss the hint of sadness reflected in her words. "He was always alone, without anyone who truly understood him, or what he needed. I was the only one who could truly connect with him and support him in a way that others simply couldn't grasp."

"And how did you do that? By helping him kidnap and murder these women? Did he make you kill her?" I nod to Sarah's lifeless corpse. "

"Don't presume to understand our relationship," She hisses. "He didn't *make* me do anything."

It's beginning to make sense on why he was starting to get sloppy—he's been teaching her, molding her to be a ruthless killer just like him. But there's something different with her, where Nathan disposes of his victims shortly after death occurs, this girl keeps them and as grotesque as it is—*plays* with them like they're toys in some demented game.

Reyes glances at me, then back to the girl. "And what about you? What do you get out of this?"

"Whatever I want, silly." The girl laughs. "Tell you what. I'll give you ten minutes, agents. If you can find me, I'll go with you willingly." She promises. "But if you can't then you become my new toys." Her eyes sparkle with a type of innocence that doesn't belong here.

This girl has serious issues.

Suddenly, everything goes silent. No more, childlike voice taunting us, only quiet remains.

Reyes and I exchange a look that needs no words; we're on borrowed time now.

Our boots resound mutely against the damp ground as we match one another's pace, sweeping through the labyrinth of tunnels beneath our feet. The air is stale, suffused with the musty odor of earth long undisturbed.

"Room clear," Reyes whispers each time he checks a new space that could be hiding someone.

We've been down here too long already.

My gut clenches with the certainty that if we don't catch them now, they'll vanish into the ether, taking their twisted games across borders, leaving nothing but dead bodies and sorrow in their wake.

"Keep it tight, Cade," Reyes says, his eyes scanning the darkness ahead. "She's close—I can feel it."

Nodding, I press forward, my hand steady on the grip of my weapon.

Faint, yet there, a giggle reaches our ears and we freeze. It's impossible to pin down where it comes from, bouncing around us until it fades back to the soundlessness.

She's playing with us, enjoying the chase as much as the kill.

Sloan's voice is in my ear again, "Nathan has been apprehended. You were right. He was trying to get to a watercraft when he we picked him up. Medics are on their way to take him to the hospital for non-life threating injuries."

Reyes and I share a look of relief.

One perp down.

Time is running out, and we move faster with desperation as our fuel. We finally reach the surveillance room and its blinking monitors, showing us a patchwork of empty hallways and dark areas.

And the girl—she's gone, vanished without a trace.

"Damn it," Reyes curses.

A flicker of movement catches my attention out of the corner of my eye, but before I can shout a warning, she drops from the rafters, silent as a ghost but deadly as a viper, landing squarely on Reyes's back.

"Reyes!" My heart seizes. His body buckles under the sudden weight, the girl's arm snaking around his neck, blade glinting in the dim illumination of my flashlight.

There's no time to think, only react.

My finger tenses on the trigger. Reyes's eyes meet mine, wide and pleading, yet full of undeniable trust.

He's not dying.

Not today, not on my watch.

The shot rings out, shattering the silence like glass.

It's over.

CHAPTER SIX

Tia

A little hard work and dedication are all it takes to make your dreams come true.

You just have to believe in yourself and stick it out through the hard times, because there will be many of those.

"Tiana, darling. It's absolutely remarkable."

"Didn't I tell you, Momma?" I ask, spinning around on the elegant, marbled floors of the main dining hall. "I was going to create the biggest, fanciest restaurant in all of New Orleans, and here it is."

Here it is indeed. I paid over seven hundred thousand for the building and all of the renovations that went into opening Le Rêve Brisé, but it was worth every penny to see it all come to life.

The room glows with a dazzling radiance from the grand chandeliers, while the subtle flicker of candlelight adds a touch of warmth and sophistication to each table, creating an inviting ambiance.

"I never doubted that you would create something amazing, child," She smiles, flashing me a quick wink.

In just a few short weeks, the Grand Opening will finally arrive. I'm feeling a mixture of nerves and excitement as I eagerly await the moment to reveal my masterpiece to the world. It's a feeling unlike any other I've ever experienced before—even being a renowned chef in London pales in comparison to this.

"Do you want to whip something up in the kitchen with me, for supper? You know, just to break in the new equipment to make sure it functions properly." I ask.

"You know I do." She laughs, her dark brown eyes twinkling with amusement.

Once we're in the kitchen area, we jump straight to work, grabbing fresh vegetables, potatoes, sausage, and shrimp from the cooler, and begin chopping and sauteing with a comfortable ease that comes only from years of practice.

The clinking of pots and pans fills the space as we move around each other in perfect harmony, a dance we've performed countless times before. The savory aroma of spices fills the air, mingling with the laughter and shared stories that flow between us.

"You know, now that you have the restaurant, maybe you can find yourself a nice young man to spend your extra time with." My mother offers the suggestion, completely aware that a romantic relationship is the last thing on my mind and not exactly at the top of my to-do list.

"Momma," I groan. "Why must you insist on me dating someone?"

"Because I'm not getting any younger, and because I'm not going to be around forever—I want to know that you have someone to take care of you." She replies.

"I do! I am perfectly capable of taking care of myself, thank you, and I most certainly do *not* need a man for that." I roll my eyes but can't help but smile at her persistence.

"I know, I know," she says shaking her head in mock exasperation.

My mother chuckles under her breath, knowing better than to push the subject further. We both know how independent and headstrong I can be, traits that have served me quite well in life.

"And even if I did want a man, it certainly wouldn't be just any man," I add, stirring the steaming pot of gumbo on the stove.

"Of course not," my mother agrees, her tone conspiratorial. "It would have to be someone special, someone who can match your fire and passion."

While she's not exactly wrong in her assessment, I still find myself scoffing at the notion of romance in my life.

My focus has always been on the restaurant, on perfecting my craft and creating dishes that speak to the soul. Love has always seemed like a frivolous distraction, a luxury I can ill afford in the hustle and bustle of running a successful business.

Furthermore, there is only one man who has ever held my heart in the palm of his hands and did so with such delicacy and understanding that it almost felt as if he knew me better than I knew myself—I can't imagine anyone else ever filling that role.

"Mmhmm," I hum through the memories to acknowledge her before tipping the wooden spoon full of broth I had been blowing on to cool off, up to my lips, taking a small sip.

It needs another dash or two of hot sauce.

I tilt the hot sauce bottle over the pot, shaking it and jokingly ask my mother, "You know what I *really* could use right now?" I wave towards the cupboard of dishes. "A couple of those bowls to serve this delicious stew that's just about ready in."

"You got it, sugar," As she reaches for the bowls, her laughter fills my soul with happiness. I can see the vivacious joy she exudes as she places the bowls next to me on the counter, their delicate china making a gentle clinking sound against the smooth quartz stone.

With a large wooden spoon, I carefully scoop the steaming stew into each bowl over a bed of soft, fluffy white rice, the rich aroma filling the kitchen. My mom slices thick pieces of crusty sourdough bread from the loaf I made yesterday and sets them on a platter. With our bowls and bread in hand, we make our way to one of the smaller tables in the dining area, sitting across from each other with a clear view of the courtyard garden just outside the set of glass doors sitting in front of us.

The terrace is by far my favorite part of the property, a riot of colors showcasing all the beautiful flowers in full bloom, swaying gently in the evening breeze as the warm glow of the sinking sun casts a golden haze across the Quarter.

As we start to eat, the silence between us is comfortable, filled only with the sounds of spoons clinking against bowls and the occasional satisfied hum escaping our lips. The stew is hearty and flavorful, a perfect blend of spices and tenderness that warms me from the inside out.

"I saw an old friend of yours today." My mother shares.

I hold the spoon in my mouth, secretly hoping that she's not referring to Elliot. I take a moment to swallow, gathering my thoughts before responding with a feigned interest, "Oh yeah, and who might that be?" I ask, trying to sound genuinely curious.

She wipes her mouth and places her napkin on the table beside her bowl, "Allie, the one little blonde girl that used to help out at the restaurant on the weekends, her family hosts the street parade that happens every year right before the big Mardi Gras celebration. You two used to be so close."

A knot forms in the pit of my stomach at the mention of Allie's name.

She used to be my closest friend as a child, our summer days were spent sharing secrets, pretending to be princesses, and climbing trees in the garden until the sun dipped below the horizon and fireflies lit up the night like little specks of stardust. But then, everything shifted and changed—including myself. And now, the way things used to be will never be the same again. Not after all that has happened.

I force a smile anyway, "Oh wow! It's been so long since I last saw her. I hope she's well."

"She is do—my goodness!" She cuts her words short. "You know, I didn't think to ask the child how her mother and father were doing!"

I place my silverware down, my stomach too sour to continue eating, "Her father—he's a cop, isn't he?"

"I'm pretty sure, yes. At least he was before we moved."

Moved.

My mom's way around having to mention Papa's murder.

A small part of me is worried that her return to this place only adds to the pain she feels from losing him. Every day, as she walks down the main strip, passing all the ghosts of old memories, she is forced to relive our painful past.

"I'll have to stop in at the station one of these days and take them all some lunch."

"That's a wonderful idea, darling. I'll—" Her phone rings loudly from her purse. Her forehead pulls together as she turns the phone around, looking at its screen.

"Everything okay?" I whisper.

She nods, swiping her finger against the screen before pressing it to her ear, "Hi, Cassandra! I'll be heading that way in the next hour. I'm finishing up supper now with Tia."

I hear the other woman's muffled voice on the other line, though, I can't make out what she is saying."

"Okay. Al—Alright, hun. I'll see you there. Mhmm. Bye-bye now."

"Plans?" I ask.

A mischievous grin dances on the corner of her lips, "Cassandra invited me for drinks down at the Speak Easy over on *St. Ann Street*. And I figured, why not? I could use a night out, and you know Cassandra always has the best gossip to share," she gleams.

Cassandra was one of the few friends Momma had in this town. My memories of her are somewhat fuzzy, but I do recall her being a kind woman with long straw-colored hair and hazel eyes. She always had those little strawberry candies with the gooey centers in her oversized purse, which I simply couldn't resist as a child.

"Okay." I smile. "Have fun, Mom. You deserve it. Oh, and be careful!"

She laughs, "I will, and no promises." She jokes, still a wild card even in her older age.

It's a relief to see her genuine smile again as if all the worries in the world have disappeared, and now she's free. I love that for her—truly I do. But for me, those feelings cannot be matched, not until they all pay.

And pay, they will.

CHAPTER SEVEN

Tia

The humid air wraps around the sprawling veranda like a sultry embrace, carrying the scent of blooming magnolias that adorn our new plantation. Momma always dreamt of owning such a property, with magnificent grand pillars and wrought-iron balconies that seem to whisper secrets of the old New Orleans charm. And it's here, in this picturesque setting, where I will finally craft the closing act of a tragedy that began so many years ago.

As I slice through ripe plump tomatoes, laying them beside crispy fried shrimp on the open-faced baguette, the swinging wooden doors opening up to the kitchen creak, heralding my mother's entrance. A smile graces her thinning lips, completely oblivious to the raging storm brewing within me as she admires the spread destined for the police station.

"Smells divine, as always," she says, tying an apron around her waist to assist me.

"Thanks, Momma. Just making a little food to drop off for Alana's dad and the rest of the station before I meet her for lunch this afternoon." I reply.

Turning back to the counter, my gaze shifts to where the garlic aioli awaits its final, fatal ingredient. The tiny vial hidden in my pocket is no larger than a thimble and contains a lethal poison, a fatal concoction born from long sleep-deprived nights in a London lab with a professor whose moral compass has long since lost its true north. He did, however, understand the temptation of seeking revenge, and the desire to personally ensure that justice is served.

To this day the authorities still don't know what happened to the woman responsible for the tragic death of his wife and their unborn child, and perhaps they never will.

You see, the law didn't seem to care when a lawyer struck down an eight-month pregnant woman while driving drunk behind the wheel before fleeing the scene, but they sure cared when that same lawyer mysteriously vanished. Of course, they'll never find her, because as it turns out, hydrofluoric acid not only destroys the skin and soft tissues, but also the bone as well.

The biggest plot twist to the whole story—no one ever suspected the grieving science professor, who had just lost everything. They didn't even consider him a suspect when he suddenly left for London. Or maybe it's just that they just don't want the truth to come out—that the judicial system protected a killer and then falsified the death certificate of a deceased pregnant woman.

My hands are quick as I sneak a dash of the odorless liquid into the creamy sauce, mixing it vigorously with a fork. Each stir is a silent eulogy for my father, whose life was snuffed out far too early by the very people who swore an oath to protect it.

Yet, those sworn officers chose to betray their oaths and crush them beneath their dirty boots, extinguishing the life of an innocent man whose only intention was to protect his daughter. Now their unwarranted freedom echoes aimlessly in my mind, haunting my thoughts like a cruel and taunting specter.

"Are you alright, sugar?" my mother asks, peering at me with concern as she wraps another sandwich perfectly, placing it in one of the large baskets on the center island.

"Yes ma'am, couldn't be better." I lie, "I'm just concentrated on getting these just right," I say, brushing off her worry with a reassuring smile, but internally, my heart burns with sorrow and rage.

With meticulous care, I spread the tainted aioli onto the fluffy interior of the baguette designated for one officer in particular—officer Landry.

His complicity has sealed his fate as surely as if he had pulled the trigger himself. And though revenge may be a dish best served cold, today, it will be delivered warm and fragrant, nestled between lettuce and tomato, a delicious illustration of the lengths one will go to serve justice.

"Such a kind gesture, bringing lunch to our boys in blue," Momma chimes from somewhere behind me, oblivious to the dark undercurrent of my actions.

"Just doing my part," I reply softly, placing the top half of the bread on the sandwich, sealing the deadly deal with a gentle press. "Oh, I almost forgot to ask, did you enjoy your night out with Cassandra last night?" I look over my shoulder to see Momma's reaction as I tuck a napkin around the last of the po' boys.

The woven baskets on the counter are now filled, teasing my nose with scents of fried shrimp and freshly baked bread.

"Oh, it was marvelous!" Mama exclaims, her eyes lighting up like the string lights that drape over the gazebo in the courtyard. "The band had a trumpet player, straight from Chicago, they said. He played *'Basin Street Blues'* so soulfully, it almost brought tears to my eyes."

I chuckle, picturing the scene—Momma being in her element, lost in the music, "Sounds wonderful. And how did Cassandra fare? She's not one to shy away from dancing, if memory serves me right."

"Like a queen holding court," She laughs, tapping her foot as if the rhythm still lingered. "Had every gentleman in the place vying for a turn to twirl her around the floor."

"Of course she did!" My lips curl into a smile and an easy laugh escapes while my hands arrange the bottles of sweet teas alongside the sandwiches, each one artfully positioned, like pieces on an elaborate game board so none of them topple over during transport.

"All set to go?" Momma questions, glancing at the baskets now ready for delivery.

"Almost," I reply, fastening the lids and securing them with a flourish of ribbon. "Would you mind to help me carry these out?"

With our combined efforts, we quickly load the baskets into my sleek black Jaguar. The car gleams under the midday sun, its curves and polished finish standing out against the backdrop of the old plantation's regal oaks and hanging Spanish moss.

My mom plants a soft kiss on my cheek, just as she always does before any journey, no matter how far or near it may be, "You drive safe now, sugar."

"Always do," I respond with a grin, feeling the weight of the keys in my hand as if they were some sort of talisman. "And don't worry about tonight's dinner. I'll be back in plenty of time." I call out, sliding behind the wheel, the plush leather seat of the car hugging me like a warm embrace.

The engine purrs to life with a gentle roar that speaks of power held in check—much like the anger I carry within me. As I drive away, I leave behind the serene beauty of the estate—a facade of tranquility that mirrors my own.

Each mile closer to the NOPD tightens the coil of anticipation in my chest. The streets bustle with life, but I barely register the blur of faces and storefronts as I pass by.

Finally, I arrive, parking smoothly along the curb before stepping out and popping open the trunk. The humid New Orleans air envelops me as I reach for the first basket, jumping when I notice a youthful officer, his uniform still carrying the creases from being freshly issued, standing before me with an eagerness that reminds me of a schoolboy.

"Can I help you with those, ma'am?" he asks, gesturing towards the wicker containers filled with the aromas of New Orleans' finest.

"Why, yes. Thank you so much, officer—"

"Jenkins, ma'am"

"I'm Tia Williams," I reach out my hand, "I bought the old warehouse that's opening soon as a brand-new restaurant. I thought I'd bring a taste of what's to come to this wonderful city. I introduce myself, a well-practiced smile forming on my face.

The mere mention of food lights up his face, "That's mighty kind of you, Ms. Williams. We sure do appreciate it."

"It's nothing really. Oh, while I have you for a moment, I have a quick question," I say smoothly, "A friend of mine's father works here, and I was wondering, would you happen to know if Officer Landry is on duty today?"

"Officer Landry?" The young man's eyes widen slightly as he nods. "He's not just an officer though, ma'am; he's the sheriff here now. Took over after the old sheriff passed away a few years back. He's in his office. I can show you the way if you'd like?"

"That would be wonderful, thank you so much," I smile, handing him a basket while keeping a special one for the sheriff in my grasp.

We navigate through the maze of desks and ringing telephones until we reach a door marked *'Sheriff Landry.'* The young officer knocks, and a voice rich in years beckons us inside.

"Come in!"

Upon entering the large office space, the sight of Sheriff Landry strikes a chord in my memory, his features barely touched by time since I saw him last at Papa's funeral. His gaze lifts from the file lying on the desk in front of him, locking onto mine, and recognition flickers on his face like a candle flame in a drafty room.

"Tia? Tia Williams!" He exclaims rising from his chair, engulfing me in a suffocating embrace that fills my soul with ice.

"Hello, Mr. Landry, or should I address you as Sheriff now?" I ask with a forced smile, pulling back slightly to meet his eyes. My stomach churns, but I do my best to hide the nausea creeping up the back of my throat.

"It's been too long; I'm getting to be an old man now." He takes a step back. "How's your momma doin?"

"Eh, she's doing alright. Keeping herself busy these days."

"Does Allie know you're back in town yet?"

"She sure does! We're actually going to be meeting up for lunch after I leave here."

"Is that right?" He chuckles, the lines around his eyes deepening. "You two always were inseparable, even as kids."

"Speaking of when we were kids, I remember how much you use to enjoy Papa's cooking." I hand over the *'special'* po boy and a small box of chocolate hazelnut beignets. "Thought you might enjoy a little taste of nostalgia."

"Ah, you and your father's beignets were second to none," He croons, yet his voice holds a touch of sorrow. "Thank you, Tia. And listen...I—I'm truly sorry about your dad. He was a good man."

I can feel the tension in my throat as I quietly mutter, "Yes, that he was, Sheriff." It takes all of my acting skills to keep up the charade.

It's such a cruel twist of fate, though, that a man who has shared so many meals at our family table, who has laughed with me—with my father, will now share his fate. Not because he was the one who pulled the trigger, no, but because his silence was just as lethal as the bullet that stole my father's life. His knowledge of that night's true villain makes him complicit. And for that, there can be no forgiveness.

He settles back into the worn leather of his chair, his rather expanded belly hanging over his belt as he does, and hefts the woven basket onto his cluttered desk, pushing aside case files and pens to make room for the unexpected treat. Beaming up at me, his eyes crinkle, and he lifts the lid with the eagerness of a child on Christmas morning rubbing his hands together back and forth.

"Smells just like the old days," he enthuses, his large hands, calloused from years of service, carefully extract the neatly wrapped sandwich, tenderly placing it before him as if it's a sacred offering.

He inhales sharply, taking in all the scents of the flavors and spices, his eyes rolling back as he does, "Thank you again, Tia. You didn't have to go through all this trouble," he says.

"It's no trouble at all, Sheriff," I respond, my smile unwavering even as my heart thrums against my ribcage.

My fingers twitch at my side, longing to see the culmination of years spent plotting, and of pain that's spent years of being masked by polite smiles and feigned pleasantries.

He peels back the paper, and my breath catches in my throat. *Just eat the fucking thing already!*

I swallow hard, my eagerness almost giving away a hint of suspicion, but I correct myself before the sheriff has a chance to notice.

"Here goes nothing," he chuckles, oblivious to the shadow of death that looms over him. A low moan of pleasure escapes his lips as he savors the flavors of his past, of a time before the truth of his actions—or lack thereof—had stained our family's history.

"Oh...Mhmmm...yea, this is—this is delicious," he manages around his mouthful, his contentment echos hollowly in my ears as he licks at the aioli sauce dripping down his hand, crumbs of bread peppering his dark mustache, "I can't wait to see what this restaurant of yours brings. I'm hoping it's more of this!" He takes another bite.

"Why thank you, Mr. Landry. That's mighty kind of you," I say, my voice as soft and lethal as the concoction hidden within his meal.

"Anyway, I really should get going. Allie will be waiting for me." I add casually, turning towards the door. I pause at the threshold, casting a final glance over my shoulder. The sight of him, so vulnerable and exposed in his contentment, only fans the flames of retribution burning inside me further, awakening an even darker side of myself than I thought possible.

"Of course! I'm sorry for holding you up." He wipes his mouth before standing to offer me a hug. "I'll see you soon, Tia. Take care."

"Yes, sir. You take care of yourself too. I look forward to seeing you at the restaurant sometime." A cold smile forms on my face. He'll be dead by morning and the plant the professor found on one of his excavation trips to a land yet to be discovered by any other person but him, won't be identifiable even with modern science and toxicology tests.

The location of where he gets the plants remains a mystery even to me, as well as it will for the rest of the world—diminishing any chances of it being traced back to me. It will simply appear as though he quit breathing in his sleep—that is if the cardiac arrest doesn't kill him first. Either way, his autopsy report will show that he died of natural causes, keeping *my* hands clean.

A festival will be thrown to celebrate his life, and we will mourn him as a community—he'll be missed by many—perhaps, and Momma and I will console his wife and children as the silence he chose to carry all these years lingers on forever, with our ancestors, buried deep beneath the earth's surface as they whisper the secrets of our pasts.

Life will begin to balance itself once more, and I can move on to my next victim.

The woman I have become is foreign to me, but I can't exactly say that I'm bothered by the transformation. Though my path is one of death and destruction, I do not consider myself a killer. I have simply made difficult choices in order to honor my father's legacy and ensure his demise was not for naught.

Taking one last look at him and doing a little wave, I click the door behind me and begin my exit through the bustling precinct, "Goodbye, Sheriff Landry," I whisper under my breath as the bright sun meets my face.

Today is going to be a good day.

CHAPTER EIGHT

Agent Holloway

"Nice work, Agent Holloway."

"Thank you, Director."

How are you doing after—?"

I didn't have a choice. I was forced to make the call. It came down to her or Reyes, and as much as I would have loved to save them both, it just wasn't possible. The girl had already made her decision, and the sad truth of the matter is—she would have continued to kill with or without him. In fact, I believe she relished in it just as much as Nathan did, if not more.

"I'm okay. There wasn't anything I could have done differently, sir."

He gives a slight nod, intertwining his fingers and leaning back into the plush black leather chair situated at the head of his sturdy oak desk, "You made the right call. Still, I know it never gets easier." He speaks from experience.

Director Manchin has had his fair share of tough calls to make. One of those difficult decisions resulting in the loss of his partner, and best friend, who died during a botched raid.

One of our own had set them up and tipped off the cartel. The traitor had been working with them, feeding them information for a cut of the profit.

He cradled his dying friend in his arms, staying by his side until the very end, until the very last breath left his body. It was that moment that changed him forever.

After taking a brief leave of absence, he came back with a vengeance and proved himself to be one of the most skilled FBI agents. Over time, he worked his way up to becoming the director of the BAU, or Behavioral Analysis Unit, where he now serves as my boss.

"We do what we have to do."

His weary eyes look up at me with a mixture of empathy and pride, "I agree. Which brings me to my next subject."

Taking a brief moment to gather his thoughts, the director's eyes fixate on the window behind me, presenting a view of the city skyline.

"Sir?"

He absentmindedly strokes his chin as his mind drifts away momentarily before snapping back to our discussion in the present, "A couple of fishermen found a body in the harbor earlier this morning. We're still waiting to hear back from forensics, but I'm pretty certain it's Francisco. The body was too mangled to ID but—" He places a photo of the crime scene in front of me. "The rose tattoo, here on his temple—"

"Yeah, that's him," I confirm, my stomach twisting in knots upon the recognition.

It took much longer than we expected for his body to appear. From the gruesome state of it, it seems like they kept him alive for an extended period just to prolong his suffering before ultimately killing him.

"You know what this means then?" The director's expression hardens, his voice grave.

I let out a long, slow breath, running my fingers through my jet-black hair, "I'm their next target."

He nods, his jaw tightening, "For now, I've already assembled a team to ramp up the security around you, *and* her, beginning immediately." He quickly corrects himself.

His tall frame casts a shadow over the room as he paces back and forth.

"It seems like we're already ahead of them, and with the flash drive Fransico provided, we have all the necessary information to dismantle their entire drug organization. Once we take down the Rivera cartel, the city will finally be rid of their influence, and crime rates will drop drastically, possibly to the lowest they've been in over a decade."

"You know how big this operation is. You're a profiler, not a fucking God, Cade, and Rome wasn't built in a day." He snaps, pinching the bridge of his nose between his fingers in dismay.

The quick change in his tone catches me off-guard, "I—yes, sir. Do we have any leads on their whereabouts?" I shift the conversation—a tactic I learned early on in the academy.

Since the cartel learned of Fransisco's perfidy, we've been monitoring all known safe houses, but they've gone dark. They're operating more covertly now, making it harder for us to track them down. But we have eyes everywhere, and it's just a matter of time before we catch a break.

"There's been some progress on tracking their movements. Surveillance footage caught by one of the boat owner's cameras, down at the docks shows a couple of cartel goons disposing of Fransisco's body. Their exact whereabouts are still unknown, but the *NYPD* has been placed on high alert and you will have twenty-four-hour surveillance around you until we figure out where they are operating from."

"Sir, respectfully I don't feel like that's needed."

He stops pacing and looks directly at me, his eyes intense.

"Respectfully, Agent Holloway, it isn't a request—it's a direct order from your superior." He replies through clenched teeth.

I chose this job.

I put my life on the line every single day chasing some of the most depraved killers, so his reasoning is incomprehensible to me.

"Tactical deception, also referred to as functional deception is commonly used in the animal kingdom by using misinformation—or lies, by one animal to another in a way that propagates beliefs that are not true. So, what happened that has you so on edge that you lack faith in your team's skill and intelligence?"

"God damn it. Your too smart for your own damn good." He rattles under his breath. "She made me promise when I went to tell her you wouldn't be able to see her for a while."

In an instant, my lungs collapse, struggling against the icy tide from the sea of emotions overwhelming me, and dragging me down into the depths of my own self-pity.

Her hope of a normal life is always being put on the back burner or compromised at the mercy of my profession.

How many times have I promised her that things would get better, that I would be there more often, only to let her down time and time again?

"Did you give her the things I gave you? The letter?"

He nods.

I take a deep breath, trying to push away the guilt clawing at my insides.

"She's being moved to a safer location for the time being. You understand I can't tell you where that is right now?" He questions.

"I understand. Thank you for looking out for her," I finally manage to answer, my voice hoarse with unspoken emotions.

He takes a seat back at his desk, "Listen, there's something else." He pauses.

I quirk my brow, waiting for him to continue, but a loud explosion has us both reaching for our weapons and scrambling to assess the damage.

It came from somewhere outside the building.

We're ten stories up and we were still able to hear and feel the blast. Peering down from the glass, I can make out several plumes of smoke in multiple locations around the area.

Debris falls down from the sky like a toxic rain as the people down below scurry quickly, seeking sanctuary from the chaos unfolding around them in the overly busy streets of New York City. The panicked cries and terror show clearly on their faces, yet never actually reach my ears as they're stolen by the thick glass barricading us from the horrors they are enduring on the ground.

It's possible there may be more explosives so we need to do everything we can, as quickly as we can to get these people to safety. My instincts kick into overdrive, as does the Director's and we bolt toward the door into the disarray of agents rushing to secure the building and evacuate any civilians still inside.

The Director is barking orders into his comms unit, his face a mask of determination as he tries to maintain control and keep order amidst of all the turmoil.

I take the emergency exit stairwell, taking the steps two at a time as I race down toward the ground level, my boots echoing off the narrow walls and through the empty space.

A pungent scent of smoke invades my nostrils, mingling with the cacophony of screams and cries that nearly deafen me as I burst out onto the sidewalk. I quickly survey the surrounding vicinity, looking for the perpetrator behind this heinous act of violence, but there's no one that stands out to me.

Squinting through the smoke, I spot something that ignites a chill that hastily spreads across my skin—Fransico's wife's vehicle—the one that witness protection set her up with. She should have already made it out of town.

As I get closer, about thirty feet away, the haze of smoke clears and I realize that the car is not empty.

Francisco's wife and daughter are in there.

Savannah is hunched over her mother, tears streaming down her face. Officer Bailey, a petite brunette from the NYPD, reaches them before I do, attempting to calm the distraught girl through the slightly tinted windows of the van. But her efforts only seem to make Savannah even more frantic.

"Please, just leave us alone!" She sobs, trying to deter the officer away from the vehicle.

Where the hell is their security detail?

As I glance at the back seat, the silhouette of a man is barely visible, hidden by the clutter of boxes and clothes still in the van from the family's relocation.

That's not one of the agents.

A sinister grin spreads across his face as his eyes lock with mine. He brings his fist up; a small remote device sits just beneath his thumb.

Fuck.

He's going to blow it up.

"Officer, Bailey!" I yell out, trying to gain her attention. "Get awa—"

But it's too late. She reaches to open to door, pulling against the handle of the driver-side door, and the van explodes in a deafening blast of fire and metal, rocking the ground beneath my feet.

The force of the explosion knocks me off my feet, sending me flying backward into another car, my body cracking off the windshield and then slamming hard onto the pavement.

Blood fills my mouth, coating my tongue with the taste of iron as I cough and gasp for air. The world is a blur of fire and smoke, and my senses are left reeling from the force of the blast. My body throbs from the impact, my ears ringing profusely as I try to roll over onto my back in an attempt to regain my bearings.

I can see Officer Bailey's lifeless body sprawled out on the pavement, her uniform now a tattered mess of blood and ash. Pushing away the pain and confusion, I struggled to pull myself up, staggering to her side, and cradling her petite body in my arms.

"I really messed things up this time." She croaks, struggling to put on a smile.

"This isn't your fault," I whisper, a tear sneaking its way from the corner of my eye, down to the tip of my nose.

She struggles to take shallow breaths and her exhausted eyes meet mine, trying to form words but failing, "I—I..."

"It's okay, Michelle. You did good," I say, my throat is tight as I fight back the tears and grief threatening to consume me. "You did good, so you—you can rest now," I tell her, brushing a strand of hair away from her face.

She nods, and the tension in her body melts away, almost as if a heavy burden has been lifted from her shoulders.

I feel her hand squeeze mine gently, and then her eyes slowly drift close.

In a soft, barely audible whisper, she murmurs, "Thank you for staying with me." Before her hand falls to the ground.

Her last words echo in my ears as I cradle her limp form. I'm frozen with shock and grief, unable to take my eyes off her mangled face. And the guilt from the shattered promise I made to Fransico to protect his family if he helped us with the case, will haunt me forever. I was supposed to keep them safe—to keep them from falling into the hands of the very people we were protecting them from, and I failed.

Sirens faintly wail in the distance, getting louder as rescue trucks and ambulances race toward the scene.

Though I can't be sure without solid evidence, I'm almost certain this is a warning—a demonstration of what's to come—a message from Antonio Rivera himself...he's planning for a fucking war, and I'm his main target.

CHAPTER NINE

Tia

"I'll have a blueberry lemon mimosa and the Cajun eggs benedict with an extra side of bacon, please." I close my menu handing it to the waitress.

She's been an absolute delight, her personality is humorous, yet professional, she wears a smile and carries herself with a sense of confidence and pride—I wonder if she's looking for a new job. I'd love to have her at Le Rêve Brisé.

"Oh, Tia!" Allie squeals, "I still can't believe you're back! I've missed you something fierce, girl. I sent you so many letters. Why did you stop writing back?"

Shame heats my face, "I guess I just got busy with school and work, I neglected any semblance of a social life." I let out a nervous chuckle.

The waitress returns with our drinks, setting them down on the table with a bright smile. I take a sip of my mimosa, the tangy sweetness hitting my taste buds in just the right way.

Allie's eyes widen as she takes a sip of her own drink, letting out a contented sigh, "Well," She begins, "I sure am happy to have you back now. We have so much to catch up on! Wait till I tell you about Emily and Brad." She snorts, grabbing a crouton off the top of her salad and popping it into her mouth.

I lean in with anticipation, eager to hear all the juicy details. Allie has always been the town gossip, but I can't help but revel in the drama of it all. She has a way of spinning a tale that keeps me on the edge of my seat, hanging on her every word.

She launches into the latest scandal involving Emily and Brad—our old middle school classmates who have been on again, off again since the first grade.

I focus all of my attention on Allie's animated storytelling, waves of nostalgia flooding over me as she relives the drama between Emily and Brad. She pauses strategically, waiting for my expected gasps of shock at each key point in her story.

It's funny how some things never seem to change no matter how much time has passed.

Allie finishes her tale with a flourish, her eyes dancing with mischief as she waits for my reaction. I lean back in my chair, shaking my head in mock disbelief. "I can't believe they're still at it after all these years," I chuckle, taking another sip of my mimosa. "And he cheated on her with not one, but *two* of Summer's teachers? Oh no, honey. Not me."

"At this point, they both cheat so much on one another that they might as well just have an open relationship. Most of the townsfolk already know and talk about all the drama they create, it's like a never-ending soap opera." She remarks, rolling her eyes.

"It seems like it." I nod in agreement, knowing all too well the small-town gossip mill never stops churning.

"Okay, enough about them. Girl, what about you? You leave me here all alone to go become some big fancy chef in London?" She beams. "Tell me all about what it was like living in London."

I take a moment to collect my thoughts, the memories of bustling London streets and aromatic kitchens flooding back to me. "London was both exhilarating and challenging," I begin, swirling the straw in my drink absentmindedly. "The culinary scene there is unlike anything I've ever experienced. The flavors, the techniques...it was all so magical." I breathe. "I made a few friends—one in particular. Her name is Alice, and let me tell you, she is a wildcard." I laugh.

"Any handsome suitors there vying for your attention?" Allie asks, waggling her eyebrows.

I shake my head.

"Come on, you can't tell me that the entire time you were gone you didn't date or fall in love unless—OMG! Tia, are you a virgin?"

Mimosa sprays from my nostrils the moment her words brand my ears, much to Allie's delight. I cough and sputter, trying to compose myself as she laughs uproariously at my expense.

Once I finally catch my breath, I glare at her playfully. "No, I am not a virgin, thank you very much," I retort, joining in her laughter despite my burning cheeks. "There was one man, actually," I admit. "His name was Oliver. Tall, with eyes like liquid silver and a smile that could disarm even the coldest of hearts."

Allie leans in eagerly, her eyes sparkling with curiosity.

"I was in love with him...too much perhaps."

"What happened?" She questions.

"I fell for him, and he fell for someone else." I shrug. "Don't get me wrong, I've had my share of companions, but relationships just haven't been a priority of mine. I enjoy coming and going as I please without anyone to answer to—it suits me and my life." I say, smiling at the waitress as she places my food down in front of me. "Okay, now it's your turn."

"There just aren't any good men down here in the Quarter." She pouts, pushing out her bottom lip.

Despite her playful demeanor, I can detect a hint of longing in her voice, a yearning for something more than just casual flings and fleeting romances.

"Well, who needs men anyway when you have beignets like these?" I say with a wink, biting into the not-so-fluffy pastry, my nose crinkling in disgust as my teeth struggle to bite through the dense toughness of the greasy dough.

Allie giggles, her mood shifting as quickly as the sunlight filtering through the café windows.

"The food here is decent but stay away from the deserts." She says, sticking out her tongue. "No one can make them the way you and your daddy do."

My fork falls from my hand, clanking off the porcelain plate in front of me before clambering to the floor.

"Oh, Tia! I'm so sorry! Fragging damn it, Allie, why do you have to have such a big mouth?" She curses herself as she picks up my fork, wiping it off on a napkin before handing it back over to me.

I wave off her apology as though the mention of him didn't just tear me apart, "It's alright, I'm still as clumsy now as I was as a pre-teen." I offer the lie, taking a deep breath, trying to push away the memories that Allie's words have brought back to the surface.

"I thought I said something wro—"

"Not at all. You are *fine*, sugar! I promise." I assure her, glancing down at the face of the gold watch hugging my wrist. "Shoot. I really do need to get going, though. I promised Momma that I'd help her repaint and treat the front deck today since we have all those storms coming in over the next few weeks according to the weatherman."

"They're going to miss us," Allie states with confidence. "I've been manifesting it, so Mardi Gras isn't ruined." She grins before polishing off the rest of her meal.

"I'm with you there. Keep manifesting it, girl. I need sunshine and blue skies for opening day." I laugh, grabbing my purse off the back of my chair as I stand up and smooth out my dress.

"Once I'm crowned princess of Mardi Gras, I'm coming to the restaurant to celebrate."

"Princess, huh?"

She squares her shoulders, "Crowned princess for five straight years in a row." A big toothy smile spreads across her gorgeous face.

It doesn't surprise me she's won so many times. Allie is—*pure talent.*

Even when we were little, she excelled at everything; always more athletic, always had the prettiest voice in the church choir, always had the perfect skin and the perfect smile—she had a natural charm that attracted people, drawing them in, like moths to a flame.

"Please, forgive me, your highness." I curtsy, mockingly bowing my head as I do.

"Oh, stop it!" She scolds, giggling as she playfully shoves my arm before hugging me goodbye.

I chuckle as I make my way out of the restaurant, waving to Allie as she calls out, "Don't forget about our girls' night next Friday!"

"Wouldn't dream of it!" I call back to her.

I'm not being dishonest; I genuinely am excited for our girls' night. But deep down, I know there's a good chance we'll end up at an unplanned funeral instead.

What a pity.

CHAPTER TEN

Tia

I weave through the clusters of mourners, their somber whispers mingling with the low drone of organ music that fills the air of Allie's childhood home—a grand plantation house nestled just outside the French Quarter, standing tall with large white pillars that support a grand entrance and balcony overlooking the sprawling grounds. The parlor is bathed in elongated shadows from the sun, and the antique furnishings are adorned with memories, much like the moss that clings to the ancient oaks just outside this set of walls.

"Excuse me," I murmur, gently slipping past a huddled group of Allie's relatives.

Their faces are etched with grief, though my heart remains untouched by their sorrow. After what feels like an eternity, I reach Allie, who stands with indefatigable strength amidst the ocean of sympathy.

"Hey," I say softly, and her gaze locks onto mine. There's a vulnerability in her eyes that pulls at something deep within me, something I thought was long extinguished. I pull her into an embrace, feeling the rigidness of her posture melt slightly. "I'm so sorry about your dad," I whisper, and she nods against my shoulder, her breath hitching with silent sobs.

"Thank you so much for being here, Tia." She whispers.

"Of course."

After a moment, I step back, watching Allie as she tries to compose herself. With a tight smile, I turn away from her pain and approach the open casket where Sheriff Landry—her father—lies in eternal slumber. The dim light glazes over his features, giving them a waxy pallor.

I reach inside the folds of my dress and produce a single white lily—the symbol of innocence, though the irony isn't lost on me. I lay it gently on the sheriff's chest, right above his stilled heart. Standing up straight, I let my fingers graze the lapel of his suit, the same hands that had sealed his fate.

No guilt gnaws at me; no remorse clouds my thoughts.

He got what he deserved, and the satisfaction of knowing I've enacted the first act of my fastidiously planned retribution is a thrill that pulses through my veins. The sheriff was just the beginning, the first thread pulled from the tapestry of lies and corruption that he helped to weave.

It's time for justice to claim its next due, I muse, casting a final glance at the still figure before me. A shiver of anticipation tingles down the length of my spine. My plan is in motion, and there's no turning back now.

I find myself escaping from the heavy atmosphere and seeking refuge in the kitchen.

Allie's here too, her delicate hand trembling slightly as she brings a glass of pink champagne to her lips. The bubbles rise and pop, like the silent whispers of condolences being exchanged in the next room.

"Hey," she says, noticing my presence. Her smile is fragile, cracked like a porcelain dolls. "Join me in a drink?" She gestures to an open bottle on the counter.

"Thanks." I pull out one of the high chairs from under the breakfast bar and settle onto its cushioned seat. My fingers curl around the stem of the flute she hands me, but I don't drink.

"I—I can't believe he's gone..." Her voice trails off, choked by grief.

"Me neither," I lie smoothly, letting empathy soften my face. "I'm so sorry you have to go through this, Allie."

In all honesty, I hate that things had to turn out like this. But what other option did I have?

She nods, her eyes glistening with unshed tears. "You always understood loss...ever since..." Her voice trails off again.

"Yea, I know. Too well in my opinion," I reply quietly, thinking of my own father's untimely demise, anger sinking deep into my bones.

Allie pours herself another glass, her movements quick and careless. The liquid sloshes over the rim and drips down the side.

Quickly, she downs it in one long swallow, seeking courage at the bottom of the glass.

"I just...I can't shake the feeling that something's not right," She confesses, wiping her mouth with the back of her hand. "Daddy was healthy, you know? He ran every morning, ate clean—most of the time. Even the medical examiners are stumped. They're waiting on the toxicology report, but that won't be ready for weeks."

"Did they mention anything at all?" I prod gently, feigning ignorance and concern.

It is essential to always be a step ahead and for me to anticipate any doubts that may arise.

"Nothing. They say it looks like cardiac arrest, but..." She shrugs helplessly. "I need answers, Tia. I need to know why."

"Of course, that's to be expected." I soothe, placing a comforting hand over hers. "And if there's anything suspicious, I'm sure they will find it. Technology has come such a long way."

She nods, looking somewhat reassured, but the seed of doubt has already been planted. I watch her fill her glass yet again, knowing full well that the truth will remain buried, just like both our fathers.

"Thanks again for being here," she murmurs, her gaze heavy with gratitude and pain.

I give her a gentle smile, bringing the small glass of champagne to my lips, taking a sip, "I wouldn't have missed it for the world."

The procession snakes through the heart of the city, a sinuous line of mourning and celebration staggering between the living and the dead.

The languid strains of a trombone slur against the wail of a clarinet, the notes hanging thick in the humid air like the ghostly cries of the departed.

I walk leisurely down the road, trailing after the horse-drawn carriage that carries the casket of the sheriff. The casket is covered with the American flag, and I can't help but be awestruck by the splendor of the procession.

Men and women—some in uniform, some in festival costumes, others in cheerless attire—step to the rhythm of the music. Their feet tap off the cobblestone streets, a syncopated beat that pulses with the heartbeat of NOLA.

Despite the gravity of the occasion, there's an undercurrent of something more, something profound and uniquely New Orleans: a tribute not just to a man's end, but to the spirit he carried through a lifetime.

As we round the corner onto hallowed ground, the cemetery appears like an ancient city itself, a labyrinth of stone and marble rising to greet us.

The band softens their playing, the music melting away as the NOPD officers, resplendent in their dress blues, approach the carriage. With solemn precision, they lift the casket, their movements polished and reverent.

All eyes follow them as they carry Allie's father to his final resting place beneath the shade of a sprawling magnolia tree, its blossoms a stark white against the backdrop of gathered mourners.

The pastor, a man whose weathered face tells of countless farewells, steps forward. His voice, soothing and rich, fills the silence left by the absent jazz.

"Friends, family, colleagues," he begins, his gaze sweeping over the crowd before settling on Allie, who stands next to me like a Bayou reed swaying in a storm of grief. "We are here to honor a man who served his community with strength and dedication…"

My attention drifts from the pastor's words, instead focusing on Allie. Her sorrow is almost touchable, vibrating in the air between us.

It strikes me, watching her fragile form, that the pain she bears is a twin to my own—a mirror reflecting the anguish of two daughters—two childhood friends that in the past, would have done anything for one another.

"Let us now share our memories of the late Sheriff, that his legacy may be etched not only into stone but also in our hearts," The pastor concludes, motioning towards the podium.

One by one, people rise to speak. Their voices paint a vivid picture of a man larger than life, a protector and hero of the community.

Allie takes her turn, her voice breaking as she recounts tales of a father's love intertwined with duty, and of lessons learned and laughter shared.

As Allie speaks, her words are filled with both love and sadness. Memories dance in her eyes, flickering like candlelight in the dimming mid-evening sun. She speaks of moments I had witnessed and others that were shared only between her and her father.

I can only watch, my heart a paradox of ice and fire, struggling to contain the tempest of emotions swirling within me.

Each anecdote transpires into the next, creating a tapestry of his existence, I stand silent among the throng, my own story remaining locked away, a secret chapter written in the darkness, waiting for the right moment to be revealed.

Soon, the last words of comfort are whispered, and the final tear-stained embraces are shared.

I press my hand into Allie's, squeezing tightly before letting go.

"Take care of yourself and your momma. I'll stop by soon," I murmur, my voice threaded with an empathy born of dark secrets and shared grief. She nods, her eyes brimming with fresh tears as she hugs me tightly.

"Momma, I'll catch up with you back at home," I call out to her right after she finishes speaking with Allie's mother, Shannon. "I just want to visit Papa for a bit."

She gives me a knowing look and blows a kiss in my direction, "See you after while. Love you."

"Will do, and I love you too."

Traversing the rain-softened earth, I make my way toward Papa's grave. There, amidst the whispering grass, an old man is hunched over, his wrinkled and calloused hands pulling at the weeds that encroach upon the sacred space.

"Evenin', young miss," He greets without looking up, his voice a gravelly echo of days gone by.

"Good evening," I reply, curious, looking around the vast grounds. "Do you...Do you work here?"

"Sure do," he says, rising to his full height, dusting soil from his worn hands before offering me one, "I've been working these grounds for as long as I can remember. Your daddy," He nods to the gravestone, "Was knee-high to a grasshopper when he first came around here." His gaze meets mine, and a glint of something unspoken passes between us. "Shame the police never did catch the one who took him from you."

His words stir a familiar ache, a melding of sorrow and simmering fury.

I take the man's hand in a firm shake, feeling the roughness of his dark skin against mine, "You knew my father?"

"Sure did. He had a love for the old stories of this city. Would come by every week just to listen to an old man spill hot air. His favorite tales being of the magic entombed into the very ground of this here mausoleum, and of the voodoo queens murmuring spells beneath a crescent moon deep in the heart of the Bayous." He laughs. "Your daddy had a thirst for adventure and a heart as big as the Louisiana sky."

"He was a good man," I say softly, my thoughts drifting to the stories he used to tell me at bedtime, tales of magic and mystery that seemed so real under the glow of the moon. "He used to tell me the same stories almost every night."

The man chuckles softly.

"I don't ever recall seeing you around," I tell him.

"Oh, no, young miss. I stick out here where the noise doesn't reach me. I prefer to keep to the shadows, tending to the forgotten corners of this place where the spirits linger and the wind sings the forgotten songs of our ancestors." His eyes seem to glimmer with an otherworldly light as he speaks.

"You have a way with words." I smile, the corners of my lips turning up despite myself.

The old man's grin widens, revealing a row of weathered teeth. "Well, storytelling is an old art around these parts, and words is all I got left, Miss. And even that ain't much in this world of silence and blight." His tone takes on a more serious undertone.

"Well, it was enough for me. And who knows, you may have even made another believer." I wink.

"Magic does have a way of showing up when you least expect it," He muses, casting a long look at the sky as clouds gather above us.

No sooner do the words leave his lips than rain begins to fall, gentle at first, then growing insistent, urging the living to seek shelter and leave the dead to their peace.

"Better head on home before this gets worse," The old man advises, nodding toward the gates.

"Thank you," I say, grateful for the warning. "Oh, um...I didn't catch your name?"

With nothing more than a smile, he responds, "Take careful now."

As I turn to walk away, the rain leaves a cool layer of droplets on my skin, but something inside me urges me to turn back. I want to know his name, to hold onto this small sliver of thread connecting me to Papa.

But when I turn around to ask him once more, the spot where he was standing is now vacant, leaving only the freshly disturbed soil, and the absence of weeds around the gravestone as evidence of his recent presence.

My heart stutters, caught between disbelief and the eerie sensation that perhaps, in the heart of New Orleans, magic isn't just lore after all.

A TASTE OF REVENGE

CHAPTER ELEVEN

Agent Holloway

Heat envelops us, Layla Sloan's breath a syncopated counterpoint to my own labored inhales. The mattress beneath us squeaks in protest, springs worn from clandestine encounters that bear the weight of our secrets as much as our bodies.

Sweat slicks our skin, a testament to the urgency with which we seek solace in each other—solace from a world splintered by violence and vendettas.

Her sweet moans fill my ears as her pussy tightens around me, milking my cock. Her legs tremble, clenching around my waist as she loses herself in the heat of the moment.

The sound of our skin slapping together sings through the room like a percussive beat, her body moving upward, meeting mine at just the right time, her nails biting into my shoulders, drawing tiny droplets of blood as she claws for leverage with each forceful thrust.

Our lips meet in a fervent kiss, tongues dancing and exploring, mirroring the frenzied motion of our bodies. I can feel the tension coiling, winding tighter within me, as if my body knows it's about to be robbed of this one illicit pleasure.

It's been almost two weeks since the bombing—a maelstrom of fire and shrapnel that tore Francisco's family apart—and here we are, desperately trying to piece together fragments of normalcy with every carnal collision.

My fingers trace the curve of her hip, feeling the faint scar from the night she was attacked by a group of men when she was a teenager before moving up to her hardened nipple, squeezing it between my fingers.

Her moans are low and guttural now, raw emotion pouring from her throat as she loses control to me completely. Suddenly, she cries out—a long, drawn-out moan that tells me she's reached her peak. Her pussy convulses around my cock, her nails digging into my skin even harder.

I thrust into one last time and my own climax crashes over me, bright and blinding, and I'm catapulted over that razor-thin edge into oblivion.

As I come back down to earth, Layla collapses beside me, her chest heaving, strands of dark hair plastered to her forehead.

My heart is still beating rapidly, but now my mind can process beyond the basic instinctual response, and I feel a surge of frustration.

"I still can't believe it," I pant out, voice edged with disbelief and anger. "It's bullshit that the Director pulled me off the Rivera case."

Layla props herself up on one elbow, her gaze meeting mine with a calmness that seems at odds with the storm that just passed between us. She brushes a damp lock of hair from my forehead, her touch gentle despite the strength I know she wields.

"Hey," she says softly, her voice steady, reassuring. "The director cares about you, Cade. He doesn't want to lose a good agent, not to some cartel vendetta."

I want to argue, to rail against the injustice of being sidelined when the fight feels more personal than ever, but I know she's right.

"Maybe," I relent, though the dissatisfaction lingers, bitter on my tongue. "But it feels like running away. I've been on this case for years, I made the connection with Fransisco, did all the dirty work, and for what?"

"Sometimes," she replies, her fingers tracing the line of my jaw, "the best choice you can make is to survive to fight another day. They'll kill you if you stay."

The mattress groans a protest as I extricate myself from the tangle of sweat-dampened sheets. My feet find the cold floor, and I walk, to the bathroom—the mirror reflecting back a man who seems a stranger, even to himself.

This old hotel room with its peeling wallpaper and the musty scent of our secret rendezvous has become a familiar haunt over these past eight months. It's been our hideaway—our divulgence into a world meant to be forbidden.

Layla...she's more than a colleague now, but less than whatever lies beyond.

I can feel her emotions tangling up, creeping around the edges of what we have, or rather, what she thinks we do. The way she looks at me sometimes, it's like she sees someone worth staying for. But for me, attachment is a language I can't decipher. My circumstance makes sure of that—keeps me safe in a bubble where romantic feelings are like radio waves from a distant star; intriguing, yet fundamentally unreachable.

I don't hear her approach, but then her arms encircle my waist, her presence a warmth at my back. She presses a kiss to my shoulder, and I catch her eyes in the mirror—those deep pools of empathy and resilience.

"Focus on healing," she murmurs, her breath warm against my skin. "Your ribs, your head...You've been through hell, Cade."

I nod, the rational part of me understanding, while the rest rebels against the notion of vulnerability. Her hands leave me then, and she steps back, reaching for her clothes that lie scattered like breadcrumbs across the floor.

"See you at work," she says, her voice carrying a note of something unsaid, something perhaps felt too deeply.

"See ya," I manage, watching as she dresses in silence, a ritual we've perfected, all the while knowing that this is where we draw the line—here in this clandestine space between duty and desire.

"Unbelievable!" I slam my fist onto the solid oak of the director's desk, the impact reverberating through the tense air of his office. "You're sending me to New Orleans?"

"Agent Holloway," The director begins, "This isn't about what you want. The local PD requested assistance from the FBI with their sheriff's case. It's sudden, his death seems suspicious, and they need the best."

"Then send someone else!" My words are hot, laced with a frustration that's been simmering since I was unceremoniously ripped from the Rivera Cartel case. "I *need* to be here, not playing detective in some backwater tragedy!"

"Enough!" His command slices through my tirade, and I'm left glaring at him, breathing hard, the fight still coursing through my veins despite the futility I sense in this battle of wills.

The director's eyes lock onto mine, a steel trap of authority. "Cade, listen to me," he says evenly, every word measured and deliberate. "You are one of our best agents, and that's exactly why we need you on this case."

My jaw clenches as I stand across from him, the room shrinking with the weight of his words. A muscle ticks in my cheek, and I can feel the cold logic within me trying to override the rush of anger. I'm good at piecing together puzzles, unraveling threads others can't see, but this? This feels like a demotion disguised as flattery.

"Sir, with all due respect, it's the Rivera Cartel that needs dismantling," I argue, struggling to keep my voice level. The deaths, the chaos they've caused—it's personal now.

He leans back in his chair, fingers steepled, his gaze unwavering. "I understand your investment in the cartel case, but consider this: your unique skill set could be what solves a sheriff's death. And let's not forget, there's a bigger picture here. The cartel knows what we have on them but they aren't stupid, they know they can't go after the entire FBI, but they can go after you and everyone you care about. Do you want them going after Rhodes or Sloan? Or, what if they come after her next?"

"You said she was safe!"

He throws up his hand, "She is, but do you see what I'm getting at now? It's not forever, Cade. It's just until we can ensure your safety along with everyone else's.

"Sir," I start again, but he raises a hand again, silencing me.

"Agent Holloway," he says firmly with a tone that brooks no argument. "This is not about assigning blame or punishing anyone. We appreciate your contributions, but this decision has been made and it is final. Your flight to New Orleans will depart in three days."

My hands ball into fists at my sides, the fight draining out of me as the reality sinks in. Three days to close the book on everything here, to step away from the hunt that's consumed me, to leave unfinished business that gnaws at my core.

"Understood, sir," I grit my teeth, the words tasting like ash in my mouth.

"Good." He nods, a finality in the gesture as his gaze meets mine. "Thank you for your time, Agent Holloway. You're dismissed."

CHAPTER TWELVE

Agent Holloway

I slam my carry-on into the overhead compartment with more force than necessary, a scowl etched onto my face like it's been carved in stone.

New Orleans.

The very thought has my blood boiling hotter than the coffee I declined at the terminal cafe. It's not just the reassignment that's got me seeing red—it's the abruptness of it, the lack of respect for the life I'm uprooting. My apartment, now someone else's space; my belongings, scarcely filling two boxes, already waiting at some cookie-cutter house that's supposed to be home.

Home?

Not by half a fucking mile.

"Sir, is everything okay?" The flight attendant's voice is soft, tinged with concern, but I barely register it over the drumming annoyance in my head.

"Fine," I grunt, strapping myself into my seat with unnecessary vigor.

"Can I offer you any food or refreshments, sir?" "Can I just a bourbon, neat? Thank you." I add at the end to sound a little less like an asshole.

"Of course!" She responds with a well-practiced smile before quickly moving on, her fleeting presence adding a graceful touch to the chaotic buzz of pre-flight chatter.

I lean back, close my eyes, and try to imagine anything other than humidity clinging to my skin like a second layer and insects the size of small aircraft. But the respite is short-lived. A few rows ahead a child's laughter pierces through my brooding, and I open my eyes to see a mop of curly hair bouncing as the boy turns around in his seat, wide-eyed and curious.

"Are you a policeman?" He pipes up, pointing directly at my badge.

"Something like that," I say, the corners of my mouth betraying me with the faintest hint of a smile.

This kid has got some guts—I'll give him that.

"Is that your gun?" He cranes his neck further, eyes alight with boyish fascination.

"Part of the job," I respond, tapping the badge lightly. "Agent Cade Holloway, FBI."

"Wow," he breathes out, all awe. "So, you catch bad guys and stuff?"

"Jordan! Leave the poor man alone." She scolds.

"No worries, ma'am. I don't mind answering a few questions."

Her lips curl up in a warm smile as she looks up at me, her eyes filled with gratitude and a touch of embarrassment. She raises her hand in a slight wave, thanking me for indulging her son's curiosity and apologizing for any inconvenience.

The boy turns back to me, "Well, do ya?"

"Yep," I answer, taking the drink the flight attendant hands me with a nod of thanks. "That's what I do."

"Do you have, like, a super cool code name?" He's practically bouncing in his seat now, every bit of him thrumming with excitement.

"Just Cade," I say, though part of me wonders what moniker could possibly encapsulate the chaos of my current situation. "But hey, you might want to strap in. We're about to take off."

"Okay, Agent Cade!" He gives me one last grin before turning around, and I think to myself that maybe, just maybe, this flight won't be as long as I'd feared after all.

***

The wheels touch down with a jolt that snaps me back to the present moment. I catch a glimpse of Jordan and his mother in the row ahead of me. The boy is chattering animatedly about superheroes and villains, completely enveloped in his own imaginary world.

Part of me wishes I could escape to my own imaginary world—forget about this nightmare and live in a place where *she* can be with me. My heart aches. I've been unaware of her whereabouts for what feels like a lifetime already.

As passengers around me rustle and reach for their overhead luggage, I twist in my seat, offering the boy a curt nod. "Take care, kid," I say, tucking away the badge he'd been so enamored with.

He waves, his smile broad and untainted by the life that awaits me beyond this cabin, "Nice meeting you, Agent Cade!"

Dragging myself through the narrow aisle, I feel the weight of my carry-on more than usual, an anchor tethering me to the decisions I didn't make.

As I enter the terminal, I am met with a rush of cold, lifeless air that does little to ease my bubbling frustration.

"Agent Holloway?" A man in a nondescript suit steps forward, extending his hand. I take it out of habit, not interest. "I'm Agent Forester. Welcome to New Orleans."

His hand off is swift—a set of keys landing heavily in my palm. They're attached to a glossy red key fob, the emblem of luxury I neither asked for nor wanted.

He points towards where the sunlight gleams off a cherry red Audi, a flawless machine that seems untouched by any difficulties. Its glossy finish mirrors the surroundings perfectly, and the wheels are polished to perfection. "Your ride," he announces, motioning towards it.

"Great," I mutter, all but throwing my bag into the trunk.

The car might be a beauty to some, but to me, it's just another facet of my upheaval, a shiny trinket meant to distract me from all this...bullshit—to be simply put.

Forester hands over a manila envelope, thick with paperwork and information. "You'll find everything you need here—case files, your new address." He pauses, his eyes softening just enough to show a sliver of empathy. "Look, I know this isn't easy, but we appreciate you stepping in. The district could really use someone with your expertise."

"Appreciate it," I reply, though my tone suggests anything but gratitude.

I slide into the driver's seat, the leather cool against my skin, but no amount of comfort can ease the resentment that's festering within me.

I turn my head back to the agent standing outside my door, "Did you know that many animals, such as dogs, can become stressed or anxious when faced with changes in their environment? This can include things like moving to a new home, changes in routine, or event changes in their social structure. Dogs are a creature of habit and can find comfort in familiarity, so sudden changes can be unsettling for them."

At first, he looks at me like I'm crazy before busting into laughter, "You Northern folk are peculiar ones. That's for sure." He breaks his uptight facade and his thick southern draw ripples to the surface. "But yea, I get what you're saying. MayBell—my beagle, ripped through three couches, two divider gates, and about a million pairs of shoes when we first moved in with my girlfriend and her cat. It was some nasty business." He chuckles.

"Animals are more perceptive than we give them credit for," I remark, the tension between us easing as we share a moment of understanding. Clearing my throat, I shift the car into gear. "Well, thank you for...everything."

"Good luck, Holloway." He pats the top of the car, backing away from my window. "See you soon."

With a nod, I start the engine, the purr of the Audi mocking me as I navigate through the myriad of cars. There seems to be a small festival of sorts, though Mardi Gras is still a week and a half away.

The moisture in the air seeps into my pores, creating a sticky layer on my skin. Each inhale is a struggle, as if I am swimming through thick, warm soup. Insects buzz with a maddening zest, celebrating my discomfort.

I roll the windows up, and turn on the air conditioner, flipping through the radio channels as I whizz pass trees and overgrown shrubbery lining the road.

The road stretches out endlessly before me, a monotonous ribbon of asphalt bordered by the dense Louisiana swampland.

The scenery blurs together, a dizzying mix of greens and browns until I reach a slightly rural area with rows of quaint southern homes.

The closer I get to the city the more the roads begin to come alive with vibrant hues of flowers blooming in almost every yard and the sweet scent of magnolias perfuming the warm moist air. It's as if the whole world is pulsing with energy and life, while I am stuck in a void of my own making.

As I drive into the heart of the city, the streets are teeming with life—a small similarity to the Big Apple. Tents line the sidewalks, dazzling colors flapping in the breeze, and the smell of frying food, spices, and sweetness wafts through the open car window.

My stomach growls, an involuntary reminder that I haven't eaten since...When did I last eat?

Slipping out of the car, I try to keep my focus narrow, dodging between clusters of laughing festival-goers. The noise, the crush of bodies—it sets my nerves on edge, each brush and jostle a friction against my already strained composure.

A bistro, tucked away from the main roadway, offers a promise of escape.

The sign is quaint, the interior dimly lit and inviting. I push through the door, letting the murmur of conversation and the clinking of cutlery envelop me. Seated at a corner table, I finally allow myself a moment, a deep breath, and the chance to plan my next move over something that doesn't come with a side of regret.

"The Cajun Eggs Benedict has easily become one of my favorites," The soft, velvety voice of a woman at a nearby table catches my attention.

My head turns in every direction but the correct one. Her laughter tinkles like wind chimes in a summer breeze, finally drawing my gaze towards her.

She sits alone, a book open in front of her, her enchanting green eyes, like diamonds of the sea, meet mine as she gestures to the open menu in my hand.

"Oh, um...thank you. I—I'll give it a try." I nod my thanks.

She smiles and my heart leaps up to the back of my throat, skipping a beat. For a moment, I forget the weight of my troubles, swept away by the warmth in her gaze. Her dark skin is like polished mahogany, her curls cascading around her shoulders like a waterfall of silk as her head tilts back down to focus on her book.

As I place my order with the waiter, I steal glances at her from across the room. Every once in a while, she'll look up from her book to take a sip of water, her eyes never meeting mine directly but always making my heart race.

Before I even finish my meal, she's standing up and gathering her things. As she passes by my table, a whiff of jasmine and vanilla trails in her wake, leaving me momentarily breathless.

It would seem that New Orleans has some hidden gems after all.

Agent Holloway

I pull up the gravel driveway, my tires crunching as they roll over the loose stones before I come to a stop. The sight of my new home unfolds before me, its grandeur both tranquilizing and contemptuous in equal measure as though it is daring me to enter and discover its secrets hidden within.

The agency has provided me with everything I need, and then some for this re-location. They could likely afford to do so, considering the lower cost of living in this area compared to New York.

A small pond winks at me under the sun's caress, surrounded by weeping willows that seem to guard the serenity of the water like old, and wise warriors. Vibrant flowers, an explosion of colors really, line the front porch, their petals bobbing gently in the breeze as if to welcome me—or perhaps to ensnare me in their deceptive beauty.

It's breathtaking, this little slice of paradise carved into the Louisiana landscape. But as I kill the engine and sit there for a moment, the weight of solitude presses against my chest. This beauty is meant to be shared, celebrated even, not hoisted upon the shoulders of one man. It's a love/hate relationship with every brick and blossom here; they whisper freedom and scream isolation all at once.

I wish she could be here too. She would have loved it and maybe, just maybe...it would have felt more like a home.

With a sigh, I finally swing open the door and step out.

The air is thick with the aromatic scent of honeysuckle and freshly cut grass—a fragrance that fills my lungs and tries to ease the animosity within me. I pop the trunk and retrieve my luggage, a simple duffel and a case that has seen more of the country than most people do in a lifetime.

The house, with its expansive front deck, stretching across the front of the structure, watches me approach. Adorned with a porch swing and a set of dark blue rocking chairs, its windows reflect my hesitant figure. I walk up the steps, each creak of the wood beneath my feet a welcome of sorts, and push open the front door. The coolness of the air conditioner from within rushes out to greet me, a sharp deviation to the humid embrace outside.

I take a moment to absorb my surroundings—the gleaming hardwood floors, the vintage pieces of furniture that exude Southern charm and class.

There's a parlor to my right, untouched by time, a dining room to my left, boasting a long table that could easily seat a dozen guests, and a large living area straight ahead through an arched doorway where it homes my dark leather brown sectional.

A grand staircase curls upwards, its banister gleaming from white-glove care. I ascend, feeling the grains of the wood under my palms, acknowledging the amount of detail that went into the design of the home.

The second floor reveals itself, hallways darting off in different directions. Three bedrooms, three baths. The sheer size of the home seems almost too much.

Why all this? It's just me.

I'm here because it's strategic—because it's necessary. But necessity doesn't always bridge the gap between space and comfort.

"Agent Holloway," I mutter to myself, "Welcome to your new base of operations." The words are supposed to feel like a beginning, but they hang heavy in the air—unfinished, like so much else in my life.

I drop my bag, a loud thud sounding off the floor below. The expanse of the master bedroom swallows me whole, almost too big and too empty for just me, but I decide to make it my room anyhow.

Beyond the white double swinging doors, the balcony beckons—a leisure I'm not even mad about when it's overlooking the spectacular gardens below.

I wonder who keeps up with all this stuff?

Sinking onto the bed, I feel myself give in to exhaustion. My body bounces slightly as it meets the plush mattress and I let out an exasperated groan.

Rhode's capable hands on the Rivera Cartel case should be comfort enough, but doubt gnaws at me. There's a thread loose somewhere, one that doesn't tie neatly into the bow of this whole damn operation.

A seasoned agent down without a fight?

How did they not see it coming?

These questions hammer inside my brain, relentless as the southern sun beating down on the roof above.

The agents tailing Francisco's family were trained for stealth, for observation. And yet, somehow, they were blindsided. They missed the shadow that trailed their own, and now there's blood on the ledger that won't easily wash away.

I need to cleanse my mind, strip away the layers of confusion and worriment that have settled like dust on old furniture. I make my way to the bathroom, shedding my clothes, and turn the knob on the shower.

The water heater starts up with a loud hiss, sending water rushing through pipes that have likely been dormant for more than a decade. I stand in the shower, the intense heat scorching my skin in a futile attempt to rid me of my uncertainties.

Steam curls around me, and for a minute all my troubles slip down the drain with the flow of the water, giving me a moment of peace.

And then she slips into my thoughts—unbidden but defiantly not unwelcome.

The woman from the bistro, with eyes that seem to hold secrets as deep as the ocean and a smile that could tempt even the most stoic of souls.

It's unlike me to fixate, but her image is carved too deeply into the recesses of my mind, flickering like a candle in a storm. I imagine the taste of her lips, sweet and intoxicating, the curve of her body pressing against mine.

My hand moves of its own accord, tracing paths over my chest, lower, lower, spurred on by the fantasy of her beneath me.

As the water cascades down my body, I close my eyes and let myself drift into the fantasy of her. Her laughter echoes in my mind, a melody that soothes the chaos within me. I can almost feel the softness of her skin beneath my fingertips, the warmth of her breath against my neck.

My hand grips my dick tighter as my hips thrust forward, the rhythm a match to the pounding of the water against the shower walls. With every stroke, I imagine her body writhing against mine, her lips screaming my name.

My pace quickens and so does the rapid beating of my heart against my chest. I'm lost to the moment, no longer in control of my own body. The fantasy consumes me, taking me further and further from reality with each passing second.

My breath comes in ragged gasps, my muscles tensing and then releasing in a wave of pleasure, like a ship crashing against the shore, and as I climax, her nameless face is all I see, her cries of pleasure echoing in my mind, drowning out the whispers of cartel ghosts and unanswered questions.

I grip the shower wall, my fingers digging in as if it's the only thing keeping me grounded.

The water splashes around me, mingling with the steam and the evidence of my desire. My knees buckle and I slump against the wall, completely spent.

I turn the faucet off with a decisive click, and the bathroom falls silent as droplets of water trickle down my skin. Chastising myself for the lapse in discipline, I wrap a towel from one of the floating wall shelves around my waist and wipe the fog from the mirror. The reflection before me displays a man I do not recognize—his hungry gaze seems tempered by an unusual sense of vulnerability.

"Get it together, Cade," I mutter, scraping a hand over my stubbled jaw.

I dress quickly, choosing comfort over style—a pair of worn jeans and a simple black tee that fits snugly across my chest.

The house feels different now, its newness less welcoming as I descend the stairs.

In the kitchen, I flick on the lights, and they buzz to life, illuminating granite countertops and stainless steel appliances. Upon inspection, I decide to bypass the fridge, ignoring the array of fresh produce and prepped meals. Instead, I rummage through the pantry and grab a protein bar from the box hidden in the back corner—the kind that promises sustenance but delivers only the taste of cardboard and regret.

With the bar in hand, I trudge back upstairs, my footsteps heavy against the polished wood. The bedroom is a sanctuary of familiarity, everything arranged just so—my bed, desk, and electronics all common amid the foreign walls.

I collapse onto the bed, still feeling the ghostly imprint of the day's revelations. I flip on the TV, the screen flickering to life with the exaggerated expressions of a sitcom that's been rerunning since my academy days. It's mindless, harmless, and for a moment, I allow myself to get lost in the canned laughter and predictable punchlines.

The protein bar, half-eaten, sits forgotten on the nightstand as my eyelids grow heavy. Laughter spills from the TV speakers, but it's distant, like echoes from another world. In the haze between wakefulness and sleep, I contemplate the unknown challenges and unfamiliar faces that will await me at the agency tomorrow.

"New director, new team," I whisper into the dark.
Can't fucking wait.

CHAPTER FOURTEEN

Tia

I'm posted up in my usual corner at Café du Monde. Coming here to read has become a ritual on the evenings when Momma is out on a social escapade with Camilla.

The soft buzz of conversations around me fades to a dull hum as I thumb open the crisp pages of *'The Crescent City Killer,'* a crime thriller that promises to plunge its readers into the murky depths of human depravity.

Just as the protagonist is about to uncover a crucial piece of evidence, the quaint chime of the door tugs me back into the real world.

I glance up involuntarily, noting the arrival of the handsome stranger I met a few days back. He stands by the hostess stand, exuding an air of quiet confidence, splashed with a douse of anxiousness, that doesn't quite match the laid-back atmosphere of the Quarter.

A waitress with bouncy red curls approaches him, her eyes hungrily taking him in, "Welcome to Café du Monde! How many tonight?"

"Just one, thank you." He replies.

I can see the look in her eyes—the look a woman gives when she's about to put on a flirty show for a potential suitor. It's a seasoned routine, one I've seen countless times before.

"You don't sound like you're from around here," she remarks, tilting her head to catch his response.

From my secluded vantage point, his answer is lost in the orchestra of clinking silverware and murmured voices, but his tone has a smooth, almost honeyed quality that suggests he's used to blending into various surroundings. Whatever he says next, elicits a bright laugh from the waitress, whose tits and ass are barely covered by her form-fitting uniform. She bats her eyelashes playfully, leading him towards a table not far from mine, casting furtive glances over her shoulder to ensure he's watching, but his gaze never follows.

I can't help but chuckle at the small pout on her face when she realizes.

Forcing my gaze away, I redirect my attention to the malevolent plot unfolding in my book, yet a part of me remains anchored to the newcomer's quiet energy, settling into the rhythm of the café as if he's always belonged, though the look on his face says anything but.

The waitress leans over the table, her breasts on full display right in front of him. He asks for a water and for a few moments to look over the menu.

"Anything for you, darlin!" She quips, her voice dripping with a little too much sweetness.

I catch myself chewing on the end of my pen, a heat rising in my cheeks that has nothing to do with the spicy aroma wafting from the kitchen. It's unsettling, this thread of jealousy twining through my chest. I don't even know him. Yet here I am, covertly stealing glances at his table, watching as he settles into his chair with an ease that speaks of long days and longer nights as she walks away.

His face is clean-shaven today, revealing a strong jawline that seems to be chiseled from stone. He's wearing a black button-up shirt that stretches taut across broad shoulders, paired with slacks that drape over his thick legs in a way that hints at the power beneath. Today, he opted for black leather boots that were both functional and fashionable—suiting his rugged appearance.

His muscles are not on full display, but they are certainly present, flexing and shifting beneath his clothing with every movement. I find myself wondering what demands such physical readiness.

I'm so engrossed in my silent appraisal that it takes me a moment to realize he's staring right at me. Our gazes meet, and a spark of electricity ignites between us, filling the air with a magnetic energy. But just as quickly, he diverts his gaze, attention snapping back to the menu in his hands as if I were nothing more than a fleeting thought.

Mild offense prickles at my pride, a tiny barb that prods me to retreat behind the safety of my book. I focus on the words, letting them blur into meaningless shapes as I try to regain my composure. My quiet dinner was supposed to be an escape, not a battleground for inexplicable emotions.

"Any more recommendations for an exhausted man just getting off work?" His voice carries across the short distance, roughened around the edges in a way that suggests weariness rather than disinterest.

I lift my head, a laugh escaping before I can capture it. "The jambalaya here is pretty good," I say, pointing to the description on the laminated menu. "It's got a kick but won't knock you out cold. Seems fitting for someone who looks like they've been through the wringer."

He nods, a ghost of a smile touching his lips, and I wonder if it's the dish or the small talk that's amused him. But my heart is lighter, somehow, the strange tension eased by the simple exchange. I bury my nose back in my book, clinging to the fictional world while the real one sits, elusively out of reach, just a few tables away.

The waitress scribbles down the order, and as she departs after a few moments of her brazen lewdness, I catch Cade's eyes roaming to the book spread open before me. "Ah, *'The Crescent City Killer'*," he comments with that same half-smile now fully blossomed, "A personal favorite."

"Really?" My surprise is genuine—men like him don't often share my literary tastes. We delve into a discussion about the circuitous storyline and the richness of Zafón's characters, and it occurs to me that this is the first real conversation I've had in weeks that didn't revolve around food or business plans.

As I speak, my eyes wander down to his hip where a gun holster stands out against the black fabric of his pants.

I'm curious and can't resist asking, "What kind of work do you do?"

"I was just transferred to the FBI Headquarters here from New York," he says with a touch of apathy. "But to be one hundred percent truthful, I'd take New York over this infested city any day."

His blunt honesty draws a chuckle from me. "You just need someone to show you the right spots," I retort playfully. "I could give you a tour...If you want."

My face is an inferno of embarrassment as soon as the words leave my mouth, realizing how forward it must sound. But to my surprise, Cade's expression softens, a spark of something unreadable flickering in his eyes.

"Is that so?" He raises an eyebrow, interest piqued.

"Absolutely." My offer hangs between us, bold and very uncharacteristic of me.

"I'd like that," he responds, his voice low and unexpectedly warm. Then he turns the tables and begins to interrogate me. "And you? Native to New Orleans?"

"Born here. Somewhat raised," I reply. "Spent time in London after my Papa passed. Momma just up and left one day. After my time in college and culinary school, I got a job at a big wig fine dining restaurant and trained as a head chef. Now I'm back, crafting a dream in the Quarter."

"And what might that be?" He asks.

"My own restaurant," Pride blooms in my voice, "Le Rêve Brisé"—It's a couple of blocks away, but it's not opened just yet."

"Le Rêve Brisé?" His northern accent strong as he tests the words on his tongue. "The Broken Dream." He whispers, the name sounding as sacred as a fallen angel as it spills from his lips.

Lips that I find myself desperately wanting to taste.

"Exactly." I watch his face, looking for...what?

Approval?

"I guess I shouldn't be surprised you know the language with you being an FBI agent and all."

"They wouldn't let me graduate high school without learning a second language first, so I decided it might as well be

French. I've heard the ladies love it." He winks playfully, making my heart skip a beat.

His charm is undeniable, and I can feel myself falling under his spell more and more with each passing moment.

Before the conversation can dip further, his order arrives, steaming and fragrant. The interruption is timely; I feel myself teetering on the edge of revealing too much. He's an FBI agent which means he works with the NOPD, so how do I know it's not a trap?

Does he know anything? Could he?

Impossible. I shake the thoughts from my head just as the waitress tells him to just holler if he needs anything.

He looks back at me and I smile, closing my book as I get up from my table. "I'm Tia, by the way."

He stands with a simple yet gracious fluidity and extends his hand. "I'm Cade—Cade Holloway," He introduces himself.

His handshake is strong, comforting, and slightly exhilarating, producing a spark I fear may explode like a ton of dynamite, straight down to my lady bits.

I bet his hands would make a beautiful necklace.

"Nice to meet you, Agent Holloway. Enjoy your meal." I say, "I'll see you around."

"Around the same time tomorrow?" His question flows like molasses, smooth and slow.

Temptation tugs at my resolve, but I push it down with a smile, "We'll see." I shrug, turning to leave, though deep down

I know full damn well that as much as I hate to admit it, I really hope it is.

CHAPTER FIFTEEN

Agent Holloway

I Survived.

Despite feeling like my heart was about to burst, I managed to make it through an entire conversation with her without rambling like an idiot.

Although, I must admit that half of the time my mind was not fully engaged in the conversation; instead, it was captivated by the lethality of her intense viridian eyes, shining like fireflies in the night.

My heart hammers against my ribcage, a staccato rhythm that seems to echo the fading footsteps of her retreat. I should have spoken up, should have woven words into a net to capture the moment and extend it just a little longer. But fear, that insidious little bitch—clings to my tongue whenever I attempt to converse with someone, especially someone such as Tia—radiant, graceful, effortlessly charming.

As I see her disappear behind the closing door, a silent plea forms in my chest, hoping that this won't be the last time I have the pleasure of spending time with her.

"I hope you find your meal to be to your liking," The waitress's voice pulls me from my reverie, placing a plate before me that steams with the hearty aroma of spices and promises of Southern comfort.

I glance at the dish—jambalaya clustered with shrimp and sausage, a golden cut of fried chicken resting alongside. The scent is intoxicating, a blend of cayenne, garlic, and something indefinably warm. My stomach growls in anticipation, and I can't help but think how this meal, vibrant and bold, is much like Tia herself. It's a culinary leap of faith I wouldn't have taken without her nudge.

I lift a forkful of jambalaya to my lips, the heat of the dish seeping into my palate before I even taste it. The flavors burst upon my tongue, a harmonious blend of savory and spicy notes dances through my senses, erasing any regret of not settling for the bland safety of mashed potatoes and corn. I savor each bite, finding serenity in the layers of intricacy within the dish, a small dissent to the unexpected joys of stepping outside one's comfort zone.

As the warmth of the meal fills me, I let the sound of Tia's name play silently in my mind, rolling the syllables over like marbles. It strikes me then, like a bolt of lightning on a clear day, that perhaps Tia is the adventure I never knew I craved.

Pushing the now-empty plate aside, I lean back in my seat with a contented sigh. The corners of my eyes crinkle as I watch the small wavy blonde waitress weave through the maze of tables, her movements efficient yet weighed down by an invisible weight.

I reach for my wallet, extract a crisp hundred-dollar bill, and place it neatly under the edge of my water glass. It's a modest gesture, but I hope the eighty-dollar tip might ease some of the strain that seems etched into the lines of her young face. In my line of work, I've learned to read people, and every hurried step she takes speaks volumes of a life racing against unspoken challenges. I trust this token of appreciation will silently communicate my gratitude, not just for the meal, but for her tireless hustle.

With a final glance around the cozy interior of the restaurant, I stand and head toward the exit, the faint clink of dishes and murmured conversations dissolve behind me as I step out into the refreshing and surprisingly cool, night air.

At home, I pull out my briefcase and grab the files I was given today and soon the familiar sight of manila folders and scattered paperwork greets me. I flick on the desk lamp, casting a pool of light over the sheriff's case files I was assigned upon transferring here.

My eyes dart across the pages, absorbing information, and connecting dots that seem increasingly misaligned the deeper I delve. I nod to myself, a silent affirmation that there's merit to the unease that's been gnawing at his daughter's gut—the situation is definitely suspicious, and the FBI's involvement isn't just warranted, it's crucial.

I feel the heaviness of exhaustion settling in my bones after many hours of forming a web of intrigue that promises to ensnare the unwary across the large corkboard on the left side of the wall next to my desk.

The soft glow of the desk lamp flickers, casting eerie shadows across the corkboard filled with photographs, and red strings crisscrossing between faces and locations. I lean back in my creaky office chair, rubbing my tired eyes and trying to make sense of the pandemonium displayed before me. But even this disciplined mind can't stave off exhaustion forever.

I know I need rest, but the incessant feeling that time is slipping through my fingers like sand keeps me rooted in my chair. The longer this case sits untouched, the more difficult it will be to solve—that is, if it even needs solving.

Before I jump to conclusions, I must carefully consider all possibilities and avoid making assumptions. It is important to approach the situation with caution and not rush to any hasty judgments. This could just be a fluke and he really did go into cardiac arrest while sleeping. The human body is extremely complex, and sometimes even the most skilled medical professionals can miss crucial signs of underlying conditions.

At some point, the files on my desk start to blur together, and I find myself drifting off to sleep right here in my chair, my last conscious thought a passing hope that tomorrow might bring Tia's gorgeous smile back into my orbit.

CHAPTER SIXTEEN

Jia

K arma stole my revenge with the man who pulled the trigger on my father. But that won't be the case for Carl.

It took time, patience, and research to find out his whereabouts these days—his life, much different than the one he led before.

I've watched from a distance, my gaze fixed on the sleek glass facade of Carl's new venture, GreenScape Innovations. The sun everyday glints off the windows as if to highlight the success of his thriving lawn care business that sits smugly about fifteen minutes away from the quarter.

It's hard not to feel a twinge of irony; Carl, who once prided himself on personal sweat and soil-stained boots, now relegates himself to an air-conditioned office. There, he presides like some kind of suburban king, issuing edicts from behind a lacquered desk while others tend to the grass and gardens that made him big in the first place.

My thoughts shift from Carl's empire to his office assistant, Emma, whose routine I've painstakingly learned. She's punctual, predictable—traits I can exploit.

Her taste in coffee, though, is anything but ordinary. At precisely nine a.m., she'll waltz into Bayou Bean Cafe, her steps as sure as the hands of the clock. Emma will order a vanilla bean latte with quirks that seem to mirror her own: an extra shot for vigor, one pump of blueberry for sweetness, and coconut milk, perhaps for a touch of maverick flair.

Next in line is Carl, whose order couldn't be more different from Emma's vibrant concoction. Plain black coffee, large, no room for cream or sugar, as if he's too robust for such frivolities. It's then accompanied by egg bites and a lemon poppyseed muffin, it's a breakfast that screams efficiency over enjoyment. A hot shot, he must imagine himself, savoring simplicity amidst subtlety, or merely indulging in the bland assurance of routine.

The anticipation coils within me like a spring, ready to release at the perfect moment. Carl's kingdom has flourished, but kingdoms have a way of underestimating the pawns. And I, am no mere pawn. I have a well-thought-out plan, and Emma is unknowingly a piece of it.

As the minute hand aligns with the hour, my vigilance pays off. There she is, pulling into her usual parking spot, just as I knew she would. It's time to make my move, and I eagerly envision what lies ahead.

I ease the car into a shadowed spot, my gaze fixed on the Bayou Bean Cafe across the street. The morning bustle hasn't yet peaked, but there's an energy in the air, a current I intend to ride. Four cars separate me from my destination, a calculated distance, close enough to pounce, distant enough to observe. Like clockwork, Emma emerges—a punctual little bird unaware of the trap laid out for her.

Slipping out of the driver's seat, I let the cool vigor morning air kiss my cheeks. My boots meet the pavement with a soft click, each step brisk as I cross the street, synchronizing my pace with my racing heart. She's just ahead, framed by the glow of the cafe's welcoming sign.

I trail behind her, a silent specter on a mission.

The chime of the door announces our arrival, and the ambiance wraps around us like a warm shawl. The line inside stretches long, a serpent coiled amidst the oasis of the cafe's interior. A miniature pond ripples gently, echoing the bayou's whispers, while vibrant greenery breathes life into the space.

The wooden beams above me form a sturdy arch, much like the foundations of Carl's powerful empire, and I'm prepared to make that foundation crumble.

"Isn't this place lovely?" I murmur, more to myself than to Emma, though she's my intended audience.

She glances back, a flicker of surprise in her eyes before recognition dawns, and a small smile graces her lips.

"Every morning, it's like stepping into a different world," She agrees, her voice light, betraying nothing of the weight she carries as Carl's assistant. "It's probably one of the best parts of my day."

As sad as that sounds, I believe her.

"That dress you're wearing—it's beautiful," I continue, letting my words weave the first thread between us. "Just perfect for the lovely Spring weather, isn't it?"

Emma's smile broadens, a flower of satisfaction in response to the compliment.

"Thank you," She says, smoothing the fabric self-consciously. "I do love the colors. It makes getting up for these early runs a bit more bearable."

"Ah, the sacrifices we must make," I quip, my tone conspiratorial.

We share a chuckle, two women making the best of our lots in life, a camaraderie blooming under the guise of casual banter.

She remains oblivious to the truth lurking beneath my friendly demeanor, a cunning scheme gradually revealing itself, as lethal and fragile as the web of a black widow.

Our laughter melds with the background hum of the café as we inch forward, the queue shortening with each friendly exchange that passes between us. Emma's face brightens when she speaks, her light-heartedness infectious despite the early hour.

"Vanilla bean latte, extra shot, one pump of blueberry, and coconut milk, please," She recites to the barista, the order rolling off her tongue like a practiced tune.

"That sounds uniquely delicious," I comment, my curiosity genuine. "Mind if I treat you? It's the least I can do for the company." I flash a warm smile, reaching for my wallet before she can protest.

"Really?" Emma's eyebrows lift, touched by the gesture. "That's incredibly sweet of you, Tia."

"Not a problem, sugar. Hopefully, it gives you a better start to your day before you have to go into work," I wink and nod to the barista. "And I'll have the same, thank you."

While the barista sets to work, Emma leans in closer, dropping her voice to a conspiratorial whisper. "You know, my boss might think he's a big deal, but he can be such a pain. Always demanding, never satisfied." She rolls her eyes, and I sense the strain of many unspoken grievances lining her words. "But isn't that most men?"

I offer a sympathetic tilt of my head, "Oh, absolutely. Men can be insufferable at times, especially when they're your boss. So full of themselves at times. As a sous-chef in London, I faced this issue daily as I worked my way towards becoming the head chef in a male-dominated industry."

"Emma and Tia!" the barista calls out, snapping us back to the present, our shared commiseration suspended in the air.

"Thanks again, Tia," Emma says, collecting her concoction.

"Hey, before you go," I say, pulling out one of my business cards, and handing it to her. "I'm having a grand opening for my restaurant soon. I'd love to see you there."

"Wow, that's super exciting! I'll definitely try to make it," She responds, pocketing the card with a promise in her eyes.

"Great!" I beam, picking up my own drink. "Take care, Emma. Try not to let the man bring you down."

She laughs and gives me a little wave, "Bye, Tia!"

I step out into the bright sunlight. The heaviness of my intentions, following me silently back to my car.

The first sip of my latte is an adventure, the unexpected flavor profile somehow fitting perfectly with the morning's intrigue. The taste lingers, an echo of success on my tongue as I slide behind the wheel of my car, the world around me innocent and unsuspecting.

I flick the ignition, the car purring to life under my touch. My hand pauses on the wheel, fingers tapping a silent tempo as the morning's encounter replays in my head.

The coffee in my cup holder catches my eye—an accidental trophy from an exchange well played. A smirk dances across my lips, and I lift the cup to my lips for another sip. The bittersweetness suits the moment, a reminder that not all victories are loud and boastful. Some are quiet, like the subtle satisfaction of realizing the power of connection and the art of strategy.

As the liquid warmth slides down my throat, the memory of Emma's focused eyes—oblivious to everything but our conversation and Carl's coffee—reasserts itself.

She hadn't seen it, the swift sleight of hand that turned my ring inward, exposing the hidden chamber within. Crafted with care, the small space nestled in the stone held a secret as deadly as it was delicate—the same floral nectar that sent the sheriff to his untimely end.

Emma's innocence, her trust in a stranger's kindness, had been the perfect cover. And now, Carl would be served a last bitter cup, courtesy of the very assistant he took for granted.

I watch the bustling crowd through the windshield. They move about their day, unaware of the chess game unfolding silently around them. I have moved each of my pieces with precision, and the checkmate is near.

"Another one bites the dust," I whisper into the quiet cabin of my car.

With a contented sigh, I slide the gear into drive, pulling off to head to the restaurant to finish the last-minute preparations before opening day. With yet another player soon to be removed from the board, I'll be one step closer to the inevitable conclusion of this tragic story.

And Papa can finally find peace knowing that his killers have been held accountable for their actions.

I can find peace.

The road stretches before me, inviting, as the sun climbs higher in the sky, casting long shadows and heralding the dawn of a new chapter.

Two down, only one more to go.

CHAPTER SEVENTEEN

Tia

I stand shoulder to shoulder with Momma, the vibrant energy of Mardi Gras pounding around us as we watch the grand parade float by.

The air is thick with the aroma of sweet, sugary beignets, mingling with the distant sounds of jazz. In front of us, the parade unfurls in a kaleidoscope of colors, floats dotted with revelers throwing beads into the eager crowd. My heart races with the same enthusiasm; today isn't just any celebration—it's the grand opening of my restaurant.

"Momma, can you believe it?" I shout, my voice barely rising above the brass band's crescendo. "After all these months, it's finally happening."

She squeezes my hand, her eyes reflecting the pride I feel deep in my bones.

A subtle emotion stirs in my chest—guilt? Cade's face floats into the third eye of my mind, and a spark of yearning blooms within me.

"To say I'm excited would be an understatement. Momma says, pulling me back to the moment. Her gaze dances over the crowd, searching for familiar faces. Most likely, Camille. "Nervous too, I bet?" She adds.

"Like a cat in a room full of rocking chairs," I admit, chuckling at the old saying, even as my stomach performs acrobatics.

The grand opening feels like a tightrope walk without a safety net.

"Remember, you've got a great team behind you." Her voice steadies me, as it always does. "Especially now that you've brought on that young waitress from the bistro—what's her name again?"

"Aurora," I reply, a smile breaking through. "She's been incredible, Momma. She's been learning the ropes faster than the other hires." I admit, shamelessly.

The girl is a diamond in the rough with a heart of gold—I'm lucky to have recruited her.

Mom nods in approval, "You were right to hire her; she has a commendable work ethic." She glances at the clock, changing the subject, "Allie should be arriving soon, correct?"

My smile falters for a moment.

Allie, my friend and the current reigning princess of Mardi Gras, struggling to cope with the weight of her grief.

"Yeah, she said she wouldn't miss it for the world. It's been tough on her, losing her dad like that. I just hope today can lift her spirits some."

Mom watches as another float passes, her expression softening. "Life throws us curveballs, sugar. All we can do is keep swinging."

"Too true." I give a small laugh, but inside, I hope the day's festivities will offer Allie a reprieve, a chance to shed the weight of sorrow, if only for a little while.

And as for myself, amidst the excitement and nerves, a part of me whispers that maybe, just maybe, Cade might find his way here too.

My mom's face lights up with excitement as she grabs my attention and points to a tent draped in luxurious purples and golds. "Tia, look!" She exclaims. "There's a tarot card reader. We have to go!"

A little laugh escapes my lips. "You're not actually going to buy into that nonsense, are you?"

"I am, without a doubt," She responds with a mischievous spark in her eyes, exuding both playfulness and certainty. "You know the stories about the witches of the Quarter, right? Magic runs deep here, pumping deep within these city's veins. And those who still have a connection to their ancestor's magic, can tap into it."

Despite my skepticism, the earnestness in her voice nudges me toward intrigue. "Okay, if it means that much to you." I relent with a playful roll of my eyes.

As we enter the tent, a foreign sensation washes over me like stepping into a bubble where the air feels denser and charged with energy.

I glance back, half-expecting to see the world we left behind distorted or vanished, but the sight of the parade, a tesserae of color and sound, assures me everything's normal out there.

"This is weird." I comment, trying to shake the eerie feeling as I look around.

"Oh, nonsense, child." Momma grins, noticing my discomfort.

The space inside is unnaturally large, defying the modest dimensions I saw outside. My practical mind searches for a logical explanation, finding none. The side-eye I give Momma earns me nothing but her quiet laughter.

"Magic," She whispers with a hint of reverence, as if reading my thoughts.

"Or clever design," I counter, but even my own words sound hollow in the face of the impossible.

We stand there for a moment, waiting for our eyes to adjust to the dim lighting, the incense-laden air weaving its spell around us. It's then I realize that I'm not just here for my mother's sake, but also to indulge a curiosity I didn't know I harbored. A part of me wonders if the cards could reveal anything about Cade, his sudden importance in my life feeling as mysterious as the tent we're standing in. But I push that thought aside, attributing it to pre-opening jitters and unacknowledged hopes.

The scent of incense grows stronger, thickening the air in my lungs, as the mysterious figure emerges from the shadows. An older woman steps into view, her long dreads cascading like midnight silk, each strand woven with glints of gold and jeweled adornments that catch the flickering candlelight.

"Welcome, Tia, Mrs. Williams," She intones, her voice rich with the timbre of the earth itself.

How she knows our names is a bit creepy, but I try to push the unease away, reminding myself that this is all just a show and it's a small town.

The shrunken skull around her neck sways gently, as she walks, its empty sockets seem to be gazing into the depths of my being.

Okay, now that is fucking weird.

"Are you sure you want to do this?" She asks, an undercurrent of warning threading through her words. "This reading will change your lives, and disappointment may be all you find here today."

I look at my mom and search her face, hoping to find any hint of doubt or disbelief. Yet, all I see are the signs of weariness etched into her features like roads on a map.

"Let's just see what the cards say," I dismiss, addressing the woman with a forced smile. "It's all part of the Mardi Gras experience, right?"

She simply nods, the corners of her mouth twitching with an unreadable expression, and gestures for us to sit. "As you wish, but remember, I did warn you," She murmurs, her hands deftly rearranging the worn tarot cards, their edges softened by the countless shuffles that took place before ours.

My mother takes her seat first, hands folded in her lap, eyes fixed on the spread that begins to take shape before her. "Remember, we can stop at any time," the reader offers one last time, but Momma shakes her head.

"Please, go on," She says surprisingly calmly.

Card after card flips over, revealing archaic symbols and intricate illustrations. The woman's eyes darken as she interprets them, her fingers tracing the air above the images as if weaving an unseen thread.

"Devastating secrets lie ahead of you," She says, her gaze never leaving the cards. "Ahhhh, yes, and soon, very soon, you shall become a grandmother."

A cold laugh escapes me before I can stifle it—a reflex to the absurdity.

I had a partial hysterectomy in high school after the doctor's found cancer in the lining of my uterus. I had been in the hospital for an injury I received playing soccer and had to have a CT scan of my abdomen and pelvic area. It's absolutely impossible for me to become pregnant. And seeing how I'm the only child my parents had—my mother will never get a grandchild from me.

Biology had written its own story for me long ago.

"Well, that's quite the performance," I say, trying to lighten the mood.

My laughter feels out of place, echoing oddly against the tent's fabric walls. But the look in my mother's eyes isn't one of amusement. It's something deeper, a mix of fear and confusion that makes my heart skip a beat.

"Your turn, Tia," The woman says, gathering the cards once more.

I slide into the chair opposite her, my earlier bravado waning under the intensity of her stare.

"Let's see what the cards have to say about you, shall we?" Her hands glide over the cards as she mixes them, but there's a gravity to her touch that wasn't there before.

A shiver runs down my spine as her fingers touch the first card, and I brace myself for whatever act comes next.

But before she flips it over, she turns her gaze to me once more. "You are certain you wish to continue?" She pries once more.

With a dismissive flick of my wrist, I nod, "Let's just get this over with," I half say to myself.

The woman's eyes, dark hazel pools of mystery, fixate on mine. She flips the first card, placing it back down with a soft thud that seems to echo through the tent.

My heart pounds against my chest, but I try to convince myself that it's just the rush of adrenaline from all the grand opening festivities, not because of this deceitful act of knowing.

She turns over one card, the image on it sends a chill down my spine—a skull, adorned with roses and surrounded by thorns.

Death.

She then flips another, and another revealing what fate has in store for me.

The images are foreign to me, but there's something unsettlingly familiar in the patterns they form. My skepticism falters as her expression shifts; no longer the theatrical mask of a performer, but something starker, graver.

"This path of yours is quite dark," She says slowly, her voice hushed, almost godly. "And the truth you carry is heavy."

A chill snakes down my spine.

"Murder...Betrayal..." She whispers, her dreadlocked head tilting slightly as if listening to a voice only she can hear.

My breath catches in my throat. I shoot a glance at my mother, searching for a sign that she thinks this lady is just as full shit as I do. But her face is drained of color, her lips parted in a silent gasp of horror.

"Momma, are you ok—," I start to say, but she cuts me off.

"What have you done, my child?" Her voice is a broken thing, fragile and splintered with suspicion.

The room spins, the festive sounds from outside dissipating until there's nothing but the thunderous beat of my heart and the weight of my mother's question anchoring me to the spot.

I want to laugh, to tell her it's all part of the act, but the conviction in the tarot reader's eyes tells me she sees through the facade I've carefully built. She sees the darkness that I've harbored, the secret scheme that was never meant to see the light.

I open my mouth, but no words come out.

How do you explain the unexplainable?

The truth is laid bare, not by confession, but by the silent testimony of ink on cardstock. And in this very moment, under the intense gaze of the old tarot lady and the horrified stare of my mother, I am rendered utterly speechless.

CHAPTER EIGHTEEN

Agent Holloway

My heart hammers against my ribs, each beat echoing the pounding rhythm of the Mardi Gras parade. I weave through a sea of people, their bodies slick with sweat and spirits. The air is thick with the intoxicating scent of spilled beer, a heady combination of hops and malt that clings to your nose hairs. You can almost taste the smoky notes of saxophones and trumpets, mingling with the lingering scent of cigars.

I've never seen anything like it—the streets are alive, cloaked in a vibrant display of streamers and glimmering lights.

"Whoooo!" A girl's shout cuts through the noise as she dangles from a balcony above, her bead-laden arms flung wide.

The crowd roars its approval, a beast with a thousand voices, as more shirts are shed in exchange for strands of colorful plastic. Nearby, a group of guys with sunburnt faces and boisterous laughter man a kegstand so massive it seems to have its own gravitational pull, attracting partygoers with the promise of free-flowing alcohol.

It's magical and beautiful, but also a sensory overload that has me on the verge of retreating.

Just as I'm about to turn back, feeling like an outsider in this riotous celebration of excess, I spot her—Tia—emerging from a vendor tent with a fluttering sign that reads *'Madame Laveau's Tarot.'*

The sight of her is like a sudden break in the clouds, a moment of clarity and familiarity amidst the crowd. She's unaware of the effect she has on me, how her presence can still the storm inside.

I pause, uncertainty rooting me to the spot as I watch her brush a stray lock of hair from her face, her curls bouncing around with each step she takes.

The last time we spoke had been at the cafe. I worry that maybe I might have been a bit too forward.

Did I overstep?

A frown creases my brow as I recall the easy banter, wondering if I crossed the line or said something to offend her.

She invited you to the Grand Opening, didn't she?

My mind races, trying to parse intention from politeness. But there's a chance that it was all professional courtesy, nothing more. Still, the way she looked at me then, the way her eyes held mine...

"Go talk to her," I mutter to myself, a private pep talk.

I take a deep breath, squaring my shoulders as I step toward her, pushing through the last remnants of doubt that cling like the humid New Orleans air. It's now or never.

The tremor in my hand isn't visible, but it's there. A cornered mouse might scamper, but a honey badger—fearless even when outmatched would saunter forth, intent on claiming its prize.

"Tia!," I call out, my voice nearly lost in the raucous laughter and music around us.

She's deep in conversation with an older woman—her mom, I presume from the alikeness—heads close, expressions serious. But at the sound of her name, Tia turns, her face lighting up as if someone flipped a switch.

"Momma, can we please finish this later?" There's a gentle firmness in her voice.

Her mother throws me a cursory glance before sweeping into the restaurant with a grace that suggests she's no stranger to commanding a room.

"Sorry about that," Tia says, her attention now fully on me. "Family drama, you know how it is?"

"Of course." I nod, trying to appear nonchalant as I take in the sight of the restaurant.

It's a striking contrast to the riotous street scene, all poised elegance with its iron-wrought sign spelling out 'Le Rêve Brisé' in elaborate script—an intricacy against the red brick. "You've outdone yourself, Tia. This place—it's immaculate."

"Why, thank you, Agent Holloway." She beams, her accent a mix of southern twang and a subtle hint of London sophistication. "I wish I could've gotten away to see you at the cafe, but I got so caught up in this Grand opening madness."

"That's understandable. I was worried, though," I admit, letting a teasing note color my tone, "Thought maybe I'd scared you off."

"Scared me off?" She laughs, light and musical. "Not at all! In fact, I was hoping you'd make it by today."

"Is that so?" I ask, a smile tugging at my lips, suddenly thankful for the courage of small, brave animals and the pull of curiosity that had me stepping into this lively celebration.

"Truth is," I start, the clamor of the parade fading into a backdrop for a moment, "I nearly didn't come today. There's this case...it has me spinning in circles."

Tia's eyes, as always, are pools of curiosity. "A case?" She leans in closer, her voice barely above the clatter around us. "Can you talk about it?"

"Only in broad strokes," I confess, my gaze flickering to ensure no eavesdroppers loiter within earshot. "It involves the death of a local businessman. The details...they're uncanny. It's so similar to another case I'm working on. So much in fact, that I find myself questioning if they might be connected somehow."

Tia's brow furrows in concern as she processes my words, a shadow flitting across her features, "Do you think they were murdered? My friend—Allie—she's the sheriff's daughter—the one who died recently. She believes there is more to the sheriff's death, though, grief sometimes can make us think and feel irrationally." There's a wisdom to her words that tells me she is speaking from experience.

I nod thoughtfully, my hand meeting the stubble forming along my jaw, "It's always wise to consider all angles, especially when the circumstances seem too strange to ignore." I'd almost been convinced that it was just a simple tragedy...that is until another man in near perfect health died the same way as Sheriff Landry.

In addition, both men had prior knowledge of one another and experience working together. The family of my new case said they were good friends—played poker together every Friday night.

"So, Allie could be right?" Tia questions.

"I can neither acknowledge nor deny," I say, knowing I need to tread carefully with my words.

"My goodness," She breathes, her hand coming up to cover her mouth. "The idea that someone could be...that there might be a killer lurking in the city." Her voice trails off.

"Hey, I'm sorry." I reach out, resting a reassuring hand on her shoulder. "I shouldn't have dumped all that on you. Today's about celebration, right? Besides, I want to know about you."

Tia takes a deep breath, her eyes shimmering with unshed tears as she tries to collect herself. "I appreciate you trusting me with this," She gives a weak smile. "Okay, what about me do you want to know?"

"Everything."

Tia's smile widens, the sorrow from our previous conversation momentarily forgotten.

"Hmmm." She taps her finger against the point of her small chin. "You already know about this place." She waves toward the restaurant. "What else...Oh, I play violin."

"Really?" I ask, impressed.

"Yep, sure can." She grins. "It's been a while since I last played though."

"I'd love to hear you play sometime."

She kicks at a rock with her toe before looking up at me, "Tell me something about you now, Agent Holloway."

The sound of laughter and music filled the air as we pushed our way through the packed crowd. Suddenly, a surge of people almost carried us apart. Tia grips my hand tightly, ushering me toward a narrow alleyway, where the noise from the street fades away and is quickly replaced by cool, quiet serenity.

Up ahead on the next street, nestled between two buildings, a food truck emits the sizzling sounds of cooking and the enticing sounds of sizzling food and the delicious scent of street-style cuisine.

"Look," Tia gasps, nudging me with her elbow, excitement brightening her emerald eyes. "Care to join me in a funnel cake, Agent Holloway?"

"Lead the way," I laugh, allowing her to pull me closer to the source that's teasing our noses, and our bellies.

"Two funnel cakes, please!" Tia calls to the vendor when it's our turn to order, a smile dancing on her full lips.

"Are there any toppings that y'all would like to add?" The lady behind the counter asks.

"Yes. May I have the apple pie filling, cinnamon sugar, and light whip?"

"Absolutely! And for you, sir?"

My eyes scan over the choices with over twelve flavors to choose from, "I don't recall there being so many options when I was a kid." I laugh, rubbing the back of my neck nervously.

Chocolate has always been my go-to, but today I'm feeling adventurous. Instead of my usual chocolate syrup, I want to step into Tia's world of flavors and taste something new and different.

"I'll take the Huckleberry Smores."

"That's one of my favorites." The lady smiles.

Tia removes her wallet from the gold designer purse looped across her shoulder, "Please, let me." I insist, already grabbing cash to hand the cashier.

She concedes with a playful spark in her eye, "Just this once!"

Exchanging money for food, the vendor hands us our funnel cakes, the warm pastries dripping with toppings that make my mouth water.

We find our way lean against the wall of the alley, the noise of the festivities, now not so intimidating standing here with her. "Not quite the grand opening feast, I came here for," I remark, taking a bite, "But it's perfect."

"Everything has its own place," Tia replies. "Even a messy funnel cake in a quiet alley. But don't you go filling yourself up too much, now. You still have a restaurant opening to attend."

Our detour through the alley comes to an end as we emerge back into the street, the brightness of the sinking sun hitting us in full force. The crowd still hums with electricity, the presence entangling with music and laughter.

Tia's voice carries a tone of awe as we draw near to a tent decorated with strings of beads and an assortment of shimmering gems. "This is absolutely beautiful," She exclaims, taking in all the different items on display.

Her hand brushes against a small table draped in velvet, fingers dancing over the jewelry like a pianist lost in a sonata.

I linger by the entrance, my gaze fixed on a jade necklace burrowed among the tangles of jewelry that had caught her attention in the first place.

The deep green stone is a correlation of her eyes—beautiful and full of a quiet strength that demands attention without shouting for it.

My decision is swift. I reach for my wallet and slip the vendor the money for it, as Tia laughs from her position on the other side of the tent, trying on sun hats that match her whimsical personality.

She looks up just as the vendor hands me a small velvet pouch and I slip it into the front pocket of my pants, the secret inside now mine to give later this evening.

"Ready to go?" Tia asks, after settling on a pair of sunglasses that framed her eyes like twin crescents of the night sky.

"Yep, I'm all good here."

As we continue our stroll, time slips by unnoticed, ceding to the easy flow of conversation and shared smiles. Eventually, though, Tia glances down at her watch, a delicate frown creasing her brow.

Oh, shit!" Her sudden outburst of foul language drawing a smirk from me. "I need to get back. There's still much to do before tonight."

"Of course," I nod, my feet shuffling the same rhythm as hers.

"Will you be there?" Her question hangs between us, optimistic.

"I wouldn't dream of missing it," I assure her, my hand lightly caressing the velvet pouch in my pocket.

I hope the fact that I feel like I'm going to throw up doesn't show.

Every time I'm in her presence, it's like my heart is sprinting a marathon, my hands are competing in a wet t-shirt contest, and my stomach is doing backflips like an Olympic gymnast. It's enough to make me feel lightheaded and dizzy as if the world has suddenly become a carousel spinning out of control.

"Great, I'll see you tonight, then." Tia smiles warmly, a touch of something indecipherable in her eyes as she turns to leave. "Oh, by the way, Agent Holloway..." She stops, turning back for just a moment. "Thank you for a wonderful time." Her body sways as she leaves, the jeans she has on hugging her ass in a way that leaves me biting my fist and re-arranging my swollen cock.

As she disappears around the corner, I exhale a breath I didn't realize I was holding. I'm helpless—a swooning fool against the power of her allure.

The chokehold this woman already possesses on me is a dangerous one, like a vice squeezing the oxygen from my lungs, yet I find it deliciously exhilarating.

She's forbidden fruit...And I can't wait to have a taste.

CHAPTER NINETEEN

Tia

The brisk chill of the cooler nips at my skin as I stack the last crate of fresh vegetables. We've got fifteen minutes before the restaurant doors swing open, and already the aroma of simmering gumbo and fried catfish is laced through the air.

Momma stands beside me, her eyes tracing a bead of condensation down the wall. She's been quiet since we stepped in here, away from the pre-opening bustle.

"Tarot cards, really Momma?" I start, breaking the silence with a hint of exasperation. "You can't be serious. That old lady is just spinning stories for all the tourists. There's no truth in bones thrown on velvet or cards dealt by wrinkled hands."

Momma shakes her head slowly, her gaze never leaving the droplet's path. Tears well in her eyes, and she turns to me. "Baby, you don't understand," She whispers, her voice thick with emotion.

I frown, crossing my arms over my chest. "Understand what? That some back-alley fortune teller claims to see my destiny in her trinkets—my murderous ways?" My voice rises with incredulity—or guilt? "It's nonsense, all of it. There's no such thing as tarot readings, witches, or magic."

But she's crying now, real heavy tears that streak her caramel cheeks and make her dark eyes shimmer with sorrow. She reaches for the locket she always wears, the one that Papa bought her on their fifth anniversary. Her fingers tremble as she pops it open, revealing the tiny photo inside.

"You were so little—so innocent. Not yet touched by the darkness this world has to offer."

I examine the photo.

It's old and worn, the edges curled with age. In it, a young version of Momma smiles, her arm around a small child with curly hair and bright, curious eyes; me as a toddler, nestled between her and Papa, a wooden spoon in my hand, dripping with the beginnings of a roux. We're laughing, a snapshot of love and happiness frozen in time.

"Without magic..." Her voice cracks, "That moment wouldn't have happened. You...Tia, you wouldn't have happened."

I'm struck silent, the protest dying on my lips as I take in the image, the locket, the tears. The love in that picture is real, as tangible as the cold air around us. But magic?

It can't be.

And yet, looking into Mama's eyes, I see something raw and earnest that plants the seed of doubt deep within me—making me question everything I know to be true.

The wintry air of the cooler bites at my skin with sharp, frigid teeth, but it's nothing compared to the chilling confusion that creeps up my spine as Momma begins unraveling the past.

She grips her hands together, knuckles turning pale from the pressure. It's almost as if holding onto the story is a source of strength for her, or maybe it keeps her grounded in a harsh reality she desperately wants to break free from.

"Your Papa and I...we wanted you so much, Tiana," She begins, and I can see a distant pain flickering behind her eyes. "But God had other plans for us, plans that didn't include children." She swallows hard, looking away, and I can feel my heart contract with each word. "He met a man...when he was a worker down on the railroad, said he'd been through the same heartache with his wife."

I open my mouth to interject, but no words come out, just a silent plea for this to be some bullshit tale.

"They found help, not from a doctor, but someone—someone else," She continues, her gaze returning to mine.

"Help? What kind of help?" The question feels foolish even as it escapes my lips.

"Magic, baby. Dark magic," She confesses, her voice almost drowned by the humming of the refrigeration unit. "The witch doctor they visited was no ordinary man. Your father and I, we were desperate, and desperation can blind even the purest souls."

I struggle to understand, to bring together the image of my mother as I know her —the one who comforted me through broken toys, scraped knees, and chased away my nightmares —with the woman standing in front of me, shrouded in hidden truths and sorrow.

"Dark magic?" I echo, my skepticism fighting against the rising tide of dread within me.

"Dark voodoo—shadow magic," she corrects, a tremor in her words. "That night, we made a choice. We believed that sacrificing our morals—would lead to our happiness, to the possibility of having you in our lives. But we sacrificed more than just our morals—we sold our souls, to a devil in disguise."

My breath catches, a sob threatening to break free. This can't be real. It just can't.

Despite any doubts I may have, the unwavering conviction etched into every line on Momma's face makes it clear that this is her truth.

"Sold your souls to the devil?" My whisper echos her decree.

She nods slowly, fresh tears brimming in her eyes. "Not all magic is good, Tia. But all magic comes with a price. That price—it's haunted us ever since."

The world I thought I knew crumbles, leaving me to grapple with the fragments of a legacy far darker than I could have ever imagined.

Tears blur the harsh fluorescent light of the cooler, turning everything into a watery mirage. The chill in the air bites at my skin, or maybe it's the truth that leaves me feeling cold and exposed.

"What happened next?" My voice quivers, betraying the fear of pearls of wisdom yet unspoken.

Momma's gaze drifts to the crates of root vegetables beside us. "Your grandma...She was a witch too," She pauses, her hands trembling as they find mine. "But her magic, it was differ-ent—pulled from the soil, from the spirits of our ancestors."

"So, like good magic?" I utter in a hushed tone.

"Yes," she says. "Magic with a balance, paid for with sacri-fices—sprigs of hair, a few drops of blood, or an animal's spirit given to the ancestors whilst its body was used for sustenance. It was respectful, tethered to the natural order. But..." She swal-lows hard, pain etching deeper lines around her mouth. "It could not give life where none was meant to be."

"So, that's why you went to the shadow man?"

She nods, wiping away a stray tear, "We were desperate. Your father and I...we were so happy when we learned I was carrying twins—a boy and a girl." A wistful smile touches her lips, but it's laced with sorrow. "But happiness is short-lived when built on a foundation of darkness."

"Twins?" My heart stutters.

I am an only child—I've always been an only child.

"What happened to—"

"Your brother, he didn't survive," Momma cries, each word laden with a grief that has no expiration date. "That witch doctor, he promised us a child, but he never told us what the true cost would be—never said that your father's line would end with you and that another life would be taken."

A sob rips from my chest, loud and raw.

This inheritance, this cursed bloodline has seeped into every corner of my being, staining the future I never even had that chance to dream up.

I'm the last.

The final result of a family tree marked by desperation and deceit. Amidst the anger, the betrayal, there's an understanding too—a resonance with the longing that drove them to such lengths.

"Momma," I whisper, the word fractured, "Why?"

"Simple. Because we wanted you, sugar," She says, her voice breaking as she pulls me into her embrace. "We wanted you more than anything."

"Why—Why didn't you just adopt?" The question feels more like an accusation than curiosity as it slips off my tongue.

"Baby," She says with a sigh that carries the weight of decades, "Back then for folks like us, adoption wasn't just hard—it was damn near impossible." She fiddles with the hem of her apron, a nervous habit when she's about to confess something she wishes she could bury forever.

"Then after you lost my brother, what made you go back to him? To that witch doctor?"

The chime above the back door tinkles in a soft breeze. Probably one of the chefs taking out trash.

It's fifteen minutes till opening time, and here we are—frozen in the cooler, wrapped in a past that won't let us go and a present that could possibly tear us apart.

"Life got tough." She replies, wrapping her arms around her small waist, her face sunken in self-contempt. "Your papa lost his job; You fell sick—so sick we thought we might lose you too. And our home was slipping away from us—foreclosure already impending. We were fools once more, with very little left to offer as payment." Her voice breaks on the last word, and her hand trembles as it rises to cover her mouth. "We turned to that shadow magic again."

The cooler feels colder, or maybe it's the chill of realization making me shiver. "Oh, Momma..."

She doesn't meet my gaze. "You got better. And suddenly, there was money—a small lottery win. Enough to save us, to start anew. Your papa opened this restaurant afterward. For a while, we believed it was a blessing."

"Until Grammy got sick," I finish for her.

My father would often mention them when he was still with us—how he wished they could see his little princess, Tiana. He said the day he lost Grammy was the day he lost his Papa too.

"Yes." A single tear escapes her eye, carving a path through her foundation. "Your Papa and Grandpapa—they prayed for a miracle. But only one person heard their prayers. The shadow man."

"Grandpapa died too, didn't he?"

"Not...exactly," She says, sitting down on one of the wooden crates nearby. "He begged to take her place, slaughter a million wild animals, to do anything just to be with her again. But that witch doctor, he was tricky—molding people's wishes to suit his sick, twisted agenda."

She takes a deep breath, closing her eyes.

I let her take a small reprieve from the haunting memories she's reliving inside the prison of her own mind.

"The witch doctor wanted freedom," She continues, her voice hollow.

"Freedom," I repeat, tasting the bitterness of the word.

The shadow man had been playing a long game, and my family was entangled in his wicked scheme, bound to a cycle of debts paid in broken souls and endless grief.

My life, my family's fortunes and misfortunes, all woven by unseen, sinister threads.

My mind is reeling. My entire life—I had no idea about any of this. Momma always seemed so reserved—so strong, even when the weight of the world threatened to crush her spirit.

For all these years, she had to bear the burden of our family's dark secret and endure the pain and agony alone. Despite her struggles, she never gave any indication that she was struggling.

Momma draws in a quivering breath, her eyes dark pools of sorrow as she clutches the locket, its chain imprinting into her weathered hand.

"I never wanted you to carry this burden, T—Tiana," She hiccups, "But now I'm afraid your path is just as dark as the one I have walked."

I hang my head, knowing that she's right. Murder was never something I ever thought I'd be capable of, yet I have the stains of two deaths already on my hands. But doesn't our family deserve some kind of peace—some kind of redemption from all this loss, all this pain?

The blood in my veins turns hot, searing my skin as fury rises within me. I won't let this damn curse control our lives any longer. Allen's death holds the final solution to ending this relentless nightmare.

It has to end with him—it has to.

"My path was never mine to walk in the first place." I clench my fists tightly, feeling my nails dig into my skin.

"I'm so sorry, Tia!" Momma weeps softly. "This was never the life we wanted for you. That's why I left New Orleans after your father's murder. When your Grandpapa agreed to that—that bastard's terms..." Hearing my mother curse is not something I am accustomed to, so her choice of words takes me by surprise. "He never imagined that the life he traded would be the one of his only child's—only son's rather than his, nor that being with your grandma meant being chained to her grave, and to the very demons that took her from us."

"What do you mean?"

"Our family has suffered while the witch doctor walked away free, laughing at the misery he left behind. He made a deal with the shadows. In exchange for his freedom, he would find them another host."

The finality of the shadow man's deception settles like lead within me. My heart is an anvil, slowly sinking in my chest, the weight of these horrendous revelations almost too much to bear.

Grandpapa, consumed by loss, had been ensnared by a promise as ephemeral as smoke, one that stole more than it could ever return.

"There was this man—down at the cemetery that was cleaning Papa's grave...Was that—is he—?"

"Your Grandfather?" Momma nods her head, "Yes, it was."

My lungs feel as if they're collapsing, all the oxygen in the room ceases to exist and I'm suffocating in a thick cloud of sorrow and rage.

"He could have brought them back. He could have brought them both back!" I yell the last word.

Momma gets up from her place on the wooden makeshift chair and walks over to me. My entire body trembles as her hands cup my face and she places her forehead against mine.

"I made a promise to your father. We both did." She pulls away to look me in the eyes. "I held your father in my arms the night he died, begging him to let me take him to his father so he could save him. Your father refused. He didn't want to be a part of any more deals with that man. He knew the cost was too high, even for the chance to watch his daughter grow up to become the amazing woman he was certain you would become."

Her eyes mirror the same pain I feel, clawing away at my insides. I want to scream, to cry, to—*fuck*—I don't even know anymore.

"I swore to your father that I would take you away from all of this and give you a normal life—the best life I could. He knew how his father would react. Likely, wanting to bring him back himself since he did possess such power, but he also knew that his father would respect his dying wish—no more shadow magic. He made me promise to sell the restaurant and the house, so that's exactly what I did."

"Why? Why didn't you say something when I told you I wanted to move back here?" I ask.

"This restaurant was a dream you once held with your father. I couldn't take that away from you."

Tears pour from my eyes, a ball of sorrow forming in the back of my throat, "I just wish he was here to see it with me. I wish he could taste the dishes we created together, feel the warmth of the kitchen, hear the laughter of our customers. I wish he could be a part of this—a part of his dream."

Momma pulls me into a tight embrace, her arms a lifeline in the storm raging inside me, "Oh, Tiana, baby. Your father lived his dream. He had everything he ever needed and more, because he had you. You were his greatest joy, his pride, and his hope for the future. He may not be here physically, but his spirit lives on in every dish you cook, in every smile you bring to a customer's face, in every beat of your heart. He is just as much a part of this restaurant as you are."

I cling to her words, letting them sink into my soul, a healing balm for my shattered heart. As I pull away from the comfort of her embrace, I square my shoulders, take a deep breath, and wipe away the tears staining my cheeks.

"You're right," I smile, smoothing my hands down my blouse in a rushed attempt to make myself more presentable. "Okay...time for the big opening. Are you ready?"

"I am. But um, Tia—"

"Yes, ma'am?" My brow arches high on my face.

"Whatever dark path you have found yourself on, sugar, whatever *actions* you've been taking, it's time to put an end to them, okay."

My eyes widen slightly, a flicker of surprise and guilt dancing in their depths. No words escape my mouth—mainly because I have none to offer. So, with fingers crossed, I nod giving in to her silent agreement, and exit the large, cold, metal room.

But I know I can't stop now. The time for that has long passed. The only way this can end now is with Allen taking his final breath.

Sorry, Momma.

CHAPTER TWENTY

Agent Holloway

The neon glow of Le Rêve Brisé's sign casts a halo over the darkened street, the charge of the crowd's anticipation conspicuous.

I lean against the cool brick exterior, my black attire feeling like a second skin, tailored to every contour. The subtle sheen of the watch on my left arm catches the reflections from the street lamps as I flick my gaze down.

Three minutes to go.

I adjust the bouquet of vibrant flowers in my hand, their petals soft and fragrant—a last-minute addition to my ensemble.

"How exciting! We should stop in tomorrow and try this place out." Murmurs a passerby to the person walking next to them.

As if cued by an unseen director, a young man materializes at the restaurant's double doors. With a quick, hefty sweep of his arms, he pushes the barrier open, revealing a sliver of light from within that cuts through the evening's dim.

"Welcome to Le Rêve Brisé! I am thrilled to reveal that we are officially open for business!" He announces, his voice carrying over the excited chatter of the crowd.

A collective step forward ripples through the line, and the wait—this purgatory of nerves and excitement—begins to dissipate. My heart paces with each tick of my watch, and with each guest that disappears beyond those welcoming doors.

Finally, the space before me clears, the last couple ahead offering me a polite smile as they pass on their way out, and it's my turn to go inside.

A large number of people behind me still wait patiently for their turn to enter, eager to experience the allure for themselves.

I'm greeted by the clink of fine crystal and a hum of subdued conversations as I step across the threshold.

The chandeliers shimmer with crystal drops, casting a soft glow over the rich marbled floors. Delicate lotus flowers and fragrant Parisian roses adorn the tables, their scents mingling together to create an intoxicating blend. The walls are painted in soft pastel colors, reminiscent of the colorful buildings in New Orleans' French Quarter.

Tia's touch is everywhere, harmonizing the things she loves most. Amongst the decor, I spy hints of London—a vintage Underground sign, a framed photo of the Thames at dusk—little pieces of her journey woven into the tapestry of this place.

Overall, the atmosphere exudes both comfort and luxury, capturing both the warmth of Southern hospitality and the elegance of French sophistication.

The young woman at the host stand smiles, waving me forward, as she grabs a menu and leads me to my table.

"Your server will be with you shortly." She says, handing me the menu.

"Mr. Cade, nice to see you made it," The blonde waitress I've grown accustomed with from my dine-ins at the cafe, welcomes me with her thick accent which I haven't quite been able to place.

Her smile is familiar, yet it blossoms anew in the warmth of Le Rêve Brisé.

"I see you decided to make the switch," I state the obvious.

"Miss Tia gave me an offer I just couldn't resist." She smiles with flushed cheeks, guiding me to a table near the window overlooking the courtyard. "Besides, this place is way nicer, but don't tell Lonna I said that."

Lonna being the owner of the small cafe.

"Indeed," I reply, my eyes still roving the details of Tia's achievement. "She's outdone herself."

"She has." The girl agrees. "Please, enjoy a complimentary appetizer on behalf of tonight's grand opening," She offers with a flourish of her hand toward the menu.

"Thank you, Aurora." My gaze settles on an item I've had many times back home. "I'd like the Smoked Salmon Canapés, please, and a glass of Chardonnay."

"An excellent choice," She notes. "Please take a moment to look over the menu while I grab your drink."

Left to my own devices, I scan the scene before me.

It's only the first hour, and already the place whirrs with life. Couples toast to future memories; friends laugh, their joy spilling over like the wine in their glasses.

Every table is a small celebration of Tia's vision made real.

A quick glance at the clock on the wall informs me that today's business hours are off-kilter, with the opening time pushed forward. It's a wise decision, given the influx of Mardi Gras celebrants seeking new experiences and festivities.

I inwardly praise Tia's intelligence and sharp thinking, her talent for seamlessly incorporating opportunity into the very essence of her ambitions.

She is more than just a chef or a business owner; she's an alchemist, turning aspirations into gold.

The moment her hand graces the railing, my breath hitches.

Tia stands atop the staircase, a vision in dark green that clings to her form like ivy around a tree. The dress—a luxurious one-shoulder affair—is daring with its thigh-high slit, revealing just enough to quicken a man's pulse. Her curls, a waterfall of obsidian piled atop her head, loose strands framing her face with an artist's precision.

She catches my eye from her elevated perch, and the room, with all its chatter and clinking glasses, fades away. Our gaze locks—an electric thread spun between us—and she descends each step with a sultry confidence that sets my heart galloping like a wild stallion.

My palms grow damp as I watch her, every inch the queen of her court, turning heads and drawing all eyes to her as she moves with a grace that can only be described as otherworldly.

As she reaches the final step, a playful smile tugs at the corners of her lips and I'm on my feet before I know it, drawn by some magnetic pull as she navigates through the mass of tables.

Her smile doesn't waver as she approaches, and I feel a prickle of sweat at my brow, the intensity of her presence rendering me both awestruck and absurdly nervous.

"Congratulations, Tia," I manage to say, voice steadier than I feel, offering her the bouquet.

The flowers pale in comparison to her, but her eyes light up in genuine appreciation.

"Thank you, Agent Holloway" Her voice is the melody that fills the gaps in my composure.

With a deep breath, I reach into my pocket, fingers closing around the velvet box that houses the jade necklace. I present it to her, watching as surprise flits across her features, giving way to delight.

"You got this for me?" She asks, her tone threaded with wonder. "How did you know?"

"I'm an FBI agent. It's my job to notice things." I joke, clicking open the box.

Her hands flutter to her chest as she admires the necklace, then she turns, lifting her hair in silent invitation.

I take the cue, draping the cool stones against her skin, their hue echoing the richness of her gown. The clasp gives a small click as it fastens, and I can't help but let my fingers linger for a moment longer than necessary.

"Perfect," I breathe out, stepping back to admire how the necklace lays against her collarbone.

It's as if it was made for her—and perhaps, in some cosmic sense, it was.

The evening air clings to my skin, the humidity more admissible with her by my side. Tia's hand brushes mine, setting off a chain reaction in my body, like the crackling of fire through dry kindling.

The restaurant's lights twinkle behind us, a small beacon of her successful night.

"The place is incredible, and the food—my God—the food. I don't think I've ever had anything that tastes so fucking good," I rave.

Her laughter is a soft chime in the night. "Thank you so much for being here tonight, Cade. It means the world." A yawn escapes her, betraying the fatigue she must feel. "Care to join me for a celebratory drink back at my place?"

I hesitate, the invitation tempting every fiber of my being, but responsibility anchors me down. "I'd love nothing more, but I've got an early day tomorrow."

"Of course," She nods, understanding lighting her tired eyes. "Rain check?"

"Definitely." Relief blossoms along with small butterflies in my chest.

"Sooo...Next week," I dare to ask, "Would you let me take you out? To celebrate properly?"

Tia tilts her head, "Are you sure you want to see me again so soon?"

"More than anything," I confess, my voice steady despite the nerves dancing under my skin. "Even if I were to see you every single minute of every day, it wouldn't be enough. I would still want more time with you."

A blush creeps onto her cheeks, and my nerves spin out of control. My mind goes blank, leaving me at a loss for words. It feels like my thoughts have abandoned me in this moment. The lid I had securely fastened on my jar of self-assurance suddenly comes loose, and all of my eccentricities spill out.

"Did you know octopuses have three hearts? And when they swim, the heart that delivers blood to the rest of the body actually stops beating."

Laughter bubbles from her lips, and she counters with, "Well, did you know that honey never spoils? They've found pots of it in ancient Egyptian tombs, perfectly edible."

"Is that so?" I muse, captivated by the spark in her eye, the effortless way she matches my playful banter and doesn't even bat an eye at my random outburst.

"I guess some things are just timeless." She winks.

We reach her car, the soft glow of the street lamps casting halos around us. Her hand slips from mine, and I'm already counting the seconds until I can hold it again.

Tia steps off the curb, her heels clicking sharply off the pavement, a soft counterpoint to the distant sounds of revelry that still sing through the now scarce streets.

"Let me," I say, reaching for the handle before she can protest, swinging the driver's side door open with a smooth motion.

The gesture feels like a dance step we've rehearsed in another lifetime—a silent harmonization of movements and unspoken words that somehow synchronize perfectly between us.

"Thank you," Her smile is the response I crave, a slow flowering of warmth that lights up her features more than any streetlamp ever could.

I linger there, caught in the gravity of her gaze. "Anytime," I reply, meaning every shade of that one simple word.

As she leans into the car, the scent of her perfume wraps around me. It's intoxicating, a fragrance I want to commit to memory. She turns back, one hand bracing herself against the frame, as I grab her other one, and place a kiss on the back of it.

"Goodnight, Cade," She says, and there's a question in her eyes, a quiet invitation that I can't ignore.

"Goodnight," I whisper, drawn forward by the allure of her presence. Our lips meet in a kiss that's tentative at first, an exploration that quickly deepens as I give into her.

The world around us falls away, leaving only the sensation of Tia's lips moving against mine, her fingers tangled in my hair, pulling me closer as if I might vanish at any given moment.

We break away, breathless, and for a moment, we simply stand here, sharing the same breath—the same heartbeat.

"Next week can't come soon enough," The taste of her lingers on my lips.

"Neither can sunrise," She replies with a playful smirk, "But all good things are worth the wait."

And with that, she slips into the driver's seat, the door closing softly behind her, sealing away the warmth of our goodbye.

I step back, watching as she starts the engine. The car pulls away, leaving me with the indelible imprint of her kiss and the luminous trail of her taillights.

CHAPTER TWENTY-ONE

Tia

The flicker of candles casts dancing shadows upon the walls as I sink deeper into the warmth of the bubble bath. I bask in the quartet of pops and crackles emanating from the wicks, a beautiful score to accompany my solitude.

Here, in my clawed tub, I am momentarily removed from the world's chaos, cocooned within the antebellum elegance of my southern plantation home.

"Congrats again, Allie," I say, my voice echoing slightly off the high ceiling as I cradle the phone between my shoulder and ear. "Mardi Gras Princess suits you."

"Thanks, Tia," Allie's voice sounds tinny yet cheerful through the speaker. "You know I just showed up for the crowning. It was...it was Dad's favorite event." The merriment in her tone slips, a dress hem catching on a splintered boardwalk.

I hesitate, tracing the rim of the tub with pruned fingertips. "How are you holding up, really?" I venture gently, knowing the facade she wears for the world often weighs heavy.

There's a pause long enough for me to hear her exhale shakily. "It's been rough," she admits, and I imagine her tucking a loose strand of hair behind her ear, a nervous habit when confronted with discomfort. "Mom's not...well, she's drinking more than ever."

The words hang between us, unadorned and vacant, like the bare branches of the live oaks after winter takes its toll. I picture Allie, standing strong like those resilient trees, weathering storms with roots dug deep into both tradition and sorrow.

"Hey, you've got me, okay?" I offer, the statement floating amid the steam and heartache. "Anytime you or your mom need anything."

"Thanks, Tia," She whispers back, and I can almost feel the fleeting smile that graces her lips.

We drift into safer waters, the conversation buoyant with trivialities: a new recipe I'm trying out, the latest gossip from the town's socialites, and the jasmine that's begun to climb the trellis outside my bathroom window. But curiosity is a persistent itch, and soon enough, I'm circling back to the shadow that's been cast over Allie since her father's death.

"Any news on your dad's case?" I ask, tentative, not wanting to pry too deep but unable to ignore the elephant lounging in my bathwater.

Allie sighs, a sound that ripples through the line. "Finally, Tia," She says, and there's a steeliness in her voice that wasn't there before. "The police are taking it seriously now. The FBI got involved last week."

"Wow, the FBI," I murmur, impressed despite the grim context. "Have they found any—" I catch myself, rephrasing— "Do they have any suspects?"

"None that they've told us about." Her tone is laced with frustration, a cocktail of hope and helplessness. "But at least it feels like we're getting somewhere, you know?"

I nod before remembering she can't see me. "Yeah, I get it. That's got to bring some comfort."

There's another pause, and then Allie clears her throat, steering us back away from the dark currents. "Oh, Tia, I'm so sorry I missed your restaurant opening! How did it go?"

"Please, don't worry about it," I assure her quickly, eager to latch onto something brighter. "It went better than I could've dreamed. The place was packed, and everything just... fell into place perfectly." I sink deeper into the warmth of the tub, the memory alone enough to make me feel bubbly all over again.

"Really? Tell me everything!" Allie demands, her voice hungry for good news.

A laugh escapes me, a bubble rising to the surface. "Well, I met someone," I confess, the words tinged with a giddy sort of shyness. "He came to the opening."

"Met someone?" There's an infectious excitement in her voice.

"Yup," I say, a smile spreading across my face. "He's a bit mysterious, but in a charming sort of way," I continue, relishing the details as I paint a picture for Allie. "He has this old-fashioned charm about him, like he doesn't quite belong in this century."

"Give me all the tea!" Allie wines.

"Okay, okay, details," I say, swirling a finger through the mountain of bubbles that threaten to spill over the edge of the tub.

"So, mom and I, we were at the parade, right? And I hadn't expected to see him there, but low and behold, he shows up and finds me. Mind you, we have only ever seen each other down at the diner before this, but I swear it's almost as we've known one another our whole lives.

As I gush about my encounter with the mysterious stranger, Allie's gasps and giggles fill the air, mingling with the gentle sound of the bubbling water around me.

"So, we ended up ducking into this little alley—just away from the madness—and we got funnel cakes from one of the vendors there. I still can't believe he never had one before." I laugh, leaning back and closing my eyes as I recall the powdered sugar dusting his fingers, and the way he laughed when I got some on my nose.

"Funnel cakes are the way to a girl's heart," She quips, and I can tell she's living for this story.

"Then, he showed up at the opening and surprised me with flowers—purple irises. Oh, and this jade necklace that he caught me admiring as we were walking and looking through tents." My fingers instinctively touch the cool stone resting against my collarbone. Ugh, He was so thoughtful, Allie." I gush like a high-school schoolgirl.

"Stop it, girl! This is straight out of a romance novel!"

"Wait, wait, there's more." I giggle, feeling the excitement bubble up inside me once again. "After the opening, he stayed behind, helped me lock up, and walked me to my car. It was...sweet."

"Sweet? Girl, that's downright swoon-worthy!" Allie squeals, and I can imagine her bouncing on the balls of her feet, the way she does when she can't contain her joy.

"Right?! Oh, and we exchanged numbers. He even asked to take me out next week," I add, the prospect sending a flutter through my chest.

"Next week? That's ages away!" Allie protests playfully. "You better call me the second you get home from your date. I need to live vicariously, you know?"

"Of course," I promise, warmth spreading through me at the thought of sharing every minute detail with my best friend.

"Good. Now go conquer that lunch rush, chef extraordinaire." She's all cheers and encouragement, the friend I don't deserve.

"Thanks, Allie. Talk soon," I say, setting the phone aside before rising from the bath, ready to face the day.

"Bye, Tia. Good luck!"

With the call ended, I quickly dry off, throw on some clothes, and pull my hair into a practical bun.

The restaurant beckons, and along with my team of dedicated chefs, today's lunch rush won't stand a chance.

CHAPTER TWENTY-TWO

Agent Holloway

The hum of the air conditioning in the New Orleans FBI headquarters is a steady backdrop to my focus. I'm hunched over the sheriff's files, papers strewn across my desk like casualties of a battle for clarity.

As the dim afternoon light filters through the blinds, I pore over each detail, knowing something lurks between the lines—something crucial.

"Hey, Cade," Forrester's voice rips through my concentration.

I don't have to look up to know he's leaning casually against my desk, that nonchalant pose belying the sharpness of his mind.

"Are we ready to give the local PD an unsub profile?" His question is pointed, impatient for progress.

I sit back, stretching muscles tight from hours of tension. "Yes," I nod, feeling the significant impact of this breakthrough in my chest. "And I think we've got more than just a profile."

"Oh?" His eyebrow arches, curiosity piqued as he scans my face for confirmation.

"Pretty sure we have our first suspect." The words hang between us, charged with the potential of being the turning point in this case.

Forrester's eyes narrow slightly, analytical gears already turning. "What did you find?"

"Connections," I say, tapping the file before me.

I get up from my seat, feeling a surge of excitement coursing through me.

Each step I take towards the case board feels electrifying, as if building up to a powerful storm.

I pin a photo to the cork surface—Emma, Carl's assistant, her eyes seeming to follow us with a quiet intelligence.

"Emma," I begin, voice echoing slightly in the hushed room, "Has ties with both victims." My finger taps on her photo then drags to two others already on the board. "And both men have ties with one another as well."

Agent Forrester leans in, scrutinizing the connections drawn in red yarn as if they might reveal deeper secrets.

The rest of the team gathers around, their collective focus tightening around the visage of the woman now at the center of our investigation.

"Let's build her profile," I say, and I sense the shift in atmosphere—a group of minds converging into a single, analytical entity.

"Female unsub," I start, and there are nods of agreement around me. "The nature of the deaths suggests something personal, intimate even." I look at each agent for a moment, ensuring we're all on the same page. "We're thinking poison—or something similar."

Forrester's forehead creases with thought. "But toxicology came back clean," he points out, echoing the thoughts of the rest of us.

"Yes, for drugs. Which means," I continue, feeling the weight of every gaze, "They will have to begin checking other sources. We're possibly looking for something that hasn't been considered yet. Thallium, Cyanide, Ricin...something to those effects. However, we won't know for sure until toxicology gets back to us."

The team absorbs this, the silence pregnant with contemplation.

We're on the brink, I can feel it—the precipice of understanding that will lead us to the heart of this darkness. And Emma, with her still, paper gaze, seems to dare us to dive deeper.

I pin another photo to the board, this one a faded snapshot of two men in uniform, taken years ago. "Both victims," I state, "Used to work as deputies under old Sheriff Whitmore."

"Until he died," Agent Forrester adds, his voice low, and I nod.

"Right. And when Landry stepped in as the new sheriff, Carl bailed out on law enforcement altogether. Started his own landscaping business." The room is quiet, save for the shuffling of papers and the occasional scratch of pen on notepad as agents take notes.

"Emma," I continue, my finger hovering over her image, "She kept Carl's schedule. Every Friday night, she had it cleared. Poker night with Landry, Allen Parker, and Parker's son."

"Seems cozy," someone murmurs from behind.

I can't help but roll my eyes at the clear inexperience of the new agent.

That's when a lady agent, a sharp profiler named Jensen, tilts her head, considering the web of relationships tacked up before us. "What's her angle, Holloway? Why would Emma be involved in any of this?"

"Blackmail," I say, and the word hangs heavy in the air. "Tech team recovered a deleted video—Carl and Emma. It wasn't meant for public viewing." I catch Jensen's eye, and there's a flicker of understanding there.

"Recorded without her consent?" She asks, a frown creasing her brow.

"Seems likely," I reply. "And Emma's engaged to the mayor's son, which complicates the picture even more. If Carl was holding that over her..."

"Desperate measures," Forrester concludes with a nod.

"Exactly."

"But that still doesn't connect her to the Sheriff."

"But doesn't it? These two men have been friends for years, and Emma attended quite a few of these poker nights—the sheriff knew."

The atmosphere in the room is heavy with unspoken accusations, causing us to huddle together with bowed heads like co-conspirators.

Forrester's eyes are sharp, alert as I lean in, my voice low but firm, "Forester, I need you back at the lawncare firm. Grill the employees again—I'm willing to bet someone knows more than they're letting on."

"Got it." He nods.

I turn to Agent Cash, who's been quiet. "Cash, visit Emma's place. See if she's there and what you can find out. But be unobtrusive for now. We don't have enough evidence to officially consider her a suspect yet, so we're following this lead carefully. We don't want to reveal our suspicions prematurely, just in case we're wrong."

"Understood," She replies, and with a tight-lipped expression, she gathers her things swiftly and exits the room.

My eyes meet Mack's, "Let's head to the mayor's office, see what light he can shed on this tangled mess," I state, already reaching for my suit jacket draped over my chair.

"Right behind ya," Mack confirms, grabbing his keys and he's on my heels.

"You won't be needing those," I say.

He gives me a questioning glance from the corner of his eye. "Old habit." I shrug. "Respectfully, I'll be the one driving this time."

Chapter Twenty-Three

Tia

Standing before the open closet, I scan through an array of dresses, searching for that perfect one which whispers confidence and sexiness.

The floral print catches my eye, too casual. The black velvet, too somber. Then, like a spotlight in the dim room, the red silk dress calls to me—a statement piece that promises more than just an ordinary evening. It's decided then; red it is.

I slip into the fabric, feeling it cling to my curves, fitting snugly in all the right places.

At the salon earlier today, they worked magic with my hair, weaving delicate scalp braids across the crown of my head while allowing my natural curls their freedom to dance upon my shoulders.

I take one final look at my dress in the mirror, adjusting the straps to sit just right on my shoulders.

The final touches are almost ceremonial.

Dangling diamond earrings, a souvenir from a Parisian adventure, catch the light as I fasten them. They are accompanied by a matching necklace, both pieces elegant yet understated. A dab of rose-tinted lip gloss to compliment my dress, and I'm nearly complete. Lastly, I reach for the small handbag, just large enough for essentials.

Descending the stairs, the soft murmur of a television drama reaches my ears. There, curled up under the comforting expanse of a large Afghan, is my mother. Her eyes glisten, reflecting the flickering angst of her favorite Lifetime channel melodrama.

"Momma, crying over fictional heartbreak again?" I jest lightly, my voice teasing the edges of our familiar banter.

She looks up, wiping away a stray tear with a little embarrassed smile and nods. "You know me too well," She admits, surrendering to the moment's levity amidst the on-screen tragedy.

The corners of my mouth lift into a knowing smile. I'm the same way with my books.

Rising from the couch, my mother brushes the Afghan aside and stands before me, her eyes scanning over my carefully curated ensemble.

She steps closer, a loving warmth radiating from her that has nothing to do with the tear-jerkers she indulges in. Her hands cup my face gently, and her lips press a tender kiss to my cheek.

Oh, darling, you're prettier than a thousand sunsets," She whispers.

A wistful smile plays on her lips as she takes a step back, her gaze lingering on me as if trying to capture this moment in her memory.

"I'm so happy for you, sugar. And this Cade...he seems like a good one." Her smile turns mischievous, a twinkle in her eye. "And he has a really nice butt."

"Momma!" I laugh, the sound bubbling up from deep within.

I wrap my arms around her in a quick hug, feeling her squeeze me back.

"Go on now," She says, releasing me with an affectionate pat. "Have a wonderful time."

"That's what I'm hoping." I wink, blowing her a kiss.

Stepping outside, the cool evening air kisses my skin. Angelo, ever the professional, holds open the limo door for me, his stoic face breaking into a smile upon seeing me.

"You look lovely this evening." He tips his all-black driving hat.

"Thank you, Angelo," I smile as I slide into the plush interior of the car.

The drive is smooth, and before I know it, the limo pulls up to the restaurant where Cade awaits.

Angelo steps out first, moving to open my door. I emerge, catching sight of Cade standing there, looking every bit the part of a man swept away by nerves.

"No need to wait up tonight. Cade will be bringing me home." I tell Angelo.

"Of course, Miss Williams," He replies, a knowing smile playing at the edge of his mouth and closes the door behind me with a soft thud.

Cades cheeks are a rosy hue of red that extends to his ears, only endearing him more to me. He stammers over his words, the sight so charmingly human that it draws a giggle from me. His nervousness is infectious, but in a way that makes my heart swell.

"Wow, Tia...You're—you're just..." Cade struggles to find the words, his hands gesturing vaguely in the air before he finally locks his gaze with mine. "You're the image of perfection."

"Thank you," I reply, my cheeks warming.

It's not just the compliment that has me flustered—it's honestly his eyes, the intensity of his gaze making my knees weak, as though I'm standing on unsteady ground.

Stepping through the velvet-draped entrance of the steakhouse, the soft croon of jazz greets us.

A singer, clad in sequins and feathers reminiscent of a bygone era, sways to the rhythm, her voice the perfect accompaniment to the sizzle and clink that fills the air.

"Quite the atmosphere," I murmur, taking in the rich black oak bar and the flicker of candlelight from each table.

"I would say only the best for our first date, but we both know that wouldn't be entirely true, would it?" Cade grins, his earlier nervousness replaced with a shy pride as he guides me to our reserved spot, a corner table with an intimate view of the live performance.

Ever such the gentleman, Cade pulls out the chair for me to sit on before making his way over to his own.

A server, moving with the finesse of someone who knows their craft, lays out an array of silverware before us, each piece glinting under the low-hung lights. His hands are deft, almost reverential, as if every placement is part of a sacred ritual.

"Someone will be with you soon to take your order," The server says, stepping back to allow us room.

"Perfect, thank you," I reply.

The server makes a discreet exit, only to be replaced by another, who presents a small wooden board laden with artisan breads. The aroma is intoxicating, a blend of earthy olives, rich butters, and sharp cheeses, inviting us to indulge while we peruse the menu. Beside them, tiny dishes of infused olive oil capture the light, shimmering like little pools of liquid gold.

"Champagne?" Cade suggests.

"Absolutely," I reply with a smile, feeling the bubbles of excitement match those soon to fill our glasses.

We signal for the waiter who, upon hearing our choice, offers a nod of approval that tells me Cade's selection is exceptional.

"Take your time to look over the menu," He advises, "For tonight's specials are particularly enticing."

The server then takes his leave.

"Everything looks delicious," I say, turning the heavy pages of the menu. "I can't decide."

"Neither can I," Cade admits, stealing a glance at the flapper singer as she hits a particularly sultry note.

His brows are pinched in concentration, his mouth moving with silent words as he reads over the options.

Peeking out from the corner of his menu, he sneakily steals glances at me, our eyes playing a flirtatious game every time they cross paths. Every time I glance up from the menu, I catch him in the act. His eyes quickly dart back to scanning the list of entrees, his face showing the cutest hint of distress, and I try to conceal my amusement behind the leather-bound offerings of the steakhouse.

Poorly, if I might add.

"So..." I start, placing the menu down with a decisive pat. "I've already chosen your dinner a few times already." His eyebrows lift, curiosity piqued. "This time, *you're* picking for both of us."

A flush creeps up his neck, proof of his fluttering nerves that I find quite charming. "Really? But what if you don't lik—"

"There are no wrong choices," I interrupt gently, reassuring him with a smile as warm as the candlelight between us. "Trust me, I've eaten my way through more countries than I can count on both hands. Surprise me."

"I accept that challenge," He declares, shutting the leather-bound menu with a snap.

The waiter materializes beside us. "Good evening once more," He says. "Have you made your decision?"

"Indeed, we have," Cade affirms, his voice steady despite the red tips of his ears.

He launches into an order that's ambitious enough to feed an ensemble cast of gourmands: "We'll start with oysters on the half shell topped with caviar, followed by escargot. Then, bring us the duck and andouille gumbo to share."

The waiter scribbles notes with a flourish, and Cade continues, undeterred by the scale of his request. "For the main course, let's do the butter poached lobster with black truffle gnocchi, a ten-ounce cut of the Japanese Wagyu, and the lamb chops with spicy apricot chutney."

There's a pause, a moment where the waiter's pen hovers over the pad, perhaps waiting for Cade to say he's joking.

But he isn't.

And neither is his final flourish: "For dessert, the hummingbird cake with pineapple ice cream, and don't forget the bourbon pecan pie."

My eyes widen—not in alarm, but in sheer delight at his audacity. The waiter's expression mirrors mine, though etched with the professional restraint of someone who's seen it all. "A good start," I smile, my voice threaded with mirth.

"Yes, all excellent choices, sir," The waiter commends, and with a bow of his head, he retreats to relay the feast Cade has conjured.

"Wow, Agent Holloway," I chuckle, reaching for the bread as a preemptive strike on our banquet. "You do realize we're going to need a wheelbarrow to roll out of here, right?"

Cade's sheepish grin tells me he's fully aware.

My fork hits my plate with a light clank, and I lean back in my chair, a satisfied sigh escaping my lips. Across from me, Cade watches with an expression that mingled admiration and surprise.

"Can't believe you kept pace with me," He says, his voice tinged with awe. "Most people would have tapped out."

I laugh softly, dabbing the corner of my mouth with a napkin. "Oh, this is nothing," I tell him. "You should have seen my dad eat. The man was like a garbage disposal—could put away food like it was nobody's business."

A shadow passes over my face as the laughter fades, replaced by a familiar ache. My eyes drop to the table, tracing the intricate patterns of the white linen tablecloth.

Cade's hand reaches across the table, "I'm sorry for your loss," He whispers gently.

My eyes trail back up to his face, perplexed. "How did you know?"

"Because I've been there too," He confesses, the pain evident in his eyes. "When I was seven," He pauses, swallowing hard, as if the words themselves torment him. "My mom and my dad were going through a divorce. My mother began seeing someone new, which infuriated my father, so one night he broke into our house while we were watching a movie and he snatched my mom off the couch, dragging her to the bedroom. I tried to fight him off, to help her but—" He trails off, not finishing the sentence, the muscle in his jaw twitching from the force of how tightly his jaw is clenched.

My voice is barely audible when I whisper, "God, Cade. I can't even imagine".

"He threw me against the hallway wall when I jumped on his back to stop him, Cade continues. "Locked the door behind him. I threw myself into the door, tried to beat it down, but there wasn't anything I could do except to listen to her cries until they finally ceased to exist." The pain in his eyes deepens as he looks away, his hands trembling slightly on the tabletop. "

I reach out, covering his hand with mine, squeezing gently. The connection is silent but strong; two souls scarred by past tragedies, finding solace in each other's understanding.

"You were brave," I murmur, "Not everyone could have done that, even tried to fight."

Cade's eyes meet mine again, a flicker of remorse swimming behind them.

"Not brave enough," He sighs. "As soon as I heard the door unlock, I sprinted to the living room and hid inside the cabinet.

But he eventually found me and beat me half to death. It was nothing compared to the brutal treatment he gave my mother, though. After he was finished with me, he went back to my mother's bedroom and took both of their lives. I thought I was going to die there with them, but luckily the neighbor woke up and heard the disturbance and decided to call the police."

"Thank heavens for that neighbor," I breath, the horror of his story clinging to me like a cold mist.

My grip tightens on his hand, an attempt to anchor him back from the dark memories.

"No one should ever have to experience something so cruel. I'm so sorry you had to go through that, Cade."

Cade forces a tight-lipped smile, a weak attempt to mask the agony that clearly lingers beneath.

"Yeah, that neighbor... I owe her my life." He takes a deep breath, trying to compose himself. "After that night, everything changed. I was put into foster care. Moved from one home to another. Never really settled anywhere long enough to care, but I knew without a doubt that I wanted to pursue a career in law enforcement and protect others just like my mom. I figured if I could stop even one person from experiencing what I did, it would be worth it."

Tears brim in my eyes, a reflection of the sorrow and pain that Cade's story has unearthed. A fragile bridge of shared grief spans between us, "I don't talk about it often," I confess, the words slipping from me like broken shards of glass. "When I was a little girl, my father was killed. But the police seemed to have given up all together on solving his case because to this day, they still have yet to make an arrest for his murder."

Cade's gaze softens, and with a tenderness that wraps around my heart, he brushes away the tears that escape down my cheeks.

"I apologize, Tia. I didn't intend for our first date to take such a ruminative turn," He mumbles.

A small laugh escapes me, though it carries no joy. "It's okay, really. It means a lot that you'd share something so personal. I like that we can talk about anything."

He looks at me, vulnerability etched across his features. "I don't know why, but with you, I want to share everything. It's strange; I've never felt this comfortable with anyone before."

"I know what you mean," I say, lifting my flute of champagne to my lips as I flash him a quick grin.

The waiter appears by our table, a welcomed interruption as he fills our glasses with sparkling water and brings us dessert. Fortunately, his sudden presence redirects our attention from the dark corners of our pasts, and to the mellifluous moments of the present and the mouth-watering treats that will conclude our meal.

The hummingbird cake sits nestled next to the creamy pineapple ice cream, its sugary scent a promise of indulgence.

Cade picks up his fork and slices a piece of the hummingbird cake, the spices mingling with the aroma of sweet pineapple and pecans. "Let's make a deal," He says suddenly, his voice firm yet inviting. "Tonight, we turn the page. New chapter, fresh beginnings. What do you say?"

"I say, here's to fresh beginnings." I lift my glass in salute.

Cade meets my glass with his own, a soft clink resounds between the two glasses, a simple yet delicate sound that seems to seal our little agreement.

As we dig into the dessert, the conversation lightens, drifting to lighter topics—favorite movies, books, and a shared passion for quirky music bands.

I laugh as he recounts his first concert blunder, where he had a little too much to drink and ended up falling into a muddy pit right before his favorite band came on stage.

"It was horrendous at the time, but now it's just fucking hilarious," He chuckles, his eyes crinkling at the corners.

When the time comes to settle the bill, we enter into a playful tussle of generosity. "I've got this," I insist, reaching for my purse.

"No, allow me," Cade counters, his hand already on his wallet.

"Let's just split it," I propose, and after a brief moment of mock-outrage, he relents with light laughter.

"Fine, but next time it's on me."

CHAPTER TWENTY-FOUR

Agent Holloway

The glow of the porch light spills over the driveway as I put the car in park, the engine's chatter stuttering into silence. We linger in the cocoon of the vehicle, the warmth of our shared laughter fogging up the windows.

I sneak glimpses at her, admiring how the streetlight dances on her face, accentuating the gentle slope of her cheeks.

"Sorry for making the wrong turn," I say, a self-deprecating smile dancing on my lips. "I swear I'm extremely good with directions, but I must admit, I was quite distracted this evening."

She giggles, her hand finding mine on the center console. "The scenic detour was an unexpected adventure."

I can't help but drown in the richness of her voice and how it envelops me in its sweet, honeyed tones.

"Well in that case, you're welcome." My sarcastic remark earning me an eyeroll and a playful nudge, but her laughter lets me know it's all in good fun.

With a reluctant sigh, I unfold myself from the driver's seat and round the car to open Tia's door. The crisp night air brushes against my skin, carrying with it the scent of impending rain. Tia steps out, grace personified, even in the simple act of leaving a car.

As we make our way towards the porch, her hand finds mine and fits perfectly. We walk leisurely on the gravel path, savoring every step as we both silently wish for the night to never end.

"So, if I didn't ruin my chances, is there a possibility of you allowing me the privilege of taking you on another date?"

"Really, Cade, you didn't ruin anything," She reassures me, her eyes catching the faint moonlight, giving them a celestial shimmer. "I had a wonderful time tonight, and yes, I would love to go out with you again."

We reach the steps leading up to her front door, the moment hanging between us like a delicate pendulum. I turn to face her, my heart thudding a rhythm of a wild stallion running free.

"Good. Because I would hate to think this evening will be our last," I reply, the words almost catching in my throat as I try to maintain a semblance of calm amidst the storm of emotions inside me.

I lean in hesitantly, my intent clear, and when she leans in too, I press a soft kiss to her lips—a fleeting caress, like the touch of a butterfly's wings.

Where my kiss was meant to be a whisper, hers became a declaration. Tia's fingers thread through my hair, pulling me back to her with a surprising fervor that sets my pulse racing.

Our kiss deepens, the world around us fading into a blur of forgotten shadows and whispered winds, as our breath mingles, becoming one in the cool night air. And when we part, the warmth of her lips lingers on mine, a treasure that feels stolen, yet one I will cherish for an eternity.

"Come inside?" She speaks with a husky tone, her words laced with an unmistakable invitation that matches the rapid beating of her heart.

Her hands tremble with anticipation as she fumbles to find the key to her front door, betraying her nervous excitement.

"I mean. if you insist." I choke out, my voice equally roughened, betraying my composure.

I follow her into the darkness of the house, where only the faintest glow of a nightlight outlines the hallway. She tiptoes through the living room, peeking around the corner. Earlier on, she had mentioned she and her mother lived together, so I can only assume she's making sure the coast is clear.

College.

I think the last time I felt the exhilaration of sneaking around at night like a lovesick puppy, was during college. It's a feeling that brings a youthful glee that I thought I had long outgrown.

Turning back to me with a predatory gleam in her eye, Tia launches herself at me, her arms wrapping tightly around my neck, and her legs coiling around my waist with an urgency that left no room for doubt.

I catch her without thinking, my own desire igniting like a flame to dry twigs. In this instant, we are two untamed creatures, unbound and guided by raw, animalistic desire.

My back hits the cool plaster of the hallway wall, a contrast to the heat emanating from Tia's body as she molds against me. My hands find purchase beneath her thighs, supporting her weight as our mouths collide.

Her fingers rake through my hair before descending to claw at the fabric of my shirt. The intensity of her touch sends shivers racing through me, the rough scrape of her nails nip at my back and it takes everything in me not to take her right where we are.

"Wait," I breathe out between our heated kisses, my voice a low rumble that vibrates against her lips. "Do—do you really want this?" I pull back just enough to search her eyes, the intensity of my gaze asking for honesty. "Because I won't take advantage—if this isn't what you want."

Her eyes, dark pools of desire, meet mine with a seductiveness that pauses the breath in my chest. "I. Want. You," She affirms, each word punctuated.

The tension in my shoulders release, my restraint crumbling under the weight of her words. It's all the confirmation I need. With a growl of approval, I shed my jacket, letting it fall forgotten to the floor, and Tia's nimble fingers make quick work of the buttons on my shirt, revealing the hunger in her touch as each one pops free.

Our ascent up the stairs is a stumbling ballet of need and impatience. Halfway up, we pause, our progress halted not by fatigue, but by my need to taste her. I peel away her dress, the fabric falling down her body, pooling at her feet.

As my mouth descends to the exposed skin of her collarbone, my lips trail a path of fire down to the swell of her breast. My tongue swirls around her nipple, eliciting a cascade of soft moans that fill the stairwell. Her head tilts back, her eyes fluttering shut in surrender as my hands roam over the contours of her body, tracing the arc of her ribs and the curve of her waist.

With a firm grip I lift Tia onto the balcony rail, her breath catching in her throat at the sudden elevation. "I've got you, lucoile." I murmur against her ear, "Do you trust me."

She nods, a breath whooshing from her lungs as she relaxes slightly.

I nip at her jawline, her body jerking with every small nibble rubbing against my cock. Her every move is a siren call to my senses, each breathless sigh more intoxicating than the last. I lean in, claiming her lips again in a searing kiss that renders everything else meaningless.

"Third door to the right," She whispers.

I respond without hesitation, my arms enveloping her petite frame as I carry her tucked close to my chest.

The door to her room looms ahead, and with a flick of my toe, I nudge it closed behind us, sealing away our problems and the rest of the world outside.

I place Tia on the silken sheets, and she reclines, her gaze locking on mine as she watches me intently, pinching her perked nipples between her fingers.

I stand, still and silent, taking in her ethereal beauty, my hardness threatening to bust from my clothes.

She notices, reaching out, her fingers softly tugging at my waistband.

I shed the rest of my clothes, clutching my cock as I kneel on the bed in front of her.

As she moves to sit, I stop her with a hand on her thigh.

"No, lie back," I command, stroking myself as she glares at me with hungry eyes, her tongue snaking across her bottom lip.

Obediently, she complies, her chest rising and falling in quickened breaths as she lies back on the sheets, her legs parting slightly in invitation. The room is suffused with the heady scent of jasmine and musk, draping us in an intimate veil.

She is a goddess amidst the plumes of silk, a Venus amongst glittering stars, a luscious temptation, beckoning me to explore every inch of her exquisite flesh.

My self-control wavers, teetering on the edge of oblivion as I trace a path along her thigh, her skin quivering with anticipation. I admire my effect on her, gazing at her dew-kissed valleys and peaks with increasing arousal.

It's a moment of pure worship, where I am the humble supplicant, and she my divine idol. Her body is my temple, and I am the devoted acolyte, my every touch a prayer, every kiss a sacrament.

She gasps as my fingers graze her center, a soft moan escaping her lips, "Please…" She murmurs, arching her back beneath my touch, seeking more.

"Patience, luciole. I'm just getting started."

With a grin, my hand stops its teasing torment and instead explores the arches and valleys of her elegantly sculpted body. The rich scent of her arousal is intoxicating; it drives me to the edge of sanity, fueling my desires.

Her eyes are closed, lips slightly parted as she writhes under the ministrations of my skilled fingers.

My mouth follows the tantalizing trail blazed by my hand, each taste of her flesh sending waves of desire crashing through me.

My hand strokes faster, my palm tightening on my shaft as the sight of her pleasure fuels my own. Her fingers clutch the sheets, her body undulating under my touch

"Tell me what you want," I murmur against the silken skin of her inner thigh, my breath causing a shiver to ripple through her.

"I—I want..." She stammers, her mounds bouncing with every trembled breath. "I want your tongue on my pussy." Her voice poised precariously on the edge of a sigh and a plea.

Fuck.

Gotta love a girl who knows what she wants.

The corners of my lips curl upwards, a devilish smirk playing on my face. "As you wish," I growl against her, my words sending a shudder through her body.

She tastes of sweetness, of heady desire, of every sinful pleasure under the heavens. My tongue eagerly delves into her depths, savoring the slickness of her desire.

She bucks against me when I suck her clit into my mouth and let it pulse between my lips, her soft whimpers filling the silence of the room. I can feel her body tense up as my tongue continues its erotic dance, writhing and twirling in her molten core.

Her hands grip my hair, her fingers tangling in the locks as she squirms beneath my grip.

"Ohhh fuuuuckkk," She rides out the words, her body tensing when I insert my fingers inside her, her wetness squelching as my hand pumps at a steady pace.

Her soft cries escalate into full-bodied moans, and her hips buck and crash up into me as I continue my assault, each sweep of my tongue and thrust of my fingers designed to push her further into the abyss of pleasure.

"More," She gasps, her legs clamping tighter around me, pulling me deeper into her. Her plea is throaty, desperate, and filled with the kind of unrestrained need that makes my own body thrum with excitement.

Adding a third finger, I burrow deeper, my fingers dancing along her slick walls as my tongue continues its relentless pursuit. She bucks beneath me, her body convulsing as her orgasm rips through her, ripping a guttural moan from her throat as she arches her back off the bed, her body taut as a bowstring. "Oh, fuck, yes!" She screams, her voice echoing off the bare walls of our room.

I keep my mouth on her, burying my face, cutting off my own oxygen, just to drink her all in.

She shakes beneath me, her breath coming out in ragged gasps and whimpers.

"St—stop," She finally manages, "Too much," She breathes out, her body still twitching with the aftershocks of her orgasm.

As the tremors subside, Tia lifts onto her knees, licking her lips, "Your turn."

Our eyes meet, hers heavy-lidded and filled to the brim with satisfaction as she wraps her hands around my cock, parts her lips, and lowers her head, taking me into the warmth of her mouth.

Her movements are slow and deliberate, her tongue swirling around my length as her eyes bore into mine. She swallows me down, her throat contracting around me with every thrust I make into the velvety cavern of her mouth. Her hands, still shaking from her release, cradle my balls, the soft pad of her thumb rubbing circles into the sensitive skin.

She knows exactly how to touch me, knows just the pressure and speed that drives me wild. And every movement, every lick sends me on a journey through the cosmos, she's a supernova and I'm caught in her gravitational pull.

A low growl rumbles in my chest as her pace quickens, the sight of her on her knees before me, her mouth on me—sucking, tasting—has my head spinning.

My hips arch uncontrollably, my fingers knitting through her hair, tugging gently at the strands as I push myself deeper down her throat.

Her eyes water as I push her limits, but she doesn't shrink away. Instead, they flash with a defiant spark before she redoubles her effort, taking me deeper, harder.

"I could spend a lifetime watching you choke on my dick."

Her response is a gurgle, spit spilling out the sides of her mouth and down her face. With a wicked grin, she pulls back, letting my throbbing length slip from her mouth with an obscene *'pop'*. Her hands stay on me, delicate fingers wrapping around me, pumping in rhythm as she leans up to capture my lips.

As she pulls away her teeth graze my bottom lip before releasing it with a bite that leaves me gasping.

Fuck this. I can't wait anymore. I need to sink my cock into her pretty little pussy—so tight, so wet for me, almost begging me to fill it and stretch it until she can't take it anymore.

With one swift move, I lean back, pulling her on top of my lap. Surprise flickers in her eyes, but quickly dissipates, replaced by a gaze of pure, unadulterated lust.

Her body trembles when I slide between her folds, teasing her before positioning myself at her entrance.

"Look at me." I order softly, "I want to see your gorgeous face as your coming on my cock."

I grip her hips tightly, the muscles of my arms straining as I guide her down. Her eyes glaze over and she gasps, a little noise that's half pleasure, half pain as I slowly push into her. The feeling is almost too intense. Her walls clench around me like a vice, her body writhing atop mine as I fill her completely. Her nails dig into my shoulders, leaving indents that will no doubt mark me for days to come.

"Fuck, you feel so good," I groan, gritting my teeth, thrusting deeper, losing myself to the sensation.

She clings to me, her fingers digging into the flesh of my back, her teeth biting down on the meat of my shoulder to stifle the screams she refuses to let go.

But I won't allow that. I want to hear her, I want her to hear herself, I want her to be fully aware who's making her scream and moan like this. As selfish as it is, I want to wreck her, ruin her—the only dick she'll ever crave again, will be mine.

Releasing her hip, my hands find their way to her breasts. They're full, and perky, her perfectly round nipples tout against my palms as I knead and stroke them.

"Oh, Cade!" She moans so loud I could swear I felt the wall shake.

I thrust into her again, harder this time, causing the breath to hitch in her throat before she yells my name again.

That's it.

That's the sound I've been craving, the sweetest melody to my ears.

"That's right, luciole," I growl. "Moan my name just like that."

I rock into her again and again, each thrust met with an exquisite gasp rippling from her lips that sends a hot rush of satisfaction coiling deep within me.

Every inch of her skin and mine is slick with sweat. I watch as her pussy swallows me whole, and I press my thumb to her swollen clit and draw lazy circles.

"God, yes!" She cries out, her voice a rasp against the heavy stillness of the room.

She shakes on top of me, her shudders vibrating down my shaft, her walls clenching—she's on the cusp of release.

And so the fuck am I.

"Open your eyes." I command, needing to see the swirl of emotions in her gaze as we teeter on the edge.

Her eyes flutter open, her gaze glassy with lust. They're the most beautiful shade of green, twinkling against her flushed cheeks.

I thrust into her one last time and together we shatter, our bodies seizing at the same time before she collapses against my chest, spent and sated.

I wrap my arms around her, holding her close, letting our heated bodies cool down against each other. Her hair is plastered to her forehead with sweat, her cheeks are flushed a beautiful rosy color, and her lips are swollen from our feverish kisses.

"Damn. You're perfect." I whisper.

"I could say the same about you." She retorts.

"You could." I say, "But then you'd just be lying."

"Oh, shut up, Cade!" Tia laughs, falling off of me, and burying her face in my chest.

I chuckle, brushing the hair from her face.

My heartbeat is a lullaby in her ear, easing her into a peaceful slumber. The darkness of the night surrounds us, and I finally give in to the pull of sleep as my consciousness slips away to the comforting sound of Tia's snores.

CHAPTER TWENTY-FIVE

Tia

I'm elbow-deep in the Sunday brunch rush, the clanging of pots and hiss of frying pans filling the restaurant.

The air is thick with the scents of buttery croissants and sizzling bacon. Servers navigate through packed tables, balancing towers of pancakes and omelets on their arms like seasoned acrobats. When we open for brunch from ten a.m to one p.m on weekends, it's always hectic.

My fingers work mechanically, plating up eggs Benedict with an artful drizzle of hollandaise, but my mind is elsewhere, tangled in a web of frustration.

How am I going to kill him?

The question gnaws at me, relentless as the ticking clock above the pass-through window.

It's been a game of cat and mouse ever since I came back to town. Allen's become a shadow, slipping through the cracks just when I think I've cornered him. I think he can feel it, that his days are numbered ever since his two friends met their untimely ends.

The clang of a bell snaps me back to the present.

Order up.

My hand steadies, but inside, the turmoil churns. Time is running out, and Allen is nowhere to be found.

With each passing order, every scramble of eggs, every pour of coffee, I feel the tension tightening in my chest, a constricting band of steel.

This isn't just about revenge; it's about justice.

"Table six needs a refill on coffee!" Someone calls out, punctuating my brooding thoughts.

"I Got it!" Melissa, a newer girl shouts.

I glance towards her, her apron stained with maple syrup and tidbits of pancake. Her hair is coming loose from its bun, a few stray locks swinging in front of her face as she moves. She looks as frazzled as I feel.

The brunch rush wanes eventually, and I begin dinner prep before I take my leave of absence for the day.

The blade glides through the duck breast, silver against crimson, and I trim away the excess fat with precision.

The restaurant hums with the clinking of dishes and the murmur of satisfied patrons, but my thoughts are far from the common racket.

Allen's wife had the sense to leave him before their baby drew its first breath, driven away by infidelity and secrets.

It's funny how some people can escape their demons while others, like me, have to face them head-on.

But good for her. She deserves better than a lowlife such as him.

I slide the trimmed duck breasts into a prep pan, layering them neatly, one beside the other and begin the pineapple-orange jerk marinade for the duck breasts.

As I lean my weight against the cold, hard surface of the stainless-steel prep counter, I contemplate the enigma that Allen has become. A man who once walked so boldly through life is now skittish, scarce—a ghost haunting the fringes of his own existence.

He's afraid.

He may not know who is coming for him, but he knows someone will.

My hands had stayed clean through the demise of his two cronies, wrapped in alibis as tight as the cling film that seals our leftovers. But Allen—Allen will be different.

Harder.

I need to get close enough to slip him the poison, but how do I approach a man who has made himself untouchable?

Garlic has a pungent odor that always catches me off guard no matter how many times a day I chop it. The flavor is impeccable, the smell, not so much.

It's a main ingredient to the marinade, along with freshly squeezed oranges, pineapple juice, soy sauce, ginger, brown sugar, ground allspice and some other spices, and finally, a few fiery Scotch bonnet peppers for that extra Cajun kick.

The clock ticks down to one pm, the end of brunch service. I shake thankful fists above my head as the last of the brunch-goers filter out of the restaurant, their satisfied chatter silencing as the door swings closed behind them.

The post-rush quiet is a welcome break, and I take a moment to bask in it.

My plan is like a perfect dish, but it's missing one crucial ingredient. I need to find a way to make Allen vulnerable, just long enough for me to serve him his final course.

He had sat there, at table seven, during his second visit. Allen's eyes had met mine across the crowded room—a flicker of recognition, then quickly veiled by feigned indifference. But the slight tightening of his jaw told me everything.

He knew who I was, and perhaps he even knew why I'd come back to town.

Is there any shred of conscience left in him? When he held his own child, did the ghost of my father ever pass through his mind? Does he ever think about the life he stole, all for the sake of preserving his pristine reputation? Or has time allowed him to bury his sins so deep that they're nothing more than forgotten echoes of a past he no longer acknowledges?

"Everything okay, Tia?" The dinner hostess brushes past me with a concerned look, snapping me out of my thoughts.

I force a smile, "Just exhaustion getting to me, sugar."

But it's not the exhaustion at all; it's the burden of inequity that pushes on my spirit.

Ralph's words reverberate in my memory, uttered with such cold certainty.

No one would believe us.

It was the word of a colored woman and her traumatized daughter against his—the sheriff, the paragon of virtue in this small town.

How quickly they accepted his narrative, how eagerly they turned a blind eye to the truth. And now, the chances of ever solving my father's murder have dwindled and the case has grown colder, fading from the possibility of ever being solved.

"Stay focused, Tia," I whisper to myself, clearing a table as discreetly as possible. "There's work to be done."

When I find my opening to reach Allen, I'll make him feel the bite of consequence for his actions. For my father, for myself, for the truth that refuses to stay silent, even as it lies buried under years of lies and hypocrisy.

Momma may believe it's a curse that killed Papa, brought on by her and Papa's dealings with the shadow man...but maybe there is no curse, no shadow man lacing misfortune into our lives.

Maybe the world is already full of monsters, hiding in plain sight, cloaked in badges and smiles.

Maybe these are the predators who walk among us, their hands not blackened by shadow magic, but rather stained with blood and corruption.

I wipe my hands off on a dish towel, all has been prepped for the dinner crowd and I can finally go home. Momma and I have dinner planned together before she leaves for her girl's trip with Camilla, and I still have much to do before then. But then it's back to the drawing board.

As much as I want to deny it, Allen's death is unavoidable. But I have to be cautious and make sure I don't get caught.

I know that I promised my mother I would stop after Carl, but I need her to understand that I'm not just doing this for us.

I'm doing it for every unheard scream, every unheeded plea, and every silenced truth that deserved to be roared.

CHAPTER TWENTY-SIX

Tia

The dappled sunlight filters through the latticework of the gazebo, casting a prism of light and shadow on the picnic blanket.

I stretch my legs out before me, the blades of grass tickling the backs of my knees. Cade is beside me, his laughter mingling with the soft rustle of leaves in the breeze. Around us, the plantation's pond mirrors the sky, its surface disturbed only by the occasional darting of a dragonfly or the concentric ripples from a jumping fish.

The gardens are a riot of color; reds, yellows, and purples in a thousand different shades bloom with abandon. The sweet fragrance of honeysuckle hangs heavy in the air, and it mixes with the heady scent of gardenias from the nearby bushes.

"Ugh, this is perfect," I sigh, closing my eyes for a moment to bask in the warmth of the sun on my skin.

Comfort seeps into my bones, and I can't help but feel that everything is as it should be.

"Almost too perfect," Cade teases, and my eyes flutter open just in time to see him pluck a cupcake from the basket.

"Hey, I made those," I say, playfully indignant.

"Which is exactly why I'm eating one." His smile is easy, and there's a light in his eyes that wasn't there when we first met.

"Well, I didn't say you could have one." I quip, snatching one of the delectable treats up.

"Too damn bad." He retorts, shoving the entire thing in his mouth.

I laugh before I take a bite of my own cupcake, the pineapple coconut flavor exploding on my tongue, the icing rich and sweet.

In my eagerness, a dollop of vanilla mango frosting finds its way onto the tip of my nose.

He chuckles at the sight, and I cross my eyes trying to see the offending blob.

"What?" I ask, feigning ignorance.

"Nothing, just—" His hand reaches out, his thumb gently swiping across my skin, removing the icing.

The touch lingers for a heartbeat longer than necessary, sending a shiver down my spine despite the warm air. And then his lips are on mine, soft and insistent, tasting faintly of sugar and spice.

We break apart, and for a few moments, we simply sit in contented silence.

"So," I begin, brushing a crumb from my dress, "How's work going? Any more thoughts on transferring back to New York?"

"Actually," Cade admits, "It's not so bad anymore. Agent Forrester, my partner for the most part—I think we've finally hit our stride. He's invited me out for drinks in a couple of days."

"Really?" I can't hide the surprise in my voice.

Cade had been less than thrilled about his new posting in New Orleans at first. To hear him speak positively about it now feels like a win for both the city and for me.

"Looks like you're settling in after all."

"Seems like it," He agrees, leaning back on his hands and gazing up at the clear blue sky. "Thanks to you, I might add."

I feel a blush creep up my cheeks, pleased by the acknowledgement.

"Not just a couple of weeks ago, weren't you complaining about how awful the humidity is here? Didn't you say the city was personally out to get you," I tease, nudging his side with my elbow.

He grins, a sheepish look crossing his face. "I might have over-reacted a tad," He concedes. "But in my defense, it took meeting one extraordinary person to change my entire perspective."

"Is that so?" My voice is light, playful, but inside, warmth blooms like the flowers in the garden around us.

"Absolutely," Cade affirms, his gaze locking onto mine. "It's all thanks to this amazing woman I met on my first day. She turned the Big Easy into something—well, really easy to love."

I laugh, amused by the turn of phrase, and reach for another cupcake, savoring the tangy sweetness.

Our lunch had been divine—the grilled shrimp and veggie skewers perfectly charred, the succotash and potato salad vibrant and comforting in equal measure, and the peach cobbler a delectable homage to the season.

Now, only crumbs and empty dishes remain.

Stretching my legs out before me, I lean back on my palms, relishing the caress of the sun on my skin.

The wide brim of my sunhat flutters in the breeze, and my sundress, airy and soft, billows slightly around my thighs. I watch as Cade, dressed in a form fitting T-shirt and cargo shorts, follows the movement with an appreciative eye.

"Careful," I warn him, though my tone is anything but stern. "You keep looking at me like that, and you'll have me thinking I'm more interesting than your detective work."

"Trust me," He says, reaching over to brush a stray curl from my face, "You are."

I catch the glint of mischief in his eye and decide to prod it further. "You know, my mom's out of town, and we've got this whole place to ourselves," I say, tilting my head toward the pond as I give him a playful grin. "And it's such a beautiful day. Perhaps we should go for a swim?"

"Is that an invitation?" Cade's voice is laced with interest, his gaze flitting to the shimmering water and back to me.

"Maybe it is," I tease, rolling onto my knees and standing.

"Then how can I refuse?" He says, rising to join me.

The soft fabric brushes against my skin as I lift the sundress over my head, the sunhat tumbling off as the dress drifts away. Underneath, a tiny bikini clings to me, making me feel almost scandalous with its boldness. Cade's breath hitches, and I revel in the heat his gaze drapes over me.

"Damn," He mutters, and I laugh, the sound mingling with the rustle of leaves and distant birdcalls.

"Like what you see?" I challenge, stepping closer.

"More than like," He growls, pulling me against his chest, our lips colliding like two comets in the night.

My fingers find the hem of his shirt, tugging it up and over his head in one smooth movement. His skin is hot to the touch, and the contact sends a jolt through me, electrifying the air between us.

"You keep kissing me like that, and we might never make it to the pond." I pant.

"Would that be such a bad thing?"

"Perhaps not," I purr, my fingers tracing the ripple of his abs.

I nibble the hard muscle of his neck, my breath skating over his flesh, and then with a flick of my wrist, Cade's shirt blooms in the air before landing over his head.

I kick off my sandals, feeling the grass between my toes, my laughter ringing out as I take off, running toward the sparkling water, "Last one in the pond does the dishes!" I yell over my shoulder.

The thrill of the challenge pulses through me, but Cade is quick on his feet. His laugh, deep and infectious, chases after me.

He's close—too close—and then his arms are wrapping around me, lifting me off the ground. My squeals are playful, echoing against the tranquil backdrop of the plantation as he spins me around.

"Cheater!" I accuse with mock indignation, kicking my legs as we near the pond's edge.

"Strategy, Tia. All is fair in romance and swimming," Cade counters, his grin as wide as the horizon.

And with that, he launches me into the cool embrace of the pond.

The water envelopes me, a delicious shock to my warm skin. I resurface with a splash, wiping droplets from my eyelashes just in time to see Cade take a running leap, cannonballing beside me, and sending waves rippling across the surface.

Our bodies glide through the water, moving with a sense of playfulness and freedom. The pool creates a world of its own, one filled with nothing but laughter and joy. Then, suddenly, Cade vanishes beneath the surface.

My heart leaps in a blend of delight and anticipation, and I scan the pond, poised for his surprise emergence.

"Where did you—" His hands find my waist underwater, and I yelp, jerking away, only for him to pop up right in front of me, his eyes alight with roguery.

Without a word, he pulls me close, and his lips pressing into mine. The kiss is a spark in the cool water, igniting a warmth that spirals through me, leaving me breathless and craving more.

Our kisses deepen, growing hotter with each passing second. Cade's arms slide beneath my knees, lifting me effortlessly. Water cascades down my back as we move together, breaking the surface.

With each step he takes, he carries us closer to the gazebo, until the softness of the large blanket beneath me replaces the liquid caress of the pond.

I look up at him through heavy lashes, the world seeming to spin slightly as the heat between us transforms into something tender yet intense, a connection that goes beyond the physicality of what we have together.

My hands reach up to the string around my neck, my fingers grasping it, pulling the bow so that my bikini top falls, and my breasts spill out.

A shiver of anticipation runs across my skin as Cade's eyes darken, unable to tear his gaze away from me. The world seems to hold its breath, the crickets quieting their symphony, the soft rustling of the trees ceasing.

I take notice of the uneasy look on his face as his eyes scan the area.

"Relax," I coo. "Nobody can see us out here."

His hand brushes through his hair as he grins, "You have a point."

He lowers himself down to the blanket, his chest pressed against mine as he places a tender kiss on my skin. His fingers trace a trail from my hip up to my bare breasts, his fingers grazing over the sensitive peaks.

I close my eyes, my breath hitching as I arch into his touch. Cade's lips follow the path his fingers trace, causing my heart to skip a beat each time he kisses me.

"Cade," I moan, my nails clawing at his biceps when he bites down on the soft flesh between my neck and shoulder.

He hums in response, the vibration of his voice sending tingling sensations down my spine.

His mouth goes to move lower, but the shrill tone of a phone slices through our taboo paradise.

My heart sinks when Cade checks his caller ID and says, "Damn. It's my boss."

His dark eyes stare at me apologetically, regret etched clearly on his handsome face, but I nod my understanding.

"Ever the tease." I chide playfully, picking up a plump blueberry from our scattered picnic and lobbing it at him, the fruit bouncing off his chest and tumbling back onto the blanket.

He winks at me, grinning as he picks up the phone and swipes to answer the call, "Cade speaking."

He listens intently for a moment, the bright playful look on his face, ceasing its existence. His brow furrows, his gaze meeting mine in silent communication, letting me know that something has come up.

"Of course, sir," He replies curtly, pushing himself off from our picnic blanket. He walks a few yards away, his voice quieting to where I can no longer make out his words.

Watching him, his back turned to me as he paces back and forth across, I let out a sigh of disappointment, and lie back on the blanket, my fingers outlining the impressions on my body that his had left.

Obviously, I understand. But that doesn't make it any less unfortunate.

He comes back after his hangs up the call, "I'm so sorry. I have to get to the agency."

"I figured," I reply, giving him a small supportive smile. "Some international crisis that needs the handsome, top-secret agent to swoop in and save the day?" I tease, picking up a strawberry from the picnic basket, and popping it into my mouth.

"You know it." He grins, tossing his shirt back on. "I'm just a regular Clark Kent." His voice oozes charm, the lopsided smile and crinkled eyes stripping away the professional exterior he'd been forced into moments before.

"I suppose our secret rendezvous will have to wait until the world is safe yet again?"

He chuckles, a warm sound that softens the disappointment in my chest. "I swear it won't be long, luciole." He says, leaning down to kiss my head.

"Promise you'll be back for dinner?" I ask, pushing out my bottom lip as he lifts me up and we begin walking to his car.

His fingers draw invisible lines across his chest, a silent promise hiding in his eyes, "Cross my heart."

CHAPTER TWENTY-SEVEN

Agent Holloway

I stand in the threshold of the director's office, a space that feels more like an expertly curated museum than a place of work. The door clicks shut behind me, sealing away the chaotic hum of headquarters, leaving only the subtle creak of leather as the director shifts in his seat.

"Ah, agent Holloway," He greets, his voice gravelly yet not unkind.

His eyes flick to the mirrored glass pane that separates us from the rest of the floor. "Emma's fiancé is stewing in interrogation. I want you in there asking the questions."

Nodding, I step further into the room, my boots sinking momentarily into the plush rug. It's a statement piece, just like everything else in here—the walls lined with awards and commendations, the shelves stocked with texts on criminal psychology and cold case files, each bound in dark leather that speaks of age and wear.

But it's the massive wooden globe in the corner that always commands attention.

It's an antique, rich lacquered wood with a glossy sheen that catches the light, and continents and oceans mapped out in exquisite detail.

He walks over to it, his fingers brushing over the equator before he opens it with a flourish to reveal its secret—a tabletop with a crystal decanter set and glasses.

"Care for a bourbon?" He offers, already reaching for the crystal with practiced ease. Sunlight dances across the facets of the decanter as he fills one glass, then another.

"Sure," I say, accepting the glass. The liquid inside is the color of burnished gold, catching the light as I hold it up slightly, the scent of charred oak rising to meet me.

"Neat okay?" He asks, as if there could be any other way.

I nod.

The bourbon slides down my throat effortlessly, leaving a pleasant heat behind. It's a temporary escape from the impending storm of interrogation awaiting me.

I set the empty glass back onto the world globe, the map blurring slightly through the crystal. "Thank you."

He grunts in acknowledgement, a gesture I've come to understand as his way of expressing approval. He straightens up his back and returns to the other side of his desk, settling back into the worn leather chair.

His fingers begin to drum a solemn tune on the desk, "Landry and I, we go back," He says. "Our kids, they shared classes, played on the same little league team." A sigh escapes him, and he leans back in his chair. "I never thought we'd be here, Cade. This whole mess—it's got me spinning."

I catch a glimpse of the man behind the badge, the friend mourning a loss, even as the gears of duty churn within him.

"I get it," I reply, the words resolute yet not void of empathy. "I'll get to the bottom of it. If he really was murdered, like we think, you can guarantee we'll find out."

"As we should, or we shouldn't be calling ourselves agents." He grumbles.

His gaze turns back to the glass of bourbon in his hands, the liquid moving gently as he rotates the glass. He takes a deep swig before setting it aside with a soft clink.

His eyes find mine, a steely determination flickering in them, "I want this son-of-a-bitch behind bars, Cade."

The door to the interrogation room clicks shut behind me. The young man before me, Benson, lounges in the hard metal chair with an air of casual defiance that doesn't quite reach his eyes. I can see the tightness in his jaw, the way his hands grip the table.

"Need anything before we start? Water, coffee?" I offer, knowing the small comforts won't be offered again.

"No," he snaps, his voice sharp like broken glass. "Do you know who I am? Who my fucking father is? Mayor Jonathan Hargrove. Which means this—" He waves a dismissive hand, "Is all bullshit."

I ignore the attempt at intimidation; it's a move I have seen played out too many times. "Was just making sure you're comfortable," I say cooly, pulling out the chair across from him and sitting down.

"Comfortable?" A sneer pulls at the corner of his mouth. "What part of me sitting here looking like a fool in this dump makes you think I would be comfortable?"

I lean forward, forearms on the table, locking eyes with him. "Did you know about Emma and her boss, Benson? That their...closeness might be the reason for her recent raise at work?"

His sneer vanishes as if slapped off his face, replaced by a flush of anger that creeps up his neck. "Lies," he spits out, each word laced with venom. "Emma wouldn't— She's loyal. And money? Please." He laughs, but it's hollow, lacking any real humor. "I can give her anything she needs. There's no way she'd betray me for some extra cash."

"Okay," I say, noting the brittle edge of desperation to his denial. "Just something we needed to clear up."

He slumps back, arms crossing defensively, but his arrogance has been punctured, leaving a quivering uncertainty that he tries to mask with bravado. "You're barking up the wrong tree, agent," He mutters, though, his voice is less sure, his earlier confidence seeping away like water through cracks.

I press a button on the remote, and the screen on the wall flickers to life. The grainy footage shows Carl's office suite, a place of leather and clad that reeks of money, even in its pixelated form. On the desk, amidst the clutter of a high-powered executive, two figures are in plain sight. Emma—her hair bouncing around her face as Carl—a middle-aged man with a belly that speaks of too many lunches in expensive restaurants—fucks her from behind, his hand entangled in her hair as he forces her to watch her discrepancies.

"Her motive," I say, my voice steady despite the turmoil that must be wreaking havoc in poor Benson's mind. "Carl has been blackmailing her. He recorded their encounters, and it's been going on for months—almost a year to be exact."

Benson's face drains of color, his eyes riveted to the damning evidence. The video continues playing, reinforcing the room's silence with its sordid spectacle.

"N-no," He stammers, a hand clawing at his tie as though it's stuck in his throat. "This—this can't b-be. Why? Why would she do this?"

"She killed him, Benson, didn't she?"

He shakes his head back and forth, "Emma isn't capable of murder. She loves all things—won't even squish a fly."

I wait, giving him the silence his pain deserves, watching as the man before me grapples with a truth that shatters the image of the woman he loves.

His eyes, wild with devastation, flicker to mine, searching perhaps for a sign of falsehood. Finding none, he rests his head in his hands and succumbs to a fit of silent tears. I turn off the screen. The sordid sight does not need to be replayed any further.

"I'm sorry you had to find out like this, Benson."

"No, you're not. No, the fuck you're not!" He yells, slamming his hands on the table.

"Thank you for your time. We'll be in touch if there are any more questions."

"Fuck you." He sneers, flipping his tie as he walks out.

My phone rings, "Cade speaking." I answer, pressing the phone to my ear.

"Agent Holloway," A woman's voice is on the other line, "It's Dr. Halsey from toxicology. We've completed the preliminary screenings on both men. As stated on the previous report, no drugs were present at the time of death."

"So, there was nothing at all?" My grip on the phone tightens, hope for an easy answer slipping away.

"Almost nothing. We found trace amounts of a substance we're having trouble identifying."

"Poison?" I question.

It's a possibility, but it's going to take additional tests, more research. It could be another week or two before we have something concrete."

"Understood," I reply, "Keep me updated, thanks."

I hang up and slowly walk over to the suspect board. The faces pinned across the cork stare back at me in silent accusation, their secrets locked behind lifeless eyes.

My fingers interlock behind my head as I lean back slightly, gazing at the constellation of connections, leads, and dead ends.

Emma's photo hangs there too, her innocence now tainted by the tape's revelations. Yet something doesn't fit; the puzzle remains incomplete, the image fragmented.

"Maybe we're chasing shadows," I murmur, the idea that we're pursuing phantoms, and concocting motives out of thin air, gnawing at me.

Is the answer really as complicated as it seems, or is it just being obscured by layers of unnecessary complexity?

"Any new leads?" Forester asks, popping up behind me.

He rubs at the stubble on his chin, a nervous tic I've come to recognize.

Snow shakes her head, pushing herself off the edge of her desk, strands of her blonde hair escaping the confines of her ponytail. "Town's still reeling from Landry's passing. Everyone's a suspect and no one is, all at once at this point."

I nod, my eyes fixed on the board. "We need to consider everyone linked to Landry and Carl. Anyone who might have wanted them gone."

"Speaking of having ties," Snow begins, shifting nervously from foot to foot, "That girl you've been seeing, her father was murdered a long time ago. He used to cater the police balls and parties hosted by the department."

"Yeah, I heard." My voice comes out flat, almost distant.

"Landry and Carl both dug into her father's murder, couldn't pin anything down though." She pauses, locking her gaze with mine, searching for a reaction. You think her mother could be involved? It's strange that she returned and now two of the investigators, who were looking into her husband's death, are dead as well."

"Doesn't add up," Forester interjects, "She was alibied out by half the speakeasy. I was there, remember? Saw her myself."

"Right," I reply, the corner of my mouth twitching involuntarily. "Alright, team," I sigh, clapping my hands together and glancing between my two colleagues. "Let's keep digging."

Forester grunts in agreement while Snow just nods, her eyes remaining on the board long after I've started to turn away.

This case—it's personal for all of us, in ways we never expected.

Agent Snow's shoulders slump as she concedes, the lines of her face softening into resignation. "You're right, it doesn't sound plausible," She admitted, and I could tell the dead ends were starting to weigh on her too. "Without anything new from toxicology or a fresh lead, we're just running in circles."

"Feels like we're chasing our own tails, I know," I reply, the weariness in my voice matching hers, as I rub at the tension knotting my neck.

I glance at the wall clock—it shows that not only had the sun set, but that we've also overstayed our welcome in the now-silent bureau. "It's getting late," I announce, "Let's call it a night. This place closed almost an hour go."

"Hey, Cade," Forester calls out as we descend down the front steps, "You ready for that drink now? My treat."

"Can't tonight," I reply, giving him a half-smile. "Got dinner plans with Tia."

"Ah," He says, an understanding nod accompanying his words. "Say no more, my friend."

"Typical, Forrester," Snow chimes in mockingly from beside us, her arms crossed over her chest. "Never even thought about inviting me, did you, asshole?"

"How about we all grab a bite this weekend?" I throw out.

"Sounds like a plan to me," Forester says.

Snow pretends to check the calendar on her phone before laughing and saying, "I'm here for it."

With a final wave, we say our farewells and I head to my car. My mind's a jumbled mess from the case, I can't barely think straight, and as I slide behind the wheel, I allow myself a moment of silence, sinking into the soft leather seat.

That's when it dawns on me, hitting me like a punch to the gut—the surveillance footage from the coffee shop's security camera, the day Carl died.

Tia had been there that day. She spoke to Emma, bought her coffee...could Snow be right about a connection, but be placing blame on the wrong Williams woman?

Tia had also brought lunch over to the Sheriff's office, merely hours before his unexpected demise.

My grip tightens on the steering wheel, the leather groaning under the strain.

It's ludicrous, the thought of her being involved, isn't it?

I try to shake it off, to dispel the absurdity clouding my judgment. She's not capable of this. She's not a murderer.

But doubt, once planted, is a weed that doesn't willingly retreat, and it's clawing its way deeper into my consciousness with every block I put between me and the agency.

"Damn it," I mutter.

Could Tia really be tied to all of this?

Would those same hands that comforted, that cooked dinners, and held mine in the quiet moments, be capable of—No, there must be a different explanation. There always is. But what if—No, I can't entertain those thoughts. Pull yourself together, Cade. You're stronger than this.

The amber lights above me flicker, creating long shadows that sway across my car's dashboard.

I've got to see her, look into her eyes, and find the truth there. Because the alternative—that's a possibility my heart refuses to entertain.

CHAPTER TWENTY-EIGHT

Jia

We're on our way to the FBI agency, and the notion feels surreal—a thick fog of disbelief clings to my thoughts as I steal a glance at my mother sitting beside me. Her eyes are fixed on the road ahead, hands gripping the steering wheel as if it's a lifeline. She hasn't said much, but the tension in her jaw speaks volumes.

We're being questioned today, about people we know, about things that have happened. It's like we've been sucked into some bizarre crime drama, only there's no screen to separate us from the reality of our predicament.

"Remember what Cade said," I murmur, trying to convince myself as much as her. "It's just routine. They're talking to everyone connected to Sheriff Landry and Carl."

"Of course, sugar," She replies, breaking her piercing stare from the road just long enough to give me a tight smile.

Her southern accent adds a touch of warmth to her words, but it doesn't fool me. I can hear the worry bubbling beneath the surface.

"Just answer their questions and don't volunteer anything else," She continues, twisting her hands together in her lap.

Even though Cade's assurance does little to settle the nerves dancing beneath my skin, I cling to it anyway.

The sheriff and Carl were well-known figures in town, their presence as constant as the tide.

It shouldn't surprise me that their sudden, inexplicable disappearance was shaking everything up, even in such a busy city.

I turn to watch the scenery blur past the window, buildings and trees melding into streaks of color as we approach our destination. The FBI agency looms ahead, and I can almost hear the soft reassurance of Cade's voice in my head, telling me there's nothing to worry about.

But it's hard to keep the skepticism at bay, hard not to feel like we're two moths being drawn unwittingly toward a flame that promises warmth but delivers destruction.

Glancing sideways, I catch my mother's gaze, her eyes are rimmed with a fatigue that goes deeper than sleeplessness.

It's been there since we huddled together in the restaurant cooler, our breaths fogging the cold air as secrets unspooled between us. She hasn't mentioned that night again.

Neither have I.

I know she suspects the truth about me, about what happened to them. But silence has become our fragile truce.

No new victims have surfaced—yet—a fact that does nothing to ease the coil of anxiety tightening within me.

Allen is still out there, and my chances to get closer to him have been thwarted at every turn. When he did visit the restaurant, Cade was always there, an unwitting chaperone, or the timing was just off.

"Momma," I start, fighting back the queasiness that threatens to betray my calm exterior. "What do you feel like doing after all this is over?" I force my lips into the shape of a smile, practiced and perfect.

My manager can handle the evening rush, so tonight, I'm free. Free to pretend that life is normal, even just for a few hours.

She turns to me, the lines around her eyes deepening as she attempts a smile of her own. "Let's not plan too far ahead, sugar. Let's just get through this first."

"Of course," I reply, nodding. "But we *are* innocent, and we've got nothing to hide, so I'm sure it will be over in no time."

The lie tastes bitter on my tongue.

We're both playing our parts in this twisted performance, aren't we?

Pretending that everything is fine, that we're just two ordinary women on their way to a routine meeting, and not enmeshed in a web of deception and death.

The security gates part for us, and we are led through the process with clinical detachment. The corridors we walk down are lacking in any personal touches, smelling only of harsh industrial cleaner and something else.

Fear?

Anticipation?

It lingers in the air, coating the walls like a sticky residue.

We reach a fork in the pathway, and an agent gestures for my mother to follow him to the left. Our eyes meet, a temporary connection before she's swallowed by the branching hallway.

My escort leads me right, towards my own private interrogation, and I'm shown into a room that feels both claustrophobic and bare, with a table, two chairs, and a mirror that doesn't fool anyone.

I sit on the hard metal chair, its surface cold and unforgiving against the fabric of my jeans.

This is utter nonsense. I shouldn't even be here.

Another lie.

My foot begins to tap, the sound echoing in the hollow room. With every second that ticks by, my frustration mounts.

How long will they keep me waiting? Do they expect me to sweat, to squirm? If so, they'll be disappointed.

Underneath the irritation, though, there's a thread of re-lief—Cade's absence means time to strategize.

Allen, that beguiling figure who haunts the edges of my life, floats through my thoughts. Without the ever-present buffer of Cade's company, perhaps tonight I can finally construct a path closer to him.

But how?

I shake my head subtly, as if to dispel the thoughts.

First things first, I need to get through this charade. The tapping of my shoe grows more insistent, a metronome to the racing of my heart. I fold my hands in my lap, schooling my features into a mask of composed indifference.

They think they can rattle me? Let them try.

The door swings open with a resolute creak, and Cade enters, his presence filling the sterile space. The stack of paperwork he clutches feels like a physical weight from across the table.

Among the files, I spot the familiar one, a dossier that has haunted my family for years—my father's case.

"Good afternoon, Ms., Williams," He greets me, but the formality in his tone strips any warmth from the words.

He takes a seat opposite me, the chair scraping against the floor. His movements are precise as he arranges the papers be-fore him, a ritual of preparation.

"Before we begin," He says, his voice steady, "You have the right to remain silent. Anything you say can and will be used against you in a court of law. You have the right to an attorney—" The Miranda rights, recited as if they're a lullaby and not the precursor to an interrogation.

"Understood," I reply, my voice betraying none of the turmoil that churns inside me.

"Let's start with the basics," He continues, unfazed by the formalities. "Full name?"

It's kind of hot seeing him thrive in his own familiar territory.

"Tianna Marie Williams."

"Occupation?"

"Owner and head chef at Le Rêve Brisé."

"Phone number?"

I rattle off the digits, each one echoing slightly in the room.

"Home address?"

"2140 River Rd," I answer with ease.

He nods, making notes, then looks up again, locking eyes with me. We've moved beyond the preliminaries now; this is where the real dance begins.

"Can you tell me where you were on the night of September 3rd?" Cade's gaze is unyielding.

"Of course," I say with a confidence I do not feel. "I was at the restaurant, overseeing the dinner rush. We had a full house that night."

My exterior remains calm, but my heart races as I feed him the alibi I've rehearsed countless times in my mind. With every word, I'm acutely aware of the thin ice beneath my feet.

"Anyone who can corroborate your whereabouts?"

"Several staff members. And customers. It was a busy night, like I said." The words coat my tongue like honey, sweet but dangerous.

Cade leans back, considering my response, his eyes never leaving mine. My pulse throbs in my ears, a drumbeat of anxiety.

Does he detect the falsehoods knotted into my truth?

"Thank you, Tia." He finally says, setting down the folder in his hand. "Excuse me for a moment."

I draw in a slow breath, steadying myself. This is just the beginning.

Cade's footsteps recede, the click of the door signaling his brief departure. I pinch the bridge of my nose, trying to massage away the tension that has taken up residence there.

He returns promptly, his presence filling the room with an intensity that makes my skin prickle. He moves to the cameras mounted on the wall, fingers slyly flicking switches, and the red recording lights blink out one by one.

Cuffs glint in his hand as he returns to the table, threading them through the metal bar with an ominous clink.

"Wait—what are you doing?" I ask, my voice sharper than I intend.

"Additional questions, luciole," He says simply, securing the cuffs around my wrists with a firmness that sends an unexpected surge of heat through me. "Procedure."

I'm cuffed to the table, a captive audience to whatever comes next.

My mind races—this isn't standard protocol, is it?

But despite the uncertainty, something about the situation ignites a strange excitement within me.

Cade begins to pace around the small room, his arms crossed over his chest. His gaze is a like a physical touch, tracing the contours of my face, the line of my shoulders. He rounds the corner of the table for the third time, and when he speaks, his voice is low, authoritative.

"You've been a bad girl, luciole. And you know what happens to bad girls, don't you?"

I swallow hard, my mouth suddenly dry, my heart pounding an erratic rhythm against my ribcage as I shake my head in response.

"They need to be punished." He growls.

This is dangerous territory, yet I can't deny the allure, the dark thrill that unfurls within me.

"Is that so?" I manage, injecting a note of defiance into my reply, even as I feel my cheeks flush.

The cold metal of the handcuffs bite into my wrists, but the bite is nothing compared to the shockwave that rips through me as I register Cade's intentions.

With every predatory circle he makes around the table, my body tenses, the air in the room seeming to thin and my pulse quickens.

"Mhmm." He hums.

"And what exactly are you going to do about it?" I ask, my lips parting to draw in a shaky breath, and I find myself licking them, watching his reaction with bated anticipation.

Cade stopped pacing, and he leans forward, elbows braced on the table, close enough for me to feel his breath fan across my face.

"We're going to play a little game," He mewls, and I can almost taste the words as they fall from his lips. "Every time you answer one of my questions," He continues, "I'll grant you a touch. Wherever you want." His gaze holds mine captive, intense and unshakeable. "But our little convergence ends with the timer. Then it's back to business."

His control over the situation is intoxicating—maddening. I nearly leap at the offer, my body screaming yes before my mind can even catch up.

"Fine," I manage to say through clenched teeth, the word barely more than a whisper, yet it blasts through the tension-filled room like a starting pistol at the beginning of a race.

Cade straightens, his expression unreadable as he fetches a small digital timer from his pocket and places it on the table where I can see the red digits blinking to life.

A silent countdown begins, and with it, the realization that perhaps this game has higher stakes than anything I've ever played before.

"Did you have anything to do with the murders?" His voice is low, a rumble that vibrates through the sterile air of the interrogation room.

I draw in a sharp breath, feeling his eyes bore into me as if he could peel away layers of my soul.

"No," I exhale, my gaze dropping to the prominent bulge straining against the fabric of his slacks.

"Touch me. Here," I point, emboldened by the lust that has all my sense of reason teetering on the edge of oblivion.

Cade doesn't hesitate. His large hand reaches for me, and even through the denim barrier of my jeans, his touch sends jolts of electricity straight to my core. He begins to rub, slow lazy circles, that have my hips curving towards him, seeking more of that sweet friction.

The pressure of his fingers builds, turning my rigid posture into a pliant arch of surrender. His touch is exactly where I want it, yet not enough to fully sate the craving that has captured my senses.

"Time's almost up," He grumbles, his voice laced with a satisfaction as intoxicating as the finest bourbon.

His breath against my ear is a sweet torment. It's a battle of wills, and I'm losing, crumbling under his touch like an ancient ruin.

But isn't that what this game is all about? The crumbling, the ruin, the inevitable fall?

I can't bring myself to care either way, because in this moment, under Cade's commanding touch, I am both lost and found and there's no other place I'd rather be.

CHAPTER TWENTY-NINE

Agent Holloway

I slam my hand down on the table next to Tia's face, the sharp smack echoing off the empty walls.

Bent over the cold surface, her eyes flash a mix of fear and something darker, more inviting.

"Why were you at that coffee shop the same day Emma was there—the day Carl died?" My voice is a low growl, demanding an answer.

Tia's body jolts, a startled gasp slipping from her lips. But the fear in her eyes morphs quickly into a glinting arousal, her chest heaving against the tabletop. I watch, almost hypnotized, as she presses her thighs tightly together, the subtle shift of her hips betraying the intensity of her need.

The insatiable desire within her pulsates relentlessly, practically radiating off her body and engulfing me in a carnal heat that leaves a trail of sweat on my skin.

I watch her chest rise and fall, her breaths uneven but her voice steady as she finally answers, "It's the only coffee shop I go to, Cade."

I can't ignore the truth in her words, as they hang in the air between us. Memories of the empty latte cups strewn across the floor of her car come flooding back, a clear confirmation of what she is saying.

"Where?" The single word comes out more like a snarl than a question as I try to navigate through the fog of lust clouding my judgment.

I'm so fucking turned on right now, my dick feels like it's going to rip through my pants.

She straightens up slowly, her movements serpentine and slightly provocative. Emerald eyes lock onto mine and her lips part.

"Kiss me," Tia demands, her voice a mixture of satin and steel.

For a moment, I stand motionless, caught in the tempest of her gaze. Then, I press myself against her delicious ass, enjoying the way her curves feel against me before my hand reaches around her, grabbing her chin. My brow lifts as I challenge her silently with a smirk, tipping her face up to meet mine.

Our lips meet, and it feels like an apocalypse, the end of everything I thought I knew. Her mouth is a cataclysmic event, obliterating every shred of self-control I possess. My hands find her waist, pulling her closer, needing to feel the heat of her body against mine to anchor me in this harrowing storm of pleasure.

I wrench myself away to catch my breath, my head reeling from the high of her taste. Her lips are slightly swollen from our kiss, her cheeks flushed a delicate shade of rose.

For a heartbeat or two, I forget why we're here, what questions I still need answers to. All that exists in this moment is Tia and the undeniable connection that pulls taut between us, threatening to snap and unravel us both.

I clear my throat, removing my body from her, though it feels like tearing away a second skin, "And the sheriff's office? Why were you there?"

Tia repositions herself so she can look at me, "Visiting an old family friend," She says, as if discussing the weather. "Allie and I grew up together, long before Tom became the sheriff."

I raise an eyebrow, skeptical, but her story checks out in my head. There's an honesty in her eyes that I can't ignore, a vulnerability that strips away the barriers between us like tearing through cobwebs.

I let out a sigh, running my hand through my hair.

"Agent Holloway," Tia's voice dips into a sultry tone that sends shivers down my spine. She meets my gaze, those green eyes like emerald fires, licking her full lips in a way that damn near derails my train of thought. "On your knees."

I blink, once, twice, her words ricocheting in my skull.

For a moment, I'm stunned into silence, incapable of doing anything other than staring at her with wide eyes. The soft command was so unexpected, it takes me several heartbeats to comprehend what she wants me to do. But when it does sinks in, a low chuckle rumbles in my chest.

"You're full of surprises, aren't you?" I manage to say, keeping my voice steady despite the fluttering in my stomach.

She steps back just enough, offering me space to move between her and the table. With hands that betray none of my inner turmoil, I slide her pants and pink lace thong down her toned legs, revealing the glistening folds of her arousal.

"Mon dieu—" The words slip from my mouth in reverence. "You look so delicious, luciole."

Tia tilts her head back, a smirk playing on her lips. "That was the point," She teases, her voice a caress all by itself. "Now, lick."

I don't need to be told twice. Diving in, I bury my face between her thighs, tasting her, the sweetest nectar I've ever known.

The whimper she releases when my tongue touches her core is a symphony to my ears, and I delve deeper into her, exploring the contours of her intimate flesh like a map leading me straight to heaven.

I pull back, the taste of her still lingering, a mix of sweetness and sin that's branded itself onto my tongue. Her breath is ragged, matching the thunderous beat of my own heart. I can't hold back any longer—not with her looking like a deity I'd gladly spend a fucking eternity on my knees for.

"More, Holloway," She breathes out.

"Ah, ah, ah." I tsk, wiping my mouth with the back of my hand. "Patience, luciole."

There's a flash of annoyance in her eyes, quickly replaced by heavy-lidded desire as I run my thumb over the sensitive bundle of nerves of her clit. Her hips buck against my hand, a choked sound escaping her as I press a little harder. "Cade," She pleads this time, her voice a ragged whisper of need.

"Good girl. Beg for me," I demand.

"Cade, please," The word trembles from her lips along with a shuddering breath.

A slow, roguish grin spreads across my face at her submission. "There it is," I coo, my voice low and thick with desire.

My slacks hit the ground with a soft thud, leaving nothing between us but the anticipatory air of desire and bare flesh.

My cock, hard and insistent, demands her attention. "Tell me," I say, stroking her entrance with the tip, "Do you want me?"

"Yes," She gasps. the desperation clear in her green depths, making my heart pump faster.

"Say it," I growl, teasing her further until she's writhing beneath me.

The sight of watching her squirm is absolutely mind blowing.

"Please, Cade." Her voice is thick with desire. "I—I want you to fuck me."

I smile in triumph, and with a rough jerk of my hand, I arch her back further, creating the perfect angle, aligning myself at her entrance.

The tip of my cock pushes past her entrance, stretching her slowly and deliciously.

"Fuck, you feel so good," I hiss, picking up my pace.

The rhythm we create is almost savage, a wild expression of our intense desire for one another that threatens to consume us both.

My hands roam over her, possessive and hungry, as I watch myself disappear and reappear between the tight clasp of her pussy. The sight is like a drug, intoxicating and addictive, driving me to thrust harder, deeper—awakening the beast within me.

Beads of sweat trail down my brow, dripping onto her flushed skin. Her wrists tug at the cuffs, trying desperately to find purchase on the slick surface of the interrogation table as I plunge inside of her over and over, each thrust more powerful than the last.

Her breathy moans have me on the cusp of cloud nine—my head spinning with pleasure, my senses heightened, devouring every detail of this moment.

"I—Cade," She moans, her voice hitching when I hit just the right spot.

There's a wild look in her eyes that tells me she's close. Her lips part as we move in unison, our bodies colliding and our ragged breaths intermingling.

With one hand I trace the curve of her hip, the dip of her waist before sliding around to press against the throbbing bundle of nerves hidden between her legs.

The surprised gasp she lets out is nearly my undoing, and I growl low in my throat. Her head falls back, my hand no longer tangled in her hair so she can move it freely now.

My fingers find their rhythm against her, pushing her higher, closer to the edge. She's whimpering now, her body trembling under mine with every thrust and stroke, her responses driving me wild.

I can feel my own climax surging to the surface and when she cries my name and announces her release, I shudder violently, surrendering to the powerful waves of ecstasy that crash over me in synchrony with hers.

As the ripples of pleasure fade, I collapse over her, still buried inside her. I'm left breathless, my heart pounding in my chest like a drum. "Fuck," I rasp, pressing my lips to the damp skin of her neck.

She hums in response, her body still quivering beneath me.

A few moments pass before she speaks again.

"Am I free to go, agent?" Tia breathes out, the ghost of a smirk touching her lips.

"For now," I reply, my voice still husky.

But despite the satiation, a nagging suspicion lingers—that she knows more than she's saying. Though, that could just be my own paranoia.

With a shake of my head, I discard the thought for the moment and reach for her wrists, unlocking the cuffs. I grab the box of tissues on the metal table, cleaning us both with a care that belies the roughness of moments before.

Leading her through the corridor, we reach the lobby where her mother waits. Concern flickers across the older woman's face, but it's not exactly like we can tell her what took so long, so I give her a reassuring nod.

"See you tomorrow?" I ask Tia, leaning against the wall.

Tia raises an eyebrow at my query, a smirk curving her lips, "I'm at the restaurant until seven, but you can pick me up there."

"Thank you, ladies, for coming in today. I apologize for any inconvenience but we're trying to do everything we can to solve this case." I nod.

"Oh, it was my pleasure, Agent." Tia responds, her voice sultry, whilst looking over her shoulder at me as she walks away.

It's a struggle to keep my eyes focused on her face instead of letting them wander lower, but I manage.

Just.

As I watch her leave, her hips sway enticingly with each step, and a mix of professional necessity and personal desire fights for dominance within me.

I know that mixing personal involvement with a case can lead to dangerous compromises, but with Tia, the lines are already blurred beyond recognition.

And now, it's too late for an easy escape because I'm already entangled—a bug caught in a web of lust and law.

CHAPTER THIRTY

Agent Holloway

The scratch of my pen halts mid-sentence, a frown creasing my brow as I lean back in my weathered chair.

My home office, usually a sanctuary of solace and concentration, feels unusually oppressive tonight. The case file for Tia's father lies open before me on the desk, a jigsaw of statements and reports that just don't fit together. I thumb through the pages once more, eyes narrowing at the scrawled notes from the sheriff and his deputies.

As I trace a finger along the timeline of events, I can't help but mutter to myself, sensing that something is not quite right.

The differences may seem small and easily dismissed as human error, but they still feel like jagged edges cutting into my skin, like a serrated knife slicing through a ripe tomato.

I pull out the autopsy summary and lay it flat, the starkness of black ink on white paper declaring facts that should be irrefutable.

Wait.

There were two autopsy reports?

I scan the document again, confirming what I just read, but where is the first one?

The second autopsy report is accounted for, clinical, precise, and in my hand. The other?

Gone.

"Surely even without today's technology—" I start, my voice trailing away into silence.

My gaze flits around the disorganized desk, its surface covered in an array of scattered papers that seem to have been swept up by an invisible tornado.

Could it have been misplaced?

There shouldn't have been this many mistakes, not unless...

"Unless someone wanted them there," I whisper, a chill skittering down my spine.

I push myself up from the desk, the wheels of the chair squeaking a protest. The case file stares up at me, its secrets cloaked in half-truths and vanished evidence.

The realization hits me like a ton of bricks, and I know that this rabbit hole goes far deeper than I had ever anticipated.

I flick open the laptop, its screen casting a pale glow in the dimness of my office. The keys clack under my fingers as I navigate through digital archives, pulling up dusty pages of newsprint now converted into pixels and bytes. There it is, an old article dated back to the time of Tia's father's murder, with a photograph of a younger Tia, her eyes haunted beyond her years.

"Even if I remembered, no one would believe me," the caption quotes from her interview.

The article explains how her memories were supposedly repressed due to the traumatic experience of watching her father's murder.

However, I can't fully believe that statement. I've spent time with children who have truly lost themselves after a traumatic experience; they have this hollow look in their eyes, as if they are constantly searching for something just beyond their grasp.

Tia's look is different; it's as if she held a secret too heavy for her young shoulders, one that she couldn't fully comprehend, let alone share.

Every time we've discussed her father, her eyes flicker with an undefined apprehension, but not the vacant stare of forgotten pain.

Shifting in my seat, I scroll to another article—a detailed account from the sheriff and his deputies. They claim to have been close by when the gunshot shattered the evening calm, followed by the piercing scream of a child. Mr. Williams was found moments later, according to their timeline, bleeding out from a fatal chest wound.

I zoom in on the text, where the sheriff recounts his desperate attempts at life-saving measures. *"Time of death approximately thirty to forty minutes after the shot,"* The coroner estimated.

My brow furrows.

If Mr. Williams survived that long, how swift were these officers really in responding to his plight?

Another click brings up Allen's report, the outlier. He states Tia wasn't there when they arrived—she'd run for help. Yet the sheriff's statement, backed by two other deputies, claims both Tia and her mother were at the scene, and frantic calls to emergency services were already underway.

"Which is it?" I mumble, rubbing the stubble on my chin in thought.

Two reports, two autopsies—one missing—and now, two different versions of a little girl's worst nightmare.

I lean back, the chair creaking under the shift of weight as my mind spins with the contradictions.

It's clear that the pieces aren't fitting together, and I can't shake the feeling that Tia, despite her silence, holds the keystone.

A realization slams into me like a rogue wave, leaving my thoughts drenched in cold suspicion.

Cover-up?

It's as if the word itself injects a dose of adrenaline straight into my veins. The reports, the discrepancies—they aren't just mistakes; they're intentional, a smokescreen to mask a deeper truth. Mr. Williams' murder—there's more to it, I'm sure now.

Staring at the faces of the officers in the fading newspaper print, a chilling thought creeps in. The only ones who truly knew what happened that night are being picked off one by one, all after Tia's return to New Orleans.

My contemplation is shattered by the sharp rap of knuckles against the front door. I jump, causing the papers resting on my lap to scatter like a flock of startled birds as I stand up to answer the door.

I glance at the clock—she's here.

"Hey," greets Tia, as she steps through the threshold as places a kiss on my cheek.

"Sorry about the mess," I mutter, gesturing to chaos I normally would call a living room.

"Oh, Please, Cade, don't even worry about it," She dismisses with a casual wave of her hand, her eyes reflecting understanding rather than judgement. "I know you have a lot on your plate. Besides if I was worried about something so trivial such as a messy home, if I were you, I wouldn't want to date me." She laughs.

"Speaking of plates." I let out a panicked smile, trying to shift gears from detective to dinner host.

I lead her toward the kitchen where the scent of sizzling meat fills the small space, cursing myself in my head.

One job, Cade. You had one job.

"Smells good in here." Tia says, sniffing the air. "What did you make?"

"Hotdogs."

"Hotdogs?" She asks, a playful quirk to her brow.

"New York staple," I say, almost apologetically.

I didn't exactly go gourmet, but given the lack of my culinary skills, it's a small victory to present anything semi-homemade at all.

The premade salad mix sits alongside the baked beans, a humble attempt at a well-rounded meal. I check the air fryer, relieved to find the fries not yet turned to charcoal.

Rubbing the back of my neck, I give her an awkward grin, embarrassment creeping in, "I know it's not five-star dinner, but I hope you'll consider it at least a three-star effort."

Laughter spills from her, genuine and unforced, filling the room and easing the tension coiled within me. She stands, strides toward me with grace, and wraps her arms around my neck. Her kiss is reassuring, affirming.

"I love hotdogs," She whispers against my lips, "And I can't wait to eat."

CHAPTER THIRTY-ONE

Tia

The chill of the hardwood floor seeps into the soles of my feet as I gingerly peel back the covers, careful not to disturb the warm cocoon where Cade slumbers beside me. Night has cloaked his room in near obscurity, save for a sliver of moonlight that sneaks through the gap in the curtains.

The need is pressing; I have to pee.

I slide out of bed, my body heavy with the reluctance of interrupted sleep, and pad silently toward the door. It creaks open with the faintest protest, and I wince, holding my breath, listening for any shift from Cade that might indicate I've woken him. Nothing but the steady rhythm of his breathing reassures me, and I step out into the hallway.

It's completely dark.

I shuffle forward, arms outstretched, seeking the familiar contours of the wall to guide me. My hip bumps against the corner of a side table, eliciting a soft thud that quickens my heartbeat with the fear of discovery. But no sound comes from the bedroom behind me—Cade sleeps on.

Counting steps becomes a silent litany in my head, a mantra to navigate this alien terrain. One, two, left foot, right foot. The wall under my fingertips is cool, unyielding. I reach the second door—or what I think is the second door—and hesitate, my mind snagged on the uncertainty of direction.

Is it the one to the right or to the left?

I bite my lip, the pressure in my bladder mounting, making it hard to concentrate.

I lean slightly to the left, then right, straining my ears for any clue that might steer me correctly. The house remains silent, indifferent to my dilemma. With a resigned sigh, I edge toward the left, hoping memory serves me right.

My fingers fumble along the wall for the doorknob, every nerve ending alight with the urgency of my predicament and the fear of being wrong.

My hand skims the wall, seeking the familiar plastic rectangle of salvation—a light switch. The small click under my fingertips breaks the stillness as I flip it on, and the room floods with an invasive brightness that makes me flinch. Blinking away the spots in my vision, I take in my surroundings, confusion quickly replacing relief.

This isn't a bathroom.

It's Cade's office, which is laid out like the guts of some police procedural drama. My gaze sweeps over the suspect board clinging to the wall next to his desk; it bristles with photographs and strings like a cobweb holding memories instead of prey. And on the whiteboard at the back, names and places are scrawled in a frenzy of dry-erase marker, each one shouting its significance from the wall.

I edge closer to his desk, where papers lie scattered, my fingers hover before descending upon the documents, tracing the edges of my father's life spelled out in ink.

His name, his records—it's all here, laid bare.

Why the hell does Cade have these?

They interviewed everyone connected to the sheriff and Carl, sure, but my father's case? A chill races up my spine, and a sour taste coats my tongue.

Oh shit!

Could Cade be onto me?

Panic crawls up my throat, clawing for release, but I swallow it down. If Cade is suspicious, what does that mean for me? For us?

My pulse throbs in my ears, a drumbeat of dread that threatens to consume me. My eyes dart across the room, searching for answers in the chaos of clues pinned and written on every surface.

I have to get back to bed. I have to pretend that none of this exists. But as I turn to leave, the questions remain, festering like a wound. Why does Cade have my father's files? What does he suspect? Or worse—what does he know?

I shut off the light with a flick of my trembling hand and spin on my heel, eager to escape the room. But in my haste, my shoulder brushes against something metallic—a trophy or a paperweight, maybe—and it topples with a damning clang that shatters the silence.

"Damn," I hiss under my breath, frozen for a heartbeat, listening to the echo of my mistake.

The next instant is a blur of motion and sound. Cade comes flying out of the bedroom like a specter born of shadows and adrenaline, his gun poised in a practiced grip that speaks volumes of his training. He's in straight agent mode—every inch of him alert, ready for confrontation.

"Jesus, Tia! Are you okay?" He asks, lowering his weapon, his voice a mix of concern and relief when he sees it's just me.

I force a laugh, though it feels brittle in my throat.

"Yeah, just a clumsy moment. I thought this was the bathroom. I'm super sorry," I say, trying to keep my voice light.

"You never have to apologize to me," He says earnestly. "This is your home too."

He blushes then, the tan of his skin not quite concealing the red hue that spreads across his cheeks. Stammering slightly, he adds, "That is if you want that. We're not officially anything, I know—not like boyfriend and girlfriend, I mean."

His awkwardness is endearing, a stark contrast to the steely agent who had just appeared, gun in hand. It's a glimpse of the man beneath the badge, the one who might just care more about me than the case.

"Thank you." I whisper, tamping down the panic still clawing at my insides. "I do still need to pee though.

He laughs, "Right there." He says, pushing the real bathroom door open with his foot.

I relieve myself and find him still waiting in the hall.

"Couldn't leave a lady in destress unescorted in a strange house again," He says, offering me his arm after he tucks the gun away.

"Why thank you, kind sir." I joke, curtseying in my babydoll then taking his bicep.

The warmth of his skin seeps into my palms as I embrace him, the earlier panic melting away under the soft glow of his eyes. "So, you wanting to make this thing with us official?" I tease.

He tenses, like a deer caught in headlights, his gaze flickering left and right, searching for words or perhaps an escape route.

However, true to his nature, Cade begins an impromptu monologue.

"Did you know that some animals," He begins, voice hitching slightly, "They live alone, isolated, until they find their mate. And sometimes...just sometimes, from that very first encounter, they know that they're meant to be together."

My heart swells, and I giggle, more at the earnestness in his voice than his attempt at awkward, romantic zoology.

"I—I guess what I'm trying to say," He continues, stuttering almost every syllable.

Leaning in, I press my finger to his lips, hushing his nervous ramble.

"I wouldn't mind at all—being your mate."

A sound akin to a joyous yip escapes him, and before I can blink, I'm swept up in his arms, laughter bubbling out of me as he tosses me onto the bed, my giggles a chorus in the night's silence. Then he's there, sliding behind me, pulling me into the sanctuary of his embrace.

"I'm one happy man, luciole." He murmurs, the term of endearment tickling my neck as he nuzzles into me.

"Good." I smile.

"Goodnight." His lips press into the top of my head.

"Goodnight, Cade."

The night wraps around us, a cocoon of shared warmth, and for a moment, with his chest rising and falling against my back, the darkness doesn't feel so heavy, and the secrets I keep are just shadows waiting for the dawn.

The cadence of Cade's snores is my signal that he is asleep. I ease out from the warmth of his embrace, the cool air of the room clinging to my skin as I make my way back to the door. My fingers curl around the handle, turning it with painstaking slowness until I'm out in the hallway.

Barefoot and heart thudding, I navigate the familiar path back to his office. The soft carpet muffles my steps, and I send a silent prayer to remain unnoticed.

Once inside, I close the door with a click softer than a whisper, thumbing the light switch and wincing as the sudden brightness assaults my eyes.

With my vision adjusted, I'm back at his desk, the chaos of papers splayed before me. My fingertips dance over them, and the memories surge, unbidden, a tide of anguish washing over me. I see my father's face, hear his laughter, all of it cut short by a meaningless that still resides in my dreams, every single night.

Tears, traitors to my resolve, spill over, carving wet trails down my cheeks. I swipe at them impatiently, my attention snagging on a sticky note buried beneath case reports and crime scene photos.

It's an innocuous square of yellow, but the words scrawled across it strike like a viper's bite: *Tia motive?*

My breath hitches.

Tom and Carl's names are there too.

A sickening realization dawns on me—Cade is close, so perilously close to unearthing truths I've buried so deep.

I press the heel of my hand against my sternum, willing my heartbeat to slow, to silence its frantic drumming.

Could he have shared his suspicions?

Panic flutters within me.

I fold the sticky note, tucking it into the pocket of my shorts. Tomorrow, I'll confront him. His response...Well, it will determine everything.

My fingers find their way to the doorknob, but as I turn it and inch the door open, the hinges give a treacherous screeching sound. I freeze, but it's too late—Cade is already there, filling the doorway with his broad frame.

His brows are knotted together, the lines on his forehead deepening. "Tia, what are you doing?" His voice is groggy.

I don't think.

I can't think.

My hand snaps inside my pocket and back out again, thrusting the sticky note at him as if it's evidence in a trial where I'm both judge and defendant. "Is this why, Cade? Is this why you've let me into your life?"

He looks down at the paper, confusion clouding his eyes before realization dawns. The paper trembles slightly in his grasp. "You think—Tia, no."

"Then tell me," I demand, my voice cracking. "Is it just you, or does everyone at the agency see me as a murderer?"

Cade's hands shoot up, his mouth working wordlessly for a moment. He looks so lost, so unlike the confident agent who swore his home was mine.

"I—I was just—" He shakes his head, struggling to form a coherent sentence.

"Because earlier," I cut in, the sour taste of betrayal burning my throat, "Earlier you were talking about being together, about us being official." Each word seems to fall in a void of silence between us. "I saw my father's name," I continue, my voice barely above a whisper now, "It was on one of the files on your desk. I noticed it earlier and thought maybe there was something here that could point to his killer, so I came back."

Cade lowers his hands, and his eyes meet mine, filled with a sincerity that makes my heart ache. "Tia, I—" He hesitates, and I see the conflict there, in his eyes—the battle between the man who cares for me, and the agent trained to suspect everyone.

"Please," I whisper, the single word a plea for truth, for reassurance, for anything that might bridge the chasm of mistrust suddenly yawning wide open between us. "Say something. Anything. Do you really think I'm involved in these men's murder?"

I know I am.

"Listen, Tia"," His voice is a muffled buzz in my ears, his words attempting to stitch the rift that's tearing open inside me. "It's procedure. We look at every angle but—"

"So that's a yes."

Cade's arms envelop me in a desperate embrace, his apology a hot breath against my temple. "I never wanted you to find this...It was just a momentary thought, I swear."

But his assurances are glass fragments, sharp and fragile, breaking under the weight of everything unspoken.

Instinctively, my fingers entwine behind his neck, my touch feigning tenderness even as my heart calcifies into something cold, something hard.

There, within arm's reach, sits the geological treasures of his hobby perch on a shelf. My hand snakes out, the largest rock's jagged surface biting into my palm.

With a ferocity born from fear and fury, the rock meets flesh and bone with a sickening crunch. Cade's body crumples to the floor, his bulk hitting the ground with a thud that reverberates through the silent house.

"God, Cade," I whisper to the stillness, my voice fractured. "I didn't want it to come to this."

I shove my arms under his shoulders, hauling him with a grunt of exertion. His head lolls back, a small trickle of blood seeping from the wound.

I rip my shirt off and press it against his head. I'm half dragging, half carrying him, each step a herculean effort as we leave the sanctuary of his office for the anonymity of the hall.

The descent down the stairs is a clumsy dance of gravity and adrenaline. I lean into the pain that buds in my muscles, karma's punishment for the violence I've wrought.

Each stair conquered is both victory and defeat.

At the bottom of the staircase, I pause, panting and looking around frantically for the best path to the door.

I stumble into the cool night air, Cade's body is a dead weight against mine, increasingly heavy and cumbersome as my strength wanes.

The once comforting chirr of crickets now feels like an accusation, each chirp a reminder of the line I just crossed. My breath heaves in ragged gasps, sweat mingling with the tears that refuse to stop tracing hot paths down my cheeks.

The car is parked further away than I remember, every additional step a test of willpower. Finally, with trembling hands, I open the backseat door and maneuver Cade inside. His head tilts awkwardly against the seat, and I wince, adjusting him as gently as I can manage. There's no time for care, though; urgency nips at my heels like a persistent hound.

The engine roars to life under my shaky grip, the quiet hum of the countryside swallowed by the growl of the car as we speed towards the plantation. Trees blur past, an abstract painting of guilt and fear, the road a dark ribbon unraveling beneath us.

Arriving feels surreal, like stepping onto the set of some tragic play where I'm both the actress and audience. The wine cellar greets me with its musty scent and cool embrace, indifferent to the drama unfolding within its walls.

Cade is heavy, so much heavier than any secret I've ever carried, and it takes what strength I have left to drag him down the stone steps. My muscles scream, but I ignore them, focusing on just getting down the damn stairs.

He looks almost peaceful here in the dim light, his chest rising and falling shallowly.

It's a cruel masquerade of sleep.

I yank the cuffs I snagged from his dresser from my pocket, wrapping them around the metal leg of one of the shelving units and then clasping them around his hands.

They click shut, anchoring him to this new reality.

Pacing now, back and forth, my thoughts are in pure disarray. *What have I done?*

The question is a refrain, looping endlessly. Then, his eyes flutter open, confusion quickly giving way to anger.

"What the fuck are you doing?" Cade's voice cuts through the silence, sharp and bitter.

I freeze, words deserting me.

My mouth opens, but nothing comes out.

What can I say?

What can I possibly say to justify this?

"Answer me, Tia!" The demand is jagged, edged with betrayal.

I stand there, the enormity of my actions crashing down upon me in the suffocating space of the cellar. The wine bottles bear silent witness to our tableau, the moment stretching between us, taut as a wire.

"I—I don't know."

TIA MOTIVE?

CARL

TOM LANDRY

CHAPTER THIRTY-TWO

Tia

The knife glints under the harsh kitchen lights, and I find my gaze lingering on its sharp edge. The same knife that could so easily slice through the thick ham for Cade's sandwich could also—No!

I shake the thought away, scolding myself.

It's absurd—the notion of harming Cade. He's been like a breath of fresh air in my stagnant life, bringing laughter back into my days and warmth into my nights.

But then there's the gnawing truth, the one that tastes like bile at the back of my throat.

Cade knows too much.

And with each passing second, the line between affection and survival blurs a dangerous shade of gray.

I let out a shuddering breath, trying to steady the trembling in my hands as I pick up the plated sandwich.

It's expertly stacked—crisp lettuce, tomato, thick slices of ham, and creamy chipotle mayonnaise between two pieces of toasted bread, just how he likes it. The chips are an after-thought, scattered beside the sandwich like fallen leaves. The glass of water beads with condensation, a small puddle forming at its base.

"Get a grip, Tia," I mutter to myself, feeling the tug of war within me.

In this quiet kitchen, where spices and herbs hang from the walls and memories of cooking with mom simmer in the air, violence feels like a foreign language.

With a resolve that feels more brittle than it does sturdy, I snatch up the plate and glass.

My feet carry me across the tiles, past the family photos on the fridge, and through the back door that creaks from long-forgotten repairs.

I storm toward the wine cellar, my sanctuary turned prison, where Cade awaits. The gravel crunches beneath my boots, a metrical condemnation of each step I take—each step that brings me closer to a decision I never wanted to make.

The scent of earth and aging wood greets me as I descend into the dimly lit space. My heartbeat is a drumroll against my ribcage.

"Keep it together," I chide myself internally. "You're just bringing him food, not a death sentence." But even as the thought crosses my mind, I know it's not entirely true.

With a deep breath that does little to steady my shaking hands, the basement door swings open with an eerie creak, an unwelcome announcement of my arrival, and I press forward.

It's time to face Cade, time to face myself, and decide if the scales of justice can be balanced without more bloodshed or death.

My gaze immediately finds Cade.

He's hunched over, his head resting against the metal shelf, seemingly resigned to his fate. The way he looks up at me, nostrils flaring with disdain, sends a cold jolt through my veins.

"Hey," I murmur, even though the greeting feels absurdly out of place.

I watch his face, searching for any sign of the man I thought I knew, but all I see is the curl of his lip as he turns away. Something sharp twists inside me, a mingled pang of regret and pain that he should look at me with such contempt.

It's a reaction I'd expected but not one I had been prepared for. I push it down, bury it deep where it can't show on my face or in my eyes.

Silently, I close the gap between us, gently setting down the plate with the ham sandwich and chips in front of him. Next to it, I place the glass of water.

Then, retreating to the sanctuary of the old pool table nestled in the corner, I sit down.

My body folds into a fortress, arms crossed over my chest, legs crossed at the ankles. From this vantage point, I allow my stare to settle on Cade again. I try to read him, to understand what he's thinking, feeling, but he's become perplex to me now.

The silence is a living thing, stretching out between us like an impassable chasm. Cade's gaze meets mine—a mixture of hurt and hardened resolve.

"Doesn't have to be this way, Cade," I tell him. "Just tell me, are you the only one who knows? About the suspicions?"

His eyes narrow, "Go fuck yourself, Tia." His words are a slap to my face.

They sting, but it's the hurt and anger behind them that cuts deeper than anything else.

I flinch, not at the vulgarity but at the truth in his anger—his right to it, "I'm sorry, Cade. But if others know then—"

"Then what?" He spits out, his body tense, "You'll do what you have to, right? Isn't that how you operate?"

I swallow hard, the taste of fear thick on my tongue. The possibility looms over us, a specter neither of us can ignore, and I'm standing at its threshold, uncertain if I'm the hunter or the hunted.

"Cade," I start again, my voice steadier than my hands that tremble ever so slightly. "What did you find out? About my father?"

Silence.

"Cade, please." I beg.

He lets out a long, weary sigh, "Tia, it's—I think the cops covered it up. Or worse, they were a part of it—his murder. But you already know that, don't you?"

I blink back the sudden wetness clouding my vision, the images from that night flickering like an old film reel—the fear, the violence, the loss.

"There's more to it. So much more." My voice cracks as I force the words out, reliving the horror as I speak. "My father and I were closing shop, he went back inside to lock up the safe, I think, and I was waiting in the alley. He caught the old sheriff in the act of raping me. He came out and fought him off with a bat. But Carl and Allen were there too. One held me down while the other beat my father. And then—" A hiccup of sorrow interrupts me, "Then the sheriff shot him."

A single tear escapes, tracing a hot path down my cheek. "They knew they'd get away with it. No one would believe me or my mother. We tried, for months we tried to get someone to look into it. But there was nothing. No justice, no peace. Just this endless nightmare."

The mask of anger on Cade's face slowly fades, revealing a glimpse of the pain he shares with me through his troubled eyes.

"And Landry?" He asks. "What was his role in all this?"

"Tom Landry," I tsk. "He's the accomplice—the one who kept their secrets locked away. He protected them, made sure they were untouchable." My knuckles whiten as I grip the edge of the pool table, "Even after the sheriff was long gone, Landry held his tongue. My father—he deserves justice, Cade. These men—they've let their sins seep into the soil of this town, infecting it to its very core."

An ache throbs in my chest, like a wound that refuses to heal.

Finally, Cade looks up, his gaze piercing me with a clarity that unnerves. "I understand why you want justice," He begins, his voice steady but not unkind. "But as an agent, I'm sworn to uphold the law—to bring justice to all murderers alike, Tia."

His words hit like a gut punch, stealing the air from my lungs.

He's talking about me now.

My vision blurs at the edges, the cold truth settling like frost. "I had to do something," I insist weakly, grappling with the enormity of what I've become. "They took everything from me! What would you have done, Cade? Just stood by and let them live their lives like nothing ever happened?"

I search his face for any trace of absolution, but all I find is the stern resolve of a man bound by duty.

"So, you did kill them?" Cade's eyes narrow, his features hardening once again, "How did you do it, Tia? How did you kill them without leaving a trace?"

"With the help of an old friend, but even I don't what it truly is, only that it came from a flower—a poisonous nectar that works slowly, spreading through the body over days, mimicking a natural illness. He called it Odette's Bloom. It's a flower he found on an expedition, and it only opens under the light of the moon."

"Odette's Bloom," He repeats slowly, as if tasting the words for their truth. "Sounds like something out of a fantasy book, not reality. There is nothing like it ever recorded in any botanical or forensic records."

But what if it's not just science? What if there's something more to it?

My fingers curl around the edge of the pool table, the worn felt rough against my skin. "Do you believe in magic, Cade?" I ask.

He scoffs, a bitter laugh escaping him. "Magic? No, people make their own luck, carve their own paths. Magic has nothing to do with it. Though, delusion might."

I know this man did not just call me delusional!

"Then call it delusion." I say, pushing off from the table and standing tall. "Makes no matter to me."

My steps are loud in the quiet room.

He eyes me warily, his body rigid, "Where are you going?" He asks. "I take it you're planning on killing me too?"

The question stings more than it should.

I take a deep breath, letting it out slowly. "No, Cade. I don't *plan* on killing you." I turn toward the door, then pause, glancing back over my shoulder. "I'm going to see someone I long believed was dead, and to find out if there's any real truth to magic, because if it does exist—it might just save your life."

The stars twinkle above, oblivious to my desperate situation. The chill of the pre-dawn air surrounds me, but I cannot stop to shiver or second-guess myself. The first light of dawn is creeping closer, and time is of an essence.

I navigate through the tombs with an urgency that turns my breath ragged. Branches from old dead trees reach out as if to slow my sprint, but I dodge them, propelled forward by hope.

Finally, I'm there—stopping so abruptly at my father's grave that small clouds of dust rise around my feet.

I double over, hands resting on my knees, fighting to regain control over my lungs, sucking in the cool air as if it could cleanse away the sins I've committed.

I lift my head, scanning the pitch black for any sign of him—the man who breathed life back into these old stones weeks ago.

My grandfather.

I strain my eyes in the darkness, searching for any sign of him. But the cemetery remains guarded, and he is nowhere to be found among the gleaming marble and granite in the moonlight.

"Where are you?" I whisper to the night, almost expecting the wind to carry an answer back to me.

But there is only silence—a heavy, expectant hush that settles over the graves like a shroud.

Tears betray me, trailing unchecked down my cheeks. The sobs that escape are muffled, strangled by the weight of decisions

I never wanted to make. My hands ball into fists, knuckles white as they strike the earth above my father's resting place.

"I don't want this," I gasp between heaving breaths, speaking to the night as if it could absorb my confession. "I don't want to kill you, Cade."

I want to believe there's a way out, that this doesn't end in despair. But wishes are feeble things and pennies in a well only reach so far.

"Please," I whisper, the plea directed at the void or perhaps at the man who should be standing before me. "Just...make it stop."

A shiver races up my spine, not from the chill of the air, but from the sudden sensation of being watched. My head snaps up, eyes searching the darkness for the source.

"Quite a peculiar place to find oneself at this hour, isn't it?" The voice is gentle, almost bemused, and unmistakably his.

He stands there as though conjured from the shadows themselves, a wraith in the twilight of night and the coming dawn. His silhouette is familiar, yet out of place amongst the graves.

"Grandpa?" Relief floods my veins. "Do you know who I am?"

"Of course," He replies, his tone softening. "You're the young lady from the sheriff's funeral."

The charade grates on my already frayed nerves, and I can feel the annoyance prickling beneath my skin like a thousand tiny needles.

"Stop it," I hiss, my voice a venomous whisper. "You know exactly who I am."

He looks at me confused, as if he hasn't the faintest clue as to what I'm talking about, but I see the slightest twitch in the corner of his eye—a telltale sign.

"I'm sorry, my dear," He responds with a practiced innocence that doesn't reach the cool depths of his gaze. "I think you must be mistaken."

A roar escapes my throat, raw and uncontrollable, as I surge to my feet. The ground beneath me feels unsteady, but my resolve is as solid as the headstones that surround us. In two quick steps, I close the distance between us, my breath coming out in ragged bursts.

"Grandpa, please," I plead, standing so close now that I can see the intricate patterns of age etched into his face. "I need your help."

Chapter Thirty-Three

Tia

He leans heavily on the weathered cane clasped in his gnarled hands, "Your mother, she swore—promised—she'd never breathe a word. We were supposed to keep you away from all this darkness."

"I know." I twirl my fingertip on the dusty ground.

His eyes, clouded with age, still manage to convey a deep sorrow as they meet mine, "But it seems fate has a cruel sense of humor," He continues. "Because here you are."

I feel rooted to the spot, confusion threading through my heart like poison ivy, invasive and suffocating.

"And here I am," I echo, standing up off the ground.

He straightens as much as his old bones allow, squaring his shoulders, "Well? Go on then."

My words spill out as though I'm in confession, "I'm the one who committed the murders that the FBI has been investigating. The sheriff and his friend were my victims." My heart races as I continue, "And right now, Cade—the FBI agent I've been involved with—he's currently restrained in my basement."

"Jesus, Tiana," The old man scolds, his voice cracking like dry ground under a relentless sun. "What have you gone and gotten yourself into?"

"I had no choice," I hurry on, my words tumbling out like runaway stones down a hill. "I can't let him pin those murders on me. But I don't want to hurt him either, I just need to make sure he stays out of it until I figure things out."

"Why?" His voice is barely audible, "Why would you go to such lengths?"

"Because I couldn't let Papa's death be in vain," I say, choking on the sentence. "It's my fault he's gone. If he hadn't rushed out to save me that night—" A sob wretches its way up out of my chest.

I can still hear the echo of gunshots, still see the horror-stricken look on my father's face as he fell, his life bleeding out onto the cold wet ground. It's a memory etched into my being, a moment that has defined the course of my life.

I wipe the tears carelessly with the back of my hand, steadying my breath. "He died because of me, Grandpa. The whole mess started there, and now I'm in too deep to just walk away."

The old man reaches out, his hand trembling as it rests briefly on my arm, offering a frail comfort, "Ah, child...guilt is a heavy burden to bear, but this is not your fault, nor your burden to carry. Your daddy—" He pauses, his voice thick with a lifetime of loss. "Death was already following him like a phantom; it stalked him long before that night. You were just a little girl, Tiana. You didn't summon the reaper to our door."

"But—"

"No buts," He interjected firmly. "His choices, his actions—they set him on that path. Your father knew the risks, and he chose them all the same. As did your mother and as did I. Death came for him, yes, but not because of you. It was always going to come."

His words, though meant to console, feel like stones in my stomach.

"A life for a life," He whispers, tracing the headstones of the two he loved the most. "If there's any blame to be laid," He says, his gaze locking with mine, "Then it falls on my shoulders."

His eyes well up, shimmering with regret.

Damn.

And I thought I went through some shit but this, this completely shatters my fucking heart.

"I understand, Grandpa. I understand it all, and no one blames you. Momma and Papa wanted a family, and you—you just wanted to bring her back." My gaze shifts to my grandmother's headstone.

His old, weather-beaten eyes focused on the tombstone as though trying to summon her image from the cold marble, "I tried to play God. I meddled with things I had no right to—the laws of life and death, the very fabric of existence. And in the end, we all paid the price. Now, the three of us are trapped here—in a place where life is just a memory, and death is a constant companion."

His shoulders sag, his body suddenly seeming frailer than usual.

"We live in a graveyard of our own making, Tiana. It is a world shaped by shadows and regret. I was too blind, too arrogant, to see the truth. That life can't be gambled like chips on a poker table."

"I know, and I promise you, I won't make the same mistakes." I try my best to comfort him, but I know it's not enough.

How could it be?

"But I need your help. I need your magic."

His gaze snaps back to mine, alarm spreading across his features. "No," He states firmly. "Have you learned nothing, child? I won't. I refuse. It's too dangerous; it's nothing more than a curse disguised as a blessing."

"I need this!" I press, annoyance bubbling in my gut.

"You don't understand what you're asking for, Tiana," He responds, shaking his head, "The shadows, they are not mere tools to be wielded. They're capricious, dangerous. They play games that can cost more than you're willing to pay."

"I do understand, Grandpa," I insist. "But I need you to understand my desperation too. I am not asking as a child playing with fire. I am asking as a woman who is willing to face the flames."

"Child, you are treading on a path lined with darkness," He warns, his jaw clenching as he struggles with his decision.

"Then so be it!" I shout, falling to my knees on the damp earth, feeling the blades of grass beneath my palms.

Tears prick at the corners of my eyes, but I grit my teeth, swallowing down the lump in my throat. "I promised her, Grandpa. I swore to momma no more death would be on my hands, no more lives would be lost. But if you won't help me, then I'll have to do whatever it takes to make sure I can continue Papa's dream. And I refuse to allow anyone else find out about the truth about the murders. I can't let momma suffer because of the choices that I made."

Grandpa's face hardens as he stares at me, his dark eyes boring through me, "Who are we," He starts, his voice raspy and worn, "If not the summation of our choices, child?"

"I don't—I don't know." I admit.

"You ask for magic," His weathered fingers pinching the bridge of his nose, "But magic is not a game. Much like vengeance, it demands sacrifice, balance. It requires you to give as much as you take. What will you give, Tiana?"

"Anything." I breathe.

"Even if it means surrendering something you truly want?"

I'm going to have to give up the restaurant. I can feel it. Am I willing to relinquish the dream, the one tangible symbol of my father's legacy? The very essence of what Papa and I had strived for over the years, is it really worth the price?

After a moment of indecisiveness, I respond confidently, feeling my heart squeeze in my chest, "Yes."

"The shadows hear you. They are listening." The old man's voice deepens, his body beginning to tremble, a fine shudder that escalates into a violent shake.

Sweat beads on his brow, each drop seeming to sizzle on his skin is made of molten lava. His eyes, once a warm brown reminiscent of the earth itself, now seem to drink in the light around them, turning into endless pools of black.

"Grandpa? What do you mean they're listening?"

"Quiet, child," He coos through gritted teeth, his palms now cracked and bleeding as they hit the ground to support himself. "They're waiting, and they're starving. Desperate for the anguish and hate you carry in your soul. They feed off it. I've made them go hungry for too long, they've been famished, waiting for a feast such as this."

Okay, this shit is fucking scary.

All of a sudden, Grandpa's head snaps back, the cords in his neck standing out as he roars in pain. I take an instinctive step backward, my heart hammering against my ribs.

"Grandpa?" My voice trembles, my hand reaching out to touch him.

"I can't—" He begins, his voice now a guttural rasp, "I can't hold them off any longer."

Before I can ask another question, the shadows around us begin to swirl and thicken, pooling like dark ink spilled across the floor. They slide towards us, alive and hungry, their forms whispering of despair and forgotten dreams. I feel a cold chill seep into my bones, fear clawing at my chest.

In a blind panic, I scramble backwards, my shoes slipping on the slick ground as I scramble to get up.

Grandpa's face contorts in agony, his aging skin painted with veins that pulse darkly under the strain of whatever force he's holding at bay.

Fanged silhouettes, born of the very essence of night, encircle us. Their eyes, crimson pinpricks in the abyss, fixed on me with a predatory intensity. I try to scream, but the sound catches in my throat, strangled by the terror that grips me.

One creature, bolder than the rest, slithers forward out of the old man's body, its form coalescing into something grotesquely humanoid.

"Assssk," It hisses, "Sssspeak your desire."

The words slither into my ears, cold and menacing. My mind races, searching through every horror movie and story I've read, trying to figure out what to do. I remember something about bargaining with these creatures, but the specifics elude me, drowned out by the pounding of my heart.

"Assssk." It says again. "Assssk, or be forever marrrrked."

Marked?

What the fuck does that even mean?

I don't care. I'm not looking to find out.

"I need your help. Please!" I blurt out, the words tumbling from my lips before I can second-guess them. "I can't let anyone find out the truth, about me murdering those two men. Make it so Cade cannot trace the murders back to me, so no one can."

"Your ssssecrets can be kept...for a price."

"Done." I agree.

"Very well," Comes the raspy reply, "The deal has been made."

As the creature speaks, a sensation of icy cold slithers down my spine, wrapping around me like a serpent's coil.

With that, the shadow man sinks back into Grandpa's frail body, his skin relaxing as the veins no longer pulse with foreboding darkness.

A foul odor wafts through the vast space, so potent that I almost stumble backward, my hand flying to cover my nose and mouth. The scent is like rotting meat and sulfur, an acrid stench so thick I can almost taste it. It's invasive, stinging my eyes and crawling into my nostrils.

I blink hard against the instinctual tears that form from the stench, squinting up at the sky. Above, black clouds roil and churn, in a ceiling of despair. Lightning strikes across the dark expanse, each bolt a white-hot talon tearing at the fabric of the night. Thunder rumbles, a growl from the belly of some great beast, and the ground beneath my feet quivers in response.

The trees around me whip and bow to the incensed sky, their branches reaching out like skeletal fingers against the dimly lit backdrop. A gust of wind sweeps through the clearing, bringing with it a biting chill. I hug my arms around myself for warmth, my goosebump-covered skin pebbling against the violent cold that seeps through my clothes, gnawing at my bones.

There's something unnatural about this chill. It would never be this frigid in Louisiana, especially not at this time of year, even without the sun's warmth.

The storm rages on, each howl of wind sounding like the cries of a thousand lost souls.

I wonder if my father is one of them.

Suddenly, a bolt of lightning strikes alarmingly close, igniting the ground no more than a few feet from where I stand. The earth beneath me shakes violently, and a brief, brilliant flare of white light blinds me. When my vision clears, the world seems eerily silent, the storm's fury hushed, and the ground smolders where the lightning struck, leaving behind a charred and steaming circle.

I look around for grandpa, but he's gone, just like last time.

I didn't even get a chance to thank him.

My heart pounds in my chest, mimicking the thunder that had just roared across the sky. I glance around frantically, searching through the disarray of shadows and swaying trees, hoping to catch a glimpse of him, to find some sign that he's still here. But there's nothing.

Only me, the wind, and my newfound belief in magic remain.

A grin creeps across my face, an alien sensation in this grim atmosphere, and a laugh bubbles up from my gut.

My laughter echoes eerily, swallowed by the vast emptiness around me.

It's a wild, mad sound, tinged with both disbelief and exhilaration. My eyes well up and I let the tears fall freely, merging with the rain on my face.

On the brightside, I no longer need to kill my boyfriend. But the downside—I have no fucking clue what to expect.

CHAPTER THIRTY-FOUR

Agent Holloway

T he sound of the metallic clang of my handcuffs against the metal shelf echoing in my ears, gives me no alleviation from my current dilemma.

My head throbs where Tia's powerful swing connected, an exemplification of her surprising strength. I never would have guessed that beneath her unassuming exterior lay the force capable of knocking me clean off my feet.

I shift against the shelves, trying to ignore the dull ache in my wrists and the sharper one in my pride.

It figures, doesn't it?

Lay your heart on the line, and you get a knockout blow as a thank-you. I could almost laugh at the timing—if it weren't so damn pathetic.

"Real smooth, operator," I mutter under my breath, feeling the sting of humiliation mixing with the pain.

Angrily, I rattle the cuffs, the clinking sound mocking me in the dim basement.

Trust is a hard-earned currency in my line of work, and I thought I'd banked enough with Tia to avoid something like—well, this. But here the fuck I am, trapped, cuffed, and nursing a bruised ego.

Guess it's not just her food that packs a punch.

Pun intended.

The disgusting taste of self-pity is acidic on my tongue. Time to switch gears; Cade the Lovesick Fool has no place here, not when Cade the FBI Agent needs to be called to duty.

I scan the basement, a sigh hissing through my clenched teeth.

Wine bottles stand like soldiers at attention, useless in my current predicament. The old pool table offers no salvation, its felt surface mocking me. A workstation catches my gaze, barren of tools—another dead end. And then there are the shelves, more metal and wood offering nothing but more disappointment.

I groan aloud at my rotten luck.

"Think, damn it," I chide myself, casting my eyes about the room in frustration.

It's not the first tight spot I've been in, I remind myself, and I'm sure it won't be the last.

But time is also a luxury I don't have. Tia will be back any moment now, so I need to figure something out, and figure it out quick.

"Mother fucking shit." I curse aloud, my voice echoing in the empty space. I rattle the cuffs again, harder, my frustration mounting. But that's all they do. Rattle and mock.

With a grimace, I consider my only viable option.

"This is going to hurt like hell." I mutter, bracing my back against the shelf.

I take a deep breath and contort my thumb against its natural alignment, pain shooting up my arm in a torrent of white heat. Gritting my teeth, I push harder, the joint bending unnaturally and sickeningly.

My vision blurs at the edges, white spots dancing before my eyes. But it's over.

The cuff slips over the swollen joint, a small victory in the wake of self-inflicted torment.

My hand, once caged, is now free, granting me the mobility I need.

I flex my fingers, wincing at the fire that licks at my nerve endings. Ignoring the pain, I reach over to my other hand, feeling the cold steel of the other cuff. I grope around it blindly and pull it back through the leg of the shelf, standing as I do.

"Step one is done," I commend myself. "Now onto the next."

I survey my surroundings. The cellar's window taunting me with a sliver of freedom too narrow for me to claim.

Useless.

I forcefully pop my thumb back into place, feeling a surge of pain shoot up my arm as I bite back a curse.

A glint of metal over near the work bench catches my eye. It's a hammer, its handle worn from use but solid.

Perfect.

I grip it tightly in my hand. Time to make my own exit.

I ascend the cellar stairs, each creaking step a ticking time bomb, and reach out to the heavy wooden door barring my way. It's locked from outside, its strength mocking my feeble attempts to crack it open earlier.

"Well, let's make some noise then," I sigh.

Out of nowhere, a loud crack seizes my attention.

Instinctively, my head snaps toward the source as the room lights up with an electric blue, almost white light.

Lightning.

It's just a storm.

No matter, I can weather

it. I grip the hammer tighter in my hand, inhaling the heavy, wet scent of approaching rain that seeps through the half-rotted wood. Moving towards the cellar door, I swing the hammer hard against it. The loud thud reverberates around me, drowning in the thunderous roars from above.

For a moment, the world turns white, a blinding flash leaving me temporarily blinded.

Spots float in my vision, but I stubbornly blink them away.

I reach forward where the doorknob had been, expecting the familiar feel of jagged edges and splintered wood.

But my hand meets empty space.

Frowning, I lean closer, my eyes, still trying to adjust to the post-strike gloom, land on the shattered remnants of what used to be the doorknob. Except now, the door itself seems enormous, towering above me.

I shake my head, trying to dispel the illusion or whatever trick my mind is playing on me.

I have a concussion. That has to it.

But as I take a step back, the monolithic door continues to loom over me. It isn't an illusion. The door has grown. Or more accurately, I have shrunk.

I lower my eyes, feeling my heart pound against my chest in a desperate cadence.

A guttural sound claws at my throat, stifled only by sheer disbelief. There, extending from where my wrist should be, is a webbed foot clad in a slick mottled green skin.

Muscle memory prompts me to retreat, yet my legs betrayed me. Instead of the familiar stride of a man, I find myself executing a series of ungainly hops.

With grim determination, I hop forward again, the strange sensation of leaping rather than walking is unnerving. As if the world wishes to mock me even more, an empty wine bottle rolls toward me, showing my distorted reflection in its curved glass.

A wide head now balances atop a squat torso, while long hind legs—perfectly designed for leaping—sprout where my lean muscles used to be. My skin, once tan and smooth, has taken on the hue of pond scum, speckled with dark blotches over a stomach that glows a sickly yellow.

A frog.

I'm a fucking frog.

The scream that erupts from my throat sounds more like a croak and the horrifying realization only deepens my despair. I try to steady myself, but the sudden lack of balance sends me sprawling onto my back. The ceiling spins above me, and for a moment I lay there, stunned by the absurdity of it all.

"Ca—Cade?" Tia's voice trembles from the top of the stairs, her silhouette framed by the doorway.

I struggle to get up upon hearing her footsteps draw closer.

"Stay back!" I manage, my voice now a grating croak that belies all human origin. I attempt to scramble away, but my new body is not used to such coordinated movements. I stumble and end up on my back again, staring at the rafters above.

"You got to be fucking kidding me." I growl.

"Cade...what—" She hurries down the stairs over to where I lay on the ground, poking me with her finger before flipping me back upright.

I glare up at her with beady eyes, my human dignity slighted by the cawing laughter that bubbles out of her.

"This," She says, "This is not what I was expecting."

Tia's laughter dies in her throat as she takes in my froggy form.

"This is your fault, isn't it." I croak.

"I think so." She laughs.

"Tia?"

"Yea?"

"Fuck you."

CHAPTER THIRTY-FIVE

Jia

My eyes don't leave the small, green creature on the windowsill. Its throat bulges, and those bulbous eyes are fixed on me. "What the fuck did you just do to me?" The frog—Cade demands, and I feel every hair on my body stand on end.

I swallow hard, "So, it's really you then?"

"Of course, it's me!" Cade snaps, his legs tense as if readying to hop, "Got any other men tied up around here somewhere that I don't know about?"

I square my shoulders, leveling a glare at the amphibian accusation before me.

"Hey! I'm no floozy," I retort, feeling the sting of his implication more than I care to admit.

The frog—Cade—shifts uneasily.

In my defense, it wasn't supposed to be like this.

As I whispered my desperate plea amongst the ancient gravestones, all I had hoped for was a simple case of amnesia or something to cloud his detective's mind.

I never expected this.

"Look what you did to me," He croaks, a ribbit of outrage bubbling from his throat.

"Unintended side effects," I shrug, scooping him up in my hands.

I cradle him in my palm, his slick skin cool against my warm flesh. "So, now you going to tell me who else knows about my involvement?" I interrogate, trying to infuse my voice with more confidence than I feel.

"Nobody," He admits after a reluctant ribbit, his eyes narrowing as if resenting the confession. "Just started piecing it together this morning—" He trails off, then gathers his resolve, puffing out his chest in an absurd display of defiance. "But once I turn back, I swear, Tia, I'll put you behind bars."

"Yea, good luck with that." I retort, staring into the bulbous eyes that once scrutinized me with suspicion. "Cade Holloway, you're staying put until I can sort this mess out."

His small amphibian body is surprisingly calm in my hold, almost as if he has accepted his current situation for the moment.

I climb up the basement stairs, on a mission, but as I reach the top step, my momentum halts abruptly—there stands my mother, suitcase in hand, her arrival prematurely cutting through the veil of my flustered thoughts.

"Momma?" I blink, unprepared for her presence, her trip supposed to tether her away from home for days yet. "You're home early."

Her eyes dart from my face to the large frog in my hands, "Oh, good! You're making frog legs for dinner. Looks like I came home just in time." Her voice is light

I freeze, my eyes darting between my mother and the frog in my hands.

I open my mouth to respond, but it's Cade who breaks the silence first, his croaky voice laced with panic.

"I sure as hell hope not!" He protests, thrashing within the confines of my fingers. "I'm too young to die!"

"Quiet, Cade," I hiss under my breath, gently restraining him with a careful thumb.

My mother's gaze shifts, a wrinkle of confusion forming between her brows as if trying to reconcile what her eyes perceive against what her mind knows to be possible.

"Momma, it's complicated." I start, stumbling over an explanation I'm still struggling to believe myself. "But not to worry, no frogs—or detectives—will be harmed for dinner." A grin spreads across my face.

My mother's silence deepens, a chasm opening between us as she stares at the amphibian captive in my hands. The kitchen clock ticks loudly, marking the seconds it takes for her to find her voice. When she does, it quivers like the last leaf clinging to an autumn branch.

"Shadow magic, Tia?" Her finger trembles as she points at me, accusation in her eyes. "Tell me you haven't—"

"Momma, just let me explain." I beg.

But she's having none of it.

With a gesture of defeat, her arms fly up, and she collapses into one of the old pine kitchen chairs, "After all we've discussed. How could you?

The words sting, each one a barb hooking into my guilt. "He was investigating the murders," I blurt out, desperate to justify the situation. "Carl, the sheriff—he started to suspect me."

"Damn it, Tia," Her voice cracks with a mixture of anger and disappointment. "I thought you put an end to your foolish vendetta."

"I did! I swear!" I choke out between sobs. "I only wanted to make things right again."

I'm drowning in regret, gasping for air in a sea of unintended consequences. And with each sob, I feel the fragile threads of hope slipping through my fingers like dry sand.

My mother sighs deeply, the lines on her face seeming to deepen, "I know you meant well, Tia. But this magic, it never leads anywhere good."

"I'm sorry. My plan—"

"Ow!" I wince as Cade's tongue lashes out, striking me square in the eye.

"Your plan sucks." He croaks, his amphibious voice grating against my already frayed nerves.

"Damn it, Cade!" I yelp, reaching for the battered eyeball.

Storming into the living room, I hunt for something, anything to contain him. My eyes land on an old jewelry music box, the one with the delicate dancing ballerina atop. It's quaint and utterly unsuited for holding a man-turned-frog, but it'll have to do.

Snatching it up, I stomp back to the kitchen table and set it down with a thud. Mother's bewildered gaze follows me, but I don't meet her eyes. Not yet. With a bravura born of desperation, I flip open the lid and shove Cade inside, the ballerina twirling silently until the lid closes back down.

Cade's protests are immediate, his muffled curses barely contained by the thin wooden walls of his temporary prison. "You can't just stuff me in here!" His voice is shrill and slightly distorted, but the outrage is clear.

"It serves you right," I shoot back, snapping the lid shut. "Now be quiet! I need to think."

Turning to face Mother, my hands are trembling, my pulse racing. She regards me with a mix of exasperation and concern that only a mother could muster.

"What am I supposed to do now?" I ask her.

Mother's sigh seems to drag the very air from the room, her fingers pressing into her temples as if she can massage away the foolishness of my crisis.

"There's an old witch," She begins, her voice low and heavy, "Lives deep in the bayous."

I nod, swallowing hard. The stories Papa used to tell me about her danced on the edges of my memory—tales of a woman so intertwined with the fabric of magic that the swamp itself seemed to bend to her will

"She is powerful, and she holds ancestral magic," Mother continues, punctuating each word as if they were truths I had long forgotten. "She might be able to undo this mess you've created."

"Thank you, Momma." I wrap my arm around her shoulders.

"Now, tell something, sugar. What was the price you paid to the shadow man? What was his stipulation?"

The truth is a nasty bitch.

"The restaurant, maybe. I don't know. It felt like something big, something important." I say, still not fully aware of what I exchanged myself.

She sucks in a breath, her disappointment a cold clawed hand that wraps around my heart and squeezes, "Tia, all that hate, all that desire for revenge—I hoped you've learned it brings nothing but sorrow." Her gaze pierces me, "Dark magic is not a plaything."

I nod through the tears falling from my eyes, "I understand. I should have come to you first. I'm so sorry, Momma."

She embraces me, her arms strong and warm, "There will be time for sorries later," She says. Right now, you need to get going, fix this mess. I'll handle the restaurant. Keep it running in the meantime."

"Yea, until—"

"Until you put things right," She finishes firmly, pressing the music box back into my hands. "Now go. Find the witch. Make amends."

I hold the music box to my chest as I leave the safe comfort of my home, the screen door banging shut behind me.

I have to find her, for Cade's sake and my own.

I've taken too many risks and put too much on the line to give up now.

Failure is simply not an option.

Agent Holloway

I hurl myself against the polished antique, the smooth walls of my wooden prison offering no purchase for my webbed feet. The impact is less of a thud and more of an irksome tap, but I persist, driven by the need to be a constant pebble in Tia's shoe—or in this case, a pebble in her music box.

"Knock it off, Cade," Comes the muffled reprimand from outside, accompanied by a rhythmic tapping that matches my own disruptions.

Her finger, I imagine, admonishing me through the intricate woodwork.

The car's momentum shifts, brakes squealing softly, and I feel us lurch to a stop.

"Where are we?" I demand, pressing my green snout against the seam of the lid, and then the keyhole, seeking any sliver of light.

"Just grabbing some cash. We need a small boat," Tia replies, and I hear her struggle to stretch her short stature out the window to reach the ATM.

A boat?

Absolutely not.

The very idea of a boat churns my stomach—or whatever serves as one in this amphibious form.

The hot, sticky landscape of New Orleans had been bad enough, the city's air hanging like a wet blanket over my once human shoulders. Now she's set on dragging me out into the bayou, and just thinking about it makes my skin crawl.

Images of snakes slithering by, gators lurking beneath murky waters, and swarms of bugs flitting above the swamp surface flash through my mind.

Ugh...Bugs.

My stomach growls at the thought, which are now, disturbingly, sounding rather appetizing. I remember the sandwich and chips that Tia had brought me earlier, the food I had turned my nose up at. Regret pangs sharply, gnawing at my insides with hunger I can no longer ignore.

"Hey, Cade," Tia's voice slices through my internal lamentations, her eye peeking into the box through a crack she's pried open with slender fingers. "You know how to drive a boat?"

"Drive a boat?" I croak back incredulously, staring up at the giant iris that fills my vision.

She knows full well the extent of my current limitations. I stretch my hind legs in agitation.

"Oh, sure! Right after I finish knitting a sweater with these nifty webbed feet of mine!" I bite out. "If you wanted a captain for your aquatic escapade, perhaps transforming me into a monkey would've been more prudent, don't you think?"

The lid comes crashing down, and I swear the sound of Tia's curse is like a sledgehammer to my tiny amphibian heart. The engine revs, and we were moving again, each turn and bump magnified in my claustrophobic jail cell.

"Damn it, Tia! Let me out of here!" I yell, infuriated that I'm reduced to a creature that can hardly control his own movements, let alone navigate a boat through a bayou. "I swear, when I get my hands back, you're going to pay for this. You think you can just shove me in a box and be done with it? I'll have you behind bars so fast—"

But my threats drown beneath the sudden blast of music from the car's speakers, tunes blaring at a volume meant to silence even the most boisterous of frogs. I can imagine her, sitting there with that smug look on her face, fingers tapping on the wheel in time with the tempo.

We come to a stop, and instantly, the aroma hit me, familiar and tantalizing—Tia's restaurant.

"Committing crimes does work up an appetite, huh?" I ask sarcastically. "What now, Tia? Gonna stuff yourself with jambalaya while your cursed accomplice starves in a box?"

"Really, Cade?" Tia's voice cuts through the stillness "I think I like you better as a human. You talk less."

The car door opens, then slams shut, letting me know that I'm alone. Straining to hear any hint of what Tia is up to, I press my amphibious face against the side of the music box, but the muffled sounds of the outside world are only torture.

The minutes stretch into what feels like hours, each second ticking by with the dull throb of my frustration. The car interior heats up, turning my box into a miniature sauna.

My skin begins to feel dry, craving the moisture it now requires in this new body. The interior of the box grows stuffy, the air stale with my own recycled breaths.

Just when I'm about to accept my fate as an overcooked frog, the car door swings open and, I hear the scrape of a key in the ignition and the shift of Tia's weight as she climbs back into the car. The door closes with a soft thud, and the vehicle rocks gently with her movement.

"Did you get anything for me? Like, I don't know—water so I don't die?!" I can't resist the jab. My throat feels parched, and my skin feels like a dried sponge, but sarcasm still comes as naturally as breathing does.

Even if I do breathe through my skin now, rather than a set of lungs.

"Actually, yes," Tia replies, "A lovely ride through the bayous to find a witch."

A surge of curiosity propels me against the confines of my enclosure. "How?" I demand.

"Through Evangeline," Tia answers smoothly, as if ferrying a cursed man-turned-frog is an everyday errand. "Her fiancé owns a boat tour company that I helped them open."

"Needed a favor, did they?" The words came out sharper than intended—a blade forged in the fires of my frustration.

"Not exactly." The car starts with a lurch, settling into a smooth hum as Tia pulls off. "I gave Evangeline a bonus, off the books—to help them out before the baby arrives. They needed things, and I had the means. Now, they're doing quite well."

The revelation strikes a chord within me. Tia's generosity, her ability to care deeply for others—it's one of her traits that made me fall for her in the first place.

But even still, things change, and I mustn't allow myself to forget: this woman, capable of such kindness, has blood on her hands. The blood of two men.

Figuratively speaking.

She might kill me too.

The notion twists like a knife in my gut, yet it wars with a conflicting belief. If Tia wanted me dead, there would have been countless opportunities.

"Why does she have to have such a big heart?" I murmur to myself, the taste of irony acrid on my new amphibian tongue.

Even in this diminutive form, I can't shake the complexity of my feelings for her. They lead me adrift in a sea of uncertainty as dense as the bayou mists, we are heading into.

The car's engine cuts out, its last purr sending vibrations through the tiny prison of my music box. I brace for movement, but not quickly enough, it seems. The sudden jolt of being lifted sends me sprawling against a corner, inadvertently I issue a surprised croak.

"Could've given me a heads-up," I grumble, rubbing my sore little frog shoulder.

A giggle filters through the keyhole, "Sorry! I forgot you don't have seat belts in there."

The box jerks slightly as she walked, each rock of her hand indicating each step she takes. My world sways with her movements, and I struggle to find my footing on the polished base.

Then, comes another voice—one that I don't recognize, but has a buoyant southern draw to it.

"Hi, Miss Williams! You all set to go?"

"Ah, yes, thank you, Ray," she replies, the vibrations of her voice making the box hum softly.

Her words have an edge of nervousness, which isn't quite like her.

"Nice to see you again." Her hand must be over the box because her voice sounds far away, like she's speaking through layers of cotton.

"Likewise, ma'am. So, you got everything you need" Ray's question is casual, but I can sense an undercurrent of curiosity.

"Actually, Ray—" She hesitates, and I imagine her biting her lip in that contemplative manner of hers. This may sound weird, but have you ever heard of the bayou witch?"

Laughter bubbles up from Ray's throat, rich and genuine. "Of course, Ms. Williams. Everyone who's grown up around here knows about MamaKaze. But she ain't no witch—just an old blind lady living by herself in the bayou wilds."

I shuffle closer to the walls, straining to hear more.

"Great. I'm fucking doomed." The words slip out as a groan.

"Did that box just talk?" Ray's voice pitches high, quivering like a plucked violin string.

"Old boxes just make strange noises sometimes." Tia interjects, masking her apprehension with a forced laugh.

"This is all your fault, you know that?" I scold her.

Tia sighs, her exasperation clear, "You just couldn't shut up for a small, measly amount of time, could you?"

She clicks open the box, and bright light floods in, an onslaught against my sensitive frog eyes.

Tia's face hovers into view, her eyes rolling as she peers down at me.

My annoyance bubbles over, and I poke my head out defiantly, meeting her gaze with what I hope is a scathing look of accusation.

It must have worked because her expression softens just a fraction.

Ray, however, his face is a canvas of pure shock, mouth agape, color drained, eyes darting between Tia and me.

"Is—is that a talking frog?" He points.

"It's rude to point." I grumble, jumping slightly with enough force to make the box rock.

Ray takes a step back, his eyes never leaving me. The sight would have been comical if not for the sudden thud that follows; his body meets the ground with a graceless flop.

"Great," I mutter, flicking my tongue in irritation as I glare up at Tia's big green eyes, "Now look what you've done."

CHAPTER THIRTY-SEVEN

Tia

"Ray," I whisper, nudging his shoulder as gently as I can. His body feels like a sack of flour, heavy and unyielding against the cool floor of the boat and tackle shop. "Ray, sugar, wake up."

His eyelids flutter, revealing eyes that are clouded with confusion. They dart around, taking in the sun-bleached wood planks above us before they focus on me.

"Ms. Williams?" His voice is barely discernible, a strained croak that seems to fight its way out.

"Are you alright?" I inquire, knowing that the question is somewhat pointless.

Who would actually feel okay after experiencing something like this?

Ray's body suddenly jolts into an upright position, his arms flailing and his eyes wide and unblinking. His mouth hangs open in disbelief, his breathing quick and shallow. Every muscle in his face is tense, revealing the panic and confusion he is feeling.

Frantically, he tries to push himself up from the floor, but his hands slip on the smooth surface.

"Sorry, ma'am," Ray finally says, scratching the top of his head. "I'm not sure what came over me. Must be unwell or somethin'."

"That makes two of us," Cade's voice chimes in.

Damn you, Cade!

Ray's gaze snaps to the object, and his eyes grow even wider, if that's possible, saucers of bewilderment reflecting the flickering light from the old fluorescent bulbs hanging from the ceiling.

"Okay, Ray, please let me explain before you start freaking out," I coax, trying to infuse my tone with a calmness I don't feel.

My fingers twitch, longing to grab the box and silence Cade before he can turn this odd scene into a full-blown circus act.

But right now, soothing Ray's fears is all that matters.

Ray's nod is jittery, like he's trying to agree with something his mind can't fully accept. His throat works over a hard swallow, and I extend my hand toward him, steadying myself to help him up off the floor.

"You aren't going to pass out on me again, are you, sugar?" I keep my voice light, laced with a hint of Southern charm that I hope is comforting.

He shakes his head so fast it looks like it might unscrew from his neck. "No, no, I—I'm good," He stammers, but his eyes still hold that deer-caught-in-headlights look.

"Can I get you something to drink?" I ask as I catch sight of the water jug dispenser tucked in the corner of the lobby.

"Ummm...Yes ma'am, thank you."

I move quickly, my shoes squeaking against the floor, and grab one of the small white paper cups from the stack beside the dispenser.

The cool gurgle of water resounds as I press the lever, watching the clear liquid swirl into the cup.

With the cup full, I carefully make my way back to Ray, ensuring not to spill a drop. He accepts it with trembling hands, before taking a sip.

I steady my breath, knowing how the next words will sound.

"Okay, Ray, this is going to sound crazy, but the talking frog in the box—" I glance at the music box, its ornate carvings mocking the insanity of how this all sounds, "Well, he's kind of my boyfriend."

"Ex-boyfriend," Cade's voice rings out sharply from within the box.

I press my lips together, feeling annoyed, but I release a deep breath and carry on, "And right now, I'm trying to find the witch. The one from all the old folktales and bedtime stories—to help me fix this mess I got him in."

Ray blinks slowly, his Adam's apple bobbing as he processes my words. He then lets out a low whistle, the sound drawn out and rich with his thick accent.

"Well, I'll be damned!" He declares, shaking his head in disbelief. "My Evangeline, she would sure get a kick out of this tale. She's knee-deep into all that magic and fairytale story stuff," He chuckles lightly, the tremor in his hand subsiding as he warms to the topic. "Says we're made of stardust, she does, and that when lives are lost, they're found again rebirthed into stars—or somethin' like that. So, trust me, Ms. Williams, I've heard some pretty weird things before, but I will admit, a talking frog and a witch hunt might just top the list." He takes another sip of water, a small grin gracing his young face.

I nod, grateful for his acceptance, however baffling my story sounds.

"Evie sure is something else," I muse aloud, thinking about how her belief in the fantastical was just what I needed right now.

Ray's lips curve into a smile that crinkles the corners of his eyes, radiating pure adoration. "I know," He says, his chest puffing out. "I'm the luckiest man alive to have her. She's got this way of seeing the world that just—it makes you want to believe in the impossible. But I can't for the life of me figure why she chose me when she could've had the pick of any litter."

"Sometimes things just—are," I reply, "The world is mysterious in its ways, and perhaps that's part of what makes it so magical.

"Look, Ray," I start, apprehensively, "After all this crazy talk, I'd get it if you didn't want to take us out to the bayou now." An apology lingers on my tongue, unspoken but heavily implied.

But Ray just laughs, straightening the bill of his camouflage hat with a practiced flick of his wrist. Keys jingle as he fishes them out from his pocket, the metallic sound punctuating his next words.

"Miss Williams," He grins, shaking his head with bemusement. "I ain't about to miss out on an adventure like this. And you're right," He winks, "It does sound completely looney, and that's exactly why I'm in."

CHAPTER THIRTY-EIGHT

Agent Holloway

I'm ricocheting off the walls like a pinball, my webbed feet slipping clumsily on the polished surface of the music box. The ballerina inside with me is trying to pirouette, but her painted eyes keep shooting daggers each time I bounce into her path.

I can't help it; this confined space is driving me mad. And there's a sliver of light teasing me through the keyhole—a hint of the freedom just beyond my reach.

"When are you going to let me out of this damn thing?" I croak at Tia, my voice an angry ribbit that echoes in the tiny chamber.

"Whenever you learn to calm down," Tia retorts, her tone laced with a mirth that only fuels my aggravation. "And stop poking me in the eye with that gross little frog tongue of yours."

The accusation sends a fresh wave of fury coursing through my amphibian body.

Calm down?

That's rich coming from her.

"You turned me into a fucking frog," I snap back, ignoring the unintentional pun as my legs coil beneath me for another agitated leap. "And now you want me to calm down?"

I'm hopping mad—literally.

The injustice of my situation, the ludicrousness of being trapped in a miniature prison with a ceramic dancer giving me the side-eye—it's too much. This isn't where I'm supposed to be, not what I'm meant to be doing. I'm an agent, damn it, not some fairy-tale character relegated to croaking away his days in a child's toy.

But here I am, subject to the whims of Tia and her voodoo shenanigans, bouncing around impotently in a child's keepsake.

It's enough to make me wish I could turn her into something small and slimy, see how she likes being on the other end of a transformation. But wishes won't get me out of this box—only

Tia will. And right now, she's holding all the cards—or rather, the key.

"Technically," Tia retorts, "I didn't turn you into a frog. That was the shadow man's doing."

Ray's laughter rolls across the cramped space of the music box, a rich baritone that seems out of place in the gloom. "You two bicker like an old married couple," He chortles, oblivious to the sharp look I'm shooting him from inside the box.

Her gaze locks onto mine through the keyhole, "If I open this lid, do you promise not to bolt?"

My heart races—a peculiar sensation in this small, webbed chest—but I manage a curt nod. Freedom is inches away; I can almost taste it. "I promise," I croak out, my voice raspy and strained, still not used to the mechanics of a frog's vocal cords.

"Good enough for me." I hear, and light floods my dark enclosure as the lid swings open.

The sudden exposure makes me blink, and I'm momentarily disoriented. As my eyes adjust to the bright light, Tia's face comes into focus, framed by curls of hair that seem to defy gravity. Her expression is a mixture of amusement and caution, as if she doesn't believe I'll behave.

Not that she's wrong.

"Miss Williams," Ray begins, but Tia cuts him off gently.

"Please, sugar, call me Tia," She says, her eyes never leaving mine as I perch on the edge of the box, resisting the urge to leap into the foreboding waters beyond.

Ray nods, a furrow forming between his brows. "Ms.—Tia, is everything okay with you?" He asks, his tone suggesting his concern.

Tia lets out a short laugh, her shoulders relaxing slightly, "Of course, Ray. Why wouldn't they be?"

The engine sputters and dies as Ray turns off the boat.

"My momma said only people who carry darkness and pain inside them can have the shadows grant them what they desire in a time of desperation," He says. "And this here, he points at me, "This here screams dark magic according to Evangeline's research." He shrugs, "She texted me on the drive over here." He admits sheepishly. "And the way we see it, is you helped us when we needed it most—is there something we can do for you now, to return the favor?"

I watch Tia's face closely from my vantage point beside her, expecting defiance, anger, anything but what comes next.

Her eyes glisten with unshed tears, and suddenly, she leans into Ray, embracing him tightly.

"Oh, Ray, you're already doing so much," She smiles, wiping away a tear, "Just by giving us a ride to the bayous to get all this voodoo, black magic stuff figured out," She clears her throat, smoothing out her shirt, "I'll be fine, really." She assures him, "And Ray, I appreciate you two more than you'll ever know."

As much as I want to resent her, to hold onto my fury for the murders she's confessed to, I can't help the way my heart twists at the sight of her vulnerability.

She's been through hell, and here she is, still trying to make things right. Her pursuit of justice for her father may have skewed her moral compass, but who am I to judge?

Corruption has seeped into the very institutions that should protect us; I've seen it firsthand.

How can I hate Tia for losing her way in the fight against such darkness?

"Thank you, Ms. Tia," Ray whispers, patting her back before pulling away and starting the boat's engine again.

I settle back into the shadow of the music box, reflecting on the intricate series of events that have brought us to this very moment.

I can't let myself faulter.

Murder is murder.

She's crossed a line that I, as an agent of the law, can't ignore. And turning me into a frog? That's unforgivable. My duty is clear, even if my heart isn't on board. Tia has a piece of it, sure, but the rest is bound by honor.

I watch, waiting for my chance. The soft murmur of their conversation, Ray's concerned tone, Tia's sniffles—they mask the sound of my impatience. Then, an opening. They're deep in exchange, their backs to me.

This is it.

With a push of my hind legs, I launch from my enclosure, aiming for the wooden planks beneath. A soft thud betrays my landing.

I freeze, heart racing.

Did they hear?

But no, their words continue uninterrupted, flowing over me like the muggy bayou air.

Now's my time. I don't belong in this box, in this boat, under her spell. I need to leap away from this tangled web she's woven around us both.

I gather myself, muscles coiling, then spring forward. Out of the boat, into the wild embrace of murky waters. The swamp swallows me whole, cool against my smooth skin.

Turns out, freedom tastes like algae.

My mind spins with plans—find the witch, break this curse, and then it's all about putting an end to Tia's reckless vendetta.

Betrayal is a bitter pill, coated in false sweet smiles and southern charm. Her fate will be sealed by the law, not by the dark arts she decided to dabble in.

But first, I must survive the perils of the swamp.

My legs thrash through the water, propelling me towards my self-appointed mission. The distant echo of Tia and Ray's shouts pierces the humid air, their words indistinct blurs against the cacophony of nocturnal creatures. Their concern is white noise; my focus is singular.

I dive deeper, navigating through the tangles of roots and the occasional brush of fish against my slick skin. The surface is a world away when I sense it—the shift in water, the silent alarm that screams danger.

Instinctively, I twist my body, an agile contortion only this cursed form allows. The sight that greets me is primeval horror—a gaping maw lined with daggers; eyes dead as the void.

An alligator, nature's own assassin, lunges at what it sees as nothing more than a wayward morsel.

Adrenaline surges like electricity through my veins, and I kick away with all the force I possess. It's a dance of death, each move calculated, desperate. The beast's jaws snap shut where I was just a heartbeat ago, and I barrel through the water, my heart pounding in my tiny chest.

"Keep moving," I mutter internally, "Or you're gator grub."

Panic seizes me, a cold grip that tightens with each snap of those monstrous jaws.

My screams are nothing but gurgles beneath the swamp's surface, my desperate kicks barely keeping me out of the alligator's lethal embrace.

I lunge upward, breaking the water's surface, gasping for life, begging for salvation, "Throw me a life preserver!"

The plea comes out as a strangled croak before I'm dragged down again by gravity and fear.

Just as darkness and despair threaten to claim me, an unexpected splash signals hope—or a shared doom.

Tia's there, her body slicing into the murky depths beside me. Her legs coil around the gator with a moxie that belies her slim form.

She locks her arms in an iron grip, wrestling the beast with a ferocity that stuns both me and the predator. The alligator twists and thrashes, trying to dislodge her, but Tia holds on, her breath bubbles trailing upwards as they spin in a deadly pirouette.

"Grab the rope!" Ray's voice punches through the chaos, a lifeline thrown across the churning waters.

Tia's hand flails, seeking the promised safety, her other fist connecting with the snout of the beast. The creature's teeth snap wildly, a hair's breadth from our flesh.

With a mighty heave, Ray manages to toss the rope closer, but she can't reach it.

My heart hammers against my ribcage. Time slows, stretching into a singular moment of terror and valiance.

The gator goes under again, this time dismounting Tia, who kicks away, her legs pumping ferociously.

But the beast is on her in an instant.

I have to gain its attention.

"Hey, dummy!" I call out just as my head bobs above the water's surface. "Over here! Come on!" I urge, "I hear I taste like chicken!"

The alligator, momentarily confused by my taunts, halts its advance towards Tia and pivots towards me, its eyes glinting with predatory calculation. For a split second, I regret my decision, my heart leaping into my throat as the gator's massive form churns through the water in my direction.

Tia uses this brief respite to surface, gasping for air, her arms reaching desperately for the rope now dancing on the water's surface.

Finally, her fingers curl around the rope, and I feel her hand warp around me as Ray hauls back on the rope, our bodies lurching toward the boat.

The gator, relentless in pursuit of its claimed prize, lunges, its primordial brain unable to concede defeat.

In a stroke of frenzied inspiration, I hoist myself onto Tia's head, perching precariously so she can use both hands without worrying about me.

She snags a driftwood branch from the water, her movements honed by necessity, and drives it down, right into the predator's eye.

A deep, guttural hissing sound escapes the alligator's mouth as Ray channels every last bit of his energy, reeling us in.

Tia's leg pistons out, her heel connecting with the beast's snout in a solid thwack. It's enough to make the creature reel back in pain, its body thrashing violently in the water, creating a froth of bubbles and spray, but also giving Ray the final few seconds he needs to pull us onto the safety of the boat.

It rocks violently, the gator's maw snapping at the air where we just were, its sheer mass threatening to capsize our only refuge. But Ray is quick, his knowledge of the bayou as innate as breathing. He flings open a cooler, seizing handfuls of raw chicken legs and casting them into the swamp.

The gator takes the bait, disappearing after its consolation prize with a thrash of its tail.

"Are you insane?" Tia's voice slices through the aftermath, and she wrenches me from my sodden perch atop her head, eyes ablaze with fury and fear. "What in the actual fuck did you think you were doing? Were you trying to get yourself killed?" She barks.

I open my mouth, struggling for words, my own heartbeat still thunderous in my ears.

"I'm sorry, okay. It was stupid." The admission tastes stagnant, like the murky waters we've just escaped.

I glance up at her, expecting more anger or a scolding that I unquestionably deserve. Instead, there's a shift in her eyes—a flicker of relief that softens the hard lines of her face.

She could have left me, a small part of my mind whispers, but she didn't.

"Thank you," I manage to say, and it's more than just for pulling me to safety. It's for everything unspoken, for every danger she faces with me when she doesn't have to.

Tia exhales, her smile barely there but enough to ease the tension in my body.

"Just stay in the damn box, okay?" Her tone bears a playful scold, but beneath it is an earnest plea.

"Right," I agree, nodding my tiny frog head.

Ray, who is busy securing a makeshift bandage around his hand where a splinter from the boat gouged him during our reckless escape, chuckles dryly. "You two are something else," He mutters, shaking his head, but there's admiration in his gruff voice.

This experience has taught me a valuable lesson: this swamp is a dangerous place, and it could easily become my watery grave. But what will stick with me for the rest of my life, is Tia's bravery, her quick thinking—or her unwillingness to let me go.

CHAPTER THIRTY-NINE

Tia

I twist my fingers through my thick wet curls, pulling and squeezing the water out before I grab the towel Ray offered me. It's rough against my scalp but comforting, a small piece of normalcy as we edge further into the unknown.

The foliage around us grows denser, an impenetrable wall of greenery. Spanish moss drapes like ghostly curtains from the trees, and milkweed clusters thickly along the banks, their pods bursting with fluffy seeds ready to take flight. No hint of sunlight breaks through the canopy anymore; it's just unforgiving darkness, like the swamp has swallowed the day whole.

"Well, this looks lovely," Ray mutters, his hands steady on the wheel.

I can see the subtle tremors in his fingers—a reflection of the fear that's worming its way into my own gut.

He flicks a switch, and suddenly the boat is bathed in the harsh glare of floodlights, turning night into day in a stark, artificial way. Shadows jump and twist around us, making the trees look like they're closing in.

The boat slows, almost drifting now, and Ray swallows hard. "This is as far out as I've been before," He confesses, eyes flickering to the depth finder, then back to the hazy waters below. "Anything beyond this is off my maps."

"We'll be okay," I try to sound convincing, more for my own sake than his.

My hands clutch the edge of the seat as I peer into the eerie glow cast by the floodlights.

Then, without warning, a massive shape displaces the water beside us, sending a vibration up the hull.

The boat rocks, and I grip the side, heart thundering in my chest. My eyes strain against the blinding light to see what lurks beneath the surface, but it's useless—there's only the dark, churning water.

"What the fuck is that?" Cade gulps.

We all lean in, peering into the abyss that laps at the sides of our vessel, each of us silently praying this isn't where our story ends, devoured by some unseen leviathan in the heart of the swamp.

Ray's hand flies to the throttle, revving the engine back to life with a troubled growl. The boat lurches forward, cutting through the water as we both scan the surging waves behind us.

The trees seem to murmur warning, their voices a sibilant chorus that raises the hairs on the back of my neck.

"Go away," They hiss, *"Turn around or all will be lost."*

A sudden jerk sends the boat careening, before it comes to a complete halt, and I can't suppress the small yelp that escapes my mouth.

Ray's head snaps from side to side, flashlight beam dancing frantically over gnarled roots and drooping moss as he tries to detect what unseen force has grasped us.

"Something's out there," Cade mutters.

"No shit!" I snap, my eyes jumping to where he sits.

"Stay calm, guys," Ray breathes out, more to himself than to us, his knuckles white as they clutch the steering wheel, he no longer has control of.

We're moving again, but not from the engine—something is pushing us.

The boat groans under the strain, timbers creaking like old bones bending to a breaking point. I can feel the rumble beneath us, more powerful than any engine; something alive.

The boat takes a natural curve in the waterway, and through the curtain of darkness swathed with ghostly light, an island materializes from the gloom.

My breath catches at the sight of the colossal tree that anchors this speck of land amidst the bayou waters. Its branches, like the arms of giants, stretch skyward, cradling a structure so fantastical it seems plucked from a dream.

"Is that a treehouse?" Ray's voice is tinged with wonder, the tension briefly forgotten.

"More like a fortress," I reply, unable to tear my eyes away from the intricate wooden haven nestled in the tree's embrace.

Stained glass windows flicker with vibrant hues, seemingly crafted from glass bottles that sway gently in the breeze, their hollow songs mingling with the soft rustle of leaves. The hanging bridges that link the treehouse's many sections beckon with an otherworldly allure, promising mysteries and perhaps, even answers.

"I have never seen anything like this before." Cade whispers.

The boat thuds against the muddy bank and we come to a stop.

Then, the stillness shatters.

"Look out!" Cade shouts.

I spin around just in time to see it—an impossibility made of scaly flesh—a giant water moccasin rearing from the black water, its scales glistening in the sparse light, its eyes milky white and unseeing.

"Welcome," It hisses, towering above us as it sways back in forth.

But as sudden as it had emerged, the serpent dives back into the water, rippling waves cascading outwards from where it dove.

"Did that moccasin just speak?" Ray murmurs.

"Focus," I remind him, though my own mind reels.

The snake isn't done with us.

It breaks the surface again, this time slithering to solid ground. Its massive body coiled tightly, as if wrapping the earth itself.

"Stay back," I warn, but the words were needless, because what happens next defies all reason.

The serpent shimmers, and light bursts forth, tearing at its scaly hide. The air crackles with energy, and I throw an arm over my eyes against the blinding glare. When I dare look again, the beast is gone.

In its stead stands a woman—tall, her hair a cascade of silver flowing down her back, complement the darkness around us. She leans on an ornate cane, her posture regal, yet marked by an agelessness that contradicts her unexpected youthful appearance.

"Of course, she's the snake." Ray beams, "No one ever wants to venture this deep because of the stories of a giant snake that terrorizes the deep bayou. Incredible."

She turns, her gaze sweeping over us with a measured calm that somehow demands respect.

"You're her, MamaKaze," I exclaim.

The corners of the woman's lips turn up in an amused smile.

"I'm surprised the youngsters of these days still know about me." She tilts her head, "Tell me, do I still lure the towns' children out here to eat them?" A playful glint sparkles in her eyes. "And boil their femurs for bone stew?"

Her laughter rolls through the thick air, echoing off the trees.

With a casual wave of her hand, she beckons us, "Come now, children, we have a lot to do."

Unsure but compelled, I share a hesitant glance with Cade, his frog form somehow less startling now.

Ray and I nod in agreement before stepping off our safe haven boat and onto the soft soil of the island.

"Watch your—" But my warning cuts short. As MamaKaze steps off a large rock, a tree root surges from the ground, forming an impromptu step beneath her foot.

It's as if the entire swamp conspires to serve her.

"Okay, the trees are alive too," Cade notes, his webbed feet gripping the edge of his box, his gaze riveted to the animated root.

"Excuse me, ma'am," I begin, but I'm cut off.

"MamaKaze," The witch corrects with a twinkle in her eye. "It's like the drink Kamikaze, but I taste much better." She laughs, swinging her cane with an air of nonchalance.

Despite the surreal nature of our encounter, a small smile flutters on my lips, a response to her peculiar humor.

I gather my courage, finding strength in her mirth. "Okay, well, MamaKaze, I need your help."

"Of course you do, child," She responds without missing a beat. "Got yourself in a good mess, you did." She casts a knowing glance over her shoulder as we follow her deeper into the thicket. "Now hurry up, supper is waiting."

I should be taken aback by her anticipation of our visit, but as we step into the treehouse, I'm not.

The table is laid out with three steaming bowls of stew, a small bowl of flies for Cade in his current amphibious form, and a fresh loaf of bread sliced neatly on a wooden cutting board.

"How did you know?" Cade asks, his voice a croak of wonder as he eyes the spread before us.

MamaKaze chuckles, a sound that seems to make the very walls of the treehouse hum with energy.

"I know everything that goes on in my swamp and in the city," She says, her gaze piercing as if she can see right through us. "The land and the animals share secrets—all you have to do is shut up every once in a while, and listen."

Cade and I exchange a glance.

With a wave of her cane, she ushers us to the table. "Eat up, hunger can cloud even the wisest of minds, and we have much to discuss."

CHAPTER FORTY

Agent Holloway

I'm slurping up the flies in my bowl, and it's unsettling how my tongue practically salivates at their flavor. A shiver of disgust runs down my spine, but my stomach rumbles in appreciation—a twisted conflict of senses.

Across from me, Ray's bowl is already empty; he devoured his stew within the first few moments of our arrival. Tia, on the other hand, is savoring her meal, spooning up the rich broth

363

with an elegance that makes you forget we're high up in a tree-house and not in some grand dining hall.

"MamaKaze, this is delicious," Tia says, her voice saturated with unalloyed respect for the old woman's culinary skills.

Her gaze lifts from the remnants of her stew, and she sets her spoon down with the soft clink of wood on ceramic. She dabs her lips with the cloth napkin—ever the image of grace even in the wildest of settings—and then turns her attention to MamaKaze. Tia's eyes, filled with that hopeful spark that's so her, meet the gaze of the elder.

"Can you fix Cade?" She asks, daring to believe in miracles.

MamaKaze doesn't answer immediately. Instead, she leans on her cane and shuffles toward the collection of shelves that hug the far wall of the room. Dust motes dance in the shafts of light that filter through the leaves outside as she surveys her array of bottles and jars, each one filled with mysterious contents known only to her.

With careful fingers, she picks up a small glass bottle and places it on the countertop. Then another follows, and another, until there's a small regiment of them standing guard by her old cast-iron stove.

The tension in the room hangs thick as the silence lingers. Tia's hopeful gaze is fixed on MamaKaze, waiting for her to dispense wisdom and possibly bring a sense of resolution.

The cauldron clanks onto the stove with a thud as MamaKaze starts her mysterious alchemy. She drops in handfuls of this and pinches of that, each ingredient spiraling into the pot like tiny cyclones.

Finally looks up from her concoction, stirring slowly.

"No," She says, with absolute, her voice low and rumbling like distant thunder. "Not without the mushrooms and fresh green onions from the opposite side of the island."

Ray's chair scrapes back against the wooden floor as he stands, "I'll go," He offers.

But the old woman shakes her head, those milky eyes of hers scanning our faces. "No, child. The ones who caused this mess must be the ones to set it right."

A moment of frustration crosses her face, and she pats her apron pockets. "Well damn," She mutters, more to herself than to us. "I done went and lost my doo-hicky."

"Your what, MamaKaze?" I ask, unable to imagine what sort of thing a *'doo-hicky'* could be.

"Never you mind," She grumbles.

Then, from the shadowed rafters above, a flurry of motion catches my eye.

A squirrel.

It scampers down, nimble as a thief, and nabs something off the top shelf with his tiny mouth, before it makes a beeline for MamaKaze. It climbs her like a tree, all the way up to her shoulder, and deposits his find into her waiting palm.

"Thank you, Bennet," She pats the squirrels head, a smile touching her lips as she unfolds her hand to reveal an aged brass compass.

The needle bobs and weaves before settling steadfastly north-ward.

"Really, a squirrel named Bennet?" I can't help but laugh, slurping up the last fly in my bowl as I watch the little creature perch triumphantly on MamaKaze's shoulder.

"Aye, and you're a frog named Cade," MamaKaze retorts with a shrug that ripples her shawl. "I'm glad we are all acquainted now."

The corner of Tia's mouth twitches, and she stifles a smile behind her napkin, glancing up from twirling thumbs.

Then, the world snaps back into place with the sharp *'thwack'* of wood hitting wood. MamaKaze's cane comes down like a guillotine between Tia and me, rattling the bowls on the table. "You two up, now," She demands.

I leap to the side, stomach leaping up in my throat, "You could have squished me, woman!" I exclaim, feeling the indignance flare hot under my green skin.

MamaKaze chuckles, unfazed.

"But did you die?" She tosses over her shoulder, already striding towards the door.

I watch her back, her form haloed by the multi-colored light filtering through the stained glass as she pushes the front door open, walking out onto the bridge just beyond it.

"Watch your step," She calls without looking back.

Tia's palm lies open before me, an unspoken invitation that feels too kind. I hesitate, a part of me rearing back at the thought of her gentle touch.

Why does she have to be so nice?

It'd make things simpler if she despised me—a clean-cut case of right and wrong.

But as I look into Tia's eyes, earnest and hopeful, I can't bring myself to want her animosity. Nor can I harbor it against her, even though what she's done skews the lines of legality in ways I can't reconcile.

With a resigned flick of my legs, I spring into her outstretched hand. The warmth there is more than just physical; it's a connection I find myself both craving and condemning.

"Let's not keep MamaKaze waiting," Tia whispers, as we step onto the bridge where the old woman stands silhouetted against the twilight sky.

"See there?" She leans forward, her cane trembling slightly as she points into the distance. "That will be your journey tonight. Bring me back the onions and mushrooms from there by morning, and I'll give you a remedy."

"But how will we know where to go?" Tia's fingers tighten ever so slightly around my damp skin.

Without a word, MamaKaze draws the compass from the folds of her apron and places it in Tia's other hand. "With this, you'll always find true north." Her milky white eyes, piercing despite their cloudiness. "But if you get lost and can't find your way, just shut up and listen. The land will show you the way."

"What the hell is that even supposed to mean?" I blurt out.

MamaKaze's gnarled finger comes down on the tip of my snout like a sledgehammer, "It means that you need to shut up and listen, you rude little toad."

Indignation puffs up my throat sac. "I'll have you know that I am a frog, not a toad—thank you," I retort, emphasizing the taxonomic distinction with a huff.

Her eyes narrow, and she leans in close enough for me to see the lines etched deeply into her face.

"And I'll have you know that I can add you to my pot next," She warns.

I gulp. Her threat is as real as the creases on her face.

"Point taken."

Tia's hand encircles my midsection and hoists me onto her shoulder.

Her touch is gentle.

She pulls MamaKaze into a quick embrace.

"Thank you," Tia whispers, "For everything."

"Ah, don't thank me yet," MamaKaze responds, pulling away just enough to lock gazes with Tia and point to the horizon. "You still have to make it back before the light touches them there clouds."

Tia nods, shoving the compass into the pocket of her pants, and she takes a step back, "Ready to go?" She glances over at me on her shoulder.

"Let's do it." I confirm.

In reality, it's not that far, so this should be easy—right?

Agent Holloway

"**W**hat exactly do you think mushrooms and onions are going to do when it comes to turning me back into a human?" I ask Tia.

She shrugs, her focus more on navigating the treacherous terrain than on culinary magic. "You know as much as I do," She answers, pushing aside a curtain of moss that blocks our path like green drapes in this swampy theater.

A misstep sends her foot sliding on the slick ground, and I cling to her shoulder for dear life, my sticky pads finding purchase against the fabric of her shirt.

"That's not exactly true," I insist after steadying myself, my voice a croak in her ear. "You knew enough about magic to get me voodooed into a frog."

Her eyes roll, an exasperated sigh fleeing her mouth, "I obviously didn't know much, or we wouldn't be out here now, would we?"

She has a point.

"Touché," I reply, my laugh a guttural chuckle that vibrates against Tia's ear.

She stifles a yawn, her shoulders slumping ever so slightly as she forges ahead. Our shared exhaustion hangs between us like the heavy Spanish moss draping from the gnarled trees.

"Sit. Rest for a moment," I urge her.

"I'm okay," She insists stubbornly, but the fatigue is etched in the dark circles under her eyes and the way her voice lacks its usual fire. "Besides, we only have until morning to get back."

"Yea well, ten minutes to catch your breath isn't going to make or break this journey," I joke, just before her foot slips again.

She lets out a huff of frustration and finally yields, her body descending onto the muddy earth with less grace than either of us would care to admit, and she leans her back against a tree.

"I feel like we've been walking in circles for hours," She complains, tapping the glass face of the compass. "I'm beginning to think this thing's broke."

I watch as Tia's head drops back and leans against the rough bark of the tree behind her. She looks exhausted, but there is a certain wild beauty to her disheveled curls forming an untamed halo around her face.

The image of a fallen angel.

"Maybe it's not the compass," I suggest gently, "Maybe it's the island playing tricks on us."

A daunting thought, but not an impossible one, given the strange energies that seem to pulse through the very air around us.

With a spring and a flutter of my webbed feet, I dismount Tia's shoulder, landing on the damp underbrush with a soft squelch. My hind legs propel me back and forth in front of her, the periodic croaking accompanying each leap exposes my frustration more than any human sigh ever could.

The sky remains hidden, veiled by an oppressive ceiling of leaves, save for that one clearing where Mamakaze's tree pierces the heavens—a beacon we've yet to reach.

"Stupid island," I mutter under my breath, "Might as well be chasing our tails."

"We don't even have tails." Tia draws her knees to her chest, chin resting on them as she watches me pace.

A single tear slips from her eye, trailing down her cheek and dropping silently to the ground.

"I'm so sorry, Cade." She sniffs, "If I hadn't dragged you into this, you wouldn't—" A sob steals her words.

I stop my jumping in its tracks, drawn to her like a magnet.

If I were human, I'd envelope her in an embrace, wipe away her tears, and tell her everything is all going to be okay.

But as a frog, I lack the arms to hold her, so instead, I nudge her hand with my head, trying to convey comfort through the cool dampness of my skin.

"Hey, none of that," I say, nudging her again. "To tell you the truth, I wouldn't trade a single second of our adventure."

Her shoulders heave in a quiet sigh, the tension from our endless trek seeming to drain away. She lifts her head, meeting my gaze, "Thank you."

"Don't mention it." I assure her.

"Cade?"

"Yes?"

"Once we find what MamaKaze needs and you're human again," She hiccups, forcing a smile as her hands brush away the remnants of tears, "I'll turn myself in."

"Turn yourself in?" The words leap out before my brain has time to catch up.

Shock hits me first, jarring against the backdrop of the swamp's eternal murk.

"Yes," She murmurs, gazing at the gnarled roots that twist like serpents beneath us. "My mother always said...hatred's a heavy burden. And she's right. It's done nothing but eat me alive."

Her words linger in the air, and I catch a glimpse of her vulnerability.

For a moment, she is not the fearless woman who has endured this cursed island, but a wounded child who has suffered great losses. The unfairness of it all ignites a rage inside me that has been building since I first heard about her past.

"Listen, Tia," I begin, "You don't have to do that."

I know I'm going to kick myself later for my next words, but I say them anyway.

"There's—there's no evidence. They haven't found anything. The case, it's on the verge of being closed. The forensic lab is stumped; they believe it was natural causes because their technology cannot detect whatever flower-poison-nectar stuff, you used."

Our eyes meet, and I can sense the weight of realization settling between us. I can only imagine the flurry of thoughts racing through her head.

I should feel relief at sharing the truth, but instead, there's an ache, a longing to see justice for the wrongs she's endured, a wish to rewrite the narrative of her life into one where she isn't the villain for seeking retribution.

"Really?" She whispers.

"Really," I confirm, "You've suffered enough, luciole. You don't owe them anything more."

There's a silence then, filled only by the distant croak of my kin and the soft rustle of leaves in the breeze. Tia's eyes are wide, a tumult of emotions swirling within their depths.

It's in this moment, I realize, whatever form I wear, human or frog, my loyalty to Tia is unshaken. Whatever path she chooses, I'll hop alongside her, until the very end.

"What? I—I don't understand." Tia's voice trembles.

"Nobody else ever suspected you," I assure her, "I'm just really fucking good at my job."

Her lips curve into a weary smile, "That you are, Agent Halloway, that you are." It's an acknowledgment, a statement of fact that warms me more than any sunbeam could.

With a grunt of effort, she pushes herself off the ground, and her hands make quick work of brushing off the bits of moss and leaves clinging to her cargo pants, and offers me her hand, "Let's go get your man bits back, sugar."

I leap onto her palm, the familiarity of her skin against my webbed feet grounding me.

Together, we're a team—a mismatched duo against the world.

As she lifts me back to the safety of her shoulder, I feel that where we're heading isn't just about reversing spells or clearing consciences; it's about reclaiming our lives that have been twisted by fate and unfortunate circumstance.

And maybe, just maybe, it's about finding redemption in the unlikeliest of places.

CHAPTER FORTY-TWO

Tia

Panic gnaws at the edges of my mind. There's only a little over an hour left before dawn smears the sky in pastel hues and the cover of night slips away from us.

We were supposed to have found it by now—the place MamaKaze sent us to find—but all we've met so far are dead ends.

My fingers, shake as they fumble with the small crossover body bag slung haphazardly over my shoulder. The strap digs into my skin through the thin fabric of my shirt.

I fish out the water bottle, its surface slick with condensation from the humid air that hangs heavy around us. Unscrewing the cap with more force than necessary, I bring the bottle to my lips and tilt it back, hoping for the cool, refreshing taste of water to soothe my fraying nerves.

It's warm.

The vial liquid does little to quench my thirst or comfort me, instead adding to the list of today's disappointments.

Murky waters reflect the darkness that has swallowed the land around us.

"Nothing but swamp as far as the eye can see," I whisper, the words falling flat in the stillness of the night.

We're surrounded by nothing, but waterlogged earth and the occasional cry of a distant creature hidden within the reeds.

We're running out of time, and I'm running out of ideas.

But giving up isn't an option—not when so much is at stake. We have to find what we came for, and we have to do it before the first light of day creeps over the island.

With resignation weighing heavy in my chest, I lower myself onto the large rock at water's edge.

The stone is cool beneath me, unlike the lukewarm bottle of water clutched in my hand. Cade's silent gaze lands on me, his head tilted as if he's trying to read my expression.

"Everything alright?" His voice breaks through the quiet, but I can't muster the energy to answer.

Instead, I nod, and let my fingers wander over the surface of the boulder, tracing the delicate patterns of moss that cling to it like a living tapestry. The texture is soothing—soft and plush, a natural velvet under my touch.

Somewhere in the recesses of my mind, MamaKaze's cryptic advice echoes, urging me to listen to the land itself.

I close my eyes, focusing on her words, hoping for some revelation to pierce through the doubt clouding my thoughts.

"Are you sure you're, okay?" Cade's voice comes again.

"Uh-huh," I hum back, nothing more than a half-hearted affirmation as I slide off the rock to sit cross-legged on the damp earth.

My hands rest beside me, pushing against the ground for balance.

Listen.

I command myself to be still, to push past the anxiety that flutters in my stomach. But all I perceive is the blather of night sounds—the incessant buzz of insects, the distant call of birds, the rustle of unseen creatures that own these shadowed hours.

They blend together.

But I strain harder, seeking a sign, any guidepost hidden within the raucous singing of the swamp.

The ground beneath me vibrates faintly, a subtle pulsation. A gentle breeze caresses my face, stirring the branches into a choreographed sway above.

Animal calls puncture the night, no longer just noise but clear messages—a hiss warning of predators lurking, a chirp like a cheerful greeting, and then, I hone in on it—I can hear the land, just like she said I would."

"Holy shit," I whisper, my breath hitching as my eyes snap open.

A surge of certainty floods through me, and I grab Cade up off the swamp floor, "I know where to go!"

"What? How?" Cade's froglike eyes widen.

My forehead pinches in concentration, my feet moving on their own accord, "I—I don't know how to explain it, I just do."

I dodge a low-hanging branch, swiping it aside just before it could graze my forehead. My heart hammers with excitement, propelling us forward as the first hints of dawn threaten the horizon.

The canopy opens up, granting us a view of the pre-dawn sky. Twinkling stars blink at us from above.

I pause at the water's edge, drinking in the sight of an ethereal bayou oasis nestled within the island's heart.

It's like stumbling upon a secret garden, hidden away from the rest of the world.

"Look at this place," Cade murmurs from my palm.

Surrounded by the serenity of catacombs wave, milkweed clusters stand tall, their creamy blooms undisturbed. Lotus flowers crown the lilypads, their vibrant pinks and whites striking against the dark waters. Luminescent butterflies flit about, their wings catching the first light, creating a glimmering dance as they feast on nectar.

The sharp, earthy scent of wild onions teases my nose, guiding me further inland until my gaze lands on it—a large white mushroom cap dappled with brown spots, the mark that we've found what we were looking for.

"We did it," I exclaim, bouncing on the balls of my feet, a triumphant little hop escaping me.

"You did it," He corrects, his eyes meeting mine with something similar to pride.

Heat creeps into my cheeks as I shake my head, still bewildered by it all.

"I still don't know how to explain it," I confess, "I just felt this—pull."

Cade chuckles, rubbing his stomach. "Huh, the only thing I felt was indigestion from all those flies."

His humor breaks through my uncertainty, coaxing a laugh from deep within my gut.

But reality quickly alleviates our joyousness.

"We're gonna have to hurry if we're going to make it back in time," I warn, already scanning the horizon for the quickest path back.

"Guess I better hop to it then," Cade quips, a grin tugging at his froggy lips as he follows my lead.

Darting through the brush, our footsteps are swift. The path back to MamaKaze's is familiar now, a route imprinted into my muscle memory.

Sweat beads on my forehead, but I brush it away, the bundle of wild onions and speckled mushrooms secure in my bag.

"Almost there," I puff out, catching sight of the clearing up ahead.

We burst from the underbrush with minutes to spare, our breaths coming out in heavy, satisfied gasps. That's when a mischievous rustle from above announces Bennet the squirrel's descent. He lands deftly on my shoulder, tiny claws gripping the fabric of my shirt.

"Hey, Benn—" Before I can finish, he leans over and thumps Cade squarely on the head, then darts off, a string of chitters trailing behind him like laughter.

"What the hell was that for?" Cade bellows, rubbing the spot Bennet assaulted, a mock scowl on his face.

I stifle a giggle, just as MamaKaze's voice drifts toward us, rich with amusement.

"Ahhh...you made it. And in one piece," She laughs, her tone as warm as the morning sun now peeking through the trees.

"Of course we did," I reply, trying to keep the pride from my voice as I swing the bag off my shoulder.

MamaKaze steps closer, she examines us, a nod acknowledging our success.

"Can you help us now?" I ask, my heart hammering with hope.

She takes the bag from my hands, a knowing smile playing at the corners of her lips.

"Almost," She replies, peering into the contents. "I need to go whip something up first." She then turns on her heels, the skirts of her vibrant dress swishing around her ankles as she disappears through the mossy door of her dwelling.

Cade and I exchange a worried glance, but there is nothing more we can do.

Our part is done—for now. The rest is in the hands of an old, possibly crazy witch.

CHAPTER FORTY-THREE

Agent Holloway

T he night clings to the remnants of its reign, a dusky hue stretching its fingers to paint watercolors on the soon to be morning sky.

It's like the world is caught, between two different existences: one shrouded in the shadowy mystery of the moon and stars, the other basking in the vibrant radiance of the sun.

"Beautiful, isn't it?" Tia murmurs from beside me.

I nod, "It is." I confirm, though, I'm not talking about the scenery.

She sighs, "I mean, just look at all of this." She waves her hand gesturing to backdrop of the fading night.

I let my gaze wander across the canvas of the heavens, drinking in the sight of stars suffering their last stand against the dawn. They're like tiny holes punched in the fabric of the night, allowing glimmers of a brighter realm to shine through.

"Do you ever wish you could capture the stars—put them in a jar to keep forever?"

"Oh, no! I would never!" Tia exclaims. "Thier beauty isn't meant to be contained by just one person—it's meant to be shared, to shine bright enough for the entire universe to see. They help guide us through the darkest of times, even when the moon feels too burdened to do so."

Her confession sings a song that only I can hear, resonating down to the very core of my soul.

Damn.

I want so badly to kiss her, but that could be a little weird considering my current condition.

So instead of a kiss, I say the first thing that comes to mind when I gaze into her eyes, "You know, I never noticed the beauty in the stars, or how brightly they shine, until I met you, luciole."

"Your charm is deadly, Agent Holloway," A smile steals the place of the small frown she held only moment prior.

"Mmmm...That may be true, but I'm still not as deadly as you are, Ms. Williams." I reply coyly, then immediately regret my choice of words.

Way to ruin the moment, Cade.

But she doesn't get angry. Her face drops, melancholy—she's lost her shine.

"I'm sorry. I—I didn't mean to upset you." I stammer, my tongue tripping over the syllables.

"No, you're right. I'm no better than the murdering psychopaths you keep society safe from. I don't deserve sympathy, or love. My father gave up his life to give me the one I've been blessed with—the one I shouldn't even be entitled to."

"You're nothing like those monsters." I whisper, hating that I ever made her feel that way. "Those monsters don't feel remorse, luciole. They don't feel love. They don't sacrifice for the sake of others; not like you do."

"Don't," She breathes, shaking her head and looking away. "Don't make me out to be some kind of saint, Cade. You know what I've done."

"Hey guys," Ray waves as he opens the front door, "Am I interrupting?"

Yes.

"No, Ray, you're fine, sugar." Tia says, standing up quickly and wiping the moisture in her eyes with her balled fist.

I guess that's what we're going with then.

With a contented sigh, Ray squeezes himself into the small gap between Tia and me.

He gestures skyward, toward one of the last cluster of stars holding on to the night. "Evangeline says that cluster there formed just for us," He announces, a note of wonder threading his tone. "Says it tells a never-ending story of the love we share for one another." His grin stretches wide, his pride unmistakable as he adds, "Our little boy is part of that story now."

Tia's eyes linger on the star cluster Ray indicates, her lips curving into a small smile despite her recent tears.

"That's beautiful, Ray," She murmurs, some of her earlier sparkle returning as she gazes at the celestial spectacle.

Ray, oblivious to the undercurrent of tension, continues to ramble on until the door slams open and MamaKaze makes her presence known, "Ya'll coming or not? I ain't getting no younger."

Ray extends a hand to help me down from my perch on the banister, and together, we trail after Mamakaze into the heart of the house, the smell of breakfast growing stronger with each step.

"So, now what?" I ask her, eager for some semblance of normalcy, for a plan, for anything.

"Now we eat," She answers simply.

Tia's confusion spills out in a giant wave when she notices the omelets laid out on the table fit with cheese, onions, mushrooms, tomato, and peppers.

"What?" Anger sharpens her voice. "We were out all night searching this—stuff, and it was for omelets?!" She says, getting louder at the end of her declaration.

She's pissed.

"Indeed," Mamakaze replies, unworried by Tia's mounting fury.

"But I thought you could help turn Cade back into a human," Tia presses, her words nearly a yell now.

Mamakaze sighs, "Oh, yea. That." She waves her hand dismissively. "He just needs to be kissed by a princess."

My blood boils, a snarl twisting my lips. "A princess? A fucking princess?" I spit out the words.

"This old woman is out of her fucking mind!" My gaze sweeps the room as if a royal might be hiding in the rafters. "And where exactly am I supposed to find a goddamn princess? You expect me to hop to London to ask the queen to have one of her daughters kiss me?"

Mamakaze leans against the kitchen counter, a mystifying twinkle in her eye. "I sure would hope you wouldn't travel that far for something so close." She winks, before hobbling over to her chair and sitting down.

"Close?" My voice rises "I'm getting really tired of your riddles, woman."

MamaKaze chuckles, the sound raspy and dry like leaves skittering across a cobblestone path.

"Dearie, sometimes what you seek is hidden in plain sight," She gestures broadly with an unsteady hand, encompassing the room.

The realization that I may never take on another case, apprehend another criminal, or have the chance to hold the hand of the woman I am falling for slowly sinks in, and it's a difficult truth to accept.

And what about *her*? Will I ever see her again? Will she think that I've abandoned her?

She's been through enough heartache—I don't want to be the cause of any of her pain.

A lump forms in the back of my throat, my stomach twists with a cocktail of frustration and despair.

"Enough with the cryptic nonsense!" I shout, unable to keep the desperation out of my voice. "This was just a waste of fucking time. I'm out of here." I jump from Ray's palm.

"Cade, wait." I hear Tia call out behind me, but I'm on the verge of tears and I can't stand the idea of her seeing me like this—broken, defeated.

Since I don't have opposable thumbs, Ray takes the curtesy of opening the door so I can storm off with what's left of my pride.

I barrel down the front steps, the cool evening air stinging my amphibious cheeks as I attempt to outrun the turmoil churning inside me.

I can hear Tia's footsteps trailing behind, her calls growing more insistent, but I can't face her—not yet.

Not like this.

Maybe this is where I'll stay—out here in the bayous where I'll eventually become some creature's midnight snack.

What kind of life can I live now anyway?

The heavy scent of moss and damp earth does little to calm my racing heart as I make my way deeper into the thick under-growth, my webbed feet sloshing through the mud.

Birds flutter ahead, small animals rustle the underbrush, and the incessant croak of frogs blend into the morning dew. The sounds of the bayou should be soothing, yet they only heighten my sense of isolation.

"Cade!" Tia calls again, her voice clearer now, closer. She's catching up, despite my futile attempts to escape.

Curse her human legs.

"Please, Cade, just talk to me!" Tia pleads.

I can't deny her.

I stop, turning slowly to face her as she emerges from between the tangled webs of cypress trees, her thick curly hair tousled from the chase.

"Tia," I say, my voice shaky with emotion. "I don't know if I can do this anymore."

She steps closer, her eyes searching mine for something I'm afraid I can't give.

"You don't have to do it alone," She says softly, bending down, her hand reaching out to brush a wet leaf off my head. "Whatever *this* is, we'll figure it out together."

"Luciole, you have a long life ahead of you. You're amazing and talented and I—I'm a frog. A literal frog and we can never be together. We can never lead a normal life."

Tia's eyes well with unshed tears, but her voice is steady, resolute. "Normal is overrated, Cade. Who wants normal when they can have extraordinary?"

Extraordinary is exactly what she is.

But I refuse to let her lead a life where every day is a gamble, where every moment spent with me is a moment taken away from her potential, her future.

Isn't love supposed to be selfless?

Isn't it about wanting the best for the other, no matter what that means for yourself?

"Cade, nothing about us was ever normal," Tia continues, giving me a little poke.

Her touch, even light and teasing, sends a jolt through me. It's warmth, it's human, and it's filled with the kind of stubbornness only Tia could hold onto.

"What if we never find a way to change me back?" I ask.

"What if we do?" She retorts. "The world is full of magic, Cade. And I bet you, we've only just begun to see what it can do. If there's any chance, any possibility that we can find a cure for this, I want to take that chance with you.

Her determination rekindles a flicker of hope within me. How could it not?

"But what about everything you'll miss?" My voice cracks, laden with the weight of my fears. "What if it takes years? Decades?"

Tia picks me up off the moist earth, her hands gently cradling me, "Then I will have spent those years with you."

"But—"

"No buts. If it weren't for me, you wouldn't even be in this situation. I owe it to you to find a way out."

I know when I'm a beaten man—er, frog.

Damn, this woman possesses a spiritedness that surpasses anything I've encountered before.

She's a fierce wind that bends but never breaks, a storm in human form.

"Okay," I finally give in.

She smiles, "Ready to go back inside? Those omelets did smell pretty delicious."

I don't find her joke to be funny.

"Sorry," She says coyly. "Too soon, I know."

But her smile doesn't fade, and I find myself releasing my grip on self-pity, even if just for a moment.

After returning to the house, we find MamaKaze and Ray sit at the dining table. They're deep in conversation, their plates of food untouched before them.

"Bout time the two of you made it back." MamaKaze says, winking at Ray.

"Did you get what you needed to sort out, sorted out?" She asks.

"As much as we can for now," Tia responds. "One way or another, I am going to fix this, even if *you* can't."

The old lady rises from her seat at Tia's words, "You listen here, child. My word is not to be doubted. I've seen more than you can imagine, and I've done things beyond your wildest dreams.

But this—this is different. This ain't just about fixing something. It's about understanding it, and even respecting the powers at play here." Her voice softens, "Magic has its own ways, Tia. It doesn't adhere to our wants or timelines. Sometimes, the journey is more than just finding a solution; it's about finding yourself in the process."

Tia's brows furrow, "I know exactly who I am." She snaps. "And who I am, has nothing to do with fixing Cade."

"Doesn't it?" Another cryptic message from the old coot."

Tia's mouth moves, but no words come out as she plops down next to MamaKaze at the table and stares down at the cold egg on her plate.

"For now, let us eat." MamaKaze flicks her wrist and the omelets on each plate begin to steam.

The table fills with the warm scent of herbs and cheese as the food magically reheats itself.

Ray, always one to lighten the mood, claps his hands and grins, "Looks like breakfast is served again!" He says, grabbing his fork.

Tia forces a smile, and places me on the table, pulling the small saucer of scrambled bugs and eggs that could only belong to me, over to where I am.

As Ray and MamaKaze begin to eat, the tension slowly dissipates, the clinking of utensils against plates replacing the heaviness of earlier words.

Tia, however, eats mechanically, her fork raking at the stretchy cheese, her mind clearly elsewhere.

She's not one to easily let go of a thought once it has taken hold.

Her plate soon looks more like a battlefield than a breakfast.

As Ray laughs at some joke MamaKaze shares—something about a mischievous sprite and a misplaced potion—Tia's gaze drifts toward the window where the early morning sun warms the earth.

Suddenly, she sets down her fork, wipes her mouth with the napkin, and stands abruptly, pushing the chair back with a squeal that cuts through the lingering laughter.

"Is it necessary for this princess to come from a royal background?"

MamaKaze grins, "Ah, now those are the questions that lead to answers worth finding. Tell me, child, what does your heart say?"

Tia crosses her arms, her eyes narrowing as she processes the question. "My heart says it's tired of all these puzzles and your cryptic guidance. Can't something just be clear and simple for once?"

"Clarity is often hidden beneath layers of mystery."

"Ughhhh!" Tia groans, throwing her hands up.

Ray's smile fades a bit as he watches Tia's frustration build. He interjects with a gentle tone, trying to bridge the gap between her exasperation and MamaKaze's enigma. "Maybe what MamaKaze means is that sometimes we need to look beyond what's traditionally expected. Princesses from them fairy stories that my Evangeline likes so much—they aren't always born to it. Some of them become princesses through bravery, kindness, or even cleverness. Kind of like how a leader isn't just someone who wears a crown, but someone who acts with other people's hearts in mind."

Tia nods, relaxing slightly, "That's kind of what I'm hoping for, Ray."

"Cade, I—I want to try something."

Her hands reach out for me, and I quickly eat the rest of my food before hopping into her hand.

Tia holds me gently, her fingers warm and careful. The room falls silent for a moment, all eyes on us. She brings me closer to her face, and I can see the determination in her eyes mixed with a flicker of doubt.

"I'm taking a leap of faith," She whispers as she leans down and places a delicate kiss on my thick, mottled forehead.

A surreal, otherworldly aura envelops me, emanating from my skin like a radiant flame. Its gentle, pulsating glow reminds me of the night I was transformed into a frog, when a similar light surrounded me and changed me forever. It radiates a sense of magic and mystery, filling me with wonder and a touch of fear. As I bask in the warm glow, I can almost feel its power tingling on my skin, like tiny sparks of electricity dancing along my flesh.

It is both beautiful and unsettling.

Ray yelps and stumbles back, his chair toppling over with him in it.

My body leaves the solace of Tia's hands and I'm then levitating, hovering in midair. The light ripping through my flesh intensifies, becoming a miniature sun that implodes with a silent rush, forcing everyone to shield their eyes.

The light fades, there I am—stark fucking naked and crouched awkwardly on all fours.

Heat floods my cheeks, not from the transformation, but from a sudden modesty that was foreign to my amphibian form.

With a lunge, I grab an old, faded round couch pillow and press it against myself.

"How—How did you know that would work?" I manage, my voice hoarse with shock.

Tia's smiles, a hint of sadness dancing in her soulful viridian eyes as she replies, "I *was* someone's princess once."

CHAPTER FORTY-FOUR

Agent Holloway

Water droplets cascade off my skin as I step out from the embrace of an outdoor shower, a secret haven shielded by a curtain of leaves, vines, and moss. The air is heavy with the scent of damp earth and greenery, and the rustle of a passing breeze tickles my ears, carrying with it the chatter of distant birds hidden high up in the towering trees.

I reach for the clothes Mamakaze offered—her late husband's—a simple shirt and a pair of shorts.

With each button fastened, I feel a bit more normalcy. The fabric, worn soft by time and washed to a gentle sun-bleached hue, stretches over my skin in a comforting embrace, and as I shrug into the shorts, I am enveloped by the faint scent of wood smoke and spice—compliments of the previous owner, I'm sure.

As I enter the room I share with Tia, the soft glow of candlelight catches my eye, golden and seductive.

She's there, lying on the bed, her chest rising and falling in the serene rhythm of sleep, hand tucked beneath her head as if cradling a dream.

Ray's presence is just a muted silhouette in the living room, his form sprawled across the couch, gaining a few hours of rest before we plunge back into the chaos of the French Quarter.

I move quietly, mindful not to disturb the tranquility. My gaze lingers on Tia, the way the candlelight brushes her features, the gentle curve of her lips.

Her eyelids flutter open, and she gifts me a smile that instantly banishes the remnants of any unease.

"I have to admit, I missed you in this form," She jokes, her voice still oozing sleepiness.

"That makes the both of us," I say. "Though it does feel weird walking instead of hopping. But on the bright side, I no longer have the knack to eat flies." The last part tumbles out of me, and it's ridiculous, yet it's true.

Her grin widens, "Well, what do you have a taste for then?" She asks, tilting her head slightly, her tongue darting out to trace her bottom lip.

I stop in my tracks.

Her question is a loaded invitation.

A silent pause holds us captive, a pause heavy with the hum of insects and the distant murmur of Ray's breathing.

My cock hardens painfully, making a tent out of the oversized khakis sitting on my hips.

I close the distance between us, my fingers grazing her arm, tracing a line from her shoulder down to her wrist, and I watch, captivated, as a shiver courses through her at the contact.

This girl, as infuriating as she is irresistible, has developed a talent for catching me off guard.

"Right now?" I answer, my voice huskier than intended. "I think I'd like a bite of a little something sweet."

Her smile turns downright wicked and she flips over on her belly, propping her chin up on the palms of her hand, batting her lashes, "Something sweet, huh? Like what?" She asks, kicking her feet back and forth, innocently.

My hand moves to her thigh, tracing the hem of her shorts. I watch her eyes flash with surprise then pleasure. Her lips part slightly as she exhales softly.

A low rumble vibrates my chest, she's teasing me, and she knows it. With each flick of her eyes, each subtle shift in her body, she draws me deeper into her game.

"What if I said you?"

CHAPTER FORTY-FIVE

Tia

The presumptuousness of his question sends a pulse of heat through my belly and straight down to my already dripping pussy.

With deliberate slowness, I lick my lips, offering him a sultry gaze from under my lashes.

"I'd say I know a place for you to start," I murmur, watching his eyes widen in surprise, that cocky smirk dissolving into something far more primal.

"Then why don't you show me where to begin?" He challenges, his voice on the verge of a growl.

I catch the unmistakable bulge straining against the fabric of his shorts.

I want to touch it—taste it—but I hold back, drawing out the tension between us.

The mattress dips under his way as he climbs onto it, his hands sliding under me before he flips me over onto my back.

In one fluid motion, Cade yanks his shirt over his head, revealing a landscape of chiseled abs that glisten with a sheen layer of sweat.

My fingers twitch with the need to explore every ridge and valley of his perfect musculature. I reach out, my fingertips tracing the defined lines of his stomach, feeling the firm warmth of his skin beneath my touch.

He's a sculpture of desire, an art form in flesh and blood that pulls at every fiber of my being.

His head dips down, his lips hovering just inches from mine, the heat of his breath mingling with my own. His eyes, dark and intense, hold mine captive as he whispers, "Are you sure you're ready for this?" His voice is a seductive blend of danger and sin.

"Yes," I moan, my nails skating across his skin.

Cade's grip is firm yet tender as he draws me into his embrace, his hand encircling my throat with a possessive demand. His lips crash against mine in a relentless kiss that steals the breath from my lungs. I moan against his mouth, my body responding to his touch with an eagerness that mirrors the slick desire gushing between my thighs.

His hands roam over my body, tugging at the fabric holding it hostage until I'm naked, and exposed under his hungry gaze.

With a swift movement, Cade peels away the oversized t-shirt that MamaKaze had offered me earlier, the fabric that had smelled faintly of sun and wind now lay discarded on the floor. My skin prickles in anticipation as I lay naked before him, feeling both vulnerable and powerful under his intense gaze.

His fingers trace a line down the center of my body, pausing to torment and flick at the sensitive spots.

"You are exquisite," He praises.

My entire body is on edge, every nerve eagerly awaiting the next sensation. I am entirely his to command, lost in the spell of his touch.

His hands began their exploration, skimming over my curves with reverence, tracing the rise and fall of my hips, the dip of my waist.

My hands find their way to his hair, tugging him closer, urging him to explore further. Cade obliges with soft kisses to my thighs, the precursor of what's to come.

Cade reaches for one of the candles on the nightstand.

My heart races, my chest heaving with rapid breaths as he tilts the candle, and a single drop of hot wax falls onto my nipple.

The sensation is sharp, searing, yet utterly delicious, pulling a guttural moan from deep within me.

"Fuck," Cade exhales, the word a prayer in the dim room. "Moan like that again for me, luciole."

He shifts the candle once more, the heat hovering above my skin, before creating a trail of liquid fire that meanders torturously down towards my pulsating center. Each drop is a jolt of pleasure, and I arch into him, wanting—needing more of the exquisite torture he deals with such skill.

"Please," I whisper, the word barely a breath, yet heavy with the weight of my arousal.

Cade's playfulness, the way he delights in drawing out every moment of foreplay, only serves to stoke the inferno within me, leaving me aching for release.

His breath hitches as he watches the blend of pain and pleasure dance across my features. Another drop falls, closer now to the apex of my thighs, and I shudder, Cade's eyes alight with a passionate gleam.

He sets the candle aside and his hands return to my body, his touch now soothing the spots where the wax marked me. His mouth follows, kissing each spot tenderly, as if to worship the pain he inflicted.

His lips brand my flesh, his tongue a composer rendering me helpless under his succor. He makes his way lower—lower, his tongue sliding between my folds.

"Ahhh!" I moan, the sudden suction on my clit almost too much to bear, but he's unrelenting in his assault.

It takes no time, and an orgasm is already ripping through me. My hands grip the sheets, my knuckles turning white from the force, as waves of pleasure crash over me.

Cade's tongue continues its merciless dance, drawing out my climax until I'm gasping for breath, a string of pleas falling from my lips.

He finally eases up, his breath warm against my sensitized skin as he rises to meet my eyes. His own are dark with desire, heavy with the satisfaction of pushing me to the edge and watching me tumble over.

"Mine. Now." He sounds more like a caveman than he does a savvy FBI agent.

But I'm not ready to relinquish power just yet.

I encase him with the warmth of my mouth, starting slowly, savoring the taste of his urgency. He groans, his hands finding their way to the back of my head, urging me to go faster.

His hips thrust upward involuntarily, and I met each movement, taking him deeper.

I run my tongue over the tip of him, savoring the salty taste of him.

"Like that, Tia. Just like that," he rasps, his grip tightening, guiding me.

Unable to wait any longer, Cade gently but firmly pulls away from the warmth of my mouth, and he lifts me atop him, my body responding instinctively to the silent command.

His hands grip my hips, urging me down as I sink onto him, enveloping him entirely. The connection sears through us both, a perfect fusion of need and fulfillment. His chest rises and falls rapidly beneath me, his breaths mingling with mine in heavy, ragged gasps.

The intensity in his eyes burns hotter than the wax he'd dripped on my skin earlier.

I set the pace, slow and flirtatious initially, drawing out the length of him and then sinking back down in a languid, rolling motion.

Cade's fingers dig into my hips, his control slipping, "Stop. Fucking. Teasing. Me." His words are a growled command.

He seizes control, and drives upwards with a force that leaves gentleness, long forgotten.

My breath catches in my throat, stifled moans suffocated between my clenched teeth.

The room rings with our combined moans and the headboard smacking against the wall in time with our frantic motions. Cade's grip on my hips tightens as I feel him throb within me, signaling his impending climax. His thrusts become more erratic, more desperate. It's all the encouragement I need to let go of my remaining inhibitions. I wrap my legs around his waist and arch my hips, meeting him thrust for thrust, my core tightening around him.

I'm right there with him, teetering on the edge of paradise.

"Come with me," He growls, his breath hot against my neck as he nibbles and licks the sensitive flesh.

"I—I—yessss!"

Our orgasms crash into one another, a wave of white-hot pleasure engulfing us both. I clench around him as my entire body trembles, nails digging into his back. Cade's grip on my hips tightens even more, as if he's afraid he'll lose me if he lets go. His final thrusts are deep, claiming, and possessive.

As our breathing slows, Cade collapses beneath me, his chest heaving.

"First thing I'm doing when we get home, is making you that dinner I promised," He says, pulling me into him as he nuzzles into the crook of my neck.

"Sounds perfect," I smile and run my fingers through his hair as we lay tangled together, our hearts still racing.

"Perfect," He whispers back, leaning in to plant a soft kiss on my sweat-dampened forehead.

But the dinner can wait a little longer, because right now, I just want to savor this moment with him.

CHAPTER FORTY-SIX

Tia

Laughter bubbles up from my chest as we waltz into the restaurant, a trio of giggling misfits.

"Look at y'all!" Evangeline's voice rings out, and she waddles over, her pregnant belly leading the way.

Her arms envelop Ray in a tender embrace that speaks of homecoming, her joy infectious even through the layers of grime we wear like badges of honor.

"How was the tour?" She asks.

Ray, Cade, and I exchange glances, an entire conversation in a shared split-second smirk before we erupt into a chorus of laughter.

"It was an—adventure, Starlight," Ray manages between chuckles, pressing a kiss to Evangeline's lips. "And I can't wait to tell you all about it when I take you out for dinner tonight."

My gaze softens as I watch them, Cade's hand still warm in mine. They're a picture of love that feels both ancient and brand new, something out of time—a love that could outlast the storms and win wars simply with the strength of its bond.

I can't help but think of momma and papa, how their love was the kind that spoke in silent looks and shared laughter. It's been years since Papa passed, but this moment, with Evangeline and Ray, it's like catching a glimpse of the shadows, alive and dancing in the love before me.

"I'll be looking forward to it, darling," She murmurs with a playful wink.

"Oh, by the way, Cade," Evangeline starts, her voice carrying a lilt of hesitance as she shifts her gaze between us.

She arches an eyebrow, conveying a blend of suspicion and apology. It's as if she's about to drop a bombshell that could disrupt the fragile calm we just achieved.

"A woman who claims to be your wife is here." She finishes.

Wife?

I feel Cade stiffen beside me, his laughter cut short, as if someone has sucked the oxygen from the room.

Cade's laugh rings out, but it's hollow, devoid of any actual humor. "I've never been married," He says, the confusion in his voice barely concealing the shiver of unease that it mixes with. "Must be some mistake."

But Evangeline only shakes her head, lays her hand reassuringly on his bicep, "She seemed really certain, Cade. Even knew about your birthmark and that scar from when you fell off the swing set as a kid."

"Who is she?" I hear myself ask.

Evangeline, bless her heart, shuffles over, her pregnancy not dampening her determination. She peers through the doors to the dining room, and I follow her pointed finger to a pretty blonde woman sitting at a table.

The sight before me shakes me to my core, as if the very ground I stand on is trembling.

Beside her sits a little girl with almond eyes, no older than three or four, with long black pigtails—the kind you see on porcelain dolls in antique shop windows.

She's coloring on one of the children's menus.

My stomach twists, dropping like an anchor in the sea, my heart following in free fall.

Could Cade have a wife and child—a life—that I knew nothing about?

The thought fractures something inside me, splintering like the fragile shell of a robin's egg.

"What?" Cade's voice cracks like thunder, "She said I was her husband?"

My vision blurs with the tears threatening to spill out as I struggle to comprehend what the hell is going on in front of me.

Cade's hand wraps around mine, tugging me forward. Despite my heart wrenching in betrayal, I follow him, half-stumbling toward the woman who sits nonchalantly at the table, watching our arrival.

"Sloan?" Cade's tone drops several octaves, every syllable dripping with disbelief and a dangerous edge I rarely hear from him.

The woman—Sloan—looks up, an unreadable smile playing on her lips.

At the sound of Cade's voice, the little girl's head snaps up, pigtails bouncing.

Her brown eyes light up, "Cade! Cade!" She squeals, springing from her chair. "Did you miss me, Cade?"

"Of course I missed you, Nami!" He scoops her into his arms effortlessly, her small body melding into his embrace. "What—what are you doing here though?"

"Agent Sloan says I don't have to hide now because the bad men aren't following me anymore." Her excitement almost infectious if not for the gnawing pang of uncertainty in my chest.

I watch, a bystander in my own skin, as Cade's expression softens for a heartbeat, his protective instincts enveloping the child.

"Is that so?" Cade glances at Sloan, a level of unease creeping into his usually calm demeanor. "Why wasn't I informed?"

"Cade," Sloan's cool voice slithers into the conversation, her gaze steady on me, "I see you haven't introduced your—friend."

Cade stiffens but tries to keep the expression on his face neutral, "What do you want, Sloan?"

The moment of reunion breaks like a fragile shell as Sloan's arm jerks back, wrenching Nami away from safety. Her small frame is swallowed by Sloan's iron grip, a scream piercing the air.

"Owe, Agent Sloan, you're hurting me!" Nami's voice, moments ago bubbling with laughter, now trembles.

In a second's time, with only a flicker of movement—chilling in its casualness, Sloan reveals the gun, pressing the cold metal against Nami's temple.

"First, you're going to do everything I say, unless you want the little brat to die," Sloan snarls, her voice as venomous as the threat she poses.

"Please, you're scaring me, Agent Sloan," Nami whimpers, her plea a jagged knife to my heart.

I stand there, muscles screaming to act, but the icy grip of reason holds me still.

Any wrong move, any twitch of aggression, could spell disaster.

I'm just as confused as this poor little girl.

Cade's jaw clenches, his eyes narrowing into slits of fury, yet his stance remains calculated and steady.

We both know the delicacy of the situation, the precarious balance between life and death resting in the hands of a woman whose sanity seems to have slipped its leash.

My gaze flicks to Evangeline, catching the mix of concern and confusion painting her delicate features. I can't let her be part of this—not with the life she carries within her, ready to greet the world any day now. I nod at her slowly trying to get her attention.

It works.

"Go get help," My lips form the words without sound.

Understanding dawns in her eyes, and with it, a hint of relief. Evangeline gives a subtle nod in return before turning and grabbing Ray by the hand, as they slip out the front door.

Their departure goes unnoticed by Sloan and her captive audience.

"You must be the reason I've barely heard from Cade here," Sloan sneers in my direction, the malice in her tone thick.

Her insinuation is transparent, a dagger wrapped in velvet, aimed straight for my heart.

I meet her contempt with a steely gaze.

"Oh, bless your heart, sugar," I say, the sweetness of my southern drawl contradicting the sarcasm laced within. "But judging just by the first impression of you, I highly doubt that's why you don't hear from him."

Sloan's smile is a snake's, all fangs and false warmth.

"He always did like them feisty," She says, her eyes flicking to Cade. "Isn't that right?" She purrs.

Underneath the boiling surface of my skin, fear and anger are a tangle of thorns.

I want to leap across the room, wipe that smirk off Sloan's face, but it's Nami, small and terrified, that anchors me in place.

My hands clench into fists at my sides, nails digging into my palms as Sloan shifts her attention back to her captive.

Her fingers trace the outline of Nami's face, the action causing an audible gasp from the girl. It's a menacing display of dominance.

"Sloan, tell me what the fuck is this," Cade demands.

"Aw," She mocks, her lips curled into a sneer as she leans closer to Cade, "Poor Cade can't figure it out. I thought you were a smart boy?"

The muscles in Cade's cheek twitch.

"Enough games," Cade warns.

"By the way...Daddy sends his regards." She pauses, letting the silence hang heavy before continuing, "He said watching you fail, watching you suffer as he shattered every promise you ever made, took away everything you ever cared for—it was the greatest show of all time."

Cade's face turns an ashen shade, the blood draining from his cheeks.

My mind races, trying to connect the dots.

Wait...Could this be—The Cartel from New York, the one Cade had been so wrapped up in before he landed here, the one he's talked about so many times?

I glance at Sloan with her overdone makeup, and tight smile—she could pass for a cheap Jessica Alba knockoff if you were to squint, and the lighting was bad enough.

Disbelief floods Cade's handsome features, "Your dad is Antonio Rivera? Wha—How?"

She rolls her eyes, "He fucked my mom? Duh." She says facetiously.

"How did you get her without the FBI being alerted?" He nods at the little girl.

The cheap blonde shoves Nami's head with the barrel of her gun, Wow. You're *really* not as smart as you thought you were," She taunts. "For fucks sake, Cade, the director has been dipping into my father's deep, silk-lined pockets for years. Once I joined the FBI, it wasn't exactly like daddy gave him a choice." A giggle escapes her, high-pitched and out of place.

Cade swallows hard, "Layla," He pleads, each word he speaks weighed down with desperation, "Let Nami go. Let all these innocent people walk out of here with their lives."

"Where's the fun in that?" She asks, a twisted glee in her tone.

I watch, feeling the cold grip of fear tightening around my own heart as Cade stands helplessly before her. But there's a determination in his eyes that tells me he's far from defeated, a quiet strength in the set of his shoulders.

The crack of gunfire outside slices through the tense air, and my body jolts as if I've been struck.

The memories of my father's brutal death resurface, haunting me and blending with the havoc around me.

Layla's face splits into a grin, her eyes alight with a warped rejoice.

"Ohhhh! Sounds like daddy is here now," She sings, whirling to point her gun at Cade with an authoritative flick of her wrist. "Sit down. Daddy wants to talk to you."

Cade stands his ground, "I'm good," He counters, meeting her gaze with a challenge.

Her smile vanishes, replaced by a scowl as swift as summer lightning. With a sudden pivot, she aims the gun at me and pulls the trigger. The marbled floor erupts beside my foot, sending shards skittering across the room.

Screams from the patrons

fill the air as they duck under tables and press against walls, trying to make themselves invisible.

"Next one might not miss. Now fucking sit," She snaps at Cade.

This time, he complies sinking into the nearby chair.

Moments later, the door swings open.

A Latino businessman strides in, the epitome of power tailored into an Armani suit, his hair slicked back as if defying any notion of disarray, and he's flanked by three brutes. One casually wiping blood from his knuckles onto a white handkerchief before tucking it away.

"Run into some trouble?" Layla queries.

"No, just some kid trying to play hero," Her father chuckles, the sound grating against my nerves.

He approaches Layla, brushes a kiss on her cheek, then he turns, pulling out a chair, confronting Cade with a cold smile, "Nice to finally put a face to the man who almost shut my business down."

Cade returns the smile, "Nice to finally meet the man who thinks he's above the law."

The cartel boss's face loses all trace of emotion, and he snaps his fingers imperiously, pointing at me with a flick of his manicured hand. "The bitch that has him pussy whipped. Kill her."

CHAPTER FORTY-SEVEN

Agent Holloway

I sit frozen, my heart pounding in my chest like a jackhammer.

Tia and Nami are the most important things in my life, and I can feel them slipping away.

Losing them would mean losing a part of myself.

I promised Nami that I would keep her safe, ever since I found her that day—covered in her mother's blood, not even two years old at the time. I hadn't made it there in time to save her mother, but I did save her. Unfortunately, not before the man that murdered her mother did unspeakable acts to her.

Yet, here now, my words are fruitless—broken promises that are damned to never see the light of day.

The immense weight of grief bears down on me, reminders flooding my mind of that tragic night when my father ended both my mother's life and his own.

"Please, don't do this," I beg, my jaw clenched so tight I fear my teeth might shatter. "She has nothing to do with any of this."

My voice breaks as tears stream down my face, meeting Tia's eyes briefly before looking away.

This is going to ruin her—ruin me.

"¡Hijo de puta!" Tito, the guy Antonio just ordered to kill Tia, calls out, and the large Latino brute with a septum piercing and gold teeth grins maliciously.

He grabs Tia by the back of her hair, yanking her up from her seat.

"I want you to make her squeal. I want our friend here to hear every second of you ripping her apart." Antonio smirks.

"You got it, jefe," The big guy says in a thick Spanish accent, his cruel smile never wavering.

Tia remains stoic, refusing to give either of them the sick satisfaction they're seeking.

Watching the brute drag Tia away, my emotions surge like an unstoppable flood - fear, anger, and desperation all crashing through me at once.

I need to do something, but what?

My mind races, searching for a solution, a way to save them both, but all I see is darkness.

"Fuck!" I scream silently, praying for a miracle, for someone to step in and put an end to this nightmare.

"Know your place, agent," The cartel kingpin spits, sneering at my helplessness. "You really should have thought about that before fucking with me, ese. You fucked with my home, my business, my associates—and you fucked my daughter."

His words sear into my chest like a hot iron.

"But, enough talk," The kingpin states, pulling a cigar from his pocket. He clips it, placing it between his lips, and lights a match. As he takes a deep puff, exhaling rings of smoke, he suddenly leans forward, pressing the still-burning match against my cheek. Pain sears through me, but I refuse to cry out, even as the sickening scent of my own burning flesh fills the air.

"Stop!" A woman screams from somewhere in the restaurant.

"Keep them in line, Layla," Antonio orders, his cold eyes never leaving mine. In response, she jerks up the woman who yelled and smacks her in the face with the handle of the gun in her hand, a twisted smirk on her face.

As a woman, I would have expected Layla to be disgusted by her father's orders—murder, rape, but no—she remains undeterred, her loyalty to him clear.

Tia, her head held high and her expression one of defiance, is dragged back towards the kitchen by Tito. My heart clenches at the sight, but she still doesn't make a sound. Tito's buddy watches them eagerly, lewdly palming himself through his jeans.

"There might be some leftovers," Tito calls back to him, laughing cruelly.

"As long as she's still a little warm," his friend replies, joining in the twisted amusement.

"Stay strong, luciole," I whisper, and she nods subtly, her eyes flashing with an indomitable spirit that gives me a flicker of hope amidst the horrors unfolding around us.

Forcing down the bile that threatens to rise in my throat, I focus on the pain radiating from my cheek—using it to fuel the rage and determination that simmers deep within me.

I won't let them win.

I can't.

A wail pierces the air, shattering the fragile silence that had fallen over the room. It's Tia's voice, raw and full of pain—a sound that cuts me to my very core.

I hear her cry out again, and it feels as if someone has plunged a knife into my heart. Rage courses through my veins.

Around me, the other restaurant goers break down, some sobbing uncontrollably while others simply stare in horror. An older woman near the entrance heaves, retching violently as she succumbs to the overwhelming terror.

"Enjoying the show?" Antonio grins, taking a puff from his cigar before nodding a signal to other the two brutes behind me.

They waste no time in grabbing me, their grips like iron vices on my arms.

"Spread his hands out on the table," The drug-lord demands, his voice cold and merciless.

I don't resist, knowing that any attempt at rebellion could result in Tia or Nami's death.

I divert my attention to pinpointing the perfect opportunity to attack, to catch them off guard.

"Please, just let them go," I beg. "They've done nothing wrong."

"Shut up!" Antonio snaps, his patience seemingly wearing thin.

The two men force my fingers apart, pressing them firmly against the cold, hard surface of the table.

"Showtime," Antonio says with an evil grin, pulling out his cigar cutter.

I watch as he positions the sharp metal around the tip of my pointer finger, a bead of sweat trickling down my forehead. Pain explodes through my hand as he chops off my fingertip, but I refuse to cry out.

The agony sears through every nerve, yet I clamp my jaw tight, the taste of iron filling my mouth as I bite down on my tongue to stifle any sound.

"Your turn next, bitch," One of the brutes hisses at Nami, who trembles uncontrollably in Layla's grip.

Another scream permeates the space, radiating from the kitchen. It's door then bursts open with a violent crash, and

Tito stumbles out, his pants around his ankles, his boxers shredded, and blood pouring down both legs.

"What the fuck?" Antonio shouts, his eyes wide with disbelief.

Tia emerges from the kitchen, a wild, deranged look in her eyes that sends chills down my spine. She's gripping a large meat cleaver in one hand and a .357 revolver in the other.

Before Layla or the other brutes have a chance to react, Tia aims the gun at Layla and pulls the trigger.

"NO!" Antonio screams, but it's too late.

The bullet finds its mark—right between his daughters eyes. She crumples lifelessly to the floor, blood pooling on the ground around her.

As all hell breaks loose around us, a quick-thinking patron grabs Nami and guides her beneath a nearby table for protection.

A sense of relief floods through me as I see that she is out of harm's way.

"Antonio!" I roar, using the distraction to jab both of my thumbs into the drug lord's eyes as hard as I can.

He howls in pain, momentarily blinded, and I seize the opportunity to punch him in the face, breaking his nose.

"Here!" Tia calls out, tossing me her gun.

I manage to catch it, but not before one of the remaining brutes shoots me in the chest. Pain spreads throughout my body, shock numbing my senses. It feels like everything is slow-ing down, and I can see the horror on Tia's face as she watches blood pour from the wound.

With adrenaline coursing through my veins, I take aim and shoot the brute twice before collapsing to the ground.

"Cade!" Tia wails, her voice breaking as she tries to hold back tears. "Cade!" Her screams echo in my ears as I fall to the cold floor beneath me.

I fight to stay conscious, my vision blurring as darkness threatens to consume me. The pain is unbearable, but I can't give in, not now.

My ears are ringing, but I can still hear Tia scream my name. She bolts toward the last brute, cleaver gripped tight in her hand while his attention is on me.

He doesn't stand a chance.

With a violent roar, she swings the blade, connecting with the brute's neck, stopping just short of severing it completely.

Blood spurts out like a fountain, painting the walls and floor in a gruesome tableau. The brute's eyes widen in shock, his hands reaching up to clutch at the lethal incision as if he could somehow put himself back together.

"NO! No, please! Not again!" Tia's sobs tear through me as she runs to my side. "I can't do this again!"

She collapses beside me, her body shaking with every sob, her hands stained with blood—some mine, some not.

"Help me!" She screams at the remaining patrons. "HELP!"

She yanks a white tablecloth from a nearby table and balls it up, pressing it against my chest. The fabric quickly soaks through with my blood, but she doesn't let up, pressing harder, her tears mingling with the crimson.

"Stay with me, Cade." Her plea filled with anguish.

I fix my gaze on her face, streaked with tears. I am filled with pride knowing that she was able to save countless innocent lives, and most importantly, Nami's.

"You did good, luciole," I whisper, forcing a smile.

"Why do you call me that?" She asks, and I know she's just trying to keep me talking.

"Would you prefer I didn't?"

"No."

A laugh escapes me, and I wince feeling the stabbing pain in my chest intensify.

"Well," I manage between shallow breathes, "Fireflies are beautiful, unique, and magical—such as yourself."

I try to wink, but I'm not sure that I succeed.

Charming.

"But," I go on, gasping slightly. "It's not only because of your strength and ability to adapt and overcome whatever comes your way—it's not even your remarkable charm that captivates me. It's the way you bring brightness into the darkest corners of my heart, and hope to a soul that has long forgotten what it's like to love."

Tears stream anew down Tia's cheeks, washing faint trails through the blood that has splattered across her face. She shakes her head, a small, disbelieving laugh mingling with her cries.

"You're not allowed to make speeches like that," She chokes out, pressing the tablecloth even harder against me.

I cough, and blood fills my mouth.

Tia turns me on my side, doing her best to keep me from either bleeding out of drowning on the thick crimson fluid.

"I need you to hang on, Cade," Her hand brushes my forehead as she wipes away the matted hair. "Just a few more minute, okay?"

But my vision is already fading, darkness creeping in at the edges. My body is heavy, weighted down by blood loss and pain. As much as I want to hold on, my strength is slipping away, and the last thing I feel is Tia's warm tears falling onto my skin before everything fades to black.

CHAPTER FORTY-EIGHT

Tia

"Cade?" I whisper, my heart shattering into a million pieces, but refusing to believe he's dead, I continue to plea with him. "Please, Cade, wake up. Don't—don't leave me."

But he doesn't stir.

He doesn't blink.

And the silence is an answer I refuse to accept.

No longer the scared little girl without a clue, I brace myself above him, my hands finding the pattern of survival as I pump compressions on his still chest.

One. Two. Three. Four. Five.

Time loses all meaning as I continue.

"Come back to me, Cade."

Twenty-eight. Twenty-nine. Thirty.

Breath for breath, I force air into his lungs, praying silently that each would be the one to drag him back from wherever he has slipped away to.

I start again.

Just as my hope flickers, threatening to extinguish, the police finally burst through the door. The medics, with the urgency of angels wielding mortal tools, rush to our side.

Antonio's hands are locked in cuffs, his fate now in the hands of justice. His eyes are filled with a mixture of rage and defeat, and they linger on me for a moment too long before he's led away.

"Let us take it from here," A medic says, her voice firm yet not unkind.

Reluctantly, I step back, watching them slice through Cade's shirt with clinical precision. They expose his pale skin to the harsh lights, placing AED pads onto his silent heart.

"Everyone stand back," She commands.

The machine whirs, its electronic count punctuating the tense space.

"Clear!" With a single word, she try's bridging the gap between life and death, sending a jolt through Cade's body.

He remains motionless.

"Clear!" The medic calls out again.

My gaze is locked onto Cade as another surge of electricity animates his body with a violent twitch. The seconds stretch out, each one an unbearable eternity until—there.

Suddenly, a stuttering rhythm emerges on the monitor, a symphony to my ears: his heart has started beating once more.

"Get him on a gurney!" The medic shouts.

I'm at their heels, desperation fueling my steps. "Can I ride with him?" The inquiry escapes me, a plea wrapped in a whisper.

The medic meets my eyes, her expression softening for just a moment.

"I'm sorry, ma'am, but no. You can meet us at the hospital."

As they load Cade into the back of the ambulance, a woman medic approaches me, her intent clear.

I wave her off, insisting, "I'll be fine." My injuries are nothing; it's my soul that's been scraped raw, and there's no bandage for that."

She nods, leaving me be.

"Does anyone know where the little girl is?" I call out, suddenly remembering Nami amidst the turmoil.

"She's here. She's safe," Calls a female voice.

I see Nami then, her small frame trembling, her eyes wide with a fear too large for her years.

"Do you want some food? And—ice cream?" I ask her.

It's a simple question, but it carries the weight of a promise—to care, to mend what's been broken, if only just a little.

Nami's smile is a small light in the dark as she reaches out for me.

"Thank you for saving my friend," She says, her hug strong despite her small size.

I embrace her tightly, her gratefulness bringing comfort to the pain in my soul.

"Everything's going to be okay, now" I promise her.

"Can you keep an eye on her for a bit while I check on Cade?" I ask one of my staff members that stayed behind.

"Absolutely, Ms. Williams." She says, escorting Nami to a calmer area in the dining room. She turns around for a brief moment, "After everything you did today, you're a real-life hero," She says with awe."

I manage a faint smile at her words, though they sit uncomfortably like a crown too heavy for my head.

"I won't be long." I promise her before I turn to walk away.

I catch Evangiline staring out the front window on my way out the door, "Evangeline? Where's Ray, sugar? What happened?"

Her voice cracks as she stutters out a response, the words tumbling over one another in her panic, "I—I don't know. I've been calling him over and over and he's not answering his phone."

She clutches her mobile like a lifeline, the screen illuminating tear-streaked cheeks.

"Those men—one of them knocked me out, and when I woke up, Ray—he was nowhere to be found." Her eyes dart around, wild and desperate.

"You need to go get checked out," I insist, but she cuts me off with a fierce shake of her head.

"No!" The single word is shrewd, "Not until I find him. I need him to come with me."

I recognize that same stubborn streak in her that I see in myself—the refusal to back down when someone we love is on the line. There's no changing her mind; I can see it in the set of her jaw, the hard glint in her eyes.

"Alright," I concede, knowing it will just be a waiting game at the hospital so I have a few moments that I can spare her, "Come on, let's go see if we can find him."

We move together through the shattered front door, our feet crunching on shattered glass.

Evangeline's fingers skit across her phone, hitting redial over and over.

"Wait," She says suddenly, her voice hitching, "Do you hear that?"

I pause, straining my ears, and there it is—a faint ringing, muffled but persistent.

We follow the sound down the sidewalk, past gawkers and flashing police lights, drawn to the mouth of the alleyway near the restaurant's side door.

The ringing grows louder, guiding us like a beacon until we spot him—Ray, crumpled and discarded amongst the trash and grime in the alley.

As we draw closer, the extent of the violence inflicted upon him becomes horrifyingly clear. His body is a map of brutality; arms and legs twisted at unnatural angles, his swollen face barely recognizable.

They gave this boy one hell of a beating.

He's so still, too still, and for a moment, time itself seems to hold its breath, waiting for a sign of life that might never come.

"Is that you, starlight?" The feeble words drift up from Ray.

Evangeline's tear-stained face breaks into a fragile smile, as if his mere recognition lights a candle in the dark. "Yes, my love. It's me," She assures him, her tears falling like raindrops upon his bruised skin. "I'm right here RayRay, I'm right here baby."

Evangeline's steps falter as she reaches Ray, her pregnant belly heaving with each sob that breaks from her lips.

She lowers herself with care, cradling his head in the warmth of her lap, her gaze lifting to mine, pleading for an answer I don't have.

"Oh, Ray, what have they done to you, baby?" Her fingers tremble as they comb through his matted hair.

Draped in sorrow, she hums—a soft lullaby that speaks of better times.

He tries to smile back, but it's a grimace that twists his battered features. "Are you—are you okay? Is the—is the baby?"

Her hand finds its place over her stomach, protective and tender. "The baby is just fine," She tells him, "I'm fine. We're all gonna be just fine, darlin."

"Th—that's good," He murmurs, a slight nod causing him more pain than it should.

As I watch them, a feeling of emptiness grows within me—an endless void that threatens to consume the hope I've been holding onto. They sit on the edge of life and death, discussing a future that may never come to fruition, and I can't help but wonder if we're all just fooling ourselves.

Does happiness truly even exist?

"Evangeline?" His whisper is so faint, it's almost carried away by the breeze.

She leans closer, her face mere inches from his, "Yes, my love?"

"I'm sor—I'm sorry." His words are a like a thread, fraying with each syllable.

"Shhhh," Evangeline soothes, her voice a gentle hush as she cradles his hand against her lips.

The gesture is one of devotion, a silent vow to never let go.

"Evangeline?" He calls again, a touch of fear mingling with his weakening breath.

"Hmmm?" She's barely holding herself together, her eyes glossy pools threatening to overflow.

"I'll meet you in the stars," He breathes out, "I—I love you." There's a finality in his tone.

And then, stillness.

My throat tightens as I watch Evangelina cling to Ray, her whispered comforts now lost on ears that can no longer hear.

I can't help but ache for her, for the dreams shattered on the cold concrete, for the life inside her that will know a father only through stories and photographs.

Tears escape me, silent sobs shaking my frame as I witness the end of their shared journey, a story cut brutally short.

Somewhere in the distance, sirens wail their mournful tune, the soundtrack to our grief. But here, in this alley, under the watchful eye of the city lights, it's just us—the living and the dead—the hopeless and the heartbroken.

CHAPTER FORTY-NINE

Tia

The sterile scent of antiseptics fills my nostrils as I sit by Cade's hospital bed, listening to the quiet rhythm of the heart monitor.

His chest rises and falls with a steady pace, the aftermath of surgery lurking beneath the bandages that wrap his torso. But he's going to be okay; that's what the doctors keep saying, and I cling to those words like a life raft in choppy seas.

"Hey," Cade murmurs, his voice a hoarse whisper as his fingers find mine, giving a gentle squeeze. "Looks like you're gonna be stuck with me."

I laugh, "I've been stuck with you since the day we met, haven't I?"

His grin is weak but undeniably there, a flicker of his stubborn spirit shining through the pain.

"That you have," He concedes, his grip on my hand becoming tighter. "And you're not getting rid of me anytime soon."

I had gotten lucky that my mother had been out fetching supplies, and running a few errands, missing the hostage situation at the restaurant by mere minutes.

The memory makes my blood run cold, thinking of all the late-night calls she's made afterward, organizing cleanings and repairs while I kept vigil over Cade.

"Tomorrow's going to be tough," I say after a moment, shifting the conversation toward the inevitable.

Ray's funeral looms over us, a somber cloud in an already stormy sky.

Cade nods, a shadow crossing his face. "Yeah. The bayous were his sanctuary, weren't they? He talked about them like they were sacred."

"Because they were—to him." I can almost see Ray, standing tall amidst the cypress trees, the sounds of wildlife echoing around him. "He found peace there."

"He will also be laid to rest there too," I inform him. "Evangeline needs to know that he is where he loved to be."

We'll cast the remnants of a friend, a lover, a father, intertwining his essence with the murky waters and whispering reeds.

Even in death, Ray brings us together.

Cade presses a kiss to my hand.

I'm sure my grandpa will also be there, somewhere in the shadows.

I visited him on my way over to the hospital this morning to pick Cade up, and while he didn't say the worlds, his eyes silently screamed, *"I told you so."*

But I've sworn off shadow magic. The risk is not worth the reward, and the reward is not worth the cost.

The nurse glides into the room with a bright smile, "You two are all good to go," She announces, holding out a small stack of discharge papers.

"Thank you so much," I reply, grabbing the papers from her.

Cade's hand finds mine, giving it an affirming squeeze.

The thought of the restaurant reopening in a few weeks looms at the edge of my mind, but for now, I'm content with the idea of enjoying our time off together—Cade, Nami, and me.

"Ready to go, luciole?" Cade asks, adjusting the shoulder brace that has become his latest accessory.

"Absolutely," I answer, the nickname lighting a small fire in my chest. "I was thinking about stopping by the cafe and grabbing some lunch. Do you feel up to it?"

His stomach growls, a low rumble that bounces around in the small room.

"I could eat," He jokes, earning a giggle from me.

We find ourselves at the cafe not long after. The bell above the door jingles as my mom ushers Nami inside.

Nami rushes out to greet us, her small arms open wide. She wraps herself around Cade first, careful of his injury, then comes to me, her tiny arms closing around my neck.

"Did you have fun?" I ask, ruffling her hair as we head inside.

"Uh-huh! We made cookies!" Her excitement is contagious.

"Sounds delicious," Cade says, "I hope you saved one for me."

"I did!" She reaches in her pocket, pulling out two chocolate chip cookies, handing each of us one.

"Thank you." Cade and I say in unison.

"You're welcome." Her laugh is more like a jingle.

Watching Nami flit around the waiting area, I realize how natural this feels—caring for her, protecting her. It's an unexpected warmth that fills a void I wasn't aware existed within me.

I never realized not being able to have a child bothered me so much.

And now, with the FBI yet to decide Nami's future, the thought of her leaving knits a tightness in my chest.

"She's settled in so well," I say softly, more to myself than to Cade.

He nods, "Nami is a real trooper. Adapting to everything that's happened to her in such a short life."

"Maybe—" A thought lingers and grows—an idea taking root.

Maybe there's room in our lives for a new beginning, one that involves opening our home, our hearts, to a child in need. Maybe adopting isn't such a distant possibility.

"Maybe what?" Cade prompts, a gentle nudge toward the thoughts I've yet to voice.

"Maybe we could do this—be this—for someone else," I admit, daring to envision a future where the memories of gunshots and death are replaced by laughter and light, and where the weight of guilt is shared and, perhaps, even made lighter by the love of family.

"Maybe we could," Cade agrees, his face softening at the idea.

His gaze strays towards Nami, who's now sitting on the bench with a coloring book, her tongue poking out the corner of her mouth in concentration.

The hostess greets us next and lead us to a table, handing each of us a menu.

Nami's eyes are alight with curiosity, scanning the menu with the seriousness of a scholar, ultimately settling on a grilled cheese sandwich and apple slices.

Once we've ordered our food and taken our seats, it's then that Cade clears his throat, "I have some news," He says, and the table falls silent.

He tells us about getting my father's case reopened, the words tumbling out with a mixture of pride and incredulity. "They have Allen in for questioning," He reveals. "He told them everything."

"That's incredible!" Momma exclaims, tears bubbling in the corner of her eyes.

"Guess he didn't want to die next," He quips, a lighthearted-ness in his tone as he winks at me.

It's a joke, but the implication of truth sends a shiver through me.

Laughter bubbles up from my throat, but it's cut short when my fist connects playfully with his arm—an arm I forgot was healing.

"Ahhh!" He gasps, sucking in a sharp breath.

"Oh my goodness, Cade, I am so sorry!" I squeal.

"Hey, hey," Cade murmurs, leaning in close enough that I can feel his breath against my cheek. His lips brush mine in a feather-light kiss, carrying forgiveness and affection in equal measure. "I could spend the rest of my life being abused by you."

Epilogue

I sit rigid, the stiff fabric of the courtroom bench pressing against my back, my hand intertwined with my mother's. It trembles in mine, a delicate bird caught in a storm that's finally calming.

The judge's voice booms across the room, final and unyielding, declaring Allen's fate—life without parole. My chest constricts at the words, a culmination of anguish and relief colliding within me like tectonic plates forging new land from old sorrows.

My mother's grip tightens on mine, her other hand finding its way to cover her mouth as sobs bubble up from the depths of her soul.

Tears stream down her cheeks, but these are different from the countless ones she's shed before.

These are tears of joy, droplets of a pain released, a heavy chain of what-ifs and whys broken by the gavel's decree.

"Finally, Tia, baby," She whispers between gasps of air, "He has justice, after all these years."

I pull her into my arms, her body shaking with every sob, every shudder, a release of pent-up years of despair.

Our hug is a fortress against the past, and a sanctuary in the present.

"It feels so unreal."

She agrees.

The courtroom begins to empty, the low murmur of voices and shuffling feet becoming the soundtrack to our victory. Court is adjourned, the judge's hammer has fallen, and with it, the weight we've been carrying for what feels like lifetimes.

We rise together, my mother's arm entwined with mine, and together, step by step, we make our way out of the courthouse.

The buildings doors swing shut behind us with an air of finality, and we step into the embrace of a new day.

The heat of the sun seems to be validating, a subtle acknowledgement from the universe that justice has been rightfully served.

We've barely taken a few steps down the red brick staircase when Evangeline appears in our path.

"Congratulations," She beams, shifting the weight of her little boy on her hip—a mirror image of his daddy Ray with his tousled brown hair and curious eyes. "I'm so glad that your Papa's case was finally solved."

"Thanks, Evie," I reply,

managing a small smile despite the whirlwind of emotions inside. "It's been a long road."

She's been a steady presence during the entire ordeal, offering both practical help and emotional support to my mother and me.

She's an amazing friend.

"I still can't believe you two went through this for so many years." Her voice holds a tinge of anger as she walks beside us as we make our way to Un Nouveau Rêve, our newly opened restaurant. "It just kills me to know how corrupt our police system is."

I nod slowly, acknowledging her feelings without allowing mine to overwhelm me again.

My mother notices my struggle.

"Indeed, Evie, dear, but let's not dwell on the past anymore," My mother interjects gently, her hand resting on Evangeline's shoulder. "We have to look forward now."

Evangeline nods.

As we continue walking, the city pulses around us—people bustling by, cars honking in the distance, a street performer playing a lively tune on a violin.

It's life moving forward, and I'm finally moving with it.

We cross the street, and the familiar scent of freshly baked bread from Un Nouveau Rêve greets us even before we see the façade of the restaurant.

That's when Nami, my sprite of a daughter with energy that seems to draw from the very earth itself, tugs at my hand, pulling me back to the here and now.

"Mommy, mommy! Can we have ice-cream when we get there?" Her voice is a high-pitched peal of excitement, her small hand gripping mine with urgency.

"Of course, we can, cupcake," I laugh, picking her up and twirling around, her giggles filling up the sidewalk. "Just don't tell you-know-who." I whisper in her ear.

"Yea," Nami agrees conspiratorially, wrapping her arms around my neck as I set her down, "Daddy doesn't like us having dessert before dinner, but I won't tell him." She gives me a mischievous giggle that warms my heart.

"Good girl," I say with a wink, sharing in her moment of cheeky rebellion. It's these precious instances, simple and sweet, that really make life worth living.

"Tell me what?" Cade's voice is sudden and playful, emerging from behind us like a gentle breeze that's learned to whisper.

Nami lets out a startled scream, the sound quickly tumbling into laughter as Cade's fingers find her tiny sides, tickling her relentlessly. She squirms in my arms, her giggles infectious enough to draw a smile from even the sternest face.

It took a lot of strings being pulled and hoops being jumped through, but our adoption went beautifully. We were determined to give her the world—a home. And with Antonio Rivera behind bars and his daughter being dead, the fbi decided that Nami would be safe and well taken care of with us.

That year had been a whirlwind of court dates, emotional meetings, and endless paperwork, but it was all worth it to see Nami now, thriving and happy.

"Mommy said we can eat ice cream," She gasps between fits of laughter, her little hands trying to bat away his larger, more dexterous ones.

"Did she now?" Cade raises an eyebrow in my direction, a mock sternness in his eyes that he can never quite pull off.

There's too much warmth there, too much of the love that softens every faux reprimand.

I can't help but laugh along with them, the sound bubbling up from a place inside me that feels lighter than it has in years.

"Morning ice cream," I confirm, nodding at him as if to solidify the decision.

His arm slips around my shoulders, effortlessly pulling Nami and me into his orbit. He leans down, placing a kiss on the crown of each of our heads—a sweet gesture that fills me with a sense of belonging and contentment.

Nami's laughter fades into contented sighs as she leans back against my chest, her small hand finding mine and intertwining our fingers as she beams up at Cade, her soft brown eyes reflecting pure adoration for the man she now calls Daddy.

"You know what?" He says, a conspiratorial glint lighting up his eyes. "I think I'll have some too."

As we walk, our steps in sync, I glance up at the new sign sitting right above the entrance. Un Nouveau Rêve, it reads in bright baby blue.

A new dream, indeed—one where morning ice cream is just the beginning.

XVII
THE STAR

About the author

Amber is an author of Beautifully Broken Romance. She resides in Ohio with her amazing family and dogs. When she's not creating fantasy worlds and sinfully delicious romance, you can find her with her family, gaming, playing board games, or of course, snuggled up with a cozy blanket and a good book. Some of her favorite genres include fantasy, paranormal, mythological, ect. but she's a total sucker for any kind of romance. She has an unhealthy addiction to coffee and yes...she does believe in magic, and you can't convince her otherwise.

(Her pet dragon wouldn't allow it anyway.)

Stay up to date by following her socials or by visiting her website:

https://www.amberbunchauthor.com

Also by

Of Gods and Muses:

Bonded by Secrets
Bound by Flames
Tempted by Fate (TBD)

A Twisted Princess Collection

A Pursuit of Madness
A Taste of Revenge
A Spindle of Nightmares (2025)

Secret Project:

Title TBA (A Dark Mafia Romance)

452

Acknowledgements

This has been a long and bumpy road, but I am so grateful to have so many readers on board this crazy rollercoaster ride with me. To everyone who helped make this book go from dream to reality; thank you from the bottom of my little black heart.

XOXO – Amber